The Summer

It all begins with a lecture that introd... dents to a man who will change their lives—a wizard who will take them from Earth to the heart of the first of all worlds: Fionavar. And take them Loren Silvercloak does, for his need—the need of Fionavar and all the worlds—is great indeed.

And in a marvelous land of men and dwarves, of wizards and gods, five young people discover who they are truly meant to be. For they are a long-awaited part of the pattern known as the Fionavar Tapestry, and only if they accept their destiny will the armies of the Light stand any chance of surviving the wrath the Unraveller and his minions of darkness intend to unleash upon the world. . . .

Praise for <u>The Fionavar Tapestry</u>

"Kay's intricate Celtic background will please fantasy buffs . . . in the manner of *The Silmarillion*, the posthumous Tolkien work that Kay helped edit." —*Publishers Weekly*

"A grand galloping narrative . . . reverberates with centuries of mythic and incantatory implications—with a little Prince Hal and Falstaff on the side." —*Christian Science Monitor*

"As fine a piece of fantasy as has been published for some time." —*Winnipeg Free Press*

"Kay has an acrobatic imagination . . . one ingenious plot after another . . . well-staged and presented." —*Montreal Gazette*

"Excellent fantasy reading . . . *The Fionavar Tapestry* will deserve a place among the best of fantasy." —*Regina Leader Post*

The Summer Tree

The Fionavar Tapestry:
Book One

Guy Gavriel Kay

A ROC BOOK

ROC
Published by New American Library, a division of
Penguin Putnam Inc., 375 Hudson Street, New York, New York 10014, U.S.A.
Penguin Books Ltd, 27 Wrights Lane, London W8 5TZ, England
Penguin Books Australia Ltd, Ringwood, Victoria, Australia
Penguin Books Canada Ltd, 10 Alcorn Avenue, Toronto, Ontario, Canada M4V 3B2
Penguin Books (N.Z.) Ltd, 182–190 Wairau Road, Auckland 10, New Zealand

Penguin Books Ltd, Registered Offices: Harmondsworth, Middlesex, England

Published by Roc, an imprint of New American Library, a division
of Penguin Putnam Inc.

First Roc Printing, February 1992
First Roc Trade Paperback Printing, April 2001
10 9 8 7 6 5 4 3 2 1

ROC REGISTERED TRADEMARK—MARCA REGISTRADA

LIBRARY OF CONGRESS CATALOGING-IN-PUBLICATION DATA
Kay, Guy Gavriel.
    The summer tree / Guy Gavriel Kay.
        p.   cm.
    Originally published in the series: The Fionavar tapestry, bk. 1.
    ISBN 0-451-45822-2 (alk. paper)
    1. College students—Fiction. 2. Time travel—Fiction. 3. Wizards—Fiction I. Title.
PR9199.3.K39 S9 2001
813'.54—dc21   00-045803

Printed in the United States of America

PUBLISHER'S NOTE
This is a work of fiction. Names, characters, places, and incidents are either the product of the author's imagination or are used fictitiously, and any resemblance to actual persons, living or dead, business establishments, events, or locales is entirely coincidental.

The Summer Tree is dedicated to the
memory of my grandmother,

TANIA POLLOCK BIRSTEIN

whose gravestone reads,
"Beautiful, Loving, Loved,"
and who was all of these things.

Acknowledgments

In a labor of daunting scope an equally daunting accumulation of debts seems to have evolved. Not all can be recorded here, but there are some people who must be given their rightful place at the beginning of the Tapestry.

I would like to thank Sue Reynolds for the rendered image of Fionavar, and my agent John Duff, who was with me from the very beginning. Alberto Manguel and Barbara Czarnecki lent their editorial faculties, and Daniel Shapiro found me a Brahms sonata and helped shape a song.

Also, and most profoundly, I must name here my parents, my brothers, and Laura. With love.

Contents

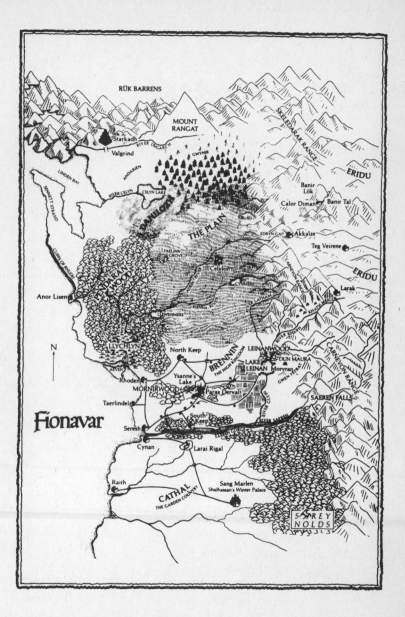

THE CHARACTERS

The Five:
KIMBERLY FORD
KEVIN LAINE
JENNIFER LOWELL
DAVE MARTYNIUK
PAUL SCHAFER

In Brennin:
AILELL, High King of Brennin
THE EXILED PRINCE, his older son
DIARMUID, younger son and heir to Ailell;
  also Warden of the South Marches

GORLAES, the Chancellor

METRAN, First Mage of Brennin
DENBARRA, his source
LOREN SILVERCLOAK, a mage
MATT SÖREN, his source, once King of the Dwarves
TEYRNON, a mage
BARAK, his source

JAELLE, High Priestess of the Goddess

YSANNE, Seer of Brennin ("the Dreamer")
TYRTH, her servant

COLL, Lieutenant to Diarmuid
CARDE
ERRON
TEGID   the men of South Keep,
DRANCE   members of Diarmuid's band
ROTHE
AVERREN

MABON, Duke of Rhoden
NIAVIN, Duke of Seresh
CEREDUR, Warden of the North Marches

RHEVA
LAESHA } ladies of the Court of Ailell

LEILA
FINN } children in Paras Derval

NA-BRENDEL, a lord of the lios alfar, from Daniloth

In Cathal:
SHALHASSAN, Supreme Lord of Cathal
SHARRA, his daughter and heir ("the Dark Rose")

DEVORSH
BASHRAI } Captains of the Guard

On the Plain:
IVOR, Chieftain of the third tribe of the Dalrei
LEITH, his wife
LEVON
CORDELIANE ("LIANE") } his children
TABOR

GEREINT, Shaman of the third tribe

TORC, a Rider of the third tribe ("the Outcast")

The Powers:
THE WEAVER at the Loom

MÖRNIR of the Thunder
DANA, the Mother
CERNAN of the Beasts
CEINWEN of the Bow, the HUNTRESS
MACHA
NEMAIN } goddesses of war

RAKOTH MAUGRIM the UNRAVELLER,
   also named SATHAIN, the HOODED ONE
GALADAN, Wolflord of the andain, his lieutenant

EILATHEN, a water spirit
FLIDAIS, a wood spirit

From the Past:
IORWETH FOUNDER, first High King of Brennin

CONARY, High King during the Bael Rangat
COLAN, his son, High King after him ("the Beloved")
AMAIRGEN WHITEBRANCH,
   first of the mages
LISEN of the Wood, a deiena,
   source and wife to Amairgen
REVOR, ancestral hero of the Dalrei,
   first Lord of the Plain

VAILERTH, High King of Brennin in a time of civil war
NILSOM, First Mage to Vailerth
AIDEEN, source to Nilsom

GARMISCH, High King before Ailell
RAEDERTH, First Mage to Garmisch,
   beloved of Ysanne the Seer

OVERTURE

After the war was over, they bound him under the Mountain. And so that there might be warning if he moved to escape, they crafted then, with magic and with art, the five wardstones, last creation and the finest of Ginserat. One went south across Saeren to Cathal, one over the mountains to Eridu, another remained with Revor and the Dalrei on the Plain. The fourth wardstone Colan carried home, Conary's son, now High King in Paras Derval.

The last stone was accepted, though in bitterness of heart, by the broken remnant of the lios alfar. Scarcely a quarter of those who had come to war with Ra-Termaine went back to the Shadowland from the parley at the foot of the Mountain. They carried the stone, and the body of their King—most hated by the Dark, for their name was Light.

From that day on, few men could ever claim to have seen the lios, except perhaps as moving shadows at the edge of a wood, when twilight found a farmer or a carter walking home. For a time it was rumoured among the common folk that every sevenyear a messenger would come by unseen ways to hold converse with the High King in Paras Derval, but as the years swept past, such tales dwindled, as they tend to, into the mist of half-remembered history.

Ages went by in a storm of years. Except in houses of learning, even Conary was just a name, and Ra-Termaine, and forgotten, too, was Revor's Ride through Daniloth on the night of the red sunset. It had *become a song for drunken tavern nights, no more true or less than any other such songs, no more bright.*

For there were newer deeds to extol, younger heroes to parade through city streets and palace corridors, to be toasted in their turn by village tavern fires. Alliances shifted, fresh wars were fought to salve old wounds, glittering triumphs assuaged past defeats, High King succeeded High King, some by descent and others by brandished sword. And through it all, through the petty wars and the great ones, the strong leaders and weak, the long green years of peace when the roads were safe and the harvest rich, through it all the Mountain slumbered—for the rituals of the wardstones, though all else changed, were preserved. The stones were watched, the naal fires tended, and there never came the terrible warning of Ginserat's stones turning from blue to red.

And under the great mountain, Rangat Cloud-Shouldered, in the wind-blasted north, a figure writhed in chains, eaten by hate to the edge of madness, but knowing full well that the wardstones would give warning if he stretched his powers to break free.

Still, he could wait, being outside of time, outside of death. He could brood on his revenge and his memories—for he remembered everything. He could turn the names of his enemies over and over in his mind, as once he had played with the blood-clotted necklace of Ra-Termaine in a taloned hand. But above all he could wait: wait as the cycles of men turned like the wheel of stars, as the very stars shifted pattern under the press of years. There would come a time when the watch slackened, when one of the five guardians would falter. Then could he, in darkest secrecy, exert his strength to summon aid, and there would come a day when Rakoth Maugrim would be free in Fionavar.

And a thousand years passed under the sun and stars of the first of all the worlds. . . .

PART 1

Silvercloak

Chapter 1

In the spaces of calm almost lost in what followed, the question of *why* tended to surface. Why them? There was an easy answer that had to do with Ysanne beside her lake, but that didn't really address the deepest question. Kimberly, white-haired, would say when asked that she could sense a glimmered pattern when she looked back, but one need not be a Seer to use hindsight on the warp and weft of the Tapestry, and Kim, in any event, was a special case.

With only the professional faculties still in session, the quadrangles and shaded paths of the University of Toronto campus would normally have been deserted by the beginning of May, particularly on a Friday evening. That the largest of the open spaces was not, served to vindicate the judgement of the organizers of the Second International Celtic Conference. In adapting their timing to suit certain prominent speakers, the conference administrators had run the risk that a good portion of their potential audience would have left for the summer by the time they got under way.

At the brightly lit entrance to Convocation Hall, the besieged security guards might have wished this to be the case. An astonishing crowd of students and academics, bustling like a rock audience with pre-concert excitement, had gathered to hear the man for whom, principally, the late starting date had been arranged. Lorenzo Marcus was speaking and chairing a panel that night in the first public appearance ever for the reclusive genius, and it was going to be standing room only in the august precincts of the domed auditorium.

The guards searched out forbidden tape recorders and waved ticket-holders through with expressions benevolent or inimical, as their natures dictated. Bathed in the bright spill of light and pressed by the milling crowd, they did not see the dark figure that crouched in the shadows of the porch, just beyond the farthest circle of the lights.

For a moment the hidden creature observed the crowd, then it turned, swiftly and quite silently, and slipped around the side of the building. There, where the darkness was almost complete, it looked once over its shoulder and then, with unnatural agility, began to climb hand over hand up the outer wall of Convocation Hall. In a very little while the creature, which had neither ticket nor tape recorder, had come to rest beside a window set high in the dome above the hall. Looking down past the glittering chandeliers, it could see the audience and the stage, brightly lit and far below. Even at this height, and through the heavy glass, the electric murmur of sound in the hall could be heard. The creature, clinging to the arched window, allowed a smile of lean pleasure to flit across its features. Had any of the people in the highest gallery turned just then to admire the windows of the dome, they might have seen it, a dark shape against the night. But no one had any reason to look up, and no one did. On the outside of the dome the creature moved closer against the window pane and composed itself to wait. There was a good chance it would kill later that night. The prospect greatly facilitated patience and brought a certain anticipatory satisfaction, for it had been bred for such a purpose, and most creatures are pleased to do what their nature dictates.

Dave Martyniuk stood like a tall tree in the midst of the crowd that was swirling like leaves through the lobby. He was looking for his brother, and he was increasingly uncomfortable. It didn't make him feel any better when he saw the stylish figure of Kevin Laine coming through the door with Paul Schafer and two women. Dave was in the process of turning away—he didn't feel like being patronized just then—when he realized that Laine had seen him.

"Martyniuk! What are you doing here?"

"Hello, Laine. My brother's on the panel."

"Vince Martyniuk. Of course," Kevin said. "He's a bright man."

"One in every family," Dave cracked, somewhat sourly. He saw Paul Schafer give a crooked grin.

Kevin Laine laughed. "At least. But I'm being rude. You know Paul. This is Jennifer Lowell, and Kim Ford, my favorite doctor."

"Hi," Dave said, forced to shift his program to shake hands.

"This is Dave Martyniuk, people. He's the center on our basketball team. Dave's in third-year law here."

"In that order?" Kim Ford teased, brushing a lock of brown hair back from her eyes. Dave was trying to think of a response when there was a movement in the crowd around them.

"Dave! Sorry I'm late." It was, finally, Vincent. "I have to get backstage fast. I may not be able to talk to you till tomorrow. Pleased to meet you"—to Kim, though he hadn't been introduced. Vince bustled off, knifing in front of him like the prow of a ship cleaving through the crowd.

"Your brother?" Kim Ford asked, somewhat unnecessarily.

"Yeah." Dave was feeling sour again. Kevin Laine, he saw, had been accosted by some other friends and was evidently being witty.

If he headed back to the law school, Dave thought, he could still do a good three hours on Evidence before the library closed.

"Are you alone here?" Kim Ford asked.

"Yeah, but I—"

"Why don't you sit with us, then?"

Dave, a little surprised at himself, followed Kim into the hall.

"Her," the Dwarf said. And pointed directly across the auditorium to where Kimberly Ford was entering with a tall, broad-shouldered man. "She's the one."

The grey-bearded man beside him nodded slowly. They were standing, half hidden, in the wings of the stage, watching the audience pour in. "I think so," he said worriedly. "I need five, though, Matt."

"But only one for the circle. She came with three, and there is a fourth with them now. You have your five."

"I have five," the other man said. *"Mine,* I don't know. If this were just for Metran's jubilee stupidity it wouldn't matter, but—"

"Loren, I know." The Dwarf's voice was surprisingly gentle. "But she is the one we were told of. My friend, if I could help you with your dreams. . . ."

"You think me foolish?"

"I know better than that."

The tall man turned away. His sharp gaze went across the room to where the five people his companion had indicated were sitting. One by one he focused on them, then his eyes locked on Paul Schafer's face.

Sitting between Jennifer and Dave, Paul was glancing around the hall, only half listening to the chairman's fulsome introduction of the evening's keynote speaker, when he was hit by the probe.

The light and sound in the room faded completely. He felt a great darkness. There was a forest, a corridor of whispering trees, shrouded in mist. Starlight in the space above the trees. Somehow he knew that the moon was about to rise, and when it rose. . . .

He was in it. The hall was gone. There was no wind in the darkness, but still the trees were whispering, and it was more than just a sound. The immersion was complete, and within some hidden recess Paul confronted the terrible, haunted eyes of a dog or a wolf. Then the vision fragmented, images whipping past, chaotic, myriad, too fast to hold, except for one: a tall man standing in darkness, and upon his head the great, curved antlers of a stag.

Then it broke: sharp, wildly disorienting. His eyes, scarcely able to focus, swept across the room until they found a tall, grey-bearded man on the side of the stage. A man who spoke briefly to someone next to him, and then walked smiling to the lectern amid thunderous applause.

"Set it up, Matt," the grey-bearded man had said. "We will take them if we can."

"He was good, Kim. You were right," Jennifer Lowell said. They were standing by their seats, waiting for the exiting crowd to thin. Kim Ford was flushed with excitement.

"Wasn't he?" she asked them all, rhetorically. "What a *terrific* speaker!"

"Your brother was quite good, I thought," Paul Schafer said to Dave quietly.

Surprised, Dave grunted noncommittally, then remembered something. "You feeling okay?"

Paul looked blank a moment, then grimaced. "You, too? I'm fine. I just needed a day's rest. I'm more or less over the mono." Dave, looking at him, wasn't so sure. None of his business, though if Schafer wanted to kill himself playing basketball. He'd played a football game with broken ribs once. You survived.

Kim was talking again. "I'd love to meet him, you know." She looked wistfully at the knot of autograph-seekers surrounding Marcus.

"So would I, actually," said Paul softly. Kevin shot him a questioning look.

"Dave," Kim went on, "your brother couldn't get us into that reception, could he?"

Dave was beginning the obvious reply when a deep voice rode in over him.

"Excuse me, please, for intruding." A figure little more than four feet tall, with a patch over one eye, had come up beside them. "My name," he said, in an accent Dave couldn't place, "is Matt Sören. I am Dr. Marcus's secretary. I could not help but overhear the young lady's remark. May I tell you a secret?" He paused. "Dr. Marcus has no desire at all to attend the planned reception. With all respect," he said, turning to Dave, "to your very learned brother."

Jennifer saw Kevin Laine begin to turn himself on. Performance time, she thought, and smiled to herself.

Laughing, Kevin took charge. "You want us to spirit him away?"

The Dwarf blinked, then a basso chuckle reverberated in his chest. "You are quick, my friend. Yes, indeed, I think he would enjoy that very much."

Kevin looked at Paul Schafer.

"A plot," Jennifer whispered. "Hatch us a plot, gentlemen!"

"Easy enough," Kevin said, after some quick reflection. "As of this moment, Kim's his niece. He wants to see her. Family before functions." He waited for Paul's approval.

"Good," Matt Sören said. "And very simple. Will you come with me then to fetch your . . . ah . . . uncle?"

"Of course I will!" Kim laughed. "Haven't seen him in *ages*." She walked off with the Dwarf towards the tangle of people around Lorenzo Marcus at the front of the hall.

"Well," Dave said, "I think I'll be moving along."

"Oh, Martyniuk," Kevin exploded, "don't be such a legal drip! This guy's world-famous. He's a legend. You can study for Evidence tomorrow. Look, come to my office in the afternoon and I'll dig up my old exam notes for you."

Dave froze. Kevin Laine, he knew all too well, had won the award in Evidence two years before, along with an armful of other prizes.

Jennifer, watching him hesitate, felt an impulse of sympathy. There was a lot eating this guy, she thought, and Kevin's manner didn't help. It was so hard for some people to get past the flashiness to see what was underneath. And against her will, for Jennifer had her own defences, she found herself remembering what love-making used to do to him.

"Hey, people! I want you to meet someone." Kim's voice knifed into her thoughts. She had her arm looped possessively through that of the tall lecturer, who beamed benignly down upon her. "This is my Uncle Lorenzo. Uncle, my room-mate Jennifer, Kevin and Paul, and this is Dave."

Marcus's dark eyes flashed. "I am," he said, "more pleased to meet you than you could know. You have rescued me from an exceptionally dreary evening. Will you join us for a drink at our hotel? We're at the Park Plaza, Matt and I."

"With pleasure, sir," Kevin said. He waited for a beat. "And we'll try hard not to be dreary." Marcus lifted an eyebrow.

A cluster of academics watched with intense frustration in their eyes as the seven of them swept out of the hall together and into the cool, cloudless night.

And another pair of eyes watched as well, from the deep shadows under the porch pillars of Convocation Hall. Eyes that reflected the light, and did not blink.

It was a short walk, and a pleasant one. Across the wide central green of the campus, then along the dark winding path known as Philosopher's Walk that twisted, with gentle slopes on either side, behind the law school, the Faculty of Music, and the massive edifice of the Royal Ontario Museum, where the dinosaur bones preserved their long silence. It was a route that Paul Schafer had been carefully avoiding for the better part of the past year.

He slowed a little, to detach himself from the others. Up ahead, in the shadows, Kevin, Kim, and Lo-

renzo Marcus were weaving a baroque fantasy of im-
probable entanglements between the clans Ford and
Marcus, with a few of Kevin's remoter Russian ances-
tors thrown into the mix by marriage. Jennifer, on
Marcus's left arm, was urging them on with her laughter, while Dave Martyniuk loped silently along on the
grass beside the walkway, looking a little out of place.
Matt Sören, quietly companionable, had slowed his
pace to fall into stride with Paul. Schafer, however,
withdrawing, could feel the conversation and laughter
sliding into background. The sensation was a familiar
one of late, and after a while it was as if he were
walking alone.

Which may have been why, partway along the path,
he became aware of something to which the others
were oblivious. It pulled him sharply out of reverie,
and he walked a short distance in a different sort of
silence before turning to the Dwarf beside him.

"Is there any reason," he asked, very softly, "why
the two of you would be followed?"

Matt Sören broke stride only momentarily. He took
a deep breath. "Where?" he asked, in a voice equally
low.

"Behind us, to the left. Slope of the hill. Is there a
reason?"

"There may be. Would you keep walking, please?
And say nothing for now—it may be nothing." When
Paul hesitated, the Dwarf gripped his arm. "Please?"
he repeated. Schafer, after a moment, nodded and
quickened his pace to catch up to the group now several yards ahead. The mood by then was hilarious and
very loud. Only Paul, listening for it, heard the sharp,
abruptly truncated cry from the darkness behind them.
He blinked, but no expression crossed his face.

Matt Sören rejoined them just as they reached the
end of the shadowed walkway and came out to the
noise and bright lights of Bloor Street. Ahead lay
the huge stone pile of the old Park Plaza hotel. Before

they crossed the road he placed a hand again on Schafer's arm.

"Thank you," said the Dwarf.

"Well," said Lorenzo Marcus, as they settled into chairs in his sixteenth-floor suite, "why don't you all tell me about yourselves? Yourselves," he repeated, raising an admonitory finger at grinning Kevin.

"Why don't you start?" Marcus went on, turning to Kim. "What are you studying?"

Kim acquiesced with some grace. "Well, I'm just finishing my interning year at—"

"Hold it, Kim."

It was Paul. Ignoring a fierce look from the Dwarf, he levelled his eyes on their host. "Sorry, Dr. Marcus. I've got some questions of my own and I need answers now, or we're all going home."

"Paul, what the—"

"No, Kev. Listen a minute." They were all staring at Schafer's pale, intense features. "Something very strange is happening here. I want to know," he said to Marcus, "why you were so anxious to cut us out of that crowd. Why you sent your friend to set it up. I want to know what you did to me in the auditorium. And I really want to know why we were followed on the way over here."

"Followed?" The shock registering on Lorenzo Marcus's face was manifestly unfeigned.

"That's right," Paul said, "and I want to know what it was, too."

"Matt?" Marcus asked, in a whisper.

The Dwarf fixed Paul Schafer with a long stare.

Paul met the glance. "Our priorities," he said, "can't be the same in this." After a moment, Matt Sören nodded and turned to Marcus.

"Friends from home," he said. "It seems there are those who want to know exactly what you are doing when you . . . travel."

"Friends?" Lorenzo Marcus asked.

"I speak loosely. Very loosely."

There was a silence. Marcus leaned back in his armchair, stroking the grey beard. He closed his eyes.

"This isn't how I would have chosen to begin," he said at length, "but it may be for the best after all." He turned to Paul. "I owe you an apology. Earlier this evening I subjected you to something we call a searching. It doesn't always work. Some have defences against it and with others, such as yourself, it seems, strange things can happen. What took place between us unsettled me as well."

Paul's eyes, more blue than grey in the lamplight, were astonishingly unsurprised. "I'll need to talk about what we saw," he said to Lorenzo Marcus, "but the thing is, why did you do it in the first place?"

And so they were there. Kevin, leaning forward, every sense sharpened, saw Lorenzo Marcus draw a deep breath, and he had a flash image in that instant of his own life poised on the edge of an abyss.

"Because," Lorenzo Marcus said, "you were quite right, Paul Schafer—I didn't just want to escape a boring reception tonight. I need you. The five of you."

"We're not five." Dave's heavy voice crashed in. "I've got nothing to do with these people."

"You are too quick to renounce friendship, Dave Martyniuk," Marcus snapped back. "But," he went on, more gently, after a frozen instant, "it doesn't matter here—and to make you see why, I must try to explain. Which is harder than it would have been once." He hesitated, hand at his beard again.

"You aren't Lorenzo Marcus, are you?" Paul said, very quietly.

In the stillness, the tall man turned to him again. "Why do you say that?"

Paul shrugged. "Am I right?"

"That searching truly was a mistake. Yes," said their host, "you are right." Dave was looking from Paul to the speaker with hostile incredulity. "Although I am Marcus, in a way—as much as anyone is. There is no one else. But Marcus is not who I am.''

''And who are you?'' It was Kim who asked. And was answered in a voice suddenly deep as a spell.

''My name is Loren. Men call me Silvercloak. I am a mage. My friend is Matt Sören, who was once King of the Dwarves. We come from Paras Derval, where Ailell reigns, in a world that is not your own.''

In the stone silence that followed this, Kevin Laine, who had chased an elusive image down all the nights of his life, felt an astonishing turbulence rising in his heart. There was a power woven into the old man's voice, and that, as much as the words, reached through to him.

''Almighty God,'' he whispered. ''Paul, how did you know?''

''Wait a second! You *believe* this?'' It was Dave Martyniuk, all bristling belligerence. ''I've never heard anything so crack-brained in my life!'' He put his drink down and was halfway to the door in two long strides.

''Dave, please!''

It stopped him. Dave turned slowly in the middle of the room to face Jennifer Lowell. ''Don't go,'' she pleaded. ''He said he needed us.''

Her eyes, he noticed for the first time, were green. He shook his head. ''Why do you care?''

''Didn't you hear it?'' she replied. ''Didn't you feel anything?''

He wasn't about to tell these people what he had or hadn't heard in the old man's voice, but before he could make that clear, Kevin Laine spoke.

''Dave, we can afford to hear him out. If there's danger or it's really wild, we can run away after.''

He heard the goad in the words, and the implication. He didn't rise to it, though. Never turning from Jennifer, he walked over and sat beside her on the couch. Didn't even look at Kevin Laine.

There was a silence, and she was the one who broke

it. "Now, Dr. Marcus, or whatever you prefer to be called, we'll listen. But please explain. Because I'm frightened now."

It is not known whether Loren Silvercloak had a vision then of what the future held for Jennifer, but he bestowed upon her a look as tender as he could give, from a nature storm-tossed, but still more giving, perhaps, than anything else. And then he began the tale.

"There are many worlds," he said, "caught in the loops and whorls of time. Seldom do they intersect, and so for the most part they are unknown to each other. Only in Fionavar, the prime creation, which all the others imperfectly reflect, is the lore gathered and preserved that tells of how to bridge the worlds—and even there the years have not dealt kindly with ancient wisdom. We have made the crossing before, Matt and I, but always with difficulty, for much is lost, even in Fionavar."

"How? How do you cross?" It was Kevin.

"It is easiest to call it magic, though there is more involved than spells."

"Your magic?" Kevin continued.

"I am a mage, yes," Loren said. "The crossing was mine. And so, too, if you come, will be the return."

"This is ridiculous!" Martyniuk exploded again. This time he would not look at Jennifer. "Magic. Crossings. Show me something! Talk is cheap, and I don't believe a word of this."

Loren stared coldly at Dave. Kim, seeing it, caught her breath. But then the severe face creased in a sudden smile. The eyes, improbably, danced. "You're right," he said. "It is much the simplest way. Look, then."

There was silence in the room for almost ten seconds. Kevin saw, out of the corner of his eye, that the Dwarf, too, had gone very still. What'll it be, he thought.

They saw a castle.

Where Dave Martyniuk had stood moments before, there appeared battlements and towers, a garden, a central courtyard, an open square before the walls, and on the very highest rampart a banner somehow blowing in a non-existent breeze: and on the banner Kevin saw a crescent moon above a spreading tree.

"Paras Derval," Loren said softly, gazing at his own artifice with an expression almost wistful, "in Brennin, High Kingdom of Fionavar. Mark the flags in the great square before the palace. They are there for the coming celebration, because the eighth day past the full of the moon this month will end the fifth decade of Ailell's reign."

"And us?" Kimberly's voice was parchment-thin. "Where do we fit in?"

A wry smile softened the lines of Loren's face. "Not heroically, I'm afraid, though there is pleasure in this for you, I hope. A great deal is being done to celebrate the anniversary. There has been a long spring drought in Brennin, and it has been deemed politic to give the people something to cheer about. And I daresay there is reason for it. At any rate, Metran, First Mage to Ailell, has decided that the gift to him and to the people from the Council of the Mages will be to bring five people from another world—one for each decade of the reign—to join us for the festival fortnight."

Kevin Laine laughed aloud. "Red Indians to the Court of King James?"

With a gesture almost casual, Loren dissolved the apparition in the middle of the room. "I'm afraid there's some truth to that. Metran's ideas . . . he is First of my Council, but I daresay I need not always agree with him."

"You're here," Paul said.

"I wanted to try another crossing in any case," Loren replied quickly. "It has been a long time since last I was in your world as Lorenzo Marcus."

"Have I got this straight?" Kim asked. "You want

us to cross with you somehow to your world, and then you'll bring us back?''

''Basically, yes. You will be with us for two weeks, perhaps, but when we return I will have you back in this room within a few hours of when we departed.''

''Well,'' said Kevin, with a sly grin, ''that should get you, Martyniuk, for sure. Just think, Dave, two extra weeks to study for Evidence!''

Dave flushed bright red, as the room broke up in a release of tension.

''I'm in, Loren Silvercloak,'' said Kevin Laine, as they quieted. And so became the first. He managed a grin. ''I've always wanted to wear war-paint to court. When's take-off?''

Loren looked at him steadily. ''Tomorrow. Early evening, if we are to time it properly. I will not ask you to decide now. Think for the rest of tonight, and tomorrow. If you will come with me, be here by late afternoon.''

''What about you? What if we don't come?'' Kim's forehead was creased with the vertical line that always showed when she was under stress.

Loren seemed disconcerted by the question. ''If that happens, I fail. It has happened before. Don't worry about me . . . niece.'' It was remarkable what a smile did to his face. ''Shall we leave it at that?'' he went on, as Kim's eyes still registered an unresolved concern. ''If you decide to come, be here tomorrow. I will be waiting.''

''One thing.'' It was Paul again. ''I'm sorry to keep asking the unpleasant questions, but we still don't know what that thing was on Philosophers' Walk.''

Dave had forgotten. Jennifer hadn't. They both looked at Loren. At length he answered, speaking directly to Paul. ''There is magic in Fionavar. I have shown you something of it, even here. There are also creatures, of good and evil, who co-exist with human-kind. Your own world, too, was once like this, though it has been drifting from the pattern for a long time now. The legends of which I spoke in the auditorium tonight are echoes, scarcely understood, of mornings when man did not walk alone, and other beings, both friend and foe, moved in the forests and the hills." He paused. "What followed us was one of the svart alfar, I think. Am I right, Matt?"

The Dwarf nodded, without speaking.

"The svarts," Loren went on, "are a malicious race, and have done great evil in their time. There are few of them left. This one, braver than most, it would seem, somehow followed Matt and me through on our crossing. They are ugly creatures, and sometimes dangerous, though usually only in numbers. This one, I suspect, is dead." He looked to Matt again.

Once more the Dwarf nodded from where he stood by the door.

"I wish you hadn't told me that," Jennifer said.

The mage's eyes, deep-set, were again curiously tender as he looked at her. "I'm sorry you have been frightened this evening. Will you accept my assurance that, unsettling as they may sound, the svarts need not be of concern to you?" He paused, his gaze holding hers. "I would not have you do anything that goes against your nature. I have extended to you an invitation, no more. You may find it easier to decide after leaving us." He rose to his feet.

Another kind of power. A man accustomed to command, Kevin thought a few moments later, as the five of them found themselves outside the door of the room. They made their way down the hall to the elevator.

Matt Sören closed the door behind them.

"How bad is it?" Loren asked sharply.

The Dwarf grimaced. "Not very. I was careless."

"A knife?" The mage was quickly helping his friend to remove the scaled-down jacket he wore.

"I wish. Teeth, actually." Loren cursed in sudden anger when the jacket finally slipped off to reveal the dark, heavily clotted blood staining the shirt on the Dwarf's left shoulder. He began gently tearing the cloth away from around the wound, swearing under his breath the whole time.

"It isn't so bad, Loren. Be easy. And you must admit I was clever to take the jacket off before going after him."

"Very clever, yes. Which is just as well, because my own stupidity of late is terrifying me! How in the name of Conall Cernach could I let a svart alfar come through with us?" He left the room with swift strides and returned a moment later with towels soaked in hot water.

The Dwarf endured the cleansing of his wound in silence. When the dried blood was washed away, the teeth marks could be seen, purple and very deep.

Loren examined it closely. "This is bad, my friend. Are you strong enough to help me heal it? We could have Metran or Teyrnon do it tomorrow, but I'd rather not wait."

"Go ahead." Matt closed his eyes.

The mage paused a moment, then carefully placed a hand above the wound. He spoke a word softly, then another. And beneath his long fingers the swelling on the Dwarf's shoulder began slowly to recede. When he finished, though, the face of Matt Sören was bathed in a sheen of perspiration. With his good arm Matt reached for a towel and wiped his forehead.

"All right?" Loren asked.

"Just fine."

"Just fine!" the mage mimicked angrily. "It would help, you know, if you didn't always play the silent hero! How am I supposed to know when you're really hurting if you always give me the same answer?"

The Dwarf fixed Loren with his one dark eye, and there was a trace of amusement in his face. "You aren't," he said. "You aren't supposed to know."

Loren made a gesture of ultimate exasperation, and left the room again, returning with a shirt of his own, which he began cutting into strips.

"Loren, don't blame yourself for letting the svart come through. You couldn't have done anything."

"Don't be a fool! I should have been aware of its presence as soon as it tried to come within the circle."

"I'm very seldom foolish, my friend." The Dwarf's tone was mild. "You couldn't have known, because it was wearing this when I killed it." Sören reached into his right trouser pocket and pulled out an object that he held up in his palm. It was a bracelet, of delicate silver workmanship, and set within it was a gem, green like an emerald.

"A vellin stone!" Loren Silvercloak whispered in dismay. "So it would have been shielded from me. Matt, someone gave a vellin to a svart alfar."

"So it would seem," the Dwarf agreed.

The mage was silent; he attended to the bandaging of Matt's shoulder with quick, skilled hands. When that was finished he walked, still wordless, to the window. He opened it, and a late-night breeze fluttered the white curtains. Loren gazed down at the few cars moving along the street far below.

"These five people," he said at last, still looking down. "What am I taking them back to? Do I have any right?"

The Dwarf didn't answer.

After a moment, Loren spoke again, almost to himself. "I left so much out."

"You did."

"Did I do wrong?"

"Perhaps. But you are seldom wrong in these things. Nor is Ysanne. If you feel they are needed—"

"But I don't know what for! I don't know *how*. It is only her dreams, my premonitions. . . ."

"Then trust yourself. Trust your premonitions. The girl *is* a hook, and the other one, Paul—"

"He is another thing. I don't know what."

"But something. You've been troubled for a long time, my friend. And I don't think needlessly."

The mage turned from the window to look at the

other man. "I'm afraid you may be right. Matt, who would have us followed here?"

"Someone who wants you to fail in this. Which should tell us something."

Loren nodded abstractedly. "But who," he went on, looking at the green-stoned bracelet that the Dwarf still held, "who would ever give such a treasure into the hands of a svart alfar?"

The Dwarf looked down at the stone for a very long time as well before answering.

"Someone who wants you dead," Matt Sören said.

Chapter 2

The girls shared a silent taxi west to the duplex they rented beside High Park. Jennifer, partly because she knew her roommate very well, decided that she wouldn't be the first to bring up what had happened that night, what they both seemed to have heard under the surface of the old man's words.

But she was dealing with complex emotions of her own, as they turned down Parkside Drive and she watched the dark shadows of the park slide past on their right. When they got out of the cab the late-night breeze seemed unseasonably chill. She looked across the road for a moment, at the softly rustling trees.

Inside they had a conversation about choices, about doing or not doing things, that either one of them could have predicted.

◆

Dave Martyniuk refused Kim's offer to share a cab and walked the mile west to his flat on Palmerston. He walked quickly, the athlete's stride overlaid by an ger and tension. *You are too quick to renounce friendship,* the old man had said. Dave scowled, moving faster. What did *he* know about it?

The telephone began ringing as he unlocked the door of his basement apartment.

"Yeah?" He caught it on the sixth ring.

"You are pleased with yourself, I am sure?"

"Jesus, Dad. What is it this time?"

"Don't swear at me. It would *kill* you, wouldn't it, to do something that would bring us pleasure."

"I don't know what the hell you're talking about."

"Such language. Such respect."

"Dad, I don't have time for this any more."

"Yes, hide from me. You went tonight as Vincent's guest to this lecture. And then you went off after with the man he most wanted to speak with. And you couldn't even *think* of asking your brother?"

Dave took a careful breath. His reflexive anger giving way to the old sorrow. "Dad, please believe me—it didn't happen that way. Marcus went with these people I know because he didn't feel like talking to the academics like Vince. I just tagged along."

"You just tagged along," his father mimicked in his heavy Ukrainian accent. "You are a liar. Your jealousy is so much that you—"

Dave hung up. And unplugged the telephone. With a fierce and bitter pain he stared at it, watching how, over and over again, it didn't ring.

———◆———

They said good-night to the girls and watched Martyniuk stalk off into the darkness.

"Coffee time, amigo," Kevin Laine said brightly. "Much to talk about we have, yes?"

Paul hesitated, and in the moment of that hesitation Kevin's mood shattered like glass.

"Not tonight, I think. I've got some things to do, Kev."

The hurt in Kevin Laine moved to the surface, threatened to break through. "Okay," was all he said, though. "Good night. Maybe I'll see you tomorrow." And he turned abruptly and jogged across Bloor against the light to where he'd parked his car. He drove home, a little too fast, through the quiet streets.

It was after one o'clock when he pulled into the driveway, so he entered the house as silently as he could, sliding the bolt gently home.

"I am awake, Kevin. It is all right."

"What are you doing up? It's very late, Abba." He used the Hebrew word for father, as he always did.

Sol Laine, in pajamas and robe at the kitchen table, raised a quizzical eyebrow as Kevin walked in. "I need permission from my son to stay up late?"

"Who else's?" Kevin dropped into one of the other chairs.

"A good answer," his father approved. "Would you like some tea?"

"Sounds good."

"How was this talk?" Sol asked as he attended to the boiling kettle.

"Fine. Very good, actually. We had a drink with the speaker afterwards." Kevin briefly considered telling his father about what had happened, but only briefly. Father and son had a long habit of protecting each other, and Kevin knew that this was something Sol would be unable to handle. He wished it were otherwise; it would have been good, he thought, a little bitterly, to have *someone* to talk to.

"Jennifer is well? And her friend?"

Kevin's bitterness broke in a wave of love for the old man who'd raised him alone. Sol had never been able to reconcile his orthodoxy with his son's relationship with Catholic Jennifer—and had resented himself for not being able to. So through their short time together, and after, Kevin's father had treated Jen like a jewel of great worth.

"She's fine. Says hello. Kim's fine, too."

"But Paul isn't?"

Kevin blinked. "Oh, Abba, you're too sharp for me. Why do you say that?"

"Because if he was, you would have gone out with him afterwards. The way you always used to. You would still be out. I would be drinking my tea alone, all alone." The twinkle in his eyes belied the lugubrious sentiments.

Kevin laughed aloud, then stopped when he heard the bitter note creeping in.

"No, he's not all right. But I seem to be the only

one who questions it. I think I'm becoming a pain in the ass to him. I hate it.''

"Sometimes," his father said, filling the glass cups in their Russian-style metal holders, "a friend has to be that."

"No one else seems to think there's anything wrong, though. They just talk about how it takes time."

"It does take time, Kevin."

Kevin made an impatient gesture. "I *know* it does. I'm not that stupid. But I know him, too, I know him very well, and he's. . . . There's something else here, and I don't know what it is."

His father didn't speak for a moment. "How long is it now?" he asked, finally.

"Ten months," Kevin replied flatly. "Last summer."

"Ach!" Sol shook his heavy, still-handsome head. "Such a terrible thing."

Kevin leaned forward. "Abba, he's been closing himself off. To everyone. I don't . . . I'm afraid for what might happen. And I can't seem to get through."

"Are you trying too hard?" Sol Laine asked gently.

His son slumped back in his chair. "Maybe," he said, and the old man could see the effort the answer took. "But it hurts, Abba, he's all twisted up."

Sol Laine, who had married late, had lost his wife to cancer when Kevin, their only child, was five years old. He looked now at his handsome, fair son with a twisting in his own heart. "Kevin," he said, "you will have to learn—and for you it will be hard—that sometimes you can't do anything. Sometimes you simply can't."

Kevin finished his tea. He kissed his father on the forehead and went up to bed in the grip of a sadness that was new to him, and a sense of yearning that was not.

He woke once in the night, a few hours before Kimberly would. Reaching for a note pad he kept by the bed, he scribbled a line and fell back into sleep. *We are the total of our longings,* he had written. But Kevin was a song-writer, not a poet, and he never did use it.

◆

Paul Schafer walked home as well that night, north up Avenue Road and two blocks over at Bernard. His pace was slower than Dave's, though, and you could not have told his thoughts or mood from his movements. His hands were in his pockets, and two or three times, where the streetlights thinned, he looked up at the ragged pattern of cloud that now hid and now revealed the moon.

Only at his doorway did his face show an expression—and this was only a transitory irresolution, as of someone weighing sleep against a walk around the block, perhaps.

Schafer went in, though, and unlocked his ground-floor apartment. Turning on a lamp in the living room, he poured himself a drink and carried the glass to a deep armchair. Again the pale face under the dark shock of hair was expressionless. And again, when his mouth and eyes did move, a long time later, it was to register only a kind of indecision, wiped away quickly this time by the tightening jaw.

He leaned sideways then to the stereo and tape deck, turned them on, and inserted a cassette. In part because it was very late, but only in part, he adjusted the machine and put on the headphones. Then he turned out the only light in the room.

It was a private tape, one he had made himself a year ago. On it, as he sat there motionless in the dark, sounds from the summer before took shape: a graduation recital in the Faculty of Music's Edward Johnson Building, by a girl named Rachel Kincaid. A girl with dark hair like his own and dark eyes like no one else in this world.

And Paul Schafer, who believed one should be able to endure anything, and who believed this of himself most of all, listened as long as he could, and failed again. When the second movement began, he shuddered through an indrawn breath and stabbed the machine to silence.

It seemed that there were still things one could not do. So one did everything else as well as the one possibly could and found new things to try, to will oneself to master, and always one realized, at the kernel and heart of things, that the ends of the earth would not be far enough away.

Which was why, despite knowing very well that there were things they had not been told, Paul Schafer was glad, bleakly glad, to be going farther than the ends of the earth on the morrow. And the moon, moving then to shine unobstructed through the window, lit the room enough to reveal the serenity of his face.

———————◆———————

And in the place beyond the ends of earth, in Fionavar, which lay waiting for them like a lover, like a dream, another moon, larger than our own, rose to light the changing of the wardstone guard in the palace of Paras Derval.

The priestess appointed came with the new guards, tended and banked the naal flame set before the stone, and withdrew, yawning, to her narrow bed.

And the stone, Ginserat's stone, set in its high obsidian pillar carved with a relief of Conary before the Mountain, shone still, as it had a thousand years, radiantly blue.

Chapter 3

Towards dawn a bank of clouds settled low over the city. Kimberly Ford stirred, surfaced almost to wakefulness, then slipped back down into a light sleep, and a dream unlike any she'd known before.

There was a place of massive jumbled stones. A wind was blowing over wide grasslands. It was dusk. She almost knew the place, was so close to naming it that her inability tasted bitter in her mouth. The wind made a chill, keening sound as it blew between the stones. She had come to find one who was needed, but she knew he was not there. A ring was on her finger, with a stone that gleamed a dull red in the twilight, and this was her power and her burden both. The gathered stones demanded an invocation from her; the wind threatened to tear it from her mouth. She knew what she was there to say, and was broken-hearted, beyond all grief she'd ever known, at the price her speaking would exact from the man she'd come to summon. In the dream, she opened her mouth to say the words.

She woke then, and was very still a long time. When she rose, it was to move to the window, where she drew the curtain back.

The clouds were breaking up. Venus, rising in the east before the sun, shone silver-white and dazzling, like hope. The ring on her finger in the dream had shone as well: deep red and masterful, like Mars.

* * *

The Dwarf dropped into a crouch, hands loosely clasped in front of him. They were all there; Kevin with his guitar, Dave Martyniuk defiantly clutching the promised Evidence notes. Loren remained out of sight in the bedroom. "Preparing," the Dwarf had said. And now, without preamble, Matt Sören said more.

"Ailell reins in Brennin, the High Kingdom. Fifty years now, as you have heard. He is very old, much reduced. Metran heads the Council of the Mages, and Gorlaes, the Chancellor, is first of all advisers. You will meet them both. Ailell had two sons only, very late in life. The name of the elder—," Matt hesitated, "—is not to be spoken. The younger is Diarmuid, now heir to the throne."

Too many mysteries, Kevin Laine thought. He was nervous, and angry with himself for that. Beside him, Kim was concentrating fiercely, a single vertical line furrowing her forehead.

"South of us," the Dwarf continued, "the Saeren flows through its ravine, and beyond the river is Cathal, the Garden Country. There has been war with Shalhassan's people in my lifetime. The river is patrolled on both sides. North of Brennin is the Plain where the Dalrei dwell, the Riders. The tribes follow the eltor herds as the seasons change. You are unlikely to see any of the Dalrei. They dislike walls and cities."

Kim's frown, Kevin saw, had deepened.

"Over the mountains, eastward, the land grows wilder and very beautiful. That country is called Eridu now, though it had another name long ago. It breeds a people once brutal, though quiet of late. Little is known of doings in Eridu, for the mountains are a stern barrier." Matt Sören's voice roughened. "Among the Eriduns dwell the Dwarves, unseen for the most part, in their chambers and halls under the mountains of Banir Lök and Banir Tal, beside Calor Diman, the Crystal Lake. A place more fair than any in all the worlds."

Kevin had questions again, but withheld them. He could see there was an old pain at work here.

"North and west of Brennin is Pendaran Wood. It runs for miles to the north, between the Plain and the Sea. Beyond the forest is Daniloth, the Shadowland." The Dwarf stopped, as abruptly as he'd begun, and turned to adjust his pack and gear. There was a silence.

"Matt?" It was Kimberly. The Dwarf turned. "What about the mountain north of the Plain?"

Matt made a swift, convulsive gesture with one hand, and stared at the slight, brown-haired girl.

"So you were right, my friend, from the very first."

Kevin wheeled. In the doorway leading from the bedroom stood the tall figure of Loren, in a long robe of shifting silver hues.

"What have you seen?" the mage asked Kim, very gently.

She, too, had twisted to face him. The grey eyes were strange—inward and troubled. She shook her head, as if to clear it. "Nothing, really. Just . . . that I do see a mountain."

"And?" Loren pressed.

"And . . ." she closed her eyes. "A hunger. *Inside*, somehow. . . . I can't explain it."

"It is written," said Loren after a moment, "in our books of wisdom, that in each of the worlds there are those who have dreams or visions—one sage called them memories—of Fionavar, which is the First. Matt, who has gifts of his own, named you as one such yesterday." He paused; Kim didn't move. "It is known," Loren went on, "that to bring people back in a crossing, such a person must be found to stand at the heart of the circle."

"So that's why you wanted us? Because of Kim?" It was Paul Schafer; the first words he'd spoken since arriving.

"Yes," said the mage, simply.

"Damn!" tried Kevin softly. "And I thought it was my charm."

No one laughed. Kim stared at Loren, as if seeking answers in the lines of his face, or the shifting patterns of his robe.

Finally she asked, "And the mountain?"

Loren's voice was almost matter-of-fact. "One thousand years ago someone was imprisoned there. At the deepest root of Rangat, which is the mountain you have seen."

Kim nodded, hesitated. "Someone . . . evil?" The word came awkwardly to her tongue.

They might have been alone in the room. "Yes," said the mage.

"One thousand years ago?"

He nodded again. In this moment of misdirection, of deceit, when everything stood in danger of falling apart, his eyes were more calm and compassionate than they had ever been.

With one hand Kim tugged at a strand of brown hair. She drew a breath. "All right," she said. "All right, then. How do I help you cross?"

Dave was struggling to absorb all this when things began to move too quickly. He found himself part of a circle around Kim and the mage. He linked hands with Jennifer and Matt on either side. The Dwarf seemed to be concentrating very hard; his legs were wide apart, braced. Then Loren began to speak words in a tongue Dave didn't know, his voice growing in power and resonance.

And was interrupted by Paul Schafer.

"Loren—is the person under that mountain dead?"

The mage gazed at the slim figure who'd asked the question he feared. "You, too?" he whispered. Then, "No," he answered, telling the truth. "No, he isn't." And resumed speaking in his strange language.

Dave wrestled with the refusal to seem afraid that had, in large part, brought him here, and with the genuine panic that was building within him. Paul had nodded once at Loren's answer, but that was all. The mage's words had become a complex rising chant. The aura of power began to shimmer visibly in the room. A low-pitched humming sound began.

"Hey!" Dave burst out. "I need a promise I'll be back!" There was no reply. Matt Sören's eyes were closed now. His grip on Dave's wrist was firm.

The shimmer in the air increased, and then the humming began to rise in volume.

"No!" Dave shouted again. "No! I need a promise!" And on the words he violently pulled his hands free from those of Jennifer and the Dwarf.

Kimberly Ford screamed.

And in that moment the room began to dissolve on them. Kevin, frozen, disbelieving, saw Kim reach out then, wildly, to clutch Dave's arm and take Jen's free hand even as he heard the cry torn from her throat.

Then the cold of the crossing and the darkness of the space between worlds came down and Kevin saw nothing more. In his mind, though, whether for an instant or an age, he thought he heard the sound of mocking laughter. There was a taste in his mouth, like ashes of grief. *Dave,* he thought, *oh, Martyniuk, what have you done?*

PART II

Rachel's Song

Chapter 4

It was night when they came through, in a small, dimly lit room somewhere high up. There were two chairs, benches and an unlit fire. An intricately patterned carpet on the stone floor. Along one wall stretched a tapestry, but the room was too darkly shadowed, despite flickering wall torches, for them to make it out. The windows were open.

"So, Silvercloak, you've come back," a reedy voice from the doorway said, without warmth. Kevin looked over quickly to see a bearded man leaning casually on a spear.

Loren ignored him. "Matt?" he said sharply. "Are you all right?" The Dwarf, visibly shaken by the crossing, managed a terse nod. He had slumped into one of the heavy chairs and there were beads of perspiration on his forehead. Kevin turned to check the others. All seemed to be fine, a little dazed, but fine, except—

Except that Dave Martyniuk wasn't there.

"Oh, God!" he began, "Loren—"

And was stopped in mid-sentence by a beseeching look from the mage. Paul Schafer, standing beside Kevin, caught it as well, and Kevin saw him walk quietly over to the two women. Schafer spoke softly to them, and then nodded once, to Loren.

At which point the mage finally turned to the guard, who was still leaning indolently on his weapon. "Is it the evening before?" Loren asked.

"Why, yes," the man replied. "But shouldn't a great mage know that without the asking?"

Kevin saw Loren's eyes flicker in the torchlight. "Go," he said. "Go tell the King I have returned."

"It's late. He'll be sleeping."

"He will want to know this. Go now."

The guard moved with deliberate, insolent slowness. As he turned, though, there was a sudden *thunk,* and a thrown knife quivered in the panelling of the doorway, inches from his head.

"I know you, Vart," a deep voice said, as the man whipped around, pale even by torchlight. "I have marked you. You will do what you have been told, and quickly, and you will speak to rank with deference— or my next dagger will not rest in wood." Matt Sören was on his feet again, and danger bristled through him like a presence.

There was a tense silence. Then:

"I am sorry, my lord mage. The lateness of the hour . . . my fatigue. Welcome home, my lord, I go to do your will." The guard raised his spear in a formal salute, then spun again, sharply this time, and left the room. Matt walked forward to retrieve his dagger. He remained in the doorway, watching.

"Now," said Kevin Laine. "Where is he?"

Loren had dropped into the chair the Dwarf had vacated. "I am not sure," he said. "Forgive me, but I truly don't know."

"But you have to know!" Jennifer exclaimed.

"He pulled away just as I was closing the circle. I was too far under the power—I couldn't come out to see his path. I do not even know if he came with us."

"I do," said Kim Ford simply. "He came. I had him all the way. I was holding him."

Loren rose abruptly. "You did? Brightly woven! This means he has crossed—he is in Fionavar, somewhere. And if that is so, he will be found. Our friends will begin to search immediately."

"Your friends?" Kevin asked. "Not that creep in the doorway, I hope?"

Loren shook his head. "Not him, no. He is Gorlaes's tool—and here I must ask of you another thing." He hesitated. "There are factions in this court, and a struggle taking place, for Ailell is old now. Gorlaes would like me gone, for many reasons, and failing that, would take joy in discrediting me before the King."

"So if Dave is missing . . . ?" Kevin murmured.

"Exactly. I think only Metran knows I went for five—and I never promised him so many, in any case. Dave will be found, I promise you that. Can I ask you to keep his presence a secret for this time?"

Jennifer Lowell had moved to the open window while the others talked. A hot night, and very dry. Below and to her left, she could make out the lights of a town, lying almost directly adjacent to the walled enclosure of what she assumed to be Paras Derval. There were fields in front of her, and beyond them rose the thick, close trees of a forest. There was no breeze. She looked upward, apprehensive, and was desperately relieved to find she knew the stars. For though the slender hand on the window ledge was steady, and the cool green eyes gave little away, she had been badly thrown by Dave's disappearance and the sudden dagger.

In a life shaped of careful decisions, the only impulsive act of significance had been the beginning of her relationship with Kevin Laine one night two years ago. Now, improbably, she found herself in a place where only the fact that she could see the Summer Triangle overhead gave her any kind of security. She shook her head and, not lacking in a sense of irony, smiled very slightly to herself.

Paul Schafer was speaking, answering the mage. "It seems," he said softly—they were all speaking quietly—"that if you brought us here, then we're already a part of your group, or we'll be seen that way any-how. I'll keep my mouth shut.''

Kevin was nodding, and then Kim. Jennifer turned from the window. "I won't say anything," she said. "But please find Dave soon, because I really am going to be very frightened if you don't.''

"Company!" Matt growled from the doorway.

"Ailell? Already? It can't be," said Loren.

Matt listened for a moment longer. "No . . . not the King. I think . . ." and his dark, bearded face twisted into its version of a smile. "Listen for your-self," the Dwarf said.

A second later Kevin heard it, too: the unsteady car-oling of someone coming down the hallway towards them, someone far gone in drink:

> *Those who rode that night with Revor*
> *Did a deed to last forever . . .*
> *The Weaver cut from brighter cloth*
> *Those who rode through Daniloth!*

"You fat buffoon!" another voice snarled, rather more controlled. "Shut up or you'll have him disin-herited for bringing you in here." The sardonic laugh-ter of a third person could be heard, as the footsteps made their tenuous way up the corridor.

"Song," the aggrieved troubadour said, "is a gift to men from the immortal gods.''

"Not the way you sing, Tegid," his critic snapped. Loren was suppressing a smile, Kim saw. Kevin snorted with laughter.

"Shipyard lout," the one called Tegid retorted, not quietly. "You betray your ignorance. Those who were there will never forget my singing that night in the Great Hall at Seresh. I had them weeping, I had—''

"I *was* there, you clown! I was sitting beside you. And I've still got stains on my green doublet from when they started throwing fruit at you.''

"Poltroons! What can you expect in Seresh? But the

battle after, the brave fight in that same hall! Even
though wounded, I rallied our—"

"Wounded?" Hilarity and exasperation vied for
mastery in the other speaker's voice. "A tomato in the
eye is hardly—"

"Hold it, Coll." The third man spoke for the first
time. And in the room Loren and Matt exchanged a
glance. "There's a guard just ahead," the light, controlling voice went on. "I'll deal with him. Wait for
a minute after I go in, then take Tegid to the last room
on the left. And keep him quiet, or by the river blood
of Lisen, I *will* be disinherited."

Matt stepped quickly into the hallway. "Good even,
Prince." He raised his dagger in salute. A vein of blue
glittered in the light. "There is no guard here now.
He has gone to bring your father—Silvercloak has just
returned with four people who have crossed. You had
best move Tegid to a safe place very fast."

"Sören? Welcome home," said the Prince, walking
forward. "Coll, take him quickly."

"Quickly?" Tegid expostulated. "Great Tegid
moves at his own pace. He deigns not to hide from
minions and vassals. He confronts them with naked
steel of Rhoden and the prodigious armor of his wrath.
He—"

"Tegid," the Prince said with extreme softness,
"move now, and sharply, or I will have you stuffed
through a window and dropped to the courtyard. Pro-
digiously."

There was a silence. "Yes, my lord," the reply came,
surprisingly meek. As they moved past the doorway
Kim caught a glimpse of an enormously fat man, and
another, muscled but seeming small beside him, before
a third figure appeared in the entranceway, haloed by
the wall torch in the corridor. *Diarmuid,* she had time
to remember. They call him Diarmuid. The younger
son.

And then she found herself staring.

All his life Diarmuid dan Ailell had been doing that

to people. Supporting himself with a beringed hand upon the wall, he leaned lazily in the doorway and accepted Loren's bow, surveying them all. Kim, after a moment, was able to isolate some of the qualities: the lean, graceful build, high cheekbones in an over-refined face, a wide, expressive mouth, registering languid amusement just then, the jewelled hands, and the eyes . . . the cynical, mocking expression in the very blue eyes of the King's Heir in the High Kingdom. It was hard to judge his age; close to her own, she guessed.

"Thank you, Silvercloak," he said. "A timely return and a timely warning."

"It is folly to defy your father for Tegid," Loren began. "It is a matter far too trivial—"

Diarmuid laughed. "Advising me again? Already? A crossing hasn't changed you, Loren. There are reasons, there are reasons . . ." he murmured vaguely.

"I doubt it," the mage replied. "Other than perversity and South Keep wine."

"Good reasons, both," Diarmuid agreed, flashing a smile. "Who," he said, in a very different tone, "have you brought for Metran to parade tomorrow?"

Loren, seemingly used to this, made the introductions gravely. Kevin, named first, bowed formally. Paul followed suit, keeping his eyes on those of the Prince. Kim merely nodded. And Jennifer—

"A peach!" exclaimed Diarmuid dan Ailell. "Silvercloak, you have brought me a peach to nibble." He moved forward then, the jewellery at wrist and throat catching the torchlight, and, taking Jennifer's hand, bowed very low and kissed it.

Jennifer Lowell, not predisposed by character or environment to suffer this sort of thing gladly, let him have it as he straightened.

"Are you always this rude?" she asked. And there was no warmth in the voice at all, or in the green eyes.

It stopped him for an instant only. "Almost always," he answered affably. "I do have some redeem-

ing qualities, though I can never remember what
they're supposed to be. I'll wager," he went on, in a
swift change of mood, "that Loren is shaking his head
behind my back right now in tragic disapproval."
Which happened to be true. "Ah well, then," he continued, turning to look at the frowning mage, "I suppose I'm expected to apologize now?"

He grinned at Loren's sober agreement, then turned
once more to Jennifer. "I am sorry, sweetling. Drink
and a long ride this afternoon. You are quite extravagantly beautiful, and have probably dealt with worse
intrusions before. Indulge me." It was prettily done.
Jennifer, somewhat bemused, found she could only
manage a nod. Which succeeded in provoking yet another sublimely mocking smile. She flushed, angry
again.

Loren cut in sharply. "You are behaving badly,
Diarmuid, and you know it."

"Enough!" the Prince snapped. "Don't push me,
Loren." The two men exchanged a tense look.

When Diarmuid spoke again, though, it was in a
milder tone. "I did apologize, Loren, do me some
justice." After a moment, the mage nodded.

"Fair enough," he said. "We don't have time to
quarrel, in any case. I need your help. Two things. A
svart attacked us in the world from which I brought
these people. It followed Matt and me, and it was
wearing a vellin stone."

"And the other thing?" Diarmuid was instantly attentive, drunk as he was.

"There was a fifth person who crossed with us. We
lost him. He is in Fionavar—but I don't know where.
I need him found, and I would much prefer that Gorlaes not know of him."

"Obviously. How do you know he is here?"

"Kimberly was our hook. She says she had him."

Diarmuid turned to fix Kim with an appraising stare.
Tossing her hair back she met the look, and the expression in her own eyes was more than a little hostile.

Turning without reaction, the Prince walked to the window and looked out in silence. The waning moon had risen—overly large, but Jennifer, also gazing out, did not notice that.

"It hasn't rained while you were gone, by the way," said Diarmuid. "We have other things to talk about. Matt," he continued crisply, "Coll is in the last room on the left. Make sure Tegid is asleep, then brief him. A description of the fifth person. Tell Coll I'll speak with him later." Wordlessly, Matt slipped from the room.

"No rain at all?" Loren asked softly.

"None."

"And the crops?"

Diarmuid raised an eyebrow without bothering to answer. Loren's face seemed molded of fatigue and concern. "And the King?" he asked, almost reluctantly.

Diarmuid paused this time before answering. "Not well. He wanders sometimes. He was apparently talking to my mother last night during dinner in the Great Hall. Impressive, wouldn't you say, five years past her death?"

Loren shook his head. "He has been doing that for some time, though not in public before. Is there . . . is there word of your brother?"

"None." The answer this time was very swift. A strained silence followed. *His name is not to be spoken,* Kevin remembered and, looking at the Prince, wondered.

"There was a Gathering," Diarmuid said. "Seven nights past at the full of the moon. A secret one. They invoked the Goddess as Dana, and there was blood."

"No!" The mage made a violent gesture. "That is going too far. Who summoned it?"

Diarmuid's wide mouth crooked slightly.

"Herself, of course," he said.

"Jaelle?"

"Jaelle."

Loren began pacing the room. "She will cause trouble, I know it!"

"Of course she will. She means to. And my father is too old to deal with it. Can you see Ailell on the Summer Tree now?" And there was a new thing in the light voice—a deep, coruscating bitterness.

"I never could, Diarmuid." The mage's tone had suddenly gone soft. He stopped his pacing beside the Prince. "Whatever power lies in the Tree is outside my province. And Jaelle's, too, though she would deny it. You have heard my views on this. Blood magic, I fear, takes more than it gives back."

"So we sit," Diarmuid snarled, stiff anger cracking through, "we sit while the wheat burns up in fields all over Brennin! Fine doings for a would-be royal house!"

"My lord Prince"—the use of the title was careful, admonitory—"this is no ordinary season, and you do not need me to tell you that. Something unknown is at work, and not even Jaelle's midnight invocations will redress the balance, until we touch what lies beneath."

Diarmuid sank into one of the chairs, gazing blankly at the dim tapestry opposite the window. The wall torches had almost burnt out, leaving the room webbed with lighter and darker shadows. Leaning against the window ledge, Jennifer thought that she could almost see the threads of tension snaking through the darkened spaces. *What am I doing here,* she thought. Not for the last time. A movement on the other side of the chamber caught her eye, and she turned to see Paul Schafer looking at her. He gave a small, unexpectedly reassuring smile. *And I don't understand him, either,* she thought, somewhat despairingly.

Diarmuid was on his feet again by then, seemingly unable to be still for any length of time. "Loren," he said, "you know the King won't come tonight. Did you—"

"He must! I won't let Gorlaes have—"

"Someone's here," Paul said sharply. He had quietly ended up in Matt's post by the door. "Five men, three with swords."

"Diarmuid—"

"I know. You haven't seen me. I won't be far," and the heir to the throne of Brennin leaped in a rustle of cloth and a moonlit flash of yellow hair through the window, reaching out, almost lazily, for a handhold on the wall outside. For God's sake, Kevin thought.

Which was all he had time for. Vart, the surly guard, appeared in the doorway. When he saw that Matt was nowhere to be seen, a thin smile flicked across his face.

"My lord the Chancellor," Vart announced.

Kevin wasn't sure what he'd expected, but it wasn't what he saw. Gorlaes, the Chancellor, was a big, broad-shouldered, brown-bearded man of middle years. He smiled generously, showing good teeth as he came sweeping in. "Welcome back, Silvercloak! And brightly woven, indeed. You have come in the very teeth of time—as ever." And he laughed. Loren, Kevin saw, did not.

The other man who came in, an armed aide close beside him, was stooped and very old. The King? Kevin wondered, for a brief, disoriented moment. But it was not.

"Good evening, Metran," Loren said deferentially to this white-haired new arrival. "Are you well?"

"Well, very well, very, very," Metran wheezed. He coughed. "There is not enough light in here. I want to see," he said querulously. A trembling arm was raised, and suddenly the six wall torches blazed, illuminating the chamber. *Why,* Kim thought, *couldn't Loren have done that?*

"Better, much better," Metran went on, shuffling forward to sink into one of the chairs. His attendant hovered close by. The other soldier, Kim saw, had placed himself by the door with Vart. Paul had withdrawn towards Jennifer by the window.

"Where," Loren asked, "is the King? I sent Vart to advise him I was here."

"And he has been so advised," Gorlaes answered smoothly. Vart, in the doorway, snickered. "Ailell has instructed me to convey his greetings to you, and your—," he paused to look around, "—four companions."

"Four? Only four?" Metran cut in, barely audible over a coughing fit.

Gorlaes spared him only the briefest of glances and went on. "To your four companions. I have been asked to take them under my care as Chancellor for the night. The King had a trying day and would prefer to receive them formally in the morning. It is very late. I'm sure you understand." The smile was pleasant, even modest. "Now if you would be good enough to introduce me to our visitors I can have my men show them to their rooms . . . and you, my friend, can go to your richly deserved rest."

"Thank you, Gorlaes." Loren smiled, but a thin edge like that of a drawn blade had come into his voice. "However, under the circumstances I count myself responsible for the well-being of those who crossed with me. I will make arrangements for them, until the King has received us."

"Silvercloak, are you implying that their well-being can be better attended to than by the Chancellor of the realm?" There, too, Kevin thought, his muscles involuntarily tensing: the same edge. Though neither man had moved, it seemed to him as if there were two swords drawn in the torchlit room.

"Not at all, Gorlaes," said the mage. "It is simply a matter of my own honor."

"You are tired, my friend. Leave this tedious business to me."

"There is no tedium in caring for friends."

"Loren, I must insist—"

"*No.*"

There was a cold silence.

"You realize," said Gorlaes, his voice dropping almost to a whisper, "that you offer me little choice?" The voice came up suddenly. "I must obey the commands of my King. Vart, Lagoth . . ." The two soldiers in the doorway moved forward.

And pitched, half-drawn swords clattering, full-length to the floor.

Behind their prone bodies stood a very calm Matt Sören, and the big, capable man named Coll. Seeing them there, Kevin Laine, whose childhood fantasies had been shaped of images like this, knew a moment of sheer delight.

At which point a lithe, feral figure, shimmering with jewelry, swung easily through the window into the room. He landed lightly beside Jennifer, and she felt a wandering hand stroke her hair before he spoke.

"Who makes this noise at such an hour? Can a soldier not sleep at night in his father's palace without—why, Gorlaes! And Metran! And here is Loren! You have returned, Silvercloak—and with our visitors, I see. In the very teeth of time." The insolence of his voice filled the room. "Gorlaes, send quickly, my father will want to welcome them immediately."

"The King," the Chancellor replied stiffly, "is indisposed, my lord Prince. He sent me—"

"He can't come? Then I must do the family honors myself. Silvercloak, would you . . . ?"

And so Loren carefully introduced them again. And *"A peach!"* said Diarmuid dan Ailell, bending, slowly, to kiss Jennifer's hand. Against her will, she laughed. He didn't hurry the kiss.

When he straightened, though, his words were formal, and both of his arms were raised in a wide gesture of ritual. "I welcome you now," he began, and Kevin, turning instinctively, saw the benign countenance of Gorlaes contort, for a blurred instant, with fury. "I welcome you now," Diarmuid said, in a voice stripped of mockery, "as guest-friends of my father and myself. The home of Ailell is your home, your

honoi is ours. An injury done you is an injury to ourselves. And treason to the Oak Crown of the High
King. Be welcome to Paras Derval. I will personally
attend to your comfort for tonight.'' Only on the last
phrase did the voice change a little, as the quick eyes,
malicious and amused, flashed to Jennifer's.

She flushed again, but he had already turned.
"Gorlaes," he said softly, "your retainers appear to
have collapsed. I have been told, in the few hours
since I've been back from South Keep, of entirely too
much drinking among them. I know it is a festival,
but really . . . ?" And the tone was so mild, so very
reproachful. Kevin fought to keep a straight face.
"Coll," Diarmuid went on, "have four rooms made
ready on the north side, please, and quickly."

"No." It was Jennifer. "Kim and I will share. Just
three." She resolutely avoided looking at the Prince.
Kimberly, watching him, decided that his eyebrows
went higher than they had any right to go.

"We will, too," said Paul Schafer quietly. And
Kevin felt his pulse leap. Oh, Abba, he thought, maybe
this will do it for him. Maybe it will.

"I'm too hot. Why is it so hot everywhere?" Metran, First of the Mages, asked, of no one in particu-
lar.

◆

The north side of the palace, opposite the town,
overlooked a walled garden. When they were finally
alone in their room Kevin opened the glass doors and
stepped out onto a wide stone balcony. The moon,
waning, was high overhead, bright enough to illumi-
nate the shrubs and the few flowers below their room.

"Not much of a garden," he commented, as Paul
came out to join him.

"There's been no rain, Diarmuid said."

"That's true." There was silence. A light breeze
had finally come up to cool the evening.

"Have you noticed the moon?" Paul asked, leaning
on the parapet.

Kevin nodded. "Larger, you mean? Yes, I did. Wonder what effect that has?"

"Higher tides, most likely."

"I guess. And more werewolves."

Schafer gave him a wry look. "I wouldn't be surprised. Tell me, what did you think about that business back there?"

"Well, Loren and Diarmuid seem to be on the same side."

"It looks that way. Matt's not very sure of him."

"Somehow that doesn't surprise me."

"Really. What about Gorlaes? He was pretty quick to call in the marines. Was he just following orders, or—"

"Not a chance, Paul. I saw his face when Diarmuid made us guest-friends. Not happy, my friend."

"Really?" Schafer said. "Well, that simplifies things at least. I'd like to know more about this Jaelle, though. And Diarmuid's brother, too."

"The nameless one?" Kevin intoned lugubriously. "He of no name?"

Schafer snorted. "Funny man. Yes, him."

"We'll figure it out. We've figured things out before."

"I know," said Paul Schafer, and after a moment gave a rare smile.

"Oh, Romeo, Romeo, wherefore art thou Romeo?" came a plaintive cry from off to their left. They looked over. Kim Ford, languishing for all she was worth, swayed towards them from the next balcony. The leap was about ten feet.

"I'm coming!" Kevin responded instantly. He rushed to the edge of their own balcony.

"Oh, fly to me!" Kimberly trilled. Jennifer, behind her, began almost reluctantly to laugh.

"I'm coming!" Kevin repeated, ostentatiously limbering up. "You two all right there?" he asked, in mid-flex. "Been ravished yet?"

"Not a chance," Kim lamented. "Can't find anyone who's man enough to jump to our balcony."

Kevin laughed. "I'd have to do it pretty fast," he said, "to get there before the Prince."

"I don't know," Jennifer Lowell said, "if *anyone* can move faster than that guy."

Paul Schafer, hearing the banter begin, and the laughter of the two women, moved to the far end of the balcony. He knew, very well, that the frivolity was only a release from tension, but it wasn't something to which he had access any more. Resting his own ringless, fine-boned hands on the railing, he gazed out and down at the denuded garden below. He stood there, looking about him, but not really seeing: the inner landscape demanded its due.

Even had Schafer been carefully scanning the shadows, though, it is unlikely that he would have discerned the dark creature that crouched behind a clump of stunted shrubs, watching him. The desire to kill was strong upon it, and Paul had moved to within easy range of the poison darts it carried. He might have died then.

But fear mastered bloodlust in the figure below. It had been ordered to observe, and to report, but not to kill.

So Paul lived, observed, oblivious, and after a time he drew a long breath and lifted his eyes from sightless fixation on the shadows below.

To see a thing none of the others saw.

High on the stone outer wall enclosing the garden stood an enormous grey dog, or a wolf, and it was looking at him across the moonlit space between, with eyes that were not those of a wolf or a dog, and in which lay a sadness deeper and older than anything Paul had ever seen or known. From the top of the wall the creature stared at him the way animals are not supposed to be able to do. And it called him. The pull was unmistakable, imperative, terrifying. Looming in night shadow it reached out for him, the eyes, unnaturally distinct, boring into his own. Paul touched and then twisted his mind away from a well of sorrow so deep he feared it could drown him. Whatever stood on the wall had endured and was still enduring a loss that spanned the worlds. It dwarfed him, appalled him.

And it was calling him. Sweat cold on his skin in the summer night, Paul Schafer knew that this was one of the things caught up in the chaotic vision Loren's searching had given him.

With an effort brutally physical, he broke away. When he turned his head, he felt the motion like a twist in his heart.

"Kev," he managed to gasp, the voice eerie in his own head.

"What is it?" His friend's response was instant.

"Over there. On the wall. Do you see anything?" Paul pointed, but did not look back.

"What? There's nothing. What did you see?"

"Not sure." He was breathing hard. "Something. Maybe a dog."

"And?"

"And it wants me," Paul Schafer said.

Kevin, stunned, was silent. They stood a moment like that, looking at each other, not sharing, then Schafer turned and went inside. Kevin stayed a while longer, to reassure the others, then went in himself. Paul had taken the smaller of the two beds that had been hastily provided, and was lying on his back, hands behind his head.

Wordlessly, Kevin undressed and went to bed. The moon slanted a thin beam of light into the far corner of the room, illuminating neither of them.

Chapter 5

All the night they had been gathering. Stern men from Ailell's own birthplace in Rhoden, cheerful ones from high-walled Seresh by Saeren, mariners from Taerlindel, and soldiers from the fastness of North Keep, though not many of these because of the one who was exiled. From villages and dust-dry farms all over the High Kingdom they came as well. For days they had been trickling into Paras Derval, crowding the inns and hostels, spilling out into makeshift campgrounds beyond the last streets of the town below the palace. Some had come walking west from the once rich lands by the River Glein; leaning on the carved staffs of the southeast they had cut across the burnt-out desolation of the grain lands to join the dusty traffic on the Leinan Road. From the grazing lands and the dairy lands in the northeast others had come riding on the horses that were the legacy of their winter trading with the Dalrei by the banks of the Latham; and though their horses might be painfully gaunt, each mount yet bore the sumptuous woven saddle-cloth that every Brennin horseman crafted before he took a horse: a weaving for the Weaver's gift of speed. From beyond Leinan they came as well, dour, dark farmers from Gwen Ystrat in their wide, six-wheeled carts. None of their women, though, not from so near Dun Maura in the province of the Mother.

But from everywhere else the women and children had come in noisy, festive number. Even in the midst of drought and deprivation, the people of Brennin were gathering to pay homage to their King, and perhaps to briefly forget their troubles in doing so.

Morning found them densely clustered in the square before the palace walls. Looking up they could see the great balustrade hung with banners and gaily colored streamers, and most wonderful of all, the great tapestry of Iorweth in the Wood, brought forth for this one day that all the folk of Brennin might see their High King stand beneath the symbols of Mörnir and the Weaver both, in Paras Derval.

But all was not consigned to high and sacred things. Around the fringes of the crowd moved jugglers and clowns, and performers doing glittering things with knives and swords and bright scarves. The cyngael chanted their ribald verses to pockets of laughing auditors, extemporizing satires for a fee upon whomever their benefactor designated; not a few revenges were thus effected in the clear, cutting words of the cyngael—immune since Colan's day from any law save that of their own council. Amid the babble, pedlars carried their colorful goods about or erected hasty booths from which to display their craft in the sunlight. And then the noise, never less than a roar, became a thundering, for figures had appeared on the balustrade.

The sound hit Kevin like a blow. He regarded the absence of sunglasses as a source of profound and comprehensive grief. Hung-over to incapacity, pale to the edge of green, he glanced over at Diarmuid and silently cursed the elegance of his figure. Turning to Kim—and the movement hurt like hell—he received a wry smile of commiseration, which salved his spirit even as it wounded his pride.

It was already hot. The sunlight was painfully brilliant in the cloudless sky, and so, too, were the colors worn by the lords and ladies of Ailell's court. The High King himself, to whom they'd not yet been presented, was further down the balcony, hidden behind the intervening courtiers. Kevin closed his eyes, wishing it were possible to retreat into the shade, instead of standing up front to be seen . . . red Indians, indeed. Red-eyed Indians, anyhow. It was easier with his eyes closed. The fulsome voice of Gorlaes, orating the glittering achievements of Ailell's reign, slid progressively into background. What the hell kind of wine did they make in this world, Kevin thought, too drained to be properly outraged.

The knock had come an hour after they'd gone to bed. Neither of them had been asleep.

"Careful," said Paul, rising on one elbow. Kevin had swung upright and was pulling on his cords before moving to the door.

"Yes?" he said, without touching the lock. "Who is it?"

"Convivial night persons," came an already familiar voice. "Open up. I've got to get Tegid out of the hallway."

Laughing, Kevin looked over his shoulder. Paul was up and half dressed already. Kevin opened the door and Diarmuid entered quickly, flourishing two flasks of wine, one of them already unstoppered. Into the room behind him, also carrying wine, came Coll and the preposterous Tegid, followed by two other men bearing an assortment of clothing.

"For tomorrow," the Prince said in response to Kevin's quizzical look at the last pair. "I promised I'd take care of you." He tossed over one of the wine flasks, and smiled.

"Very kind of you," Kevin replied, catching it. He raised the flask in the way he'd learned in Spain, years before, to shoot a dark jet of wine down his throat. He flipped the leather flask over to Paul who drank, wordlessly.

"Ah!" exclaimed Tegid, as he eased himself onto a long bench. "I'm dry as Jaelle's heart. To the King!" he cried, raising his own flask, "and to his glorious heir, Prince Diarmuid, and to our noble and distinguished guests, and to. . . .'' The rest of the peroration was lost in the sound of wine voluminously pouring into his mouth. At length the flow ceased. Tegid surfaced, belched, and looked around. "I've a mighty thirst in me tonight,'' he explained unnecessarily.

Paul addressed the Prince casually. "If you're in a party mood, aren't you in the wrong bedroom?''

Diarmuid's smile was rueful. "Don't assume you were a first choice,'' he murmured. "Your charming companions accepted their dresses for tomorrow, but nothing more, I'm afraid. The small one, Kim''—he shook his head—"has a tongue in her.''

"My condolences,'' said Kevin, delighted. "I've been on the receiving end a few times.''

"Then,'' said Diarmuid dan Ailell, "let us drink in joint commiseration.'' The Prince set the tone by commencing to relate what he characterized as essential information: a wittily obscene description of the various court ladies they were likely to meet. A description that reflected an extreme awareness of their private as well as public natures.

Tegid and Coll stayed; the other two men left after a time, to be replaced by a different pair with fresh wine flasks. Eventually these two departed as well. The two men who succeeded them, however, were not smiling as they entered.

"What is it, Carde?'' Coll asked the fair-haired one.

The man addressed cleared his throat. Diarmuid, sprawled in a deep chair by the window, turned at the sound.

Carde's voice was very soft. "Something strange. My lord, I thought you should know right away. There's a dead svart alfar in the garden below this window.''

Through the wine-induced haze descending upon him, Kevin saw Diarmuid swing to his feet.

"Brightly woven," the Prince said. "Which of you killed it?"

Carde's voice dropped to a whisper. "That's just it, my lord. Erron found it dead. It's throat was . . . ripped apart, my lord. Erron thinks . . . he thinks it was done by a wolf, though . . . with respect, my lord, I don't ever want to meet what killed that creature."

In the silence that followed this, Kevin looked over at Paul Schafer. Sitting up on his bed, Schafer seemed thinner and more frail than ever. His expression was unreadable.

Diarmuid broke the stillness. "You said it was below this window?"

Carde nodded, but the Prince had turned already and, throwing open the doors, was on the balcony and then dropping over the edge. And right behind him was Paul Schafer. Which meant that Kevin had to go, too. With Coll beside him and Carde just behind, he moved to the edge of the balcony, swung over the balustrade, hung by his hands a dizzy instant, and dropped the ten feet to the garden. The other two followed. Only Tegid remained in the room, his mountainous bulk precluding the descent.

Diarmuid and Paul had moved to where three men were standing by a stunted clump of shrubbery. They parted to let the Prince in among them. Kevin, breathing deeply to clear his head, moved up beside Paul and looked down.

When his eyes adjusted to the dark, he wished they hadn't. The svart alfar had been almost decapitated; its head had been clawed to shreds. One arm had been torn through, the shoulder remaining attached to the body only by an exposed strip of cartilage, and there were deep claw marks scoring the naked torso of the dark green, hairless creature. Even in the shadows, Kevin could see the thick blood clotting the dried-out soil. Breathing very carefully, shocked almost sober, he resisted an impulse to be sick. No one spoke for a long time: the fury that was reflected in the mangled creature on the ground imposed its own silence.

Eventually Diarmuid straightened and moved back a few steps. "Carde," he said crisply, "I want the watch doubled on our guests as of now. Tomorrow I want a report on why that thing wasn't seen by any of you. And why you didn't see what killed it either. If I post guards, I expect them to be useful."

"My lord." Carde, badly shaken, moved off with the other guards.

Coll was still crouching beside the dead svart. Now he looked over his shoulder. "Diar," he said, "it was no ordinary wolf that did this."

"I know," said the Prince. "If it was a wolf."

Kevin, turning, looked at Paul Schafer again. Schafer had his back to them. He was gazing at the outer wall of the garden.

At length the four of them walked back to the balcony. With the aid of crevices in the palace wall, and a hand over the balustrade from Tegid, they were all soon in the room once more. Diarmuid, Tegid, and Coll departed shortly after. The Prince left them two flasks of wine and an offer; they accepted both.

Kevin ended up drinking almost all of the wine himself, primarily because Paul, for a change, wasn't in a mood to talk.

◆

"We're on!" Kim hissed, prodding him with an elbow. They were, it seemed. The four of them stepped forward in response to Gorlaes's sweeping gesture and, as instructed, waved to the loudly cheering crowd.

Kimberly, waving with one hand and supporting Kevin with the other, realized suddenly that this was the scene that Loren had conjured up for them in the Park Plaza two nights before. Instinctively she looked up over her shoulder. And saw the banner flapping lazily overhead: the crescent moon and the oak.

Kevin, grateful for her arm, did manage a few waves and a fixed smile, while reflecting that the tumultuous gathering below was taking a lot on faith. At this height they could have been any four members of the court. He supposed, impressed with himself for thinking so clearly, that the public relations thing would probably focus on the nobility anyhow. The people around them knew that they were from another world—and someone seemed to be awfully unhappy about it.

His head was killing him, and some indeterminate fungus seemed to have taken up residence in his mouth. *Better shape up fast,* he thought, *you're about to meet a king.* And there was a long ride waiting tomorow, with God knows what at the end.

For Diarmuid's last offer had been an unexpected one. "We're going south tomorrow morning," he'd said as the dawn was breaking. "Across the river. A raid of sorts, though a quiet one. No one to know. If you think you can manage, you may find it interesting. Not altogether safe, but I think we can take care of you." It was the smile on the last phrase that got both of them—which, Kevin realized, was probably what the manipulative bastard had intended.

The great hall at Paras Derval had been designed by Tomaz Lal, whose disciple Ginserat had been, he who later made the wardstones and much else of power and beauty in the older days.

Twelve great pillars supported the high ceiling. Set far up in the walls were the windows of Delevan—stained-glass images of the founding of the High Kingdom by Iorweth, and the first wars with Eridu and Cathal. The last window on the western wall, above the canopied throne of Brennin, showed Conary himself, Colan young beside him, their fair hair blowing back as they rode north through the Plain to the last battle against Rakoth Maugrim. When the sun was setting, that window would blaze with light in such a fashion that the faces of the King and his golden son were illuminated as from within with majesty, though the window had been crafted almost a thousand years

before. Such was the art of Delevan, the craft of Tomaz Lal.

Walking between the huge pillars over mosaic-
inlaid tiles, Kimberly was conscious for the first time
of feeling awe in this place. The pillars, windows,
ever-present tapestries, the jewelled floor, the gem-
encrusted clothing of the lords and ladies, even the
silken splendor of the lavender-colored gown she
wore . . . She drew a deep, careful breath and kept
her gaze as straight as she could.

And doing so, she saw, as Loren led the four of
them to the western end of the hall, under the last great
window, a raised dais of marble and obsidian and upon
it a throne carved of heavy oak, and sitting upon the
throne was the man she'd only glimpsed through the
crowd on the balcony earlier in the day.

The tragedy of Ailell dan Art lay in what he had
fallen from. The haggard man with the wispy, snow-
white beard and blurred, cataract-occluded gaze
showed little of the giant warrior, with eyes like a
noonday sky, who had taken the Oak Throne fifty years
before. Gaunt and emaciated, Ailell seemed to have
been stretched thin by his years, and the expression
with which he peered forward to follow their approach
was not welcoming.

To one side of the King stood Gorlaes. The broad-
shouldered Chancellor was dressed in brown, with his
seal of office hung about his neck and no other orna-
ment. On the other side of the throne, in burgundy
and white, stood Diarmuid, the King's Heir of Brennin. Who winked when her gaze lingered. Kim turned
away abruptly to see Metran, the First Mage, making
his slow wheezing way, attendant solicitously at hand,
to stand with Loren just in front of them.

Seeing Paul Schafer gazing intently at the King, she
turned back to the throne herself, and after a pause
she heard her name being spoken in introduction. She
stepped forward and bowed, having decided earlier
that under no circumstances was she going to try any-

thing so hazardous as a curtsy. The others followed suit. Jennifer did curtsy, sinking down in a rustle of green silk, and rising gracefully as an appreciative murmur ran through the hall.

"Be welcome to Brennin," the High King said, leaning back in his throne. "Bright be the thread of your days among us." The words were gracious, but there was little pleasure in the low desiccated tones in which they were spoken. "Thank you, Metran, Loren," the King said, in the same voice. "Thank you, Teyrnon," he added, nodding to a third man half hidden beyond Loren.

Metran bowed too low in response and almost toppled over. His aide helped him straighten. Someone snickered in the background.

Loren was speaking. "We thank you for your kindness, my lord. Our friends have met your son and the Chancellor already. The Prince was good enough to make them guest-friends of your house last night." His voice on the last phrase was pitched to carry.

The King's eyes rested for a long moment on those of Loren, and Kim, watching, changed her mind. Ailell might be old, but he certainly wasn't senile— the amusement registering in his face was far too cynical.

"Yes," said the King, "I know he did. And herewith I endorse his doing so. Tell me, Loren," he went on in a different tone, "do you know if any of your friends play ta'bael?"

Loren shook his head apologetically. "Truly, my lord," he said, "I never thought to ask. They have the same game in their world, they call it chess, but—"

"I play," said Paul.

There was a short silence. Paul and the King looked at each other. When Ailell spoke, his voice was very soft. "I hope," he said, "that you will play with me while you are with us."

Schafer nodded by way of response. The King

leaned back, and Loren, seeing this, turned to lead them from the hall.

"Hold, Silvercloak!"

The voice was icily imperious. It knifed into them. Kim quickly turned left to where she'd noticed a small grouping of women in grey robes. Now that cluster parted and a woman walked forward towards the throne.

All in white she was, very tall, with red hair held back by a circlet of silver on her brow. Her eyes were green and very cold. In her bearing as she strode towards them was a deep, scarcely suppressed rage, and as she drew near, Kimberly saw that she was beautiful. But despite the hair, which gleamed like a fire at night under stars, this was not a beauty that warmed one. It cut, like a weapon. There was no nuance of gentleness in her no shading of care, but fair she was, as is the flight of an arrow before it kills.

Loren, checked in the act of withdrawing, turned as she approached—and there was no warmth in his face, either.

"Have you not forgotten something?" the woman in white said, her voice feather-soft and sinuous with danger.

"An introduction? I would have done so in due course," Loren replied lightly. "If you are impatient, I can—"

"Due course? Impatient? By Macha and Nemain you should be cursed for insolence!" The red-haired woman was rigid with fury. Her eyes burned into those of the mage.

Who endured the look without expression. Until another voice interceded in rich, plummy tones. "I'm afraid you are right, Priestess," said Gorlaes. "Our voyager here does at times forget the patterns of precedence. Our guests should have been presented to you today. I fear—"

"Fool!" the Priestess snapped. "You are a fool, Gorlaes. Today? I should have been spoken to *before* he went on this journey. How *dare* you, Metran? How dare you send for a crossing without leave of the Mother? The balancing of worlds is in her hands and so it is in mine. You touch the earthroot in peril of your soul if you do not seek her leave!''

Metran retreated from the enraged figure. Fear and confusion chased each other across his features. Loren, however, raised a hand and pointed one long, steady finger at the woman confronting him. "Nowhere," he said, and thick anger spilled from his own voice now, "nowhere is such a thing written! And this, by all the gods, you know. You overreach yourself, Jaelle—and be warned, it shall not be permitted. The balance lies not with you—and your moonlit meddling may shatter it yet.''

The Priestess's eyes flickered at that—and Kim suddenly remembered Diarmuid's reference the night before to a secret gathering.

And it was Diarmuid's lazy voice that slid next into the charged silence. "Jaelle," he said, from by his father's throne, "whatever the worth of what you say, surely this is not the time to say it. Lovely as you are, you are marring a festival with your wrangling. And we seem to have another guest waiting to be greeted.'' Stepping lightly from the dais, he walked past all of them, down to the end of the hall, where, Kim saw as she turned to watch, there stood another woman, this one white-haired with age and leaning on a gnarled staff before the great doors of Ailell's hall.

"Be welcome, Ysanne," said the Prince, a deep courtesy in his tone. "It is long since you have graced our court.'' But Kim, hearing the name spoken, seeing the frail figure standing there, felt something touch her then, like a finger on the heart.

A current of sound had begun to ripple through the gathered courtiers, and those lining the spaces between the pillars were crowding backwards in fear. But the murmur was only faint background for Kim now, because all her senses were locked onto the seamed, wizened figure walking carefully towards the throne on the arm of the young Prince.

"Ysanne, you should not be here." Ailell, surprisingly, had risen to speak, and it could be seen that, even stooped with years, he was the tallest man in the room.

"True enough," the old woman agreed placidly, coming to a halt before him. Her voice was gentle as Jaelle's had been harsh. The red-haired Priestess was gazing at her with a bitter contempt.

"Then why?" Ailell asked softly.

"Fifty years on this throne merits a journey to pay homage," Ysanne replied. "Is there anyone else here besides Metran and perhaps Loren who well recalls the day you were crowned? I came to wish you bright weaving, Ailell. And for two other things."

"Which are?" It was Loren who asked.

"First, to see your travelers," Ysanne replied, and turned to face Paul Schafer.

His responding gesture was brutally abrupt. Throwing a hand in front of his eyes, Schafer cried out, "No! No searching!"

Ysanne raised her eyebrows. She glanced at Loren, then turned back to Paul. "I see," she said. "Fear not, then, I never use the searching—I don't need it." The whispering in the hall rose again, for the words had carried.

Paul's arm came down slowly. He met the old woman's gaze steadily then, his own head held high—and strangely, it was Ysanne who broke the stare.

And then it was, then it was, that she turned, past Jennifer and Kevin, ignoring the rigid figure of Jaelle, and for the first time saw Kimberly. Grey eyes met grey before the carven throne under the high windows of Delevan. "Ah!" cried the old woman then on a sharply taken breath. And in the softest thread of a whisper added, after a moment, "I have awaited you for so long now, my dear."

And only Kim herself had seen the spasm of fear

that had crossed Ysanne's face before she spoke those quiet words like a benediction.

"How?" Kim managed to stammer. "What do you mean?"

Ysanne smiled. "I am a Seer. The dreamer of the dream." And somehow, Kim knew what that meant, and there were sudden, bright tears in her eyes.

"Come to me," the Seer whispered. "Loren will tell you how." She turned then, and curtsied low before the tall King of Brennin. "Fare kindly, Ailell," she said to him. "The other thing I have come to do is say goodbye. I shall not return, and we shall not meet again, you and I, on this side of the Night." She paused. "I have loved you. Carry that."

"Ysanne—" the King cried.

But she had turned. And leaning on her staff, she walked, alone this time, the length of the stunned, brilliant hall and out the double doors into the sunlight.

◆

That night, very late, Paul Schafer was summoned to play ta'bael with the High King of Brennin.

The escort was a guard he didn't know and, walking behind him down shadowy corridors, Paul was inwardly grateful for the silent presence of Coll, who he knew was following them.

It was a long walk, but they saw few people still awake. A woman combing her hair in a doorway smiled at him, and a party of guards went by, sheathed swords clinking at their sides. Passing some bedrooms Paul heard murmurs of late-night talk, and once, a woman cried out softly on a taken breath—a sound very like a cry that he remembered.

The two men with their hidden follower came at length to a pair of heavy doors. Schafer's face was expressionless as they were opened to his escort's tapping and he was ushered into a large, richly furnished room, at the center of which were two deep armchairs and a table set for ta'bael.

"Welcome!" It was Gorlaes, the Chancellor, who came forward to grip Paul's arm in greeting. "It is kind of you to come."

"It *is* kind," came the thinner voice of the King. He moved out from a shadowed corner of the room as he spoke. "I am grateful to you for indulging an old man's sleeplessness. The day has worn heavily upon me. Gorlaes, good night."

"My lord," the Chancellor said quickly. "I will be happy to stay and—"

"No need. Go to sleep. Tarn will serve us." The King nodded to the young page who had opened the door for Paul. Gorlaes looked as if he would protest again, but refrained.

"Good night then, my lord. And once more, my deepest well-wishes on this brightly woven day." He walked forward, and on one knee kissed the hand Ailell extended. Then the Chancellor left the room, leaving Paul alone with the King and his page.

"Wine by the table, Tarn. Then we will serve ourselves. Go to bed—I will wake you when I want to retire. Now come, my young stranger," Ailell said, lowering himself carefully into a chair.

In silence, Paul walked foward and took the other chair. Tarn deftly filled the two glasses set beside the inlaid board, then withdrew through an inner doorway into the King's bedroom. The windows of the room were open and the heavy curtains drawn back to admit whatever breath of air might slide in. In a tree somewhere outside a bird was singing. It sounded like a nightingale.

The beautifully carved pieces glinted in the light of the candles, but the face of the tall King of Brennin was hidden as he leaned back in his chair. He spoke softly. "The game we play is the same, Loren tells me, though we name the pieces differently. I always play the black. Take you the white and begin."

Paul Schafer liked to attack in chess, especially with white and the first move. Gambits and sacrifices followed each other in his game, designed to generate a whirlwind assault on the opposition king. The fact that the opposition this night *was* a king had no effect on him, for Schafer's code, though complex, was unwavering. He set out to demolish the black pieces of Ailell just as he would have those of anyone else. And that night, heartsick and vulnerable, there was even more fire in his game than usual, for he sought to hide from torment in the cold clarity of the black-and-white board. So he marshalled himself ruthlessly, and the white pieces spun into a vortex of attack.

To be met by a defence of intricate, resilient subtlety. Whatever Ailell had dwindled from, however his mind and authority might seem to waver, Paul knew, ten moves into the game, that he was dealing with a man of formidable resources. Slowly and patiently the King ordered his defences, cautiously he shored up his bulwarks, and so it was that Schafer's free-wheeling attack began to exhaust itself and was turned inexorably back. After almost two hours' play, Paul tipped over the white king in resignation.

The two men leaned back in their chairs and exchanged their first look since the game had begun. And they smiled, neither knowing, since there was no way they could know, how rare it was for the other to do so. Sharing that moment, however, as Paul raised his silver goblet to salute the King, they moved closer, across the twin gulfs of worlds and years, to the kind of bonding that might have allowed them to understand each other.

It was not to happen, but something else was born that night, and the fruit of that silent game would change the balance and the pattern of all the worlds there were.

Ailell spoke first, his voice husky. "No one," he said, "no one has ever given me a game like that. I do not lose in ta'bael. I almost did tonight."

Paul smiled for the second time. "You almost did.

You may next game—but I'm not very certain of it.
You play beautifully, my lord.''

Ailell shook his head. "No, I play carefully. All the
beauty was on your side, but sometimes plodding caution will wear down brilliance. When you sacrificed
the second rider. . . . '' Ailell gestured wordlessly. "I
suppose that it is only the young who can do a thing
like that. It has been so long for me, I seem to have
forgotten.'' He raised his own cup and drank.

Paul refilled both goblets before replying. He felt
drained, simplified. The bird outside, he realized, had
stopped singing a long time ago. "I think," he said,
"that it is more a question of style than of youth or
age. I'm not very patient, so I play the way I do.''

"In ta'bael, you mean?''

"Other things, too," Paul answered, after a hesitation.

Ailell, surprisingly, nodded. "I was like that once,
though it may be hard for you to credit.'' His expression was self-deprecating. "I took this throne by force
in a time of chaos, and held it with my sword in the
early years. If we are to be a dynasty, it begins with
me and follows with . . . with Diarmuid, I suppose.''
Paul remained silent, and after a moment the King
went on. "It is power that teaches patience; holding
power, I mean. And you learn the price it exacts—
which is something I never knew when I was your age
and thought a sword and quick wits could deal with
anything. I never knew the price you pay for power.''

Ailell leaned over the board and picked up one of
the pieces. "Take the queen in ta'bael," he said. "The
most powerful piece on the board, yet she must be
protected when threatened by guard or rider, for the
game will be lost if that exchange is made. And the
king,'' said Ailell dan Art, "in ta'bael you cannot
sacrifice a king.''

Paul couldn't read the expression in the sunken, still-
handsome face, but there was a new timbre in the
voice, something shifting far under the words.

Ailell seemed to notice his discomfort. He smiled again, faintly. "I am heavy company at night," he said. "Especially tonight. Too much comes back. I have too many memories."

"I have too many of my own," Paul said impulsively, and hated himself the instant the words were spoken.

Ailell's expression, though, was mild, even compassionate. "I thought you might," he said. "I'm not sure why, but I thought you might."

Paul lowered his face to the deep wine goblet and took a long drink. "My lord," he said, to break the ensuing stillness with a new subject, any new subject, "why did the Priestess say that Loren should have asked her before bringing us? What does—"

"She was wrong about that, and I will send to tell her so. Not that Jaelle is likely to listen." Ailell's expression was rueful. "She loves to make trouble, to stir up tensions she might find ways to exploit. Jaelle is ambitious beyond belief, and she seeks a return to the old ways of the Goddess ruling through her High Priestess, which is how it was before Iorweth came from oversea. There is a good deal of ambition in my court, there often is around the throne of an aging king, but hers runs deeper than any."

Paul nodded. "Your son said something like that last night."

"What? Diarmuid did?" Ailell gave a laugh that was actually evocative of the Prince. "I'm surprised he sobered up long enough to think so clearly."

Paul's mouth twitched. "Actually, he wasn't sober, but he seemed to think pretty clearly anyhow."

The King gestured dismissively. "He is charming sometimes." After a pause he tugged at his beard and asked, "I'm sorry, what were we speaking of?"

"Jaelle," Paul said. "What she said this morning."

"Yes, yes, of course. Once her words would have been true, but not for a long time now. In the days when the wild magic could only be reached underground, and usually only with blood, the power needed for a crossing would be drained from the very heart of the earth, and that has always been the province of the Mother. So in those days it was true that such an expenditure of earthroot, of avarlith, could only be made through intercession of the High Priestess with the Goddess. Now, though, for long years now, since Amairgen learned the skylore and founded the Council of the Mages, the power drain in their magic runs only through the mage's source, and the avarlith is not touched.''

''I don't understand. What power drain?''

''I go too quickly. It is hard to remember that you are from another world. Listen, then. If a mage were to use his magic to start a fire in that hearth, it would require power to do it. Once all our magic belonged to the Goddess and that power was tapped straight from the earthroot; and being both drained and expended in Fionavar, the power would find its way back to the earth—it would never diminish. But in a crossing the power is used in another world—''

''So you lose it!''

''Exactly. Or so it was once. But since Amairgen freed the mages from the Mother, the power will be drained from the source only, and he rebuilds it in himself over time.''

''He?''

''Or she, of course.''

''But . . . you mean each mage has . . . ?''

''Yes, of course. Each is bonded to a source, as Loren is to Matt, or Metran to Denbarra. That is the anchoring law of the skylore. The mage can do no more than his source can sustain, and this bond is for life. Whatever a mage does, someone else pays the price.''

And so much came clear then. Paul remembered Matt Sören trembling as they came through the crossing. He remembered Loren's sharp concern for the Dwarf, and then, seeing more clearly still, the dim

torches on the walls of that first room, the torches frail
Metran had so easily gestured to brightness, while
Loren had refrained to let his source recover. Paul felt
his mind stretch away from self-absorption, stiffly, as
if muscles had been too long unused.

"How?" he asked. "How are they bound to each
other?"

"Mage and source? There are a great many laws,
and long training to be endured. In the end, if there
is still willingness, they may bind with the ritual,
though it is not a thing to be done lightly. There are
only three left in Fionavar. Denbarra is sister-son to
Metran, Teyrnon's source is Barak, his closest friend
as a child. Some pairings have been strange ones:
Lisen of the Wood was source to Amairgen Whitebranch, first of the mages."

"Why was it strange?"

"Ah," the High King smiled, a little wistfully, "it
is a long tale, that one. Perhaps you may hear a part
of it sung in the Great Hall."

"All right. But what about Loren and Matt? How
did they . . . ?"

"That, too, is strange," Ailell said. "At the end of
his training, Loren sought leave of the Council and of
me to travel for a time. He was gone three years. When
he returned he had his cloak, and he was bonded to
the King of the Dwarves, a thing that had never happened before. No Dwarf—"

The King broke off sharply. And in the abrupt silence they both heard it again: a barely audible tapping
on the wall of the room across from the open window.
As Paul looked at the King in wonder, it came again.

Ailell's face had gone queerly soft. "Oh, Mörnir,"
he breathed. "They *have* sent." He looked at Paul,
hesitating, then seemed to make a decision. "Stay with
me, young Paul, Pwyll, stay and be silent, for you are
about to see a thing few men have been allowed."

And walking over to the wall, the King pressed his
palm carefully against it in a place where the stone

had darkened slightly. *"Levar shanna,"* he murmured, and stood back, as the thin outline of a door began to take shape in the seamless structure of the wall. A moment later the demarcation was clear, and then the door slid soundlessly open and a slight figure moved lightly into the room. It was cloaked and hooded, and remained so a moment, registering Paul's presence and Ailell's nod of endorsement, then it discarded the concealing garment in one smooth motion and bowed low before the King.

"Greetings I bear, High King, and a gift to remember your crowning day. And I have tidings needful for you to hear from Daniloth. I am Brendel of the Kestrel Mark."

And in this fashion did Paul Schafer first see one of the lios alfar. And before the ethereal, flame-like quality of the silver-haired figure that stood before him, he felt himself to have grown heavy and awkward, as a different dimension of grace was made manifest.

"Be welcome, Na-Brendel of the Kestrel," Ailell murmured. "This is Paul Schafer, whom I think we would name Pwyll in Fionavar. He is one of the four who came with Silvercloak from another of the worlds to join the fabric of our celebration."

"This I know," said Brendel. "I have been in Paras Derval two days now, waiting to find you alone. This one I have seen, and the others, including the golden one. She alone made the waiting tolerable, High King. Else I might have been long hence from your walls, with the gift I bear undelivered." A flame of laughter danced in his eyes, which were green-gold in the candlelight.

"I thank you then for waiting," said Ailell. "And tell me now, how does Ra-Lathen?"

Brendel's face went suddenly still, the laughter extinguished. "Ah!" he exclaimed softly. "You bring me quickly to my tidings, High King. Lathen Mistweaver heard his song in the fall of the year. He has gone oversea and away, and with him also went Laien

Spearchild, last of those who survived the Bael Rangat. None now are left, though few enough were ever left.'' The eyes of the lios alfar had darkened: they were violet now in the shadows. He stopped a moment, then continued. "Tenniel reigns in Daniloth. It is his greeting I bring you.''

"Lathen gone now, too?'' the King said, very low. "And Laien? Heavy tidings you bear, Na-Brendel.''

"And there are heavier yet to tell,'' the lios replied. "In the winter, rumor came to Daniloth of svart alfar moving in the north. Ra-Tenniel posted watch, and last month we learned that the word was not false. A party of them moved south past us, to the edgings of Pendaran, and there were wolves with them. We fought them there, High King. For the first time since the Bael Rangat, the lios alfar went to war. We drove them back, and most of them were slain—for we are still something of what we were—but six of my brothers and sisters fell. Six we loved will never now hear their song. Death has come again to us.''

Ailell had collapsed into his chair as the lios alfar spoke. "Svarts outside Pendaran,'' he moaned now, almost to himself. "Oh, Mörnir, what wrong of mine was so great that this need come upon me in my age?'' And aged he did seem then, shaking his head quiveringly back and forth. His hands on the carved arms of the chair trembled. Paul exchanged a glance with the bright figure of the lios. But though his own heart was twisted with pity for the old King, he saw no trace of the same in the eyes, now grey, of their visitor.

"I have a gifting for you, High King,'' Brendel said at length. "Ra-Tenniel would have you know that he is other than was the Mistweaver. My tidings of battle should tell you that. He will not hide in Daniloth, and henceforth you will see us more often than at the sevenyear. In token of which, and as earnest of alliance and our interwoven threads of destiny, the Lord of the lios alfar sends you this.''

Never in his life had Paul seen a thing so beautiful

as the object Brendel handed to Ailell. In the thin scepter of crystal that passed from the lios to the man, every nuance of light in the room seemed to be caught and then transmuted. The orange of the wall torches, the red flickers of the candles, even the blue-white diamonds of starlight seen through the window, all seemed to be weaving in ceaseless, intricate motion as if shuttling on a loom with the scepter.

"A summonglass," the King murmured as he looked down upon the gift. "This is a treasure indeed. It has been four hundred years since one of these lay within our halls."

"And whose fault was that?" Brendel said coldly.

"Unfair, my friend," Ailell replied, a little sharply, in his turn. The words of the lios seemed to kindle a spark of pride in him. "Vailerth, High King, broke the summonglass as a small part of a great madness— and Brennin paid a blood price for that madness in civil war." The King's voice was firm again. "Tell Ra-Tenniel that I accept his gift. Should he use it to summon us, the summons shall be answered. Say that to your Lord. Tomorrow I will speak with my Council as to the other tidings you have brought. Pendaran will be watched, I promise you."

"It is in my heart that more than watching may be needed, High King," Brendel replied, softly now. "There is a power stirring in Fionavar."

Ailell nodded slowly. "So Loren said to me some time ago." He hesitated, then went on, almost reluctantly. "Tell me, Na-Brendel, how does the Daniloth wardstone?"

"The same as it has been since the day Ginserat made it!" Brendel said fiercely. "The lios alfar do not forget. Look to your own, High King!"

"No offence was meant, my friend," said Ailell, "but you know that all the guardians must burn the naal fire. And know you this as well: the people of Conary and Colan, and of Ginserat himself, do not forget the Bael Rangat, either. Our stone is blue as it

ever was, and as, if the gods are kind, it ever will be."
There was a silence; Brendel's eyes burned now with
a luminous intensity. "Come!" said Ailell suddenly,
rising to stand tall above them. "Come, and I will
show you!"

Turning on his heel he stalked to his bedroom,
opened the door, and passed through. Following
quickly behind, Paul caught a glimpse of the great
four-postered, canopied bed of the King, and he saw
the figure of Tarn, the page, asleep on his cot in a
corner of the room. Ailell did not break stride, though,
and Paul and the lios alfar hastened to keep up as the
King opened another door on the opposite wall of the
bedchamber and passed through that as well into a
short corridor, at the end of which was another heavy
door. There he stopped, breathing hard.

"We are above the Room of the Stone," Ailell said,
speaking with some difficulty. He pressed a catch in
the middle of the door and slid back a small rectangle
of wood, which allowed them to see down into the
room on the other side.

"Colan himself had this made," the King said to
them, "when he returned with the stone from Rangat.
It is told that for the rest of his days, he would often
rise in the night and walk this corridor to gaze upon
Ginserat's stone and ease his heart with the knowledge
that it was as it had been. Of late I have found myself
doing the same. Look you, Na-Brendel of the Kestrel;
look upon the wardstone of the High Kingdom."

Wordlessly the lios stepped forward and placed his
eye to the opening in the door. He stayed there for a
long time, and was still silent when at length he drew
back.

"And you, young Pwyll, look you as well and mark
whether the blue of the binding still shines in the
stone." Ailell gestured and Paul moved past Brendel
to put his eye to the aperture.

It was a small chamber, with no decorations on the
walls or floor and no furnishings of any kind. In the

precise center of the room there stood a plinth or pillar, rising past the height of a man, and before it was set a low altar, upon which burned a pure white fire. Upon the sides of the pillar were carven images of kingly men, and resting in a hollowed-out space at the top of the column lay a stone, about the size of a crystal ball; and Paul saw that that stone shone with its own light, and the light with which it shone was blue.

Back in the room they had left, Paul found a third goblet on a table by the window and poured wine for the three of them. Brendel accepted his cup, but immediately began a restless pacing of the room. Ailell had seated himself again in his chair by the gameboard. Watching from the window, Paul saw the lios alfar stop his coiled movement and stand before the King.

"We believe the wardstones, High King, because we must," he began softly, almost gently. "But you know there are other powers that serve the Dark, and some of them are great. Their Lord may yet be bound beneath Rangat, but moving over the land now is an evil we cannot ignore. Have you not seen it in your drought, High King? How can you not see? It rains in Cathal and on the Plain. Only in Brennin will the harvest fail. Only—"

"Silence!" Ailell's voice cracked high and sharp. "You know not of what you speak. Seek not to meddle in our affairs!" The King leaned forward in his chair, glaring at the slim figure of the lios alfar. Two bright spots of red flushed his face above the wispy beard.

Na-Brendel stopped. He was not tall, but in that moment he seemed to grow in stature as he gazed at the High King.

When he finally spoke, it was without pride or bitterness. "I did not mean to anger you," he said. "On this day, least of all. It is in my heart, though, that little in the days to come can be the affair of one people alone. Such is the meaning of Ra-Tenniel's gift. I am glad you have accepted it. I will give your message to my Lord." He bowed very low, turned, and walked back through the doorway in the wall, donning his cloak and hood as he moved. The door slid silently closed behind him, and then there was nothing in the room to mark his ever having been there, save the shimmering scepter of glass Ailell was twisting around and around in the trembling hands of an old man.

From where he stood by the window, Paul could hear a different bird now lifting its voice in song. He supposed it must be getting close to dawn, but they were on the west side of the palace and the sky was still dark. He wondered if the King had completely forgotten his presence. At length, however, Ailell drew a tired breath and, laying the scepter down by the gameboard, moved slowly to stand by Paul, gazing out the window. From where they stood, Paul could see the land fall away westward, and far in the distance rose the trees of a forest, a greater darkness against the dark of the night.

"Leave me, friend Pwyll," Ailell said at length, not unkindly. "I am weary now, and will be best by myself. Weary," he repeated, "and old. If there truly is some power of Darkness walking the land I can do nothing about it tonight unless I die. And truly, I do not want to die, on the Tree or otherwise. If this is my failing, then so it must be." His eyes were distant and sad as he gazed out the window towards the woods far off.

Paul cleared his throat awkwardly. "I don't think that wanting to live can be a failing." The words rasped from too long a silence; a difficult emotion was waking within him.

Ailell smiled at that, but with his mouth only, and he continued to look out at the darkness. "For a king it may be, Pwyll. The price, remember?" He went on in a different voice, "Some blessings I have had. You heard Ysanne in the hall this morning. She said she had loved me. I never knew that. I don't think," the King mused softly, turning at last to look at Paul, "that I will tell that part to Marrien, the Queen."

Paul let himself out of the room, after bowing with all the respect he had. There was a queer constriction in his throat. *Marrien, the Queen.* He shook his head, and took an uncertain step along the corridor. A long shadow detached itself from the wall nearby.

"Do you know the way?" Coll asked.

"Not really, no," Paul said. "I guess I don't."

They passed through the hallways of the palace, their footsteps echoing. Beyond the walls, dawn was just breaking in the east over Gwen Ystrat. It was dark still in the palace, though.

Outside his doorway Paul turned to Diarmuid's man. "Coll," he asked, "what's the Tree?"

The burly soldier froze. After a moment a hand went up to rub the broad hook of his broken nose. They had stopped walking; Paras Derval lay wrapped in silence. For a moment Paul thought his question would not be answered, but then Coll did speak, his voice pitched low.

"The Summer Tree?" he said. "It's in the wood west of the town. Sacred it is, to Mörnir of the Thunder."

"Why is it important?"

"Because," said Coll, lower yet, "that's where the God would summon the High King in the old days, when the land had need."

"Summon him for what?"

"To hang on the Summer Tree and die," said Coll succinctly. "I've said too much already. Your friend is with the Lady Rheva tonight, I believe. I'll be back to wake you in a little while; we've got a long ride today." And he spun on his heel to walk off.

"Coll!"

The big man turned, slowly.

"Is it always the King who hangs?"

"Coll's broad, sunburnt face was etched with apprehension. The answer, when it came, seemed almost to be against his will. "Princes of the blood have been known to do it instead."

"Which explains Diarmuid last night. Coll, I really don't want to get you in trouble—but if I were to make a guess at what happened here, I'd guess that Ailell was called because of this drought, or maybe there's a drought because he hasn't gone, and I'd guess he is terrified of the whole thing, and Loren backs him because he doesn't trust whatever happens on the Summer Tree." After a moment Coll nodded stiffly, and Schafer continued.

"Then I'd go on to guess, and this is really a guess, that Diarmuid's brother wanted to do it for the King, and Ailell forbade him—which is why he's gone and Diarmuid is heir. Would that be a good guess?"

Coll had come very close as Schafer was speaking. He searched Paul's eyes with his own honest brown ones. Then he shook his head, a kind of awe written into his features.

"This is deeper than I can go. It would be," he said, "a very good guess. The High King must consent to his surrogate, and when he refused, the Prince cursed him, which is treason, and was exiled. It is now death to speak his name."

In the silence that followed it seemed to Paul as if the whole weight of the night was pressing down upon the two of them.

"There is no power in me," Coll said then, in his deep voice, "but if there was, I would have him cursed in the name of all the gods and goddesses there are."

"Who?" Paul whispered.

"Why, the Prince, of course," said Coll. "The exiled Prince, Diarmuid's brother, Aileron."

Chapter 6

Beyond the palace gates and the walls of the town, the depredations of drought came home. The impact of a rainless summer could be measured in the heavy dust of the road, in the thin grass peeling like brown paint on hills and tummocks, in stunted trees and dried-up village wells. In the fiftieth year of Ailell's reign, the High Kingdom was suffering as no living man could remember.

For Kevin and Paul, riding south with Diarmuid and seven of his men in the morning, the way of things registered most brutally in the pinched, bitter features of the farmers they passed on the road. Already the heat of the sun was casting a shimmer of mirage on the landscape. There were no clouds in the sky.

Diarmuid was setting a hard pace, though, and Kevin, who was no horseman and who'd had a sleepless night, was exceedingly happy when they pulled up outside a tavern in the fourth village they came to.

They took a hasty meal of cold, sharply spiced meat, bread, and cheese, with pints of black ale to wash away the throat-clogging dust of the road. Kevin, eating voraciously, saw Diarmuid speak briefly to Carde, who quietly sought the innkeeper and withdrew into another room with him. Noticing Kevin's glance, the Prince walked over to the long wooden table where he and Paul were sitting with the lean, dark man named Erron.

"We're checking for your friend," Diarmuid told them. "It's one of the reasons we're doing this. Loren went north to do the same, and I've sent word to the coast."

"Who's with the women?" Paul Schafer asked quickly.

Diarmuid smiled. "Trust me," he said. "I do know what I'm doing. There are guards, and Matt stayed in the palace, too."

"Loren went without him?" Paul queried sharply. "How . . . ?"

Diarmuid's expression was even more amused. "Even without magic our friend can handle himself. He has a sword, and knows how to use it. You worry a good deal, don't you?"

"Does it surprise you?" Kevin cut in. "We don't know where we are, we don't know the rules here, Dave's gone missing, God knows where—and we don't even know where we're going with you now."

"That last," said Diarmuid, "is easy enough. We're crossing the river into Cathal, if we can. By night, and quietly, because there's a very good chance we'll be killed if found."

"I see," said Kevin, swallowing. "And are we allowed to know why we are subjecting ourselves to that unpleasant possibility?"

For the first time that morning Diarmuid's smile flashed full-force. "Of course you are," he said kindly. "You're going to help me seduce a lady. Tell me, Carde," he murmured, turning, "any news?"

There was none. The Prince drained his pint and was striding out the door. The others scrambled to their feet and followed. A number of the villagers came out of the inn to watch them ride off.

"Mörnir guard you, young Prince!" one farmer cried impulsively. "And in the name of the Summer Tree, may he take the old man and let you be our King!"

Diarmuid had raised a gracious hand at the first words, but the speaker's last phrase brought him to wheel his horse hard. There was a brutal silence. The

Prince's face had gone cold. No one moved. Overhead
Kevin heard a noisy flap of wings as a dense cluster
of crows wheeled aloft, darkening the sun for an instant.

Diarmuid's voice, when it came, was formal and
imperious. "The words you have spoken are treason,"
Ailell's son said, and with a sideways nod spoke one
word more: *"Coll."*

The farmer may never have seen the arrow that killed
him. Diarmuid did not. He was already pounding up
the road without a backwards glance as Coll replaced
his bow. By the time the shock had passed and the
screaming had begun, all ten of them were around the
bend that would carry them south.

Kevin's hands were shaking with shock and fury as
he galloped, the image of the dead man engulfing him,
the screams still echoing in his mind. Coll, beside him,
seemed impassive and unperturbed. Save that he carefully refused to meet the glance of Paul Schafer, who
was staring fixedly at him as they rode, and to whom
he had spoken a treasonous word of his own the night
before.

◆

In the early spring of 1949 Dr. John Ford of Toronto
had taken a fortnight's leave from his residency at
London's St. Thomas Hospital. Hiking alone in the
Lake District, north of Keswick, he came, at the end
of a long day afoot, down the side of a hill and walked
wearily up to a farmyard tucked into the shadow of the
slope.

There was a girl in the yard, drawing water from a
well. The westering sun slanted upon her dark hair.
When she turned at the sound of his footstep, he saw
that her eyes were grey. She smiled shyly when, hat in
hand, he asked for a drink, and before she had finished
drawing it for him, John Ford had fallen in love, simply and irrevocably, which was his nature in all things.

Deirdre Cowan, who was eighteen that spring, had
been told long ago by her grandmother that she would

love and marry a man from over the sea. Because her gran was known to have the Sight, Deirdre never doubted what she had been told. And this man, handsome and diffident, had eyes that called to her.

Ford spent that night in her father's house, and in the quietest dark before dawn Deirdre rose from her bed. She was not surprised to see her gran in the hallway by her own bedroom door, nor to see the old woman make a gesture of blessing that went back a very long way. She went to Ford's room, the gray eyes beguiling, her body sweet with trust.

They were married in the fall, and John Ford took his wife home just as the first snows of the winter came. And it was their daughter who walked, a Dwarf beside her, twenty-five springs after her parents had been brought together, towards the shores of a lake in another world, to meet her own destiny.

The path to the lake where Ysanne lived twisted north and west through a shallow valley flanked by gentle hills, a landscape that would have been lovely in any proper season. But Kim and Matt were walking through a country scorched and barren—and the thirst of the land seemed to knife into Kim, twisting like anguish inside her. Her face hurt, the bones seeming taut and difficult within her. Movement was becoming painful, and everywhere she looked, her eyes flinched away.

"It's dying," she said.

Matt looked at her with his one eye. "You feel it?"

She nodded stiffly. "I don't understand."

The Dwarf's expression was grim. "The gift is not without its darkness. I do not envy you."

"Envy me *what*, Matt?" Kim's brow furrowed. "What do I have?"

Matt Sören's voice was soft. "Power. Memory. Truly, I am not sure. If the hurt of the land reaches so deeply. . . ."

"It's easier in the palace. I'm blocked there from all this."

"We can go back.''

For one moment, sharp and almost bitter, Kim did want to turn back—all the way back. Not just to Paras Derval, but home. Where the ruin of the grass and the dead stalks of flowers by the path did not burn her so. But then she remembered the eyes of the Seer as they had looked into hers, and she heard again the voice, drumming in her veins: *I have awaited you.*

"No,'' she said. "How much farther?''

"Around the curve. We'll see the lake soon. But hold, let me give you something—I should have thought of it sooner.'' And the Dwarf held out towards her a bracelet of silver workmanship, in which was set a green stone.

"What is it?''

"A vellin stone. It is very precious; there are few left, and the secret of fashioning them died with Ginserat. The stone is a shield from magic. Put it on.''

With wonder in her eyes, Kimberly placed it upon her wrist, and as she did, the pain was gone, the hurt, the ache, the burning, all were gone. She was aware of them, but distantly, for the vellin was her shield and she felt it guarding her. She cried out in wonder.

But the relief in her face was not mirrored in that of the Dwarf. "Ah,'' said Matt Sören, grimly, "so I was right. There are dark threads shuttling on the Loom. The Weaver grant that Loren comes back soon.''

"Why?'' Kim asked. "What does this mean?''

"If the vellin guards you from the land's pain, then that pain is not natural. And if there is a power strong enough to do this to the whole of the High Kingdom, then there is a fear in me. I begin to wonder about the old tales of Mörnir's Tree, and the pact the Founder made with the God. And if not that, then I dare not think what. Come,'' said the Dwarf, "it is time I took you to Ysanne.''

And walking more swiftly, he led her around an outthrust spur of hill slope, and as they cleared the spur she saw the lake: a gem of blue in a necklace of low hills. And somehow there was still green by the lake, and the profuse, scattered colors of wildflowers.

Kim stopped dead in her tracks. "Oh, Matt!"

The Dwarf was silent while she gazed down, enraptured, on the water. "It *is* fair," he said finally. "But had you ever seen Calor Diman between the mountains, you would spare your heart's praise somewhat, to have some left for the Queen of Waters."

Kim, hearing the change in his voice, looked at him for a moment; then, drawing a deliberate breath, she closed her eyes and was wordless a long time. When she spoke, it was in a cadence not her own.

"Between the mountains," she said. "Very high up, it is. The melting snow in summer falls into the lake. The air is thin and clear. There are eagles circling. The sunlight turns the lake into a golden fire. To drink of that water is to taste of whatever light is falling down upon it, whether of sun or moon or stars. And under the full moon, Calor Diman is deadly, for the vision never fades and never stops pulling. A tide in the heart. Only the true King of Dwarves may endure that night vigil without going mad, and he must do so for the Diamond Crown. He must wed the Queen of Waters, lying all night by her shores at full of the moon. He will be bound then, to the end of his days, as the King must be, to Calor Diman."

And Kimberly opened her eyes to look full upon the former King of Dwarves. "*Why*, Matt?" she asked, in her own voice. "Why did you leave?"

He made no answer, but met her look unflinchingly. At length he turned, still silent, and led her down the winding path to Ysanne's lake. She was waiting there for them, dreamer of the dream, knowledge in her eyes, and pity, and another nameless thing.

◆

Kevin Laine had never been able to hide his emotions well, and that summary execution, so casually effected, had disturbed him very deeply. He had not spoken a word through a day's hard riding, and the twilight found him still pale with undischarged anger. In the gathering dark the company passed through more heavily wooded country, slanting gradually downhill towards the south. The road went past a thick copse of trees and revealed, half a mile beyond, the towers of a small fortress.

Diarmuid pulled to a halt. He seemed fresh still, unaffected by the day on horseback, and Kevin, whose bones and muscles ached ferociously, fixed the Prince with a cold stare.

He was, however, ignored. "Rothe," said Diarmuid to a compact, brown-bearded rider, "you go in. Speak to Averren and no one else. I am not here. Coll is leading a number of you on a reconnaissance. No details. He won't ask anyway. Find out, discreetly, if a stranger has been seen in the area, then join us by the Dael Slope." Rothe spun his horse and galloped towards the tower.

"That's South Keep," Carde murmured to Kevin and Paul. "Our watchtower down here. Not too big— but there's little danger of anything crossing the river, so we don't need much. The big garrison's down river, west by the sea. Cathal's invaded twice that way, so there's a castle at Seresh to keep watch."

"Why can't they cross the river?" Paul asked. Kevin maintained his self-imposed silence.

Carde's smile in the gathering dark was mirthless. "That you'll see, soon enough, when we go down to try."

Diarmuid, throwing a cloak over his shoulders, waited until the keep gates had swung open for Rothe; then he led them west off the road along a narrow path that began to curve south through the woods.

They rode for perhaps an hour, quietly now, though no order had been given. These, Kevin realized, were highly trained men, for all the roughness of their garb and speech when compared to the dandies they'd met in the palace.

The moon, a thinning crescent, swung into sight

behind them as they wound out of the trees. Diarmuid halted at the edge of the sloping plain, a hand up for silence. And after a moment Kevin heard it, too: the deep sound of water, swift-flowing.

Under the waning moon and the emerging stars he dismounted with the others. Gazing south he could see the land fall sheer away in a cliff only a few hundred yards from where they stood. But he could not see anything at all on the far side; it was as if the world ended just in front of them.

"There's a land fault here," a light voice said close to his ear. Kevin stiffened, but Diarmuid went on casually. "Cathal lies about a hundred feet lower than us; you'll see when we go forward. And," said the Prince, his voice still light, "it is a mistake to make judgements too soon. That man had to die—had he not, word would be in the palace by now that I was encouraging treasonous talk. And there are those who would like to spread that word. His life was forfeit from the time he spoke, and the arrow was a kinder death than Gorlaes would have granted him. We'll wait for Rothe here. I've told Carde to rub you both down; you'll not make it across with muscles that won't move." He walked away and sat on the ground, leaning against the trunk of a tree. After a moment, Kevin Laine, who was neither a petty man nor a stupid one, smiled to himself.

Carde's hands were strong, and the liniment he used was extraordinary. By the time Rothe rejoined them, Kevin felt functional again. It was quite dark now, and Diarmuid threw back his cloak as he suddenly rose. They gathered around him at the edge of the wood and a ripple of soundless tension went through the company. Kevin, feeling it, looked for Paul, and saw that Schafer was already gazing at him. They exchanged a tight smile, then listened intently as Diarmuid began to speak, softly and concisely. The words spun into the almost windless night, were received and registered, and then there was silence; and they were moving, nine of them, with one man left to the horses, over the slope that led to the river they had to cross into a country where they would be killed if seen.

Running lightly beside Coll, Kevin felt his heart suddenly expand with a fierce exhilaration. Which lasted, growing brighter, until they dropped to a crouch, then a crawl, and, reaching the edge of the cliff, looked down.

Saeren was the mightiest river west of the mountains. Tumbling spectacularly out of the high peaks of Eridu, it roared down into the lowlands of the west. There it would have slowed and begun to meander, had not a cataclysm torn the land millennia ago in the youngness of the world, an earthquake that had ripped a gash like a wound in the firmament: the Saeren Gorge. Through that deep ravine the river thundered, dividing Brennin, which had been raised up in the earth's fury, from Cathal, lying low and fertile to the south. And great Saeren did not slow or wander in its course, nor could a dry summer in the north slake its force. The river foamed and boiled two hundred feet below them, glinting in the moonlight, awesome and appalling. And between them and the water lay a descent in darkness down a cliff too sheer for belief.

"If you fall," Diarmuid had said, unsmiling, "try not to scream. You may give the others away."

And now Kevin could see the far side of the gorge, and along the southern cliff, well below their elevation, were the bonfires and garrisons of Cathal, the outposts guarding their royalty and their gardens from the north.

Kevin swore shakily. "I do not believe this. What are they afraid of? No one can cross this thing."

"It's a long dive," Coll agreed from his right side. "But he says it *was* crossed hundreds of years ago, just once, and that's why we're trying now."

"Just for the hell of it, eh?" Kevin breathed, still incredulous. "What's the matter? Are you bored with backgammon?"

"With what?"

"Never mind."

And indeed, there was little chance to talk after that, for Diarmuid, farther along to their right, spoke softly, and Erron, lean and supple, moved quickly over to a large twisted tree Kevin hadn't noticed and knotted a rope carefully about the trunk. That done, he dropped the line over the edge, paying it out between his hands. When the last coil spun down into darkness, he wet each of his palms deliberately and cocked an eye at Diarmuid. The Prince nodded once. Erron gripped the rope tightly, stepped forward, and disappeared over the edge of the cliff.

Hypnotically, they all watched the taut line of the rope. Coll went over to the tree to check the knot. Kevin became aware, as the long moments passed, that his hands were wet with perspiration. He wiped them surreptitiously on his breeches. Then, on the far side of the rope, he saw Paul Schafer looking at him. It was dark, and he couldn't see Paul's face clearly, but something in the expression, a remoteness, a strangeness, triggered a sudden cold apprehension in Kevin's chest, and brought flooding remorselessly back the memory he could never quite escape of the night Rachel Kincaid had died.

He remembered Rachel himself, remembered her with a kind of love of his own, for it had been hard not to love the dark-haired girl with the shy, Pre-Raphaelite grace, for whom two things in the world meant fire: the sounds of a cello under her bow, and the presence of Paul Schafer. Kevin had seen, and caught his breath to see, the look in her dark eyes when Paul would enter a room, and he had watched, too, the hesitant unfolding of trust and need in his proud friend. Until it all went smash, and he had stood, helpless tears in his own eyes, in the emergency ward of St. Michael's Hospital with Paul when the death word came. When Paul Schafer, his face a dry mask, had spoken the only words he would ever speak on Rachel's death: "It should have been me," he had said, and walked alone out of a too-bright room.

But now, in the darkness of another world, a different voice was speaking to him. "He's down. You next, friend Kevin," said Diarmuid. And there was indeed the dancing of the rope that meant Erron was signaling from the bottom.

Moving before he could think, Kevin went up to the rope, wet his hands as Erron had done, gripped carefully, and slid over and down alone.

Using his booted feet for leverage and control, he descended hand over hand into the growing thunder of noise that was the Saeren Gorge. The cliff was rough, and there was a danger that the line might fray on one of the rock edges—but there was little to be done about that, or about the burning in his hands as the rope slid abrasively through his grip. He looked down only once and was dizzied by the speed of the water far below. Turning his face to the cliff, Kevin breathed deeply for a moment, willing himself to be calm; then he continued, hand and foot, rope and toehold, down to where the river waited. It became a process almost mechanical, reaching for crevices with his foot, pushing off as the rope slid through his palms. He blocked out pain and fatigue, the returning ache of abused muscles, he forgot, even, where he was. The world was a rope and a face of rock. It seemed to have always been.

So oblivious was he that when Erron touched his ankle, Kevin's heart leaped in a spasm of terror. Erron helped him step down onto the thin strip of earth, barely ten feet from where the water roared past, drenching them with spray. The noise was overwhelming; it made conversation almost impossible.

Erron jerked three times on the slack line, and after a moment it began to sway and bob beside them with the weight of a body above. Paul, Kevin thought wearily, that'll be Paul. And then another thought invaded him and registered hard over exhaustion: *he doesn't care if he falls*. The realization hit with the force of apprehended truth. Kevin looked upwards and began frantically scanning the cliff face, but the moon was lighting the southern side only, and Schafer's descent was invisible. Only the lazy, almost mocking movement of the rope end beside them testified that someone was above.

And only now, absurdly too late, did Kevin think of Paul's weakened condition. He remembered rushing him to hospital only two weeks before, after the basketball game Schafer shouldn't have played, and at the memory, his heart angled in his breast. Unable to bear the strain of looking upwards, he turned instead to the bobbing rope beside him. So long as that slow dance continued, Paul was all right. The movement of the rope meant life, a continuation. Fiercely Kevin concentrated on the line swaying slowly in front of the dark rock face. He didn't pray, but he thought of his father, which was almost the same thing.

He was still gazing fixedly at the rope when Erron finally touched his arm and pointed. And looking upwards then, Kevin drew free breath again to see the slight, familiar figure moving down to join them. Paul Schafer alighted moments later, neatly, though breathing hard. His eyes met Kevin's for an instant, then flicked away. He tugged the rope three times himself, before moving down the strand to slump against the rock face, eyes closed.

A time later there were nine of them standing spray-drenched by the river bank. Diarmuid's eyes gleamed in the light reflected off the water; he seemed feral and fey, a spirit of night unleashed. And he signalled Coll to begin the next stage of the journey.

The big man had descended with another coil of rope in the pack on his broad back. Now he unslung his bow and, drawing an arrow from its quiver, fitted an end of the rope to an iron ring set in the shaft. Then he moved forward to the edge of the water and began scanning the opposite shore. Kevin couldn't see what he was looking to find. On their own side a few shrubs and one or two thick, short trees had dug into the thin soil, but the Cathal shore was sandier, and there seemed to be nothing growing by the river. Coll, however, had raised his great bow with the arrow notched to the string. He drew one steady breath and pulled the bowstring all the way back past his ear, the gesture smooth, though the corded muscles of his arm had gone ridged and taut. Coll released, and the arrow sang into arching flight, the thin rope hurtling with it high over Saeren—*to sink deep into the stone cliff on the far side.*

Carde, who'd been holding the free end of the rope, quickly pulled it tight. Then Coll measured and cut it, and, tying the free end to another arrow, proceeded to fire the shaft point-blank into the rock behind them. The arrow buried itself into stone.

Kevin, utterly incredulous, turned to Diarmuid, questions exploding in his eyes. The Prince walked over and shouted in his ear, over the thunder of the water, "Loren's arrows. It helps to have a mage for a friend—though if he finds out how I've used his gift, he'll consign me to the wolves!" And the Prince laughed aloud to see the silvered highway of cord that spanned Saeren in the moonlight. Watching him, Kevin felt it then, the intoxicating lure of this man who was leading them. He laughed himself in that moment, feeling constraint and apprehension slip away. A sense of freedom came upon him, of being tuned to the night and their journey, as he watched Erron leap up, grab the rope, and begin to swing hand over hand, out over the water.

The wave that hit the dark-haired man was a fluke, kicked up from an angled rock by the shore. It slammed into Erron as he was changing grips and threw him violently sideways. Desperately Erron curved his body to hang on with one hand, but the wave that followed the first buffeted him mercilessly, and he was torn from the rope and flung into the millrace of Saeren.

Kevin Laine was running before the second wave hit. Pelting flat out downstream along the strand, he leaped, without pausing to calculate or look back, for the overhanging branch of one of the knotted trees that dug into the earth by the river. Fully extended in flight, his arms outstretched, he barely reached it. There was no time to think. With a racking, contorted movement he twisted his body, looped his knees over the branch, and hung face down over the torrent.

Only then did he look, almost blinded by spray, to see Erron, a cork in the flood, hurtling towards him. Again, no time. Kevin reached down, tasting his death in that moment. Erron threw up a convulsive hand, and each clasped the other's wrist.

The pull was brutal. It would have ripped Kevin from the tree like a leaf—had not someone else been there. Someone who was holding his legs on the branch with a grip like an iron band. A grip that was not going to break.

"I've got you!" screamed Paul Schafer. "Lift him if you can."

And hearing the voice, locked in Schafer's vise-like hold, Kevin felt a surge of strength run through him; both hands gripping Erron's wrist, he pulled him from the river.

There were other hands by then, reaching for Erron, taking him swiftly to shore. Kevin let go and allowed Paul to haul him up to the branch. Straddling it, they faced each other, gasping hard for breath.

"You idiot!" Paul shouted, his chest heaving. "You scared the hell out of me!"

Kevin blinked, then the too, too *much* boiled over. "You shut up! *I* scared *you?* What do you think you've been doing to me since Rachel died?"

Paul, utterly unprepared, was shocked silent. Trembling with emotion and adrenalin afterburn, Kevin spoke again, his voice raw. "I mean it, Paul. When I was waiting at the bottom . . . I didn't think you were going to make it down. And Paul, I wasn't sure if you cared.''

Their heads were close together, for the words to be heard. Schafer's pupils were enormous. In the reflected moonlight his face was so white as to be almost inhuman.

"That isn't quite true," he replied finally.

"But it isn't far wrong. Not far enough. Oh, Paul, you have to bend a little. If you can't talk, can't you cry at least? She deserves your tears. Can't you cry for her?''

At that, Paul Schafer laughed. The sound chilled Kevin to the core, there was such wildness in it. "I can't," Paul said. "That's the whole problem, Kev. I really, really can't.''

"Then you're going to break," Kevin rasped.

"I might," Schafer replied, scarcely audible. "I'm trying hard not to, believe me. Kev, I know you care. It matters to me, very much. If . . . if I do decide to go, I'll . . . say goodbye. I promise you'll know."

"Oh, for God's sake! Is that supposed to make me—''

"Come on!" Coll bellowed from the shore, and Kevin, startled, realized that he'd been calling for some time. "That branch could crack any second!"

So they moved back to the strand, to be disconcertingly enveloped by bear-hugs from Diarmuid's men. Coll himself nearly broke Kevin's back with his massive embrace.

The Prince walked over, his expression utterly sober. "You saved a man I value," he said. "I owe you both. I was being frivolous when I invited you to come, and unfair. I am grateful now that I did.''

"Good," said Kevin succinctly. "I don't much enjoy feeling like excess baggage. And now," he went on, raising his voice so they could all hear, while he buried again that which he had no answer for and no right to answer, "let's cross this stream. I want to see those gardens." And walking past the Prince, his shoulders straight, head high as he could carry it, he led them back to the rope across the river, grief in his heart like a stone.

One by one then, hand over hand, they did cross. And on the other shore, where sand met cliff in Cathal, Diarmuid found them what he had promised: the worn handholds carved into the rock five hundred years ago by Alorre, Prince of Brennin, who had been the first and the last to cross Saeren into the Garden Country.

Screened by darkness and the sound of the river, they climbed up to where the grass was green and the scent of moss and cyclamen greeted them. The guards were few and careless, easily avoided. They came to a wood a mile from the river and took shelter there as a light rain began to fall.

------◆------

Beneath her feet Kimberly could feel the rich texture of the soil, and the sweetness of wildflowers surrounded her. They were in the strand of wood lining the north shore of the lake. The leaves of the tall trees, somehow untouched by the drought, filtered the sunlight, leaving a verdant coolness through which they walked, looking for a flower.

Matt had gone back to the palace.

"She will stay with me tonight," the Seer had said. "No harm will touch her by the lake. You have given her the vellin, which was wiser perhaps than even you knew, Matt Sören. I have my powers, too, and Tyrth is here with us."

"Tyrth?" the Dwarf asked.

"My servant," Ysanne replied. "He will take her back when the time comes. Trust me, and go easily. You have done well to bring her here. We have much to talk of, she and I."

So the Dwarf had gone. But there had been little of the promised talk since his departure. To Kim's first stumbled questions the white-haired Seer had offered only a gentle smile and an admonition. "Patience, child. There are things that come before the telling time. First there is a flower we need. Come with me, and see if we can find a bannion for tonight.''

And so Kim found herself walking through shade and light under the trees, questions tumbling over each other in her mind. Blue-green, Ysanne had said it was, with red like a drop of blood at the heart.

Ahead of her the Seer moved, light and sure-footed over root and fallen branch. She seemed younger in the wood than in Ailell's hall, and here she carried no staff to lean upon. Which triggered another question, and this one broke through.

''Do you feel the drought the way I do?''

Ysanne stopped at that and regarded Kim a moment, her eyes bright in the seamed, wizened face. She turned again, though, and continued walking, scanning the ground on either side of the twisting path. When her answer came Kim was unprepared.

''Not the same way. It tires me, and there is a sense of oppression. But not actual pain, as with you. I can—*there!*'' And darting quickly to one side she knelt on the earth.

The red at the center did look like blood against the sea-colored petals of the bannion.

''I knew we would find one today,'' said Ysanne, and her voice had roughened. ''It has been years, so many, many years.'' With care she uprooted the flower and rose to her feet. ''Come, child, we will take this home. And I will try to tell you what you need to know.''

''Why did you say you'd been waiting for me?'' They were in the front room of Ysanne's cottage, in chairs beside the fireplace. Late afternoon. Through the window Kim could see the figure of the servant, Tyrth, mending the fence in back of the cottage. A few chickens scrabbled and pecked in the yard, and there was a goat tied to a post in a corner. Around the walls of the room were shelves upon which, in labelled jars, stood plants and herbs of astonishing variety, many

with names Kim could not recognize. There was little
furniture: the two chairs, a large table, a small, neat
bed in an alcove off the back of the room.

Ysanne sipped at her drink before replying. They
were drinking something that tasted like camomile.

"I dreamt you," the Seer said. "Many times. That
is how I see such things as I do see. Which have grown
fewer and more clouded of late. You were clear,
though, hair and eyes. I saw your face."

"*Why*, though? What am I, that you should dream
of me?"

"You already know the answer to that. From the
crossing. From the land's pain, which is yours, child.
You are a Seer as I am, and more, I think, than I have
ever been." Cold suddenly in the hot, dry summer,
Kim turned her head away.

"But," she said in a small voice, "I don't *know*
anything."

"Which is why I am to teach you what I know. That
is why you are here."

There was a complex silence in the room. The two
women, one old, the other younger than her years,
looked at each other through identical grey eyes under
white hair and brown, and a breeze like a finger blew
in upon them from the lake.

"My lady."

The voice abraded the stillness. Kim turned to see
Tyrth in the window. Thick black hair and a full beard
framed eyes so dark they were almost black. He was
not a big man, but his arms on the window sill were
corded with muscle and tanned a deep brown by labor
in the sun.

Ysanne, unstartled, turned to him. "Tyrth, yes, I
meant to call you. Can you make up another bed for
me? We have a guest tonight. This is Kimberly, who
crossed with Loren two nights past."

Tyrth met her eyes for an instant only, then an awkward hand brushed at the thick hair tumbling over his

forehead. "I'll do a proper bed then. But in the meanwhile, I've seen something you should know of. . . ."

"The wolves?" Ysanne asked tranquilly. Tyrth, after a bemused moment, nodded. "I saw them the other night," the Seer went on. "While I slept. There isn't much we can do. I left word in the palace with Loren yesterday."

"I don't like it," Tyrth muttered. "There haven't been wolves this far south in my lifetime. Big ones, too. They shouldn't be so big." And turning his head, he spat in the dust of the yard before touching his forehead again and walking from the window. As he moved away Kim saw that he limped, favoring his left foot.

Ysanne followed her glance. "A broken bone," she said. "badly set years ago. He'll walk like that all his life. I'm lucky to have him, though—no one else would serve a witch." She smiled. "Your lessons begin tonight, I think."

"How?"

Ysanne nodded towards the bannion resting on the table top. "It begins with the flower," she said. "It did for me, a long time ago."

The waning moon rose late, and it was full dark when the two women made their way beneath it to stand by the edge of the lake. The breeze was delicate and cool, and the water lapped the shore gently, like a lover. Over their heads the summer stars were strung like filigree.

Ysanne's face had gone austere and remote. Looking at her, Kim felt a premonitory tension. The axis of her life was swinging and she knew not how or where, only that somehow, she had lived in order to come to this shore.

Ysanne drew her small figure erect and stepped onto a flat surface of rock jutting out over the lake. With a motion almost abrupt, she gestured for Kim to sit beside her on the stone. The only sounds were the stir of the wind in the trees behind them, and the quiet slap of water against the rocks. Then Ysanne raised both arms in a gesture of power and invocation and spoke in a voice that rang over the night lake like a bell.

"Hear me, Eilathen!" she cried. "Hear and be summoned, for I have need of you, and this is the last time and the deepest. *Eilathen damae! Sien rabanna, den viroth bannion damae!*" And as she spoke the words, the flower in her hand burst into flame, blue-green and red like its colors, and she threw it, spiralling, into the lake.

Kim felt the wind die. Beside her, Ysanne seemed carved out of marble, so still was she. The very night seemed gathered into that stillness. There was no sound, no motion, and Kim could feel the furious pounding of her heart. Under the moon the surface of the lake was glassy calm, but not with the calm of tranquillity. It was coiled, waiting. Kim sensed, as if within the pulse of her blood, a vibration as of a tuning fork pitched just too high for human ears.

And then something exploded into motion in the middle of the lake. A spinning form, whirling too fast for the eye to follow, rose over the surface of the water, and Kim saw that it shone blue-green under the moon.

Unbelieving, she watched it come towards them, and as it did so, the spinning began to slow, so that when it finally halted, suspended in air above the water before Ysanne, Kim saw that it had the tall form of a man.

Long sea-green hair lay coiled about his shoulders, and his eyes were cold and clear as chips of winter ice. His naked body was lithe and lean, and it shimmered as if with scales, the moonlight glinting where it fell upon him. And on his hand, burning in the dark like a wound, was a ring, red as the heart of the flower that had summoned him.

"Who calls me from the deep against my desire?"

The voice was cold, cold as night waters in early spring, and there was danger in it.

"Eilathen, it is the Dreamer. I have need. Forgo your wrath and hear me. It is long since we stood here, you and I."

"Long for you, Ysanne. You have grown old. Soon the worms will gather you." The reedy pleasure in the voice could be heard. "But I do not age in my green halls, and time turns not for me, save when the bannion fire troubles the deep." And Eilathen held out the hand upon which the red ring burned.

"I would not send down the fire without a cause, and tonight marks your release from guardianship. Do this last thing for me and you are free of my call." A slight stir of wind; the trees were sighing again.

"On your oath?" Eilathen moved closer to the shore. He seemed to grow, towering above the Seer, water rippling down his shoulders and thighs, the long wet hair pulled back from his face.

"On my oath," Ysanne replied. "I bound you against my own desire. The wild magic is meant to be free. Only because my need was great were you given to the flowerfire. On my oath, you are free tonight."

"And the task?" Eilathen's voice was colder than ever, more alien. He shimmered before them with a green dark power.

"This," said Ysanne, and pointed to Kimberly.

The stab of Eilathen's eyes was like ice cutting into her. Kim saw, sensed, somehow knew the fathomless halls whence Ysanne had summoned him—the shaped corridors of seastone and twined seaweed, the perfect silence of his deep home. She held the gaze as best she could, held it until it was Eilathen who turned away.

"Now I know," he said to the Seer. "Now I understand." And a thread that might have been respect had woven its way into his voice.

"But she does not," said Ysanne. "So spin for her, Eilathen. Spin the Tapestry, that she may learn what she is, and what has been, and release you of the burden that you bear."

Eilathen glittered high above them both. His voice was a splintering of ice. "And this is the last?"

"This is the last," Ysanne replied.

He did not hear the note of loss in her voice. Sadness was alien to him, not of his world or his being. He smiled at her words and tossed his hair back, the taste, the glide, the long green dive of freedom already running through him.

"Look then!" he cried. "Look you to know—and know your last of Eilathen!" And crossing his arms upon his breast, so that the ring on his finger burned like a heart afire, he began to spin again. But somehow, as Kim watched, his eyes were locked on hers all the time, even as he whirled, so fast that the lake water began to foam beneath him, and his cold, cold eyes and the bright pain of the red ring he wore were all she knew in the world.

And then he was inside her, deeper than any lover had ever gone, more completely, and Kimberly was given the Tapestry.

She saw the shaping of the worlds, Fionavar at first, then all the others—her own in a fleeting glimpse—following it into time. The gods she saw, and knew their names, and she touched but could not hold, for no mortal can, the purpose and the pattern of the Weaver at the Loom.

And as she was whirled away from that bright vision, she came abruptly face to face with the oldest Dark in his stronghold of Starkadh. In his eyes she felt herself shrivel, felt the thread fray on the Loom; she knew evil for what it was. The live coals of his eyes scorched into her, and the talons of his hands seemed to score her flesh, and within her heart she was forced to sound the uttermost depths of his hate, and she knew him for Rakoth the Unraveller, Rakoth Maugrim, whom the gods themselves feared, he who would rend the Tapestry and lay his own malignant shadow on all of time to come. And flinching away from the vastness of his power, she endured an endless passage of despair.

Ysanne, ashen and helpless, heard her cry out then, a cry torn from the ruin of innocence, and the Seer wept by the shore of her lake. But through it all Eilathen spun, faster than hope or despair, colder than night, the stone over his heart blazing as he whirled like an unleashed wind towards the freedom he had lost.

Kimberly, though, was oblivious to time and place, to lake, rock, Seer, spirit, stone, locked like a spell into the images Eilathen's eyes imposed. She saw Iorweth Founder come from oversea, saw him greet the lios alfar by Sennett Strand, and her heart caught at the beauty of the lios in that vision, and of the tall men the God had called to found the High Kingdom. And then she learned why the Kings of Brennin, all the High Kings from Iorweth to Ailell, were named the Children of Mörnir, for Eilathen showed her the Summer Tree in the Godwood under stars.

The Dalrei she saw next, in a whirling away to the north and west; on the Plain she watched them in pursuit of the glorious eltor, their long hair tied back. The Dwarves delving under Banir Lök and Banir Tal she was shown, and the distant men of wild Eridu beyond their mountains.

Eilathen's eyes carried her south then, across Saeren, and she saw the gardens of Cathal, and the unrivalled splendor of the Lords across the river. The heart of Pendaran she touched, and in a bright vision, bittersweet, she saw Lisen of the Wood meet Amairgen Whitebranch in the grove and bind herself to him, first source to the first mage; and she saw her die by the sea tower, fairest child of all the turning worlds.

Grieving still for that loss, she was taken by Eilathen to see the war—the Great War against Rakoth. Conary she saw, and knew, and Colan his son, the Beloved. She saw the bright, fierce array of the lios, and the shining figure of Ra-Termaine, greatest of the Lords of the lios alfar—and she saw that brilliant company torn apart by wolves and svart alfar, and most terribly of all by the flying creatures older than nightmare unleashed by Maugrim. Then she watched as, coming too late, Conary and Colan were cut off and trapped in their turn by Sennett, and as a red sun went down on a night Conary would die, she saw, and her heart exploded within her to see, the curved ranks of the Dalrei ride singing out of Daniloth, out of the mist behind Revor into the sunset. She did not know, though Ysanne did, that she was weeping as the Riders and the warriors of Brennin and Cathal, terrible in their fury and their grief, drove the armies of the Dark back north and east through Andarien to Starkadh, where the Lion of Eridu came to join them, and where the blood and smoke cleared at last to show Rakoth beaten to his knees in surrender.

Then she was shown the binding, and knew the Mountain again for the prison it had become, and she watched Ginserat make the stones. Faster then, the images began to fly, and to Ysanne's eyes the speed of Eilathen's turning became as a maelstrom of power, and she knew that she was losing him. The joy of his release she tasted, even amid her own deep ache of loss.

Faster he spun, and faster, the water white beneath his feet, and the Seer watched as the one beside her who was no longer a girl learned what it was to dream true. To be a dreamer of the dream.

And there came a time when Eilathen slowed and stopped.

Kimberly lay sprawled on the rock, drained of all color, utterly unconscious. The water spirit and the Seer gazed at each other a long time, unspeaking.

At length, Eilathen's voice was heard, high and cold in the moonlight. "I have done. She knows what she is able to know. A great power is in her, but I do not know if she can bear the burden. She is young."

"Not anymore," Ysanne whispered. She found it hard to speak.

"Perhaps not. But it is no care of mine. I have spun for you, Dreamer. Release me from the fire." He was very close, the ice-crystal eyes gleaming with an inhuman light.

The Seer nodded. "I did promise. It was past time. You know why I needed you?" There was an appeal in her voice.

"I do not forgive."

"But you know why?"

Another long silence. Then, "Yes," said Eilathen, and one listening for it might have imagined gentleness in his tone. "I know why you bound me."

Ysanne was crying again, the tears glinting on her lined face. Her back was straight, though, her head high, and the command, when it came, rang clear. "Then go free of me, free of guardianship. Be free of flowerfire, now and evermore. *Laith derendel, sed bannion. Echorth!*"

And on the last word a sound burst from Eilathen, a high, keening sound beyond joy or release, almost beyond hearing, and the red-stoned ring slid from his finger and fell on the rock at the Seer's feet:

She knelt to gather it and, when she rose, saw through still-falling tears that he had already spun back out over the lake.

"Eilathen!" she cried. "Forgive me if you can. Farewell!"

For reply, his motion only grew faster, wilder somehow than before, untamed, chaotic, and then Eilathen reached the middle of the lake and dived.

But one listening for it—wanting, praying even, to catch it—might have heard, or imagined she heard, just before he disappeared, the sound of her name called out in farewell in a voice cold and free forever.

She sank to her knees cradling Kim, and rocked her upon her lap as one rocks a child.

Holding the girl, gazing out through almost blinded

eyes at the empty lake, she did not see the dark-haired, dark-bearded figure that rose from the cover of a sheltering rock behind them. The figure watched long enough to see her take the ring Eilathen had guarded and slip it carefully upon Kimberly's right hand, where it fit her ring finger as perfectly as the Seer had dreamt it would.

After seeing this, the watching figure turned, still unseen, and walked away from them, and there was no trace of a limp in his stride.

◆

She was seventeen that spring, not yet accustomed to men calling her beautiful. A pretty child she had been, but adolescence had found her long-limbed and coltish, prone to skinned knees and bruises from rough play in the gardens at Larai Rigal—activities ultimately deemed unfitting for a Princess of the realm. The more so when Marlen died hunting and she became heir to the Ivory Throne in a ceremony she scarcely remembered, so dazed was she by the speed of it and the death of her brother. Her knee was hurting, from a fall the day before, and her father's face had frightened her. There were no falls after that, for the play in the gardens and on the lake of the summer palace came to an end. She learned to school herself in the ways of a decadent court and, in time, to deal not unkindly with the suitors who began to come in such numbers, and she did grow beautiful, the Dark Rose of Cathal, and her name was Sharra, daughter of Shalhassan.

Proud she remained, as were all of her blood, and strong-willed, a quality rare in dissolute Cathal, though not unexpected in her father's daughter. Within her, too, there flickered yet a secret flame of rebelliousness against the demands of position and ritual that trammelled her days and nights.

Even now the flame burned, within beloved Larai Rigal, where the scent of calath and myrrh, of elphinel and alder enveloped her with memories. Memories that fired her with brighter longing than had any of the men who had knelt before her father's throne seeking her hand, with the ritual phrase: ''The sun rises in your daughter's eyes.'' She was young yet, for all her pride.

And it would have been for all of these reasons, the last perhaps more than any of the others, that when the letters had begun to appear in her room—how, she knew not—she kept them secret unto herself; deeply secret, too, she kept the suspicion, burning like a liena in the gardens at night, of who had sent them.

Of desire they spoke, and called her fair in words more strung with fire than any she had ever heard. A longing was in the lines that sang to her, and it awoke within her breast, prisoner that she was in the place she would one day rule, longings of her own: most often she yearned for the simplicity of mornings that were gone, leaving this strangeness in their place, but sometimes, when she was alone at night, for other things. For the letters grew more bold as time went by, and descriptions of desire became promises of what hands and lips might do.

Still, they were unsigned. Finely phrased, elegantly penned, they bespoke nobility, but there never was a name signed at the close. Until the last one came, as spring was spilling calath and anemone all over Larai Rigal. And the name she read at last gave shape and certainty to what she had long guessed and held in her heart as a talisman. *I know something you don't know* was the refrain that had carried her lightly, even kindly, through mornings in the reception chamber, then closely escorted afternoon walks with one suitor or another along the curving pathways and arched bridges of the gardens. Only at night, her ladies at last dismissed, her black hair brushed and falling free, could she take from its hiding place that last letter and read again by candlelight:

Bright One,
Too long. Even the stars now speak to me of you,

*and the night wind knows your name. I must come.
Death is a dark I seek not to find, but if I must walk
within its provinces to touch the flower of your body,
then I must. Promise only that should the soldiers of
Cathal end my life it will be your hands that close my
eyes, and perhaps—too much to ask, I know—your
lips that touch my cold ones in farewell.*

*There is a lyren tree near the northern wall of Larai
Rigal. Ten nights past the full of the moon there should
still be light enough at moonrise for us to find each
other.*

*I will be there. You hold my life as a small thing
between the fingers of your hands.*

Diarmuid dan Ailell

It was very late. Earlier in the evening it had rained,
releasing the scent of elphinel from below her window, but now the clouds had drifted and the waning
moon shone into her room. Gently its light touched
her face and glinted in the heavy fall of her hair.

It had been full nine nights before.

Which meant that he had somehow crossed Saeren
and was hiding somewhere in the dark of the land, and
tomorrow. . . .

Sharra, daughter of Shalhassan, drew a long breath
in the bed where she lay alone, and returned the letter
to its secret place. That evening she did not dream of
childhood or of childhood games when at length sleep
found her, twisting from side to side all night, her hair
loose and spread upon the pillows.

Venassar of Gath was so young and shy, he made
her feel protective. Walking the next morning on the
Circle Path, she did most of the talking. In yellow
doublet and hose, long-faced and clearly apprehensive, he listened with desperate attentiveness, tilted
alarmingly towards her as she named the flowers and
trees past which they walked, and told the story of
T'Varen and the creation of Larai Rigal. Her voice,

pitched low to exclude their retinue, which walked a careful ten paces ahead and behind, gave no hint of how many interminable times she had done this before.

They walked slowly past the cedar from which she had fallen the day her brother died, the day before she had been named heir to the throne. And then, following the curve of the path over the seventh bridge past one of the waterfalls, she saw the giant lyren near the northern wall.

Venassar of Gath, gangling and discomfited, essayed a series of coughs, snorts, and comments in a hapless attempt thereafter to revive a dead conversation. The Princess at his side had withdrawn into a stillness so profound that her beauty seemed to have folded upon itself like a flower, dazzling still, but closed to him. His father, he thought despairingly, was going to flay him.

Taking pity at last, Sharra carefully placed her hand on his arm as they crossed the ninth bridge, completing the Circle, and walked up towards the pavilion where Shalhassan reclined, surrounded by the scented finery of his court. The gesture launched Venassar into a state of petrified automatism, despite the predatory look it elicited from Bragon, his father, who was sitting beside Shalhassan under the waving fans of the servants.

Sharra shivered as Bragon's glance lingered on her and the smile deepened under his dark moustache. It was not the smile of a potential father-in-law. Beneath the silk of her gown, her body recoiled from the hunger in his eyes.

Her father did not smile. He never did.

She made obeisance to him and moved into the shade, where they brought her a glass of m'rae, deeply chilled, and a dish of flavored ices. When Bragon took his leave, she made sure he saw the coldness in her eyes, and then smiled at Venassar, extending a hand he almost forgot to touch to his forehead. Let the father know, she thought, with no possibility of mistake, why they would not be returning to Larai Rigal. And the anger in her almost showed.

What she wanted, Sharra thought bitterly, even as she smiled, was to climb the cedar again, past the branch that had broken under her, and, reaching the very topmost point, to turn into a falcon that could fly over the shining of the lake and the glory of the gardens all alone.

"A brute, and the son is a callow fool," Shalhassan said, leaning towards her so only the slaves, who didn't matter, could hear.

"They all are," said his daughter, "the one or the other."

The moon, thinning down, had risen late. From her window she could see it surfacing from the eastern arm of the lake. Still, she lingered within her room. It would not do to arrive on time; this man would have to learn that a Princess of Cathal did not scurry to a tryst like a servant from Rhoden or some such northern place.

Nonetheless, the pulse under the fine skin of her wrist was beating far too fast. *A small thing between the fingers of your hands,* he had written. Which was true. She could have him taken and garrotted for his effrontery. It might even start a war.

Which, she told herself, was irresponsible. Shalhassan's daughter would greet this man with the courtesy due his rank and the secrecy the passion in him deserved of her. He had come a long way through very great peril to see her. He would have gracious words to carry back north from the gardens of Cathal. But no more. Presumption such as his had a price, and this, Diarmuid of Brennin would learn. And, she thought, it would be well if he told her how he had crossed Saeren. It was a thing of no small importance to the land she would one day rule.

Her breathing seemed to be under control; the race

of her pulse had slowed. The image of the solitary
falcon in her mind fell away as on a down drift of
wind. It was the heiress of Cathal, well schooled in
duty and obligation, who descended, careful of her
skirt, down the easy branches of the tree outside her
balcony.

The lienae glowed, flying through the dark. About
her were woven the deep, disturbing night scents of
the flowers. She walked under starlight and the crescent illumination of the moon, sure of her way, for the
walled gardens, for all their miles, were her oldest
home and she knew every step of all the paths. A night
walk such as this, though, was a vanished pleasure,
and she would be severely chastised if discovered. And
her servants would be flogged.

No matter. She would not be discovered. The palace
guard patrolled the outer perimeter of the walls with
their lanterns. The gardens were another world. Where
she walked, the only lights were those of moon and
stars, and the hovering, elusive lienae. She heard the
soft chirring of insects and the plashing of the sculpted
waterfalls. There was a breath of wind in the leaves,
and somewhere, too, in these gardens there was now
a man who had written to her of what lips and hands
might do.

She slowed a little on the thought, crossing the
fourth bridge, the Ravelle, hearing the gentle sound of
tamed water over colored stone. No one, she realized,
knew where she was. And she knew nothing beyond
rumor, which did not reassure, of the man who was
waiting in the dark.

But courage was not lacking in her heart, though it
might be foolhardy and unwise. Sharra, dressed in
azure and gold, one lapis lazuli pendant hanging between her breasts, came over the bridge and past the
curving of the path and saw the lyren tree.

There was no one there.

She had never doubted he would be waiting—which,
given the hazards that had lain in his path, was absurd.

A besotted romantic might somehow bribe a servant of hers to plant letters, might promise an impossible tryst, but a Prince of Brennin, the heir even, since his brother's exile, would not dice his life away on a folly such as this, for a woman he'd never seen.

Saddened, and angry with herself for feeling so, she walked the last few steps and stood under the golden branches of the lyren. Her long fingers, smooth finally, after years of abuse, reached out to caress the bark of the trunk.

"If you weren't in a skirt, you might join me up here, but I don't imagine a Princess can climb trees anyhow. Shall I come down?" The voice came from directly above her. She checked a sudden motion and refused to look up.

"I've climbed every climbable tree in these gardens," she said evenly, over the acceleration of her heart, "including this one. And often in skirts. I do not care to do so now. If you are Diarmuid of Brennin, then come down."

"And if I'm not?" The tone, for a supposedly infatuated lover, was far too mocking, she thought, and she didn't answer. Nor did he wait. There was a rustle in the leaves above, then a thump beside her on the ground.

And then two hands took one of hers quite comprehensively, and brought it not to his forehead but to his lips. Which was all right, though he should have knelt. What was not all right was that he should turn the hand over to kiss her palm and wrist.

She snatched her hand away, horribly aware of the pounding of her heart. She still hadn't even seen him clearly.

As if reading the thought, he moved out of shadow, to where the moonlight could find his bright, tousled hair. And he did drop to a knee then—letting the light fall like benediction on his face.

And so she did see, finally. The eyes, wide-set and deep, were very blue under long, almost feminine lashes. The mouth was wide as well, too much so, and there was no softness in it, or in the lines of the beardless chin.

He smiled, though, and not mockingly. And she realized that from where he knelt she, too, was in the light to be seen.

"Well—" she began.

"Fools," said Diarmuid dan Ailell. "They all told me you were beautiful. Said it sixteen different ways."

"And?" She stiffened, anger ready as a lash.

"And, by Lisen's eyes, you are. But no one ever told me there was cleverness in you. I should have known. Shalhassan's heir would have to have subtlety."

She was completely unprepared. No one had ever said this. Off balance, she fleetingly remembered all her Venassars, so effortlessly handled.

"Forgive me," this man said, rising to stand beside her, very close. "I didn't know. I was expecting to deal with a very young woman—which you are not, not in the ways that matter. Shall we walk? Will you show me your gardens?"

And so she found herself in stride with him on the northern perimeter of the Circle Path, and it seemed foolish and young to protest when he took her arm. A question, however, insinuated itself as they moved in the scented darkness, haloed by the lienae flying all about them.

"If you thought me so simple, how could you write me as you did?" she asked, and felt her heartbeat slow again, as a measure of control came back to her in his silence. Not so easily, my friend, she thought.

"I am," said Diarmuid quite calmly, "somewhat helpless before beauty. Word of yours reached me some time ago. You are more than I was told you were."

A neat enough answer, for a northerner. Even honey-tongued Galienth might have approved. But it was well within her ability to compass. So although he was handsome and disturbing in the shadows beside her, and his fingers on her arm kept shifting very slightly, and once brushed the edge of her breast, Sharra now felt secure. If there was a twist of regret, another downward arc of the mind's falcon, she paid it no attention.

"T'Varen laid out Larai Rigal in the time of my great-grandfather, Thallason, whom you have cause to remember in the north. The gardens cover many miles, and are walled in their entirety, including the lake, which . . ." And so she went on, as she had for all the Venassars, and though it was night now, and the man beside her had a hand on her arm, it really wasn't so very different after all. I might kiss him, she thought. On the cheek, as goodbye.

They had taken the Crossing Path at the Faille Bridge, and began curving back north. The moon was well clear of the trees now, riding high in a sky laced with windblown clouds. The breeze off the lake was pleasant and not too chilly. She continued to talk, easily still, but increasingly aware of his silence. Of that, and of the hand on her arm, which had tightened and had grazed her breast again as they passed one of the waterfalls.

"There is a bridge for each of the nine provinces," she said, "and the flowers in each part of—"

"*Enough!*" said Diarmuid harshly. She froze in midsentence. He stopped walking and turned to face her on the path. There was a calath bush behind her. She had hidden there, playing, as a child.

He had released her arm when he spoke. Now, after a long, cold glance at her, he turned and began walking again. She moved quickly to keep up.

When he addressed her, it was while staring straight ahead, his voice low and intense. "You are speaking like someone scarcely a person. If you want to play gracious Princess with the petty lordlings who mince about, courting you, it is none of my affair, but—"

"The lords of Cathal are not petty, sir! They—"

"Do not, please, insult us both! That emasculated whipping-boy this afternoon? His father? I would take great pleasure in killing Bragon. They are worse than petty, all of them. And if you speak to me as you do to them, you cheapen both of us unbearably."

They had reached the lyren again. Somewhere within her a bird was stirring. She moved ruthlessly to curb it, as she had to.

"My lord Prince, I must say I am surprised. You can hardly expect less formal conversation, in this, our first—"

"But I *do* expect it! I expect to see and hear the woman. Who was a girl who climbed all the trees in this garden. The Princess in her role bores me, hurts me. Demeans tonight."

"And what is tonight?" she asked, and bit her lip as soon as she spoke.

"Ours," he said.

And his arms were around her waist in the shadows of the lyren, and his mouth, descending, was upon her own. His head blocked the moon, but her eyes had closed by then anyway. And then the wide mouth on hers was moving, and his tongue—

"No!" She broke away violently, and almost fell. They faced each other a few feet apart. Her heart was a mad, beating, winged thing she had to control. Had to. She was Sharra, daughter of—

"Dark Rose," he said, his voice unsteady. He took a step towards her.

"No!" Her hands were up to ward him.

Diarmuid stopped. Looked at her trembling figure. "What do you fear in me?" he asked.

Breathing was difficult. She was conscious of her breasts, of the wind about her, the nearness of him, and of a dark warmth at her center, where—

"How did you cross the river?" she blurted out.

She expected mockery again. It would have helped. His gaze was steady, though, and he stayed absolutely motionless.

"I used a mage's arrow and a rope," he said. "I crossed hand over hand above the water and climbed a ladder cut into the cliff several hundred years ago. I give you this as between you and me. You will not tell?"

She was Princess of Cathal. "I make no such promise, for I cannot. I will not betray you now in any way, but secrets endangering my people—"

"And what do you think I did in telling you? Am I not heir to a throne, just as you are?"

She shook her head. Some voice within was wildly telling her to run, but instead she spoke, as carefully as she could. "You must not think, my lord Prince, to win a daughter of Shalhassan, merely by coming here and—"

"Sharra!" he cried, speaking her name for the first time, so that it rang in the night air like a bell tolling pain. "Listen to yourself! It is not just—"

And they both heard it then.

The jangling clink of armor as the palace guard moved up on the other side of the wall.

"What was that?" a gravelly voice exclaimed, and she knew it for Devorsh, Captain of the Guard. There was a murmured reply. Then, "No, I heard voices. Two of you go have a look inside. Take the dogs!"

The sound of armored men walking off jarred the night.

Somehow they were together under the tree. She laid a hand on his arm.

"If they find you, they will kill you, so you had better go."

Incredibly, his gaze on hers, close and above, was undisturbed. "If they find me, they kill me," said Diarmuid. "If they can. Perhaps you will close my eyes, as I once asked." The expression changed then, the voice roughened. "But I will not leave you now willingly, though all of Cathal come calling for my blood."

And gods, gods, all the gods, his mouth on hers was

so very sweet, the touch of his hands blindingly sure. His fingers were busy at the fastenings of her bodice, and dear Goddess, her own hands were behind his head, pulling him down to her, her tongue sought his in hunger long denied. Her breasts, suddenly released, strained towards his touch, and there was an ache in her, a burning, something wild being set free as he laid her down on the deep grass and his fingers touched her here, and here, and her clothes were gone from about her, and his from him as well. And then his body along hers was all the night and garden, all the worlds, and in her mind she saw the shadow of a falcon, wings beating wide, fly across the face of the high moon.

"Sharra!"

From where they were, outside the walls, they heard the name cried out within the gardens. "What was that?" one of them exclaimed. "I heard voices. Two of you go have a look inside. Take the dogs!"

Two men moved quickly to obey the sharp command, jogging urgently in the direction of the western gate.

But only for a few jangling strides. After that, Kevin and Coll stopped running and looped silently back to the concealing hollow where the others lay. Erron, whose disguised voice had barked the order, was already there. The soldiers of Cathal were, at that moment, flanked ten minutes' walk away on either side. The timing and the plan were Diarmuid's, worked out as they lay watching and listening to the patrol in the early evening.

Now they had nothing more to do but wait for him. They settled quietly into the dark hollow. A few slept, using the time to advantage, for they would be running back north as soon as the Prince rejoined them. There was no talk. Too wound up to rest properly, Kevin lay on his back and watched the slow transit of the moon. Several times they heard the guards cross and cross again in their circuit of the walls. They waited. The moon reached its zenith and began to slide west against the backdrop of summer stars.

Carde saw him first, a black-clad, bright-haired figure on the top of the wall. Quickly Carde checked right and left for the patrol, but the timing, again, was flawless, and rising briefly to be seen, he gave a thumbs-up sign.

Seeing it, Diarmuid leaped, rolled once, and was up running lightly and low to the ground. When he dropped into the hollow beside them, Kevin saw that he was carrying a flower. Hair dishevelled, doublet loose and half unbuttoned, the Prince's eyes flashed with an intoxicated hilarity.

"Done!" he said, raising the flower in salute to all of them. "I've plucked the fairest rose in Shalhassan's garden."

Chapter 7

"He will be found, I promise it." So he had said. A rash promise, and uncharacteristic, but it had been made.

So at about the time Paul and Kevin began their ride south with Diarmuid, Loren Silvercloak was galloping north and east alone in search of Dave Martyniuk.

It was rare for the mage to be solitary—alone, he was stripped of his powers—but he'd needed Matt to stay in the palace, the more so since word had come of the dead svart in the garden. It was a bad time to be away, but his choices were limited, and so, too, were the people he could trust.

So north he rode, gradually curving eastward through the grain land amid the dry crackle of the ruinous summer. All that day and the next he traveled, and not slowly, for a sense of urgency was strong within him. He paused only to ask discreet questions in the farmyards and half-empty towns through which he passed, and to note again, and despairingly, the impact of famine on those to whom he spoke.

There was no word, though. No one had seen the tall dark-haired stranger or heard tell of him. So on the third morning Loren mounted early from where he'd passed the night in a copse of trees to the west of Lake Leinan. Looking eastward he could see the sun rising from the line of hills past the lake and he knew Dun Maura lay beyond. Even by daylight, with a blue sky above, there was for the mage a darkness about that place.

There was no love lost between the Mormae of Gwen Ystrat and the mages who had followed Amairgen's lead out from the dominion of the Mother. Blood magic, thought Loren, shaking his head, picturing Dun Maura and the rites of Liadon enacted every year before Conary came and forbade them. He thought of the flowers strewn by the maidens chanting his death and return as the spring: *Rahod hedai Liadon.* In every world, the mage knew; but his very soul rebelled against the darkness of this power. Grimly he turned his horse away from the country of the Priestesses and continued north, following the Latham on the long ride to the Plain.

He would ask aid of the Dalrei, as he had so often done before. If Dave Martyniuk was somewhere among the great spaces of the Plain, only the Riders could find him. So north he rode, a tall, grey, bearded figure no longer young, alone on a horse in the wide sweep of the level lands, and the baked earth resonated beneath him like a drum.

He was hoping, even though it was summer, to find a tribe of the Riders in the south Plain, for if he could speak to even one tribe then word would be sent to Celidon, and once his message was lodged at the mid-Plain, then soon all the Dalrei would know, and the Dalrei he trusted.

It was a long ride, though, and there were no villages now among the broad grazing lands in which he could take food or rest. And so he was still galloping alone as that third day drew towards sundown and then dark. His shadow lay long on the earth beside him, and the river had become a glimmering, muted presence to the east, when the urgency that had lain within him since he had left Paras Derval exploded into terror.

Grappling at the reins, he brought his mount to a rearing halt, then held it rigidly still. One moment he remained so, his face drawn suddenly tight with fear, then Loren Silvercloak cried aloud in the onrushing night and wheeled his horse hard to ride in the dark, back, back towards Paras Derval, where something overwhelming was about to happen.

Drumming furiously home under the stars, he gathered his mind and hurled a desperate warning southward over all the empty leagues that lay between. He was too far away, though, much too far away, and without his power. He urged his horse faster, driving like wind in the darkness, but he knew, even as he did so, that he was going to be too late.

◆

Jennifer was not happy. Not only was Dave missing, not only had Kevin and Paul ridden off that morning on some crazy expedition with Diarmuid, but now Kim had left as well, with Matt guiding her to the home of the old woman whom people in the Great Hall the day before had called a witch.

Which left her in a large room on the cooler west side of the palace, sitting in a low window seat, surrounded by a gaggle of court ladies whose principal yearning in life seemed to be to elicit all they could from her about Kevin Laine and Paul Schafer, with special and explicit focus on their sexual predilections.

Parrying the questions as best she could, she barely managed to conceal a growing irritation. On the far side of the room, a man was playing a stringed instrument under a tapestry depicting a scene of battle. There was a dragon flying over the conflict. She hoped profoundly that it was a mythical confrontation.

The ladies had all been briefly presented to her, but only two names had registered. Laesha was the very young, brown-eyed lady-in-waiting who seemed to have been assigned to her. She was quiet, which was a blessing. The other was the Lady Rheva, a striking, dark-haired woman who clearly enjoyed a higher status than the others, and to whom Jennifer had taken an effortless dislike.

Nor was this in any degree lessened when it became clear, because Rheva made it clear, that she'd spent the night before with Kevin. It was evidently a triumph in a continuing game of one-upmanship, and Rheva was exploiting it for all it was worth. It was aggravating in the extreme, and Jennifer, abandoned, was in no mood to be aggravated.

So when another of the women gave a sulky toss of her hair and inquired whether Jennifer had any idea why Paul Schafer had been so indifferent to her— "Does he, perhaps, prefer to spend his nights with boys?" she asked, with a barb of malice—Jennifer's brief laugh was entirely humorless.

"There are more obvious possibilities, I should think," she replied, aware that she was making an enemy. "Paul is somewhat discriminating, that's all."

There was a brief silence. Someone tittered. Then:

"Are you suggesting, by any chance, that Kevin is not?" It was Rheva, and her voice had gone very soft.

Jennifer could handle this. What she could not handle was having it continue. She rose abruptly from the window seat and, looking down on the other woman, smiled.

"No," she said, judiciously. "Knowing Kevin, I wouldn't say that at all. The trick, though, is to get him twice." And she moved past them all and out the door.

Walking swiftly down the corridor, she made a very firm mental note to inform Kevin Laine that if he took a certain court lady to bed once more, she would never speak to him again as long as she lived.

At the doorway to her room, she heard her name being called. Her long skirt trailing the stone floor, Laesha came hurrying up. Jennifer eyed her inimically, but the other woman was laughing breathlessly.

"Oh, my," she gasped, laying a hand on Jennifer's arm, "that was wonderful! The cats in that room are spitting with anger! Rheva hasn't been handled like that for years."

Jennifer shook her head ruefully. "I don't imagine they'll be very friendly the rest of the time I'm here."

"They wouldn't have been anyway. You are much too beautiful. On top of your being new, it's guaranteed to make them hate you for existing. And when Diarmuid put out word yesterday that you were reserved for him, they—"

"He *what?*" Jennifer exploded.

Laesha eyed her carefully. "Well, he is the Prince, and so—"

"I don't care who he is! I have no intention of letting him touch me. Who do they think we are?"

Laesha's expression had altered a little. "You mean that?" she asked hesitantly. "You don't want him?"

"Not at all," said Jennifer. "Should I?"

"I do," said Laesha simply, and flushed to the roots of her brown hair.

There was an awkward silence. Speaking carefully, Jennifer broke it. "I am only here two weeks," she said. "I will not take him from you or anyone else. I need a friend right now, more than anything else."

Laesha's eyes were wide. She took a short breath.

"Why do you think I followed you?"

This time they shared the smile.

"Tell me," Jennifer asked after a moment. "Is there any reason we have to stay in here? I haven't been outside at all. Can we see the town?"

"Of course," said Laesha. "Of course we can. We haven't been at war for years."

Despite the heat, it was better outside the palace. Dressed in an outfit much like Laesha's, Jennifer realized that no one knew she was a stranger. Feeling freed by that, she found herself strolling at ease beside her new friend. After a short while, though, she became aware that a man was following them through the dusty, twisting streets of the town. Laesha noticed it, too.

"He's one of Diarmuid's," she whispered.

Which was a nuisance, but before he had left in the morning, Kevin had told her about the dead svart alfar in the garden, and Jennifer had decided that for once she wasn't about to object to having someone watch over her. Her father, she thought wryly, would find it amusing.

The two women walked along a street where blacksmith's iron rang upon anvils. Overhead, balconies of second-floor houses leaned out over the narrow roadway, blocking the sunlight at intervals. Turning left at a crossing of lanes, Laesha led her past an open area where the noise and the smell of food announced a market. Slowing to look, Jennifer saw that even in a time of festival there didn't seem to be much produce on display. Following her glance, Laesha shook her head slightly and continued up a narrow alleyway, pausing at length outside a shop door through which could be seen bales and bolts of cloth. Laesha, it seemed, wanted a new pair of gloves.

While her friend went inside, Jennifer moved on a few steps, drawn by the sound of children's laughter. Reaching the end of the cobbled lane, she saw that it ran into a wide square with a grassy area, more brown than green, in the center. And upon the grass, fifteen or twenty children were playing some sort of counting game. Smiling faintly, Jennifer stopped to watch.

The children were gathered in a loose circle about the slim figure of a girl. Most of them were laughing, but the girl in the center was not. She gestured suddenly, and a boy came forward from the ring with a strip of cloth and, with a gravity that matched her own, began to bind it over her eyes. That done, he rejoined the ring. At his nod the children linked hands and began to revolve, in a silence eerie after the laughter, around the motionless figure blindfolded in the center. They moved gravely and with dignity. A few other people had stopped to watch.

Then, without warning, the blindfolded girl raised an arm and pointed it towards the moving ring. Her high clear voice rang out over the green:

> *When the wandering fire*
> *Strikes the heart of stone*
> *Will you follow?*

And on the last word the circling stopped.

The girl's finger was leveled directly at a stocky boy, who, without any hesitation, released the hands on either side of him and walked into the ring. The circle closed itself and began moving again, still in silence.

"I never tire of watching this," a cool voice said from just behind Jennifer.

She turned quickly. To confront a pair of icy green eyes and the long red hair of the High Priestess, Jaelle. Behind the Priestess she could see a group of her grey-clad attendants, and out of the corner of her eye, she noticed Diarmuid's man edging nervously closer to them.

Jennifer nodded a greeting, then turned back to watch the children. Jaelle stepped forward to stand beside her, her white robe brushing the cobblestones of the street.

"The ta'kiena is as old as any ritual we have," she murmured in Jennifer's ear. "Look at the people watching."

And indeed, although the faces of the children seemed almost unnaturally serene, the adults who had gathered at the edge of the square or in shop archways wore expressions of wonder and apprehension. And there were more people gathering. Again the girl in the ring raised her arm.

> *When the wandering fire*
> *Strikes the heart of stone*
> *Will you follow?*
> *Will you leave your home?*

And again the circling stopped on the last word. This time the extended finger pointed to another of the boys, older and lankier than the first. With only a brief, almost ironic pause, he, too, released the hands he was holding and walked forward to stand by the other chosen one. A murmur rose from the watchers, but the children, seemingly oblivious, were circling again.

Unsettled, Jennifer turned to the impassive profile of the Priestess. "What is it?" she asked. "What are they doing?"

Jaelle smiled thinly. "It is a dance of prophecy. Their fate lies in when they are called."

"But what—"

"Watch!"

The blindfolded girl, standing straight and tall, was chanting again:

> When the wandering fire
> Strikes the heart of stone
> Will you follow?
> Will you leave your home?
> Will you leave your life?

This time, when the voice and the dancing stopped together, a deep sound of protest ran through the watching crowd. For the one chosen now was one of the youngest girls. With a toss of her honey-colored hair and a cheerful smile, she stepped into the ring beside the two boys. The taller one placed an arm around her shoulders.

Jennifer turned to Jaelle. "What does it mean?" she asked. "What kind of prophecy . . . ?" The question trailed off.

Beside her the Priestess was silent. There was no gentleness in the lines of her face, nor compassion in her eyes as she watched the children begin to move again. "You ask what it means," she said at length. "Not much in these soft times, when the ta'kiena is only another game. That last one they now say means only that she will leave the life her family has led." Her expression was unreadable, but an irony in the tone reached Jennifer.

"What was it before?" she asked.

This time Jaelle did turn to look at her. "The dance has been done by children for longer than anyone can remember. In harsher days that call meant death, of course. Which would be a pity. She's an attractive child, isn't she?"

There was a malicious amusement in the voice. "Watch closely," Jaelle continued. "This last one they truly fear, even now." And indeed, the people around and behind them had grown suddenly quiet with strained anticipation. In the stillness Jennifer could hear the sounds of laughter from the market, several streets over. It seemed farther than that.

In the circle on the green, the blindfolded girl raised her arm and began the chant for the final time:

> *When the wandering fire*
> *Strikes the heart of stone*
> *Will you follow?*
> *Will you leave your home?*
> *Will you leave your life?*
> *Will you take . . . the Longest Road?*

The dancing stopped.

Her heart pounding inexplicably, Jennifer saw that the slim finger was pointing unerringly at the boy who had carried the blindfold. Raising his head, as if hearing some far-off music, the boy stepped forward. The girl removed her blindfold. They regarded each other a long moment, then the boy turned, laid a hand, as if in benediction, on the other chosen ones, and walked alone from the green.

Jaelle, watching him go, wore a troubled expression for the first time. Glancing at her unguarded features, Jennifer realized with a start how young the woman beside her was. About to speak, she was checked by the sound of crying, and, turning her head, she saw a woman standing in the doorway of a shop behind them in the lane; there were tears pouring down her face.

Jaelle followed Jennifer's glance. "His mother," the Priestess said softly.

Feeling utterly helpless, Jennifer had an instinctive longing to offer comfort to the woman. Their eyes met, and on the face of the other woman Jennifer saw, with an aching twist of new understanding, a distillation of all a mother's sleepless nights. A message, a recognition, seemed to pass for an instant between the two of them, then the mother of the boy chosen for the Longest Road turned her head away and went into her shop.

Jennifer, struggling with something unexpected, finally asked Jaelle, "Why is she hurting so much?"

The Priestess, too, was a little subdued. "It is difficult," she said, "and not a thing I understand yet, but they have done the dance twice before this summer, I am told, and both times Finn was chosen for the Road. This is the third, and in Gwen Ystrat we are taught that three times touches destiny."

Jennifer's expression drew a smile from the Priestess. "Come," she said. "We can talk at the Temple." Her tone was, if not exactly friendly, at least milder than hitherto.

On the verge of accepting, Jennifer was stopped by a cough behind her.

She turned. Diarmuid's man had moved up to them, sharp concern creasing his face. "My lady," he said, acutely embarrassed, "forgive me, but might I speak with you in private for a moment."

"You fear me, Drance?" Jaelle's voice was like a knife again. She laughed. "Or should I say your master does? Your absent master."

The stocky soldier flushed, but held his ground. "I have been ordered to watch over her," he said tersely.

Jennifer looked from one to the other. There was suddenly an electric hostility shimmering in the air. She felt disoriented, understanding none of it.

"Well," she said to Drance, trying to pick her way,

"I don't want to get you in trouble—why don't you just come with us?"

Jaelle threw her head back and laughed again, to see the man's terrified recoil. "Yes, Drance," she said, her tone coruscating, "why *don't* you come to the Temple of the Mother with us?"

"My lady," Drance stammered, appealing to Jennifer. "Please, I dare not do that . . . but I must guard you. You must not go there."

"Ah!" said Jaelle, her eyebrows arched maliciously. "It seems that the men here are already saying what you can or cannot do. Forgive me my invitation. I thought I was dealing with a free visitor."

Jennifer was not oblivious to the manipulation, and she remembered Kevin's words that morning as well: "There's some danger here," he'd said soberly. "Trust Diarmuid's men, and Matt, of course. Paul says be careful of the Priestess. Don't go anywhere on your own."

In the dawn shadows of the palace, it had made a good deal of sense, but now, in bright afternoon sunlight, the whole thing was rankling just a little. Who was Kevin, making his way through the court ladies, then galloping off with the Prince, to tell her to sit tight like a dutiful little girl? And now this man of Diarmuid's. . . .

About to speak, she remembered something else. She turned to Jaelle. "There seems to be some real concern for our safety here. I would like to place myself under your protection while I visit your Temple. Will you name me a guest-friend before I go?"

A frown flicked across Jaelle's face, but it was chased away by a slow smile, and there was triumph in her eyes.

"Of course," she said sweetly. "Of course I will." She raised her voice so that her words rang out over the street, and people turned to look. Lifting her arms wide, fingers spread, she intoned, "In the name of Gwen Ystrat and the Mormae of the Mother, I name you guest of the Goddess. You are welcome in our sanctuaries, and your well-being shall be my own concern."

Jennifer looked to Drance, questioningly. His expression was not reassuring; if possible, he appeared even more consternated than before. Jennifer had no idea if she'd done right or wrong, or even of exactly what she'd done, but she was tired of standing in the middle of the street with everyone watching her.

"Thank you," she said to Jaelle. "In that case, I will come with you. If you like," she added, turning to Drance, and to Laesha, who had just scurried up, her new gloves in hand and an apprehensive look in her eye, "you can both wait outside for me."

"Come, then," said Jaelle, and smiled.

It was a low-set building, and even the central dome seemed too close to the ground, until Jennifer realized, as she passed through the arched entrance, that most of it was underground.

The Temple of the Mother Goddess lay east of the town on the palace hill. A narrow pathway wound its way further up the hill, leading to a gate in the walls surrounding the palace gardens. There were trees lining the path. They seemed to be dying.

Once they were inside the sanctuary, the grey robed attendants melted away into shadow as Jaelle led Jennifer forward through another arch. It brought them into the room under the dome. At the far side of the sunken chamber Jennifer saw a great black altar stone. Behind it, resting in a carved block of wood, stood a double axe, each face ground into the shape of a crescent moon, one waxing, one waning.

There was nothing else.

Inexplicably, Jennifer felt her mouth go dry. Looking at the axe with its wickedly sharpened blades, she fought to repress a shudder.

"Do not fight it," Jaelle said, her voice echoing in the empty chamber. "It is your power. Ours. So it

was once, and will be again. In our time, if she should
find us worthy.''

Jennifer stared at her. The flame-haired High
Priestess in her sanctuary seemed more keenly beautiful than ever. Her eyes gleamed with an intensity
that was the more disturbing because of how cold it
was. Power and pride, it spoke; nothing of tenderness, and no more of her youth. Glancing at Jaelle's
long fingers, Jennifer wondered if they had ever
gripped that axe, had ever brought it sweeping down
upon the altar, down upon—

And then she realized that she was in a place of
sacrifice.

Jaelle turned without haste. ''I wanted you to see
this,'' she said. ''Now come. My chambers are cool,
we can drink and talk.'' She adjusted the collar of her
robe with a graceful hand and led the way from the
room. As they left, a breeze seemed to slide through
the chamber, and Jennifer thought she saw the axe
sway gently in its rest.

''And so,'' the Priestess said, as they reclined on
cushions on the floor in her room, ''your so-called
companions have abandoned you for their own plea-
sures.'' It was not a question.

Jennifer blinked. ''Hardly fair,'' she began, wondering how the other woman knew. ''You might say
I've left them to come here.'' She tried a smile.

''You might,'' Jaelle agreed pleasantly, ''but it
would be untrue. The two men left at dawn with the
princeling, and your friend has run off to the hag by
the lake.'' Midway through the sentence, her voice
had dipped itself into acid, leading Jennifer to realize
abruptly that she was under attack in this room.

She parried, to get her balance. ''Kim's with the
Seer, yes. Why do you call her a hag?''

Jaelle was no longer so pleasant. ''I am not used to
explaining myself,'' she said.

''Neither am I,'' replied Jennifer quickly. ''Which

may limit this conversation somewhat." She leaned back on the cushions and regarded the other woman.

Jaelle's reply, when it came, was harsh with emotion. "She is a traitor."

"Well, that's not the same as a hag, you know," Jennifer said, aware that she was arguing like Kevin. "A traitor to the King, you mean? I wouldn't have thought you'd care, and yesterday—"

Jaelle's bitter laugh stopped her. "No, not to the old fool!" She took a breath. "The woman you call Ysanne was the youngest person ever to be named to the Mormae of the goddess in Gwen Ystrat. She left. She broke an oath when she left. She betrayed her power."

"She betrayed you personally, you mean," Jennifer said, staying on the offensive.

"Don't be a fool! I wasn't even alive."

"No? You seem pretty upset about it, though. Why did she leave?"

"For no reason that could suffice. *Nothing* could suffice."

The clues were all there. "She left for a man, then, I take it," Jennifer said.

The ensuing silence was her answer. At length Jaelle spoke again, her voice bitter, cold. "She sold herself for a body at night. May the hag die soon and lie lost forever."

Jennifer swallowed. A point-scoring exchange had suddenly been turned into something else. "Not very forgiving, are you?" she managed.

"Not at all," Jaelle replied swiftly. "You would do well to remember it. Why did Loren leave for the north this morning?"

"I don't know," Jennifer stammered, shocked by the naked threat.

"You don't? A strange thing to do, is it not? To bring guests to the palace, then ride off alone. Leaving Matt behind, which is *very* strange. I wonder," said

Jaelle. "I wonder who he was looking for? How many of you really did cross?"

It was too sudden, too shrewd. Jennifer, heart pounding, was aware that she had flushed.

"You look warm," Jaelle said, all solicitude. "Do have some wine." She poured from a long-necked silver decanter. "Really," she continued, "it is most uncharacteristic of Loren to abandon guests so suddenly."

"I wouldn't know," Jennifer said. "There are four of us. None of us knows him very well. The wine is excellent."

"It is from Morvran. I am glad you like it. I could swear Metran asked him to bring five of you."

So Loren had been wrong. Someone did know. Someone knew a great deal indeed.

"Who is Metran?" Jennifer asked disingenuously. "Was he the old man you frightened so much yesterday?"

Balked, Jaelle leaned back on her own cushions. In the silence Jennifer sipped her wine, pleased to see that her hand was steady.

"You trust him, don't you?" the Priestess said bitterly. "He has warned you against me. They all have. Silvercloak angles for power here as much as anyone, but you have aligned yourself with the men, it seems. Tell me, which of them is your lover, or has Diarmuid found your bed yet?"

Which was quite sufficient, thank you.

Jennifer shot to her feet. Her wine glass spilled; she ignored it. "Is this how you treat a guest?" she burst out. "I came here in good faith—what right have you to say such things to me? I'm not aligned with *anyone* in your stupid power games. I'm only here for a few days—do you think I care who wins your little battles? I'll tell you one thing, though," she went on, breathing hard, "I'm not happy about male control in my world, either, but I've never in my life met anyone as screwed up on the subject as you are. If Ysanne fell in love—well, I doubt you can even *guess* what that feels like!''

White and rigid, Jaelle looked up at her, then rose in her turn. "You may be right," she said softly, "but something tells me that you have no idea what it feels like, either. Which gives us a thing in common, doesn't it?"

Back in her room a short while later, Jennifer closed the door on Laesha and Drance and cried about that for a long time.

———◆———

The day crawled forward webbed in heat. A dry, unsettling wind rose in the north and slid through the High Kingdom, stirring the dust in the streets of Paras Derval like an uneasy ghost. The sun, westering at the end of day, shone red. Only at twilight was there any relief, as the wind shifted to the west, and the first stars came out in the sky over Brennin.

Very late that night, north and west of the capital, the breeze stirred the waters of a lake to muted murmuring. On a wide rock by the shore, under the lacework of the stars, an old woman knelt, cradling the slight form of a younger one, on whose finger a red ring shone with a muted glimmering.

After a long time, Ysanne rose and called for Tyrth. Limping, he came from the cottage and, picking up the unconscious girl, walked back and laid her down in the bed he'd made that afternoon.

She remained unconscious for the rest of the night and all the next day. Ysanne did not sleep, but watched her through the hours of darkness, and then in the searing brightness of the following day, and on the face of the old Seer was an expression only one man, long dead, would have recognized.

Kimberly woke at sunset. Away to the south in that moment, Kevin and Paul were taking up their positions with Diarmuid's men outside the walls of Larai Rigal.

For a moment, Kim was completely disoriented,

then the Seer watched as a brutal surge of knowledge came flooding into the grey eyes. Lifting her head, Kim gazed at the old woman, Outside, Tyrth could be heard shutting up the animals for the night. The cat lay on the window sill in the last of the evening light.

"Welcome back," said Ysanne.

Kim smiled; it took an effort. "I went so far." She shook her head wonderingly, then her mouth tightened at another recollection. "Eilathen has gone?"

"Yes."

"I saw him dive. I saw where he went, into the green far down. It is very beautiful there."

"I know," said the Seer.

Again, Kim drew breath before speaking. "Was it hard for you to watch?"

At that, Ysanne looked away for the first time. Then, "Yes," she said. "Yes, it was hard. Remembering."

Kim's hand slipped from the coverlet and covered that of the old woman. When Ysanne spoke again, it was very low. "Raederth was First of the Mages before Ailell was King. He came one day to Morvran, on the shores of Lake Leinan. . . . You know what lies in Gwen Ystrat?"

"I know," said Kimberly. "I saw Dun Maura."

"He came to the Temple by the lake, and stayed there a night, which was brave, for there is no love in that place for any of the mages since Amairgen's day. Raederth was a brave man, though.

"He saw me there," Ysanne continued. "I was seventeen and newly chosen to be of the Mormae—the inner circle—and no one so young had ever been chosen before. But Raederth saw me that night, and he marked me for something else."

"As you did me?"

"As I did you. He knew me for a Seer, and he took me away from the Mother and changed my fate, or found it for me."

"And you loved him?"

"Yes," Ysanne said simply. "From the first, and I

miss him still, though all the years have run away from us. He brought me here at midsummer, more than fifty years ago, and summoned Eilathen with the flowerfire, and the spirit spun for me as he did for you last night."

"And Raederth?" Kim asked, after a moment.

"He died three years after of an arrow ordered by Garmisch, the High King," Ysanne said flatly. "When Raederth was slain, Duke Ailell rose in Rhoden and began the war that broke the rule of Garmisch and the Garantae and took him to the throne."

Kimberly nodded again. "I saw that, too. I saw him kill the King before the palace gate. He was brave and tall, Ailell."

"And wise. A wise King, all his days. He wedded Marrien of the Garantae, and named Metran, her cousin, First Mage to follow Raederth, which angered me then and I told him so. But Ailell was trying to knit a sundered kingdom, and he did. He deserved more love than he has had."

"He had yours."

"Late," Ysanne said, "and grudgingly. And only as King. I tried to help him, though, with his burden, and in return he found ways to ensure that I would be left alone here."

"A long time alone," Kim said softly.

"We all have our tasks," the Seer said. There was a silence. In the barn out back, a cow lowed plaintively. Kim heard the click of a gate being shut, then Tyrth's uneven steps crossing the yard. She met Ysanne's gaze, a half-smile tugging at her mouth.

"You told me one lie yesterday," she said.

Ysanne nodded. "I did. One. It was not my truth to tell."

"I know," said Kim. "You have carried a great deal alone. I am here now, though; do you want me to share your burden?" Her mouth crooked. "I seem to be a chalice. What power can you fill me with?"

There was a tear in the old woman's eye. She wiped it away, shaking her head. "Such things as I can teach

have little to do with power. It is in your dreams now
that you must walk, as all the Seers must. And for you
as well there is the stone.''

Kim glanced down. The ring on her right hand was
no longer shining as it had when Eilathen wore it. It
glowered, deep and dark, the color of old blood.

''I did dream this,'' she said. ''A terrible dream,
the night before we crossed. What is it, Ysanne?''

''The Baelrath it was named, long ago, the Warstone. It is of the wild magic,'' the Seer said, ''a thing
not made by man, and it cannot be controlled like the
shapings of Ginserat or Amairgen, or even of the
Priestesses. It has been lost for a very long time, which
has happened before. It is never found without reason,
or so the old tales say.''

It had grown dark outside as they talked. ''Why have
you given it to me?'' Kim asked in a small voice.

''Because I dreamt it on your finger, too.''

Which, somehow, she had known would be the answer. The ring pulsed balefully, inimically, and she
feared it.

''What was I doing?'' she asked.

''Raising the dead,'' Ysanne replied, and stood to
light the candles in the room.

Kim closed her eyes. The images were waiting for
her: the jumbled stones, the wide grasslands rolling
away in the dark, the ring on her hand burning like a
fire in the dream, and the wind rising over the grass,
whistling between the stones—

''Oh, God!'' she cried aloud. ''What *is* it,
Ysanne?''

The Seer returned to her seat beside the bed and
gravely regarded the girl who lay there wrestling with
what lay upon her.

''I am not sure of this,'' she said, ''so I must be
careful, but there is a pattern shaping here. You see,
he died in your world the first time.''

''Who died?'' Kim whispered.

"The Warrior. Who always dies, and is not allowed to rest. It is his doom."

Kim's hands were clenched. "Why?"

"There was a great wrong done at the very beginning of his days, and for that he may not have rest. It is told and sung and written in every world where he has fought."

"Fought?" Her heart was pounding.

"Of course," Ysanne replied, though gently still. "He is the Warrior. Who may be called only at darkest need, and only by magic and only when summoned by name." Her voice was like wind in the room.

"And his name?"

"The secret one, no man knows, or even where it is to be sought, but there is another, by which he is always spoken."

"And that is?" Though now she knew. And a star was in the window.

Ysanne spoke the name.

———◆———

He was probably wrong to be lingering, but the commands had not been explicit, and he was not overly prone to let it disturb him. It intoxicated them all to be abroad in the open spaces, using forgotten arts of concealment to observe the festival traffic on the roads to and from Paras Derval, and though by day the charred land dismayed them, at night they sang the oldest songs under the unclouded glitter of the stars.

He himself had a further reason for waiting, though he knew the delay could not be prolonged indefinitely. One more day he had promised himself, and felt extravagantly gratified when the two women and the man crested the ridge above the thicket.

———◆———

Matt was quietly reassuring. Kim was in good hands, and though he didn't know where Diarmuid's band had gone—and preferred it that way, he added with a grimace—they were expected back that night. Loren, he confirmed, had indeed gone in search of

Dave. For the first time since her encounter with the High Priestess two days before, Jennifer relaxed a little.

More unsettled by the strangeness of everything than she liked to admit, she had spent yesterday quietly with Laesha. In Jennifer's room the two new friends had traded accounts of their lives. It was somehow easier, Jennifer had reflected, to approach Fionavar in this way than to step out into the heat and confront things such as the children's chanting on the green, the axe swaying in the Temple, or Jaelle's cold hostility.

There had been dancing after the banquet that night. She had expected some difficulty in dealing with the men, but against her will she'd ended up being amused at the careful, almost apprehensive propriety of those who danced with her. Women claimed by Prince Diarmuid were very clearly off limits to anyone else. She'd excused herself early and had gone to bed.

To be awakened by Matt Sören knocking at her door. The Dwarf devoted the morning to her, an attentive guide through the vastness of the palace. Roughly garbed, with an axe swinging at his side, he was a harshly anomalous figure in the hallways and chambers of the castle. He showed her rooms with paintings on the walls, and inlaid patterns on the floor. Everywhere there were tapestries. She was beginning to see that they had a deeper significance here. They climbed to the highest tower, where the guards greeted Matt with unexpected deference, and, looking out, she saw the High Kingdom baking in the rigor of its summer. Then he led her back to the Great Hall, empty now, where she could gaze undisturbed at the windows of Delevan.

As they circled the room, she told him about her meeting with Jaelle two days ago. The Dwarf blinked when she explained how she was made guest-friend, and again when she described Jaelle's questions about Loren. But once more he reassured her.

"She is all malice, Jaelle, all bright, bitter malice. But she is not evil, only ambitious."

"She hates Ysanne. She hates Diarmuid."

"Ysanne, she would hate. Diarmuid . . . arouses strong feelings in most people." The Dwarf's mouth twisted in his difficult smile. "She seeks to know every secret there is. Jaelle may suspect we had a fifth person, but even if she were certain, she would never tell Gorlaes—who *is* someone to be wary of."

"We've hardly seen him."

"He is with Ailell, almost all the time. Which is why he is to be feared. It was a dark day for Brennin," Matt Sōren said, "when the elder Prince was sent away."

"The King turned to Gorlaes?" Jennifer guessed.

The Dwarf's glance at her was keen. "You are clever," he said. "That is exactly what happened."

"What about Diarmuid?"

"What *about* Diarmuid?" Matt repeated, in a tone so unexpectedly exasperated, she laughed aloud. After a moment, the Dwarf chuckled, too, low in his chest.

Jennifer smiled. There was a solid strength to Matt Sōren, a feeling of deeply rooted common sense. Jennifer Lowell had come into adulthood trusting few people entirely, especially men, but, she realized in that moment, the Dwarf was now one of them. In a curious way, it made her feel better about herself.

"Matt," she said, as a thought struck her, "Loren left without you. Did you stay here for us?"

"Just to keep an eye on things." With a gesture at the patch over his right eye, he turned it into a kind of joke.

She smiled, but then looked at him a long moment, her green eyes sober. "How did you get that?"

"The last war with Cathal," he said simply. "Thirty years ago."

"You've been here that long?"

"Longer, Loren has been a mage for over forty years now."

"So?" She didn't get the connection.

He told her. There was an easiness to the mood they shared that morning, and Jennifer's beauty had been known to make taciturn men talkative before.

She listened, taking in, as Paul had three nights before, the story of Amairgen's discovery of the skylore, and the secret forging that would bind mage and source for life in a union more complete than any in all the worlds.

When Matt finished, Jennifer rose and walked a few steps. Trying to absorb the impact of what she had been told. This was more than marriage, this went to the very essence of being. The mage, from what Matt had just said, was nothing without his source, only a repository of knowledge, utterly powerless. And the source . . .

"You've surrendered all of your independence!" she said, turning back to the Dwarf, hurling it almost as a challenge.

"Not all," he said mildly. "You give some up any time you share your life with someone. The bonding just goes deeper, and there are compensations."

"You were a king, though. You gave up—"

"That was before," Matt interrupted. "Before I met Loren. I . . . prefer not to talk about it."

She was abashed. "I'm sorry," she whispered. "I was prying."

The Dwarf grimaced, but by now she knew it for his smile. "Not really," he said. "And no matter. It is a very old wound."

"It's just so strange," she explained. "I can't even grasp what it must mean."

"I know. Even here they do not understand the six of us. Or the Law that governs the Council of the Mages. We are feared, respected, very seldom loved."

"What Law?" she asked.

At that he hesitated, then rose. "Let us walk," Matt said. "I will tell you a story, though I warn you, you would do better with one of the cyngael, for I am a poor tale-spinner."

"I'll take my chances," Jennifer said with a smile.

As they started to walk the outer edges of the hall, he began. "Four hundred years ago, the High King went mad. Vailerth was his name, the only son of Lernath, who was the last King of Brennin to die on the Summer Tree."

She had questions about that, too, but held her peace. "Vailerth was brilliant as a child," Matt continued, "or so the records from that time say, but it seems something bent in him after his father died and he came to the throne. A dark flower blossomed in his brain, the Dwarves say when such a thing occurs.

"First Mage to Vailerth was a man called Nilsom, whose source was a woman. Aideen was her name, and she had loved Nilsom all her life, or so the records tell."

Matt walked a few strides in silence. Jennifer had the feeling he was sorry to have begun the story, but after a moment he resumed. "It was rare for a mage to have a woman for source, in part because in Gwen Ystrat, where the Priestesses of Dana are, they would curse any woman who did so. It was always rare; it is rarer still since Aideen."

She looked over at him, but the Dwarf's features were quite impassive.

"Many dark things fell out because of Vailerth's madness. At length there came talk of civil war in the land, because he began taking children, boys and girls both, from their homes and bringing them into the palace by night. They would never be seen again, and the rumors of what the High King did to them were very bad. And in these deeds, in all of these deeds of darkness, Nilsom was with the King, and some say it was he who goaded Vailerth into them. Theirs was a dark weaving, and Nilsom, with Aideen by his side, had power so great none dared openly gainsay them. It is my own thought," the Dwarf added, turning his head for the first time, "that he, too, was mad, but in a cooler, more dangerous fashion. It was a long time ago, however, and the records are incomplete, because many of our most precious books were destroyed in the war. There *was* war at the last, for one day Vailerth and Nilsom went too far: they proposed to go into the Godwood and cut down the Summer Tree.

"The whole of Brennin rose up then, save for the army Vailerth had raised. But that army was loyal and strong, and Nilsom was very strong, more so than the five other mages in Brennin all together. And then on the eve of war there was only one other mage, for four of them were found dead, and their sources, too.

"There was civil war in the High Kingdom then. Only Gwen Ystrat stayed aloof. But the Dukes of Rhoden and Seresh, the Wardens of the North March and the South, the farmers and the townsmen and the mariners from Taerlindel, all came to war against Vailerth and Nilsom.

"They were not enough. Nilsom's power then, sourced in Aideen's strength and her love, was greater, they say, than that of any mage since Amairgen. He wrought death and ruination among all who opposed them, and blood soaked the fields as brother slew brother, while Vailerth laughed in Paras Derval."

Once more Matt paused, and when he resumed, there was a flatness in his voice. "The last battle was fought in the hilly land just west of us, between here and the Godwood. Vailerth, they say, climbed to the topmost towers of this palace to watch Nilsom lead his army to the final victory, after which nothing but the dead would stand between them and the Tree.

"But when the sun rose that morning, Aideen went before her mage, whom she loved, and she told him she would no longer drain herself for him in this cause. And saying so, she drew forth a knife and drained the life's blood from her veins instead and so died."

"Oh, no," Jennifer said. "Oh, Matt!"

He seemed not to have heard. "There is little after that," he said, still very flat. "With Nilsom powerless, the army of Vailerth was overrun. They threw down their swords and spears and sued for peace. Nilsom would not do so, and in the end he was killed by the last mage in Brennin. Vailerth leaped from his tower and died. Aideen was buried with honor in a grave close by the Mörnirwood, and Duke Lagos of Seresh was crowned in this hall."

They had come full circle, back to the benches under the last window, close to the throne. Overhead, Colan's yellow hair was brilliant in the sunlight that poured through the windows.

"It remains only to tell you," Matt Sören said, gazing directly at her now, "that when the Council of Mages gathers at midwinter, Nilsom's is a name whose memory we curse by ritual."

"I should think," said Jennifer, with some spirit.

"So, too," said the Dwarf softly, "is the name of Aideen."

"What?"

Matt's gaze was unwavering. "She betrayed her mage," he said. "In the laws of our Order, there is no crime so deep. None. No matter what the cause. Every year Loren and I curse her memory at midwinter and we do so truly. And every year," he added, very low, very gently, "when the snows melt in the spring, we lay the first of the wildflowers on her grave."

From that composed glance, Jennifer turned her head away. She felt close to tears. She was too far from home, and it was all so difficult and so strange. Why should such a woman be cursed? It was too hard. What she needed, she realized, was exercise, fifty hard laps in a pool to clear her head, or else, and better still. . . .

"Oh, Matt," she said. "I need to move, to *do* something. Are there horses for us to ride?"

And of all things, *that* cracked the solid composure of the Dwarf. Astonishingly, he flushed. "There are horses, of course," he said awkwardly, "but I fear I will not join you—Dwarves do not ride for pleasure. Why don't you go with Laesha and Drance, though?"

"Okay," she said, but then lingered, unwilling, suddenly, to leave him.

"I'm sorry if I have troubled you," Matt said. "It is a difficult story."

Jennifer shook her head. "More for you, surely, than for me. Thank you for sharing it. Thanks for a lot." And, bending swiftly, she kissed him on the cheek and ran from the hall to find Laesha, leaving a normally phlegmatic Dwarf in a remarkably unsettled state.

And so did it come to pass, three hours later, that the two women had galloped with Diarmuid's man to the crest of a ridge east of the town, where they stilled their tired horses in disbelief, as a small party of ethereal figures ascended the slope towards them, their tread so light the grass seemed not to bend beneath their feet.

"Welcome!" said their leader as he stopped before them. He bowed, his long silver hair glinting in the light. "This hour is brightly woven." His voice was like music in a high place. He spoke directly to Jennifer. She was aware that Drance beside her, the prosaic soldier, had tears shining on his transfigured face.

"Will you come down among the trees and feast with us this evening?" the silver-haired figure asked. "You are most welcome. My name is Brendel of the Kestrel Mark, from Daniloth. We are the lios alfar."

◆

The return to Brennin was almost effortless, as if they were being propelled homeward by a following wind. Erron, fluid and agile, went first again on the climb back up the cliff, and he hammered iron spikes into the rock face for the rest of them.

They came again to the horses, mounted, and began galloping north once more on the dusty roads of the High Kingdom. The mood was exhilarated and chaotic. Joining in the bawdy chorus of a song Coll was leading, Kevin couldn't remember feeling happier; after the incident on the river, he and Paul seemed to have been completely accepted by the band, and because he respected these men, that acceptance mattered. Erron was becoming a friend, and so, too, was Carde, singing away on Kevin's left side. Paul, on the other side, wasn't singing, but he didn't seem unhappy, and he had a lousy voice anyway.

Just past midday they came to the same inn where they had stopped before. Diarmuid called a halt for lunch and a quick beer, which became, given the prevailing mood, several slow beers. Coll, Kevin noticed, had disappeared.

The extended break meant that they were going to miss the banquet in the Great Hall that night. Diarmuid didn't seem to care.

"It's the Black Boar tonight, my friends," he announced, glittering and exhilarated at the head of the table. "I'm in no mood for court manners. Tonight I celebrate with you and let the manners look after themselves. Tonight we take our pleasure. Will you drink with me to the Dark Rose of Cathal?"

Kevin cheered with the others, drank with the others.

———◆———

Kimberly had dreamt again. The same one at first: the stones, the ring, the wind and the same grief in her heart. And again she woke just as the words of power reached her lips.

This time, though, she had fallen asleep again, to find another dream waiting, as if at the bottom of a pool.

She was in the room of Ailell the King. She saw him tossing restlessly on his bed, saw the young page asleep on his pallet. Even as she watched, Ailell woke in the dark of his chamber. A long time he lay still, breathing raggedly, then she saw him rise painfully, as if against his own desire. He lit a candle and carried it to an inner doorway in the room, through which he

passed. Invisible, insubstantial, she followed the King
down a corridor lit only by the weaving candle he bore,
and she paused with him before another door, into
which was set a sliding view-hole.

When Ailell put his eyes to the aperture, somehow
she was looking with him, seeing what he saw, and
Kimberly saw with the High King the white naal fire
and the deep blue shining of Ginserat's stone, set into
the top of its pillar.

Only after a long time did Ailell withdraw, and in
the dream Kim saw herself move to look again, standing on tiptoe to gaze with her own eyes into the room
of the stone.

*And looking in, she saw no stone at all, and the
room was dark.*

Wheeling in terror, she saw the High King walking
back towards his chamber, and waiting there for him
in the doorway was a shadowed figure that she knew.

His face rigid as if it were stone, Paul Schafer stood
before Ailell, and he was holding a chess piece in his
outstretched hand, and coming nearer to them, Kim saw
that it was the white king, and it was broken. There was
a music all about them that she couldn't recognize, although she knew she should. Ailell spoke words she could
not hear because the music was too loud, and then Paul
spoke, and she needed desperately to hear, but the music
. . . And then the King held high his candle and began to
speak again, and she could not, could not, could not.

Then everything was blasted to nothingness by the
howling of a dog, so loud it filled the universe.

And she awoke to the morning sunlight and the smell
of food frying over the cooking fire.

"Good morning," said Ysanne. "Come and eat,
before Malka steals it all. Then I have something to
show you."

———◆———

Coll rejoined them on the road north of the town.
Paul Schafer eased his horse over to the roan stallion
the big man rode.

"Being discreet?" he asked.

Above his broken nose Coll's eyes were guarded. "Not exactly. But he wanted to do something."

"Which means?"

"The man had to die, but his wife and children can be helped."

"So you've paid them. Is that why he delayed just now in the tavern? To give you time? It wasn't just because he felt like drinking, was it?"

Coll nodded. "He often feels like drinking," he said wryly, "but he very rarely acts without reason. Tell me," he went on, as Schafer remained silent, "Do you think he did wrong?"

Paul's expression was unreadable.

"Gorlaes would have hanged him," Coll pressed, "and had the body torn apart. His family would have been dispossessed of their land. Now his eldest son is going to South Keep to be trained as one of us. Do you really think he did wrong?"

"No," said Schafer slowly, "I'm just thinking that with everyone else starving, that farmer's treason was probably the best way he could find to take care of his family. Do you have a family, Coll?"

To which Diarmuid's lieutenant, who didn't, and who was still trying to like this strange visitor, had no reply at all. They rode north through the heat of the afternoon, the dry fields baking on either side, the far hills shimmering like mirages, or the hope of rain.

———◆———

The trap door under the table had been invisible until Ysanne, kneeling, had laid her hand on the floor and spoken a word of power. There were ten stairs leading down; on either side the rough stone walls were damp to the touch. There were brackets set into the walls, but no torches, because from the bottom of the stairs came a pale glow of light. Wondering, Kim followed the Seer and Malka, the cat, as they went down.

The chamber was small, more a cave than a room. Another bed, a desk, a chair, a woven carpet on the stone floor. Some parchments and books, very old by the look of them, on the desk. Only one thing more: against the far wall was set a cabinet with glass doors, and within the cabinet, like a captured star, lay the source of light.

There was awe in the Seer's voice when she broke the silence. "Every time I see this . . ." Ysanne murmured. "It is the Circlet of Lisen," she said, walking forward. "It was made for her by the lios alfar in the days when Pendaran Wood was not yet a place of dread. She bound it on her brow after they built the Anor for her, and she stood in that tower by the sea, a light like a star on her brow, to show Amairgen the way home from Cader Sedat."

"And he never came." Kim's voice, though she whispered, felt harsh to her own ears. "Eilathen showed me. I saw her die." The Circlet, she saw, was purest gold, but the light set within it was gentler than moonfall.

"She died, and Pendaran does not forgive. It is one of the deep sorrows of the world. So much changed . . . even the light. It was brighter once, the color of hope, they said when it was made. Then Lisen died, and the Wood changed, and the world changed, and now it seems to shine with loss. It is the most fair thing I know in all the world. It is the Light against the Dark."

Kim looked at the white-haired figure beside her. "Why is it here?" she asked. "Why hidden underground?"

"Raederth brought it to me the year before he died. Where he went to find it, I know not—for it was lost when Lisen fell. Lost long years, and he never told me the tale of where he went to bring it back. It aged him, though. Something happened on the journey of which he could never speak. He asked me to guard it here, with the two other things of power, until their place should be dreamt. 'Who shall wear this next,' he said, 'after Lisen, shall have the darkest road to walk of any child of earth or stars.' And he said nothing more. It waits here, for the dreaming.''

Kimberly shivered, for something new within her, a singing in the blood, told her that the words of the dead mage were true prophecy. She felt weighted, burdened. This was getting to be too much. She tore her eyes away from the Circlet. "What are the other two things?" she asked.

"The Baelrath, of course. The stone on your finger."

Kim looked down. The Warstone had grown brighter as they spoke, the dull, blood-dark lustre giving way to a pulsating sheen.

"I think the Circlet speaks to it," Ysanne went on. "It always shone so in this room. I kept it here beside the other, until the night I dreamt you wearing it. From that time I knew its hour was coming, and I feared the wakening power would call forces I could not ward. So I summoned Eilathen again, and bound him to guard the stone by the red at the heart of the bannion."

"When was this?"

"Twenty-five years ago, now. A little more."

"But—I wasn't even born!"

"I know, child. I dreamt your parents first, the day they met. Then you with the Baelrath on your hand. Our gift as Seers is to walk the twists that lie in the weave of time and bring their secrets back. It is no easy power, and you know already that it cannot always be controlled."

Kim pushed her brown hair back with both hands. Her forehead was creased with anxiety, the grey eyes were those of someone being pursued. "I do know that," she said. "I'm trying to handle it. What I can't. . . I don't understand why you are showing me Lisen's Light."

"Not true," the Seer replied. "If you stop to think,

you will understand. You are being shown the Circlet because it may fall to you to dream who is to wear it next.''

There was a silence. Then, ''Ysanne, I don't live here.''

''There is a bridge between our worlds. Child, I am telling you that which you know already.''

''But that's just it! I'm beginning to understand what I am. I saw what Eilathen spun. But I'm *not* of this world, it isn't in my blood, I don't know its roots the way you do, the way all the Seers must have known. How should . . . how could I *ever* presume to say who is to bear the Circlet of Lisen? I'm a stranger, Ysanne!''

She was breathing hard. The old woman looked at her a long time, then she smiled. ''Now you are. You have just come. You are right about being incomplete, but be easy. It is only time.'' Her voice, like her eyes, was gentle as she told her second lie, and shielded it.

''Time!'' Kimberly burst out. ''Don't you understand? I'm only *here* two weeks. As soon as they find Dave, we're going home.''

''Perhaps. There is still a bridge, and I did dream the Baelrath on your hand. It is in my heart as well— an old woman's heart, not a Seer's vision—that there may be need of a Dreamer in your world, too, before what is to come is full-woven on the Loom.''

Kimberly opened her mouth, and closed it again, speechless. Because now it *was* too much: too many things, too quickly and too hard.

''I'm sorry,'' she managed to gasp, and then, whirling, ran up the stone stairs and out the doorway of the cottage to where there was sunlight and a blue sky. Trees, too, and a path down which she could run to the edge of a lake. Alone, because no one was pursuing her, she could stand there throwing pebbles into the water, knowing that they were pebbles, only pebbles, and that no green spirit, water dripping from his hair, would rise in answer from the lake to change her life again.

In the chamber from which she had fled, the light continued to shine. Power and hope and loss were in the radiance that bathed Ysanne as she sat at the desk, stroking the cat in her lap, her eyes unfocused and blind.

"Ah, Malka," she murmured at last, "I wish I were wiser. What is the use of living so long if one hasn't grown wise?"

The cat pricked up her ears, but preferred to continue licking a paw rather than address herself to so thorny a question.

At length the Seer rose, lowering the affronted Malka to the floor, and she walked slowly to the cabinet wherein the Circlet shone. Opening the glass door, she reached in and took out an object half hidden on a lower shelf, then she stood there a long time, gazing at what lay in her hand.

The third thing of power: the one that Kimberly, throwing pebbles by the lake, had not seen.

"Ah, Malka," the Seer said again, and drew the dagger from its sheath. A sound like a plucked harpstring ran through the room.

A thousand years before, in the days after the Baøl Rangat, when all the free peoples of Fionavar had gathered before the Mountain to see Ginserat's stones, the Dwarves of Banir Lök had shaped a crafting of their own as a gift for the new High King of Brennin.

With thieren had they wrought, rarest of metals, found only at the roots of their twin mountains, most precious gift of earth to them, blue-veined silver of Eridu.

And for Colan the Beloved they had taken thought and fashioned a blade, with runes upon the sheath to bind it, and an old, dark magic spun in their caverns to make a knife unlike any other in all the worlds, and they named it Lökdal.

Very low bowed Conary's son when they handed it
to him, and silently he listened, wiser than his years,
as Seithr the Dwarf-King told him what had been laid
upon the blade. Then he bowed again, lower yet, when
Seithr, too, fell silent.

"I thank you," Colan said, and his eyes flashed as
he spoke. "Double-edged the knife, and double-edged
the gift. Mörnir grant us the sight to use it truly."
And he placed Lökdal in his belt and bore it south
away.

To the mages he had entrusted it, the blade and the
magic locked within it like a blessing or a curse, and
twice only in a thousand years had Colan's dagger
killed. From First Mage to First Mage it had passed,
until the night Raederth died. In the middle of that
night, the woman who loved him had had a dream that
shook her to the hidden places of her soul. Rising in
the darkness, she came to the place where Raederth
guarded the blade, and she took it away and hid it from
those who succeeded him. Not even Loren Silvercloak, whom she trusted with everything else, knew
that Ysanne had Lökdal.

"Who strikes with this blade without love in his
heart shall surely die," had said Seithr of the Dwarves.
"That is one thing."

And then softly, so that only Colan heard, he had
said the other thing.

In her hidden chamber, Ysanne the Seer, dreamer
of the dream, turned the bright rippling blade over and
over in her hands, so the light glinted from it like blue
fire.

On the shore of the lake a young woman stood,
power within her, power beneath her, throwing pebbles one by one.

———————◆———————

It was cooler in the wood where the lios alfar led
them. The food they were offered was delicate and
wonderful: strange fruits, rich bread, and a wine that
lifted the spirit and sharpened the colors of the sunset.

Throughout, there was music: one of the lios played
at a high-toned wind instrument while others sang,
their voices twining in the deepening shadows of the
trees, as the torches of evening were lit at the edge of
the glade.

Laesha and Drance, for whom this was childhood
fantasy made true, seemed even more enchanted than
Jennifer was, and so when Brendel invited them to stay
the night in the wood and watch the lios dance under
the stars, it was with wonder and joy that they accepted.

Brendel dispatched someone to ride swiftly to Paras
Derval and give private word to the King of their
whereabouts. Wrapped in a delicate languor, they
watched the messenger, his hair glowing in the light
of the setting sun, ride over the hill, and they turned
back to the wine and the singing in the glade.

As the shadows lengthened, a grace note of long
sorrow seemed to weave its way into the songs of the
lios alfar. A myriad of fireflies moved like shining eyes
just beyond the torches: lienae they were named,
Brendel said. Jennifer sipped the wine he poured for
her, and let herself be carried into a rich sweet sadness
by the music.

Cresting the hill west of them, the messenger, Tandem of the Kestrel, set his horse into an easy canter
towards the walled town and the palace a league away.

He was not quite halfway there when he died.

Soundlessly he fell from his horse, four darts in his
throat and back. After a moment the svarts rose from
the hollow beside the path and watched in unblinking
silence as the wolves padded up from beside them to
the body of the lios. When it was clear that he was
dead, they, too, went forward and surrounded the
fallen rider. Even in death, there was a nimbus of glory
clinging to him, but when they were done, when the
wet, tearing sounds had ceased and only the quiet stars
looked down, there was nothing left that anyone would
care to see of Tandem of the lios alfar.

Most hated by the Dark, for their name was Light.

◆

And it was in that moment, away to the north and east, that another solitary rider checked his own mount suddenly. A moment he was motionless, then with a terrible oath, and fear like a fist in his heart, Loren Silvercloak turned his horse and began desperately to thunder home.

◆

In Paras Derval, the King did not attend the banquet, nor did any of the four visitors, which caused more than a little talk. Ailell kept to his chambers and played ta'bael with Gorlaes, the Chancellor. He won easily, as was customary, and with little pleasure, which was also customary. They played very late, and Tarn, the page, was asleep when the interruption came.

◆

As they went through the open doorway of the Black Boar, the noise and smoke were like a wall into which they smashed.

One voice, however, made itself heard in a prodigious bellow that resounded over the pandemonium.

"Diarmuid!" roared Tegid, surging to his feet. Kevin winced at the decibel level engendered. "By the oak and the moon, it's himself!" Tegid howled, as the tavern sounds briefly resolved themselves into shouted greetings.

Diarmuid, in fawn-colored breeches and a blue doublet, stood grinning sardonically in the doorway as the others fanned out into the dense haze of the room. Tegid wove his way unsteadily forward to stand swaying before his Prince.

And hurled the contents of a mug of ale full in Diarmuid's face.

"Wretched Prince!" he screamed. "I shall tear your heart out! I shall send your liver to Gwen Ystrat! How *dare* you slip off and leave great Tegid behind with the women and the mewling babes?"

Kevin, beside the Prince, had a brief, hysterical vi-

sion of Tegid trying to go hand over hand across Saeren, before Diarmuid, dripping wet, reached to the
nearest table, grabbed a silver tankard, and threw it
violently at Tegid.

Someone screamed as the Prince followed up the
throw, which bounced off the big man's shoulder, with
a short rush, at the end of which his lowered head
intersected effectively with Tegid's massive target of a
girth.

Tegid staggered back, his face momentarily achiev-
ing a shade of green. He recovered quickly, though,
seized the nearest table top, and with one mighty ex-
ertion lifted it whole from the trestles, spilling mugs
and cutlery, and sending their erstwhile users scatter-
ing as raucous curses exploded around him. Wheeling
for leverage, he swung the board in a wide, lethal
sweep that bade fair to render Ailell heirless had it
landed.

Diarmuid ducked, very neatly. So, too, less
smoothly, did Kevin. Sprawling on the floor, he saw
the board whistle over their heads and, at the spent
end of its sweep, clip a red-doubleted man on the
shoulder, catapulting him into the patron beside him.
A remarkable human demonstration of the domino effect ensued. The noise level was horrific.

Someone elected to deposit his bowl of soup on the
red-doubleted gentleman's balding pate. Someone else regarded this as more than sufficient excuse to deck the
soup-pourer from behind with a hoisted bench. The innkeeper prudently began removing bottles from the bar
top. A barmaid, her skirts aswirl, slipped under a table.
Kevin saw Carde dive to join her there.

In the meantime, Diarmuid, springing from his
crouch, butted Tegid again before the mountainous one
could ready a return scything of the table top. The first
reaping had comprehensively cleared a wide space
about the two of them.

This time Tegid held his ground; with a joyous bellow he dropped the board on someone's head and enveloped Diarmuid in a bear-hug.

"Now I have you!" Tegid boomed, his face flushed with rapture. Diarmuid's features were also shading towards scarlet as his captor tightened a bone-crushing grip. Watching, Kevin saw the Prince free his arms for a counter-blow.

He had no doubt Diarmuid could manage to free himself, but Tegid was squeezing in earnest, and Kevin saw that the Prince was going to have to use a crippling retort to break the other man's hold. He saw Diarmuid shift his knee for leverage, and knew what would have to follow. With a futile shout, he rushed forward to intercede.

And stopped dead as a terrifying cry of outrage exploded from Tegid's throat. Still screaming, he dropped the Prince like a discarded toy on the sandy floor.

There came a smell of burning flesh.

Leaping spectacularly, Tegid upended another table, rescued a brimming pitcher of ale, and proceeded to pour its contents over his posterior.

The movement revealed, somewhat like the drawing of a curtain, Paul Schafer behind him, holding rather apologetically, a poker from the cooking fire.

There was a brief silence, an awe-stricken homage to the operatic force of Tegid's scream, then Diarmuid, still on the floor, began to laugh in high, short, hysterical gasps, signaling a resumption of universal pandemonium. Crying with laughter, barely able to stand, Kevin made his way, with Erron staggering beside him, to embrace the crookedly grinning Schafer.

It was some time before order was restored, largely because no one was particularly intent on restoring it. The red-doubleted man appeared to have a number of friends, and so, too, it seemed, did the soup-pourer. Kevin, who knew neither, threw a token bench into the fray, then withdrew towards the bar with Erron.

Two serving women joined them there, and the press of events greatly facilitated a rapid acquaintance.

Going upstairs, hand in hand with Marna, the taller of the two, Kevin's last glimpse of the tavern floor was of a surging mass of men disappearing in and out of the smoky haze. Diarmuid was standing atop the bar, lobbing whatever came to hand upon the heads of the combatants. He didn't seem to be choosing sides. Kevin looked for Paul, didn't see him; and then a door was opened and closed behind him, and in the rush of dark a woman was in his arms, her mouth turned up to his, and his soul began its familiar spiral downward into longing.

Much later, when he had not yet completed the journey back, he heard Marna ask in a timid whisper, "Is it always so?"

And a good few minutes yet from being capable of speech, he stroked her hair once with an effort and closed his eyes again. Because it *was* always so. The act of love a blind, convulsive reaching back into a falling dark. Every time. It took away his very name, the shape and movement of his bones; and between times he wondered if there would be a night when he would go so far that there was no returning.

Not this night, though. Soon he was able to smile at her, and then to give thanks and gentle words, and not without sincerity, for her sweetness ran deep, and he had needed badly to drink of such a thing. Slipping inside his arm, Marna laid her head on his shoulder beside his own bright hair, and, breathing deeply of her scent, Kevin let the exhaustion of two waking nights carry him to sleep.

He only had an hour, though, and so was vulnerable and unfocused when the presence of a third person in the room woke him. It was another girl, not Erron's, and she was crying, her hair disordered about her shoulders.

"What is it, Tiene?" Marna asked sleepily.

"He sent me to you," brown-haired Tiene sniffled, looking at Kevin.

"Who?" Kevin grunted, groping towards consciousness. "Diarmuid?"

"Oh, no. It was the other stranger, Pwyll."

It took a moment.

"Paul! What did—what's happened?"

His tone was evidently too sharp for already tender nerves. Tiene, casting a wide-eyed glance of reproach at him, sat down on the bed and started crying again. He shook her arm. "Tell me! What happened?"

"He left," Tiene whispered, barely audible. "He came upstairs with me, but he left."

Shaking his head, Kevin tried desperately to focus. "What? Did he . . . was he able to. . . ?"

Tiene sniffed, wiping at the tears on her cheeks. "You mean to be with me? Yes, of course he was, but he took no pleasure at all, I could tell. It was all for me . . . and I am not, I gave him nothing, and . . . and . . ."

"And what, for God's sake?"

"And so I cried," Tiene said, as if it should have been obvious. "And when I cried, he walked out. And he sent me to find you. My lord."

She had moved farther onto the bed, in part because Marna had made room. Tiene's dark eyes were wide like a fawn's; her robe had fallen open, and Kevin could see the start of her breast's deep curve. Then he felt the light stirring of Marna's hand along his thigh under the sheet. There was suddenly a pulsing in his head. He drew a deep breath.

And swung quickly out of bed. Cursing a hard-on, he kicked into his breeches and slipped on the loose-sleeved doublet Diarmuid had given him. Without bothering to button it, he left the room.

It was dark on the landing. Moving to the railing, he looked down on the ruin of the ground level of the Black Boar. The guttering torches cast flickering shadows over bodies sprawled in sleep on overturned tables and benches, or against the walls. A few men were talking in muted tones in one corner, and he heard a woman giggle suddenly from the near wall and then subside.

Then he heard something else. The plucked strings of a guitar.

His guitar.

Following the sound, he turned his head to see Diarmuid, with Coll and Carde, sitting by the window, the Prince cradling the guitar in the window seat, the others on the floor.

As he walked downstairs to join them, his eyes adjusted to the shadows, and he saw other members of the band sprawled nearby with some of the women beside them.

"Hello, friend Kevin," Diarmuid said softly, his eyes bright like an animal's in the dark. "Will you show me how you play this: I sent Coll to bring it. I trust you don't mind." His voice was lazy with late-night indolence. Behind him, Kevin could see a sprinkling of stars.

"Aye, lad," a bulky shadow rumbled. "Do a song for us." He'd taken Tegid for a broken table.

Without speaking, Kevin picked his way forward over the bodies on the floor. He took the guitar from Diarmuid, who slipped down from the window seat, leaving it for him. The window had been thrown open; he felt a light breeze stir the hairs at the back of his neck, as he tuned the guitar.

It was late, and dark, and quiet. He was a long way from home, and tired, and hurting in a difficult way. Paul had gone; even tonight, he had taken no joy, had turned from tears again. Even tonight, even here. So many reasons he could give. And so:

"This is called 'Rachel's Song,' " he said, fighting a thickness in his throat, and began to play. It was a music no one there could know, but the pull of grief was immediate. Then after a long time he lifted his

voice, deep when he sang, in words he'd decided long
ago should never be sung:

> *Love, do you remember*
> *My name? I was lost*
> *In summer turned winter*
> *Made bitter by frost.*
> *And when June comes December*
> *The heart pays the cost.*
>
> > *The breaking of waves on a long shore,*
> > *In the grey morning the slow fall of rain,*
> > *And stone lies over.*
>
> *You'll bury your sorrow*
> *Deep in the sea,*
> *But sea tides aren't tamed*
> *That easily—*
> *There will come a tomorrow*
> *When you weep for me.*
>
> > *The breaking of waves on a long shore,*
> > *In the grey morning the slow fall of rain,*
> > *Oh love remember, remember me.*

Then the music came alone again, transposed,
worked on harder than anything he'd written in his life,
especially what was coming now, with his own stupid
tears. The part where the melody hurt, it was so beautiful, so laden with memory: the adapted second
movement of the Brahms F Major Cello Sonata.

The notes were clean, unblurred, though the candles
were blurred in his sight, as Kevin played Rachel Kincaid's graduation piece and gave sound to the sorrow
that was his and not his.

Into the shadowed room it went, Rachel's song; over
the sleeping bodies that stirred as sadness touched their
dreams; among the ones who did not sleep and who
felt the pull as they listened, remembering losses of

their own; up the stairway it went to where two women stood at the railing, both crying now; faintly it reached the bedrooms, where bodies lay tangled in the shapes of love; and out the open window it went as well, into the late night street and the wide dark between the stars.

And on the unlit cobblestones a figure paused by the doorway of the tavern and did not enter. The street was empty, the night was dark, there was no one to see. Very silently he listened, and when the song came to an end, very silently he left, having heard the music before.

So Paul Schafer, who had fled from a woman's tears, and had cursed himself for a fool and turned back, now made his final turning, and did not turn again.

There was darkness for a time, a twisting web of streets, a gate where he was recognized by torchlight, and then darkness again in corridors silent save for the footfalls that he made. And through it he carried that music, or the music carried him, or the memory of music. It hardly mattered which.

He walked a matrix of crossing hallways he had walked before, and some were lit and others dark, and in some rooms he passed there were sounds again, but no one else walked in Paras Derval that night.

And in time he came, carrying music, carrying loss, carried by both of them, and stood for a second time before a door beyond which a slant of light yet showed.

It was the brown-bearded one called Gorlaes who opened to his summons, and for a moment he remembered that he did not trust this man, but it seemed a concern infinitely removed from where he was, and one that didn't matter now, not anymore.

Then his eyes found those of the King, and he saw that Ailell knew, somehow knew, and was not strong enough to refuse what he would ask, and so he asked.

"I will go to the Summer Tree for you tonight. Will you grant me leave and do what must be done?" It seemed to have been written a very long time ago. There was music.

Ailell was weeping as he spoke, but he said what was needful to be said. Because it was one thing to die, and another to die uselessly, he listened to the words and let them join the music in carrying him with Gorlaes and two other men out of the palace by a hidden gate.

There were stars above them and a forest far away. There was music in his head that was not going to end, it seemed. And it seemed he wasn't saying goodbye to Kevin after all, which was a grief, but it was a lost, small, twisting thing in the place where he had come.

Then the forest was no longer far away, and at some point the waning moon had risen as he walked, for it brushed the nearest trees with silver. The music still was with him, and the last words of Ailell: *Now I give you to Mörnir. For three nights and forever,* the King had said. And cried.

And now with the words and the music in his head, there had come again, as he had known it would, the face for which he could not cry. Dark eyes. Like no one else. In this world.

And he went into the Godwood, and it was dark. And all the trees were sighing in the wind of the wood, the breath of the God. There was fear on the faces of the other three men as the sound rose and fell about them like the sea.

He walked with them amid the surging and the swaying of the trees, and in time he saw that the path they were following had ceased to wander. The trees on either side now formed a double row leading him on, and so he stepped past Gorlaes, music carrying him, and he came into the place wherein stood the Summer Tree.

Very great it was, dark almost to black, its trunk knotted and gnarled, wide as a house. It stood alone in the clearing, in the place of sacrifice, and clutched the earth with roots old as the world, a challenge to the stars that shone down, and there was power in that place beyond the telling. Standing there, he felt it calling for his blood, for his life, and knowing he could not live three nights on that tree, he stepped forward, so as not to turn again, and the music stopped.

They stripped him of his garments then and bound him naked to the Summer Tree at the waning of the moon. When they had gone, it was silent in the glade save for the ceaseless sighing of the leaves. Alone upon the Tree, he felt within his flesh the incalculable vastness of its power, and had there been anything left to fear, he would have been afraid.

And this was the first night of Pwyll the Stranger on the Summer Tree.

Chapter 8

In another wood east of Paras Derval, the lios alfar were still singing as Jennifer drifted towards sleep. Under the stars and the crescent of the risen moon their voices wove about her a melody of sorrow so old and deep it was almost a luxury.

She roused herself and turned on the pallet they had made for her.

"Brendel?"

He came over to her and knelt. His eyes were blue now. They had been green like her own the last time she looked, and gold on the hillside that afternoon.

"Are you immortal?" she asked, sleepily.

He smiled. "No, Lady. Only the gods are so, and there are those who say that even they will die at the end. We live very long, and age will not kill us, but we do die, Lady, by sword or fire, or grief of heart. And weariness will lead us to sail to our song, though that is a different thing."

"Sail?"

"Westward lies a place not found on any map. A world shaped by the Weaver for the lios alfar alone, and there we go when we leave Fionavar, unless Fionavar has killed us first."

"How old are you, Brendel?"

"I was born four hundred years after the Bael Rangat. A little more than six hundred years ago."

She absorbed it in silence. There was nothing, really, to say. On her other side Laesha and Drance were asleep. The singing was very beautiful. She let it carry her into simplicity, and then sleep.

He watched her a long time, the eyes still blue, calm, and deeply appreciative of beauty in all its incarnations. And in this one there was something more. She looked like someone. He knew this, or he sensed it to be so, but although he was quite right, he had absolutely no way of knowing whom, and so could not warn anyone.

At length he rose and rejoined the others for the last song, which was, as it always was, Ra-Termaine's lament for the lost. They sang for those who had just died by Pendaran, and for all the others long ago, who would never now hear this song or their own. As the lios sang, the stars seemed to grow brighter above the trees, but that may have been just the deepening of night. When the song ended, the fire was banked and they slept.

They were ancient and wise and beautiful, their spirit in their eyes as a many-colored flame, their art an homage to the Weaver whose most shining children they were. A celebation of life was woven into their very essence, and they were named in the oldest tongue after the Light that stands against the Dark.

But they were not immortal.

The two guards died of poison arrows, and four others had their throats ripped apart by the black onrush of the wolves before they were fully awake. One cried out and killed his wolf with a dagger as he died.

They fought bravely then, even brilliantly, with bright swords and arrows, for their grace could be most deadly when they had need.

Brendel and Drance with two others formed a wall about the two women, and against the charge of the giant wolves they held firm once, and again, and yet again, their swords rising and falling in desperate silence. It was dark, though, and the wolves were black, and the svarts moved like twisted wraiths about the glade.

Even so, the shining courage of the lios alfar, with Drance of Brennin fighting in their midst as a man posessed, might have prevailed, had it not been for the one thing more: the cold, controlling will that guided the assault. There was a power in the glade that night that no one could have foretold, and doom was written on the wind that rose before the dawn.

For Jennifer it was a hallucination of terror in the dark. She heard snarls and cries, saw things in blurred, distorted flashes—blood-dark swords, the shadow of a wolf, an arrow flying past. Violence exploding all around her, she who had spent her days avoiding such a thing.

But this was night. Too terrified to even scream, Jennifer saw Drance fall at last, a wolf dying beneath him, another rising wet-mouthed from his corpse to leap past her to where Laesha stood. Then before she could react, even as she heard Laesha cry out, she felt herself seized brutally as the hideous svarts surged forward into the gap and she was dragged away by them over the body of Diarmuid's man.

Looking desperately back, she saw Brendel grappling with three foes at once, blood dark on his face in the thin moonlight, then she was among the trees, surrounded by wolves and svart alfar, and there was no light to see by or to hope for anywhere.

They moved through the forest for what seemed an endless time, travelling north and east, away from Paras Derval and everyone she knew in this world. Twice she stumbled and fell in the dark, and each time she was dragged, sobbing, to her feet and the terrible progress continued.

They were still in the woods when the sky began to shade towards grey, and in the growing light she gradually became aware that amid the shifting movements of her captors, one figure never left her side: and among the horrors of that headlong night, this was the worst.

Coal-black, with a splash of silver-grey on his brow, he was the largest wolf by far. It wasn't the size, though, or the wet blood on his dark mouth; it was the malevolence of the power that hovered about the wolf like an aura. His eyes were on her face, and they were red; in them, for the moment she could sustain the glance, she saw a degree of intelligence that should not have been there, and was more alien than anything else she had come upon in Fionavar. There was no hatred in the look, only a cold, merciless will. Hate, she could have understood; what she saw was worse.

It was morning when they reached their destination. Jennifer saw a small woodcutter's cabin set in a cleared-out space by the forest's edge. A moment later she saw what was left of the woodcutter as well.

They threw her inside. She fell, from the force of it, and then crawled on her knees to a corner where she was violently, rackingly sick. Afterwards, shivering uncontrollably, she made her way to the cot at the back of the room and lay down.

We salvage what we can, what truly matters to us, even at the gates of despair. And so Jennifer Lowell, whose father had taught her, even as a child, to confront the world with pride, eventually rose up, cleaning herself as best she could, and began to wait in the brightening cottage. Daylight was coming outside, but it was not only that: courage casts its own light.

The sun was high in a blank sky when she heard the voices. One was low, with a note of amusement she could discern even through the door. Then the other man spoke, and Jennifer froze in disbelief, for this voice she had heard before.

"Not hard," the first man said, and laughed. "Against the lios it is easy to keep them to it."

"I hope you were not followed. I absolutely must not be seen, Galadan."

"You won't be. Almost all of them were dead, and

I left behind ten wolves against the stragglers. They won't follow in any case. Enough of them have died; they wouldn't risk more for a human. She is ours, more easily than we might have hoped. It is rare indeed that we receive aid from Daniloth.'' And he laughed again, maliciously amused.

"Where is she?"

"Inside."

The door was flung open, letting in a dazzling shaft of sunlight. Momentarily blinded, Jennifer was dragged into the clearing.

"A prize, wouldn't you say?" Galadan murmured.

"Perhaps," the other one said. "Depending on what she tells us about why they are here."

Jennifer turned towards the voice, her eyes adjusting, and as they did, she found herself face to face with Metran, First Mage to the High King of Brennin.

No longer was he the shuffling old man she'd seen that first night or watched as he cowered from Jaelle in the Great Hall. Metran stood straight and tall, his eyes bright with malice.

"You traitor!" Jennifer burst out.

He gestured, and she screamed as her nipples were squeezed viciously. No one had touched her; he had done it himself without moving.

"Carefully, my dear lady," Metran said, all solicitude, as she writhed in pain. "You must be careful of what you say to me. I have the power to do whatever I want with you." He nodded towards his source, Denbarra, who stood close by.

"Not quite," the other voice demurred. "Let her go." The tone was very quiet, but the pain stopped instantly. Jennifer turned, wiping tears from her face.

Galadan was not tall, but there was a sinuous strength to him, a sheathed intimation of very great power. Cold eyes fixed her from a scarred, aristocratic face under the thatch of silver hair—like Brendel's, she thought, with another sort of pain.

He bowed to her, courtly and graceful, and with a

veiled amusement. Then that was gone as he turned to
Metran.

"She goes north for questioning," he said. "Un-
harmed."

"Are you telling me what to do?" Metran said on
a rising note, and Jennifer saw Denbarra stiffen.

"Actually, yes, if you put it that way." There was
mockery in his voice. "Are you going to fight me over
it, mageling?"

"I could kill you, Galadan," Metran hissed.

The one named Galadan smiled again, but not with
his eyes. "Then try. But I tell you now, you will fail.
I am outside your taught magic, mageling. You have
some power, I know, and have been given more, and
may indeed have greater yet to come, but I will still
be outside you, Metran. I always will be. And if you
test it, I shall have your heart out for my friends."

In the silence that followed this, Jennifer became
conscious of the ring of wolves surrounding them.
There were svart alfar as well, but the giant red-eyed
wolf was gone.

Metran was breathing hard. "You are not above me,
Galadan. I was promised this."

At that, Galadan threw back his fierce, scarred
head, and a burst of genuine laughter rang through the
clearing.

"Promised, were you? Ah well, then, I must apologize!" His laughter stopped. "She is still to go north.
If it were not so, I might take her for myself. But
look!"

Jennifer, turning skyward to where Galadan was
pointing, saw a creature so beautiful it lifted her heart
in reflexive hope.

A black swan came swooping down from the high
reaches of the sky, glorious against the sun, the great
wings widespread, feathered with jet plumage, the long
neck gracefully extended.

Then it landed, and Jennifer realized that the true
horror had only begun, for the swan had unnatural

razored teeth, and claws, and about it, for all the stunning beauty, there clung an odor of putrescent corruption.

Then the swan spoke, in a voice like slithering darkness in a pit. "I have come," she said. "Give her to me."

Far away yet, terribly far away, Loren Silvercloak was driving his horse back south, cursing his own folly in all the tongues he knew.

"She is yours, Avaia," said Galadan, unsmiling. "Is she not, Metran?"

"Of course," said the mage. He had moved upwind of the swan. "I will naturally be anxious to know what she has to say. It is vital for me in my place of watch."

"No longer," the black swan said, ruffling her feathers. "I have tidings for you. The Cauldron is ours, I am to say. You go now to the place of spiraling, for the time is upon us."

Across the face of Metran there spread then a smile of such cruel triumph that Jennifer turned away from it. "It has come then," the mage exulted. "The day of my revenge. Oh, Garmisch, my dead King, I shall break the usurper into pieces on his throne, and make drinking cups of the bones of the House of Ailell!"

The swan showed her unnatural teeth. "I will take pleasure in the sight," she hissed.

"No doubt," said Galadan wryly. "Is there word for me?"

"North," the swan replied. "You are asked to go north with your friends. Make haste. There is little time."

"It is well," said Galadan. "I have one task left here, then I follow."

"Make haste," Avaia said again. "And now I go."

"No!" Jennifer screamed, as cold svart hands grabbed for her. Her cries cut the air of the clearing and fell into nothingness. She was bound across the back of the giant swan and the dense, putrefying smell of it overwhelmed her. She could not breathe; when

she opened her mouth, the thick black feathers choked her, and as they left the earth for the blazing sky, Jennifer fainted for the first time in her life, and so could not have known the glorious curving arc she and the swan made, cutting across the sky.

The figures in the clearing watched Avaia bear the girl away until they were lost in the shimmering of the white sky.

Metran turned to the others, exultation still in his eyes. "You heard? The Cauldron is mine!"

"So it seems," Galadan agreed. "You are away across the water, then?"

"Immediately. It will not be long before you see what I do with it."

Galadan nodded, then a thought seemed to strike him. "I wonder, does Denbarra understand what all this means?" He turned to the source. "Tell me, my friend, do you know what this Cauldron is all about?"

Denbarra shifted uneasily under the weight of that gaze. "I understand what is needful for me to know," he said sturdily. "I understand that with its aid, the House of Garantae will rule again in Brennin."

Galadan regarded him a moment longer, then his glance flicked away dismissively. "He is worthy of his destiny," he said to Metran. "A thick-witted source is an advantage for you, I suppose. I should get dreadfully bored, myself."

Denbarra flushed, but Metran was unmoved by the gibe this time. "My sister-son is loyal. It is a virtue," he said, unconscious of the irony. "What about you? You mentioned a task to be done. Should I know?"

"You should, but evidently you don't. Give thanks that I am less careless. There is a death to be consummated."

Metran's mouth twitched at the insult, but he did not respond. "Then go your way," he said. "We may not meet for some time."

"Alas!" said Galadan.

The mage raised a hand. "You mock me," he said with intensity. "You mock us all, andain. But I tell you this: with the Cauldron of Khath Meigol in my hands, I will wield a power even you dare not scorn. And with it I shall wreak such a vengeance here in Brennin that the memory of it will never die."

Galadan lifted his scarred head and regarded the mage. "Perhaps," he said finally, and very, very softly. "Unless the memory of it dies because everything has died. Which, as you know, is the wish of my heart."

On the last words, he made a subtle gesture over his breast, and a moment later a coal-black wolf with a splash of silver on its head ran swiftly westward from the clearing.

Had he entered the forest farther south, a great deal of what ensued might have been very different.

At the southern edge of the woodcutter's clearing a figure lay, hidden among the trees, bleeding from a dozen wounds. Behind him on the trail through the forest the last two lios alfar lay dead. And ten wolves.

And in the heart of Na-Brendel of the Kestrel Mark lay a grief and a rage that, more than anything else, had kept him alive so far. In the sunlight his eyes were black as night.

He watched Metran and his source mount horses and swing away northwest, and he saw the svarts and wolves leave together for the north. Only when the clearing stood utterly silent did he rise, with difficulty, and begin his own journey back to Paras Derval. He limped badly, from a wound in the thigh, and he was weak unto death from loss of blood; but he was not going to let himself fall or fail, for he was of the lios alfar, and the last of his company, and with his own eyes he had seen a gathering of the Dark that day.

It was a long way, though, and he was badly, badly hurt, so he was still a league from Paras Derval when twilight fell.

———◆———

During the day there were rumblings of thunder in the west. A number of the merchants in the city came to their doorways to look at the heavens, more out of habit than out of hope. The killing sun burned in a bare sky.

On the green at the end of Anvil Lane, Leila had gathered the children again for the ta'kiena. One or two had refused out of boredom, but she was insistent, and the others acceded to her wishes, which, with Leila, was always the best thing to do.

So she was blindfolded again, and she made them do it double so she truly could not see. Then she began the calling, and went through the first three almost indifferently because they didn't matter, they were only a game. When she came to the last one, though, to the Road, she felt the now familiar stillness come over her again, and she closed her eyes behind the two blindfolds. Then her mouth went dry and the difficult twisting flowered inside her. Only when the rushing sound began, like waves, did she start the chant, and as she sang the last word everything stopped.

She removed the blindfolds and, blinking in the brightness, saw with no surprise at all that it was Finn again. As if from far away she heard the voices of the adults watching them, and further still she heard a roll of thunder, but she looked only at Finn. He seemed more alone every time. She would have been sad, but it seemed so destined that sadness didn't fit, nor any sense of surprise. She didn't know what the Longest Road was, or where it led, but she knew it was Finn's, and that she was calling him to it.

Later that afternoon, though, something did surprise her. Ordinary people never went to the sanctuary of the Mother, certainly not at the direct request of the High Priestess herself. She combed her hair and wore her only gown; her mother made her.

◆

When Sharra dreamed now of the falcon, it was no longer alone in the sky over Larai Rigal. Memory burned in her like a fire under stars.

She was her father's daughter, though, heir to the Ivory Throne, and so there was a matter to be looked into, regardless of fires in her heart or falcons over-head.

Devorsh, Captain of the Guard, knocked in re-sponse to her summons, and the mutes admitted him. Her ladies murmured behind fluttering fans as the tall Captain made obeisance and gave homage in his un-mistakable voice. She dismissed the women, enjoying their chagrin, and bade him sit in a low chair by the window.

"Captain," she began, without preamble, "certain documents have come to my attention raising a matter I think we must address."

"Highness?" He was handsome, she conceded, but not a candle, not a candle. He would not understand why she was smiling; not that it mattered.

"It seems that the archival records make mention of stone handholds cut many years ago in the cliff above Saeren due north of us."

"Above the river, Highness? In the cliff?" Polite incredulity infused the gravelly voice.

"I think I said that, yes." He flushed at the rebuke; she paused to let it register. "If those handholds exist, they are a danger and we should know about them. I want you to take two men you trust and see if this is true. For obvious reasons"—though she knew of none—"this is to be kept very quiet."

"Yes, Highness. When shall I—"

"Now, of course." She rose, and so, of necessity, did he.

"My lady's will." He made obeisance and turned to go.

And because of the falcons, the moon-touched memory, she called him back. "Devorsh, one thing more. I heard footsteps in the garden the night before last. Did you notice anything by the walls?"

His face showed real concern. "Highness, I went

off duty at sundown. Bashrai took command from me. I will speak to him of this without delay."

"Off duty?"

"Yes, Highness. We take turns, Bashrai and myself, in leading the night watch. He is most competent, I suggest, but if—"

"How many men patrol the walls at night?" She leaned on the back of a chair for support; there was a pressure behind her eyes.

"Twelve, Highness, in peacetime."

"And the dogs?"

He coughed. "Ah, no, my lady. Not of late. It was felt unnecessary. They have been used on the hunt this spring and summer. Your father knows about this, of course." His face was animated by unconcealed curiosity. "If my lady feels they should—"

"No!" It was intolerable that he be in the room another moment, that he continue to look at her like this, his eyes widening in appraisal. "I will discuss this with Bashrai. Go now and do as I have told you. And quickly, Devorsh, very quickly."

"I go, my lady," he said in the distinctive voice, and went. After, she bit her tongue, tasting blood, so as not to scream.

Shalhassan of Cathal was reclining on a couch, watching two slaves wrestling, when word was brought to him. His court, hedonistic and overbred, was enjoying the sight of the oiled bodies writhing naked on the floor in the presence chamber, but the King watched the fight, as he heard the news, expressionlessly.

Raziel appeared just then in the archway behind the throne with the cup in his hand. It was mid-afternoon then and, taking the drink, Shalhassan saw that the jewelled goblet was blue. Which meant that the northerner's stone still shone as it should. He nodded to Raziel, who withdrew, their private ritual observed, as every day it was. It would never, ever do for the court to find out that Shalhassan was troubled by dreams of red wardstones.

Turning his thoughts to his daughter, Shalhassan drank. He approved her headstrong nature, indeed he had nurtured it, for no weakling dared sit on the Ivory Throne. Tantrums, though, were irresponsible, and this latest. . . . Tearing apart her chambers and whipping her women were one thing; rooms could be restored and servants were servants. Devorsh was a different matter; he was a good soldier in a country with remarkably few, and Shalhassan was not pleased to hear that his Captain of the Guard had just been garrotted by his daughter's mutes. Whatever the insult she might say he had given her, it was a rash and precipitate response.

He drained the blue cup and came to a decision.

She was growing too undisciplined; it was time to have her married. However strong a woman might be, she still needed a man by her side and in her bed. And the kingdom needed heirs. It was past time.

The wrestling had grown tedious. He gestured and the eidolath stopped the fight. The two slaves had been brave, though, he decided, and he freed them both. There was a polite murmur from the courtiers, an approving rustle of silk.

Turning away, he noticed that one of the wrestlers was a little tardy in his obeisance. The man may have been exhausted, or hurt, but the throne could not be compromised. At any time, in any way. He gestured again.

There *were* appropriate uses for the mutes and their garrottes. Sharra would just have to learn to discriminate.

———◆———

The knowledge of approaching death can come in many shapes, descending as a blessing or rearing up as an apparition of terror. It may sever like the sweep of a blade, or call as a perfect lover calls.

For Paul Schafer, who had chosen to be where he

was for reasons deeper than loss and more oblique than empathy for an aged King, the growing awareness that his body could not survive the Summer Tree came as a kind of relief: in this failure, at least, there could be no shame. There was no unworthiness in yielding to a god.

He was honest enough to realize that the exposure and the brutal heat, the thirst and immobility were themselves enough to kill him, and this he had known from the moment they bound him.

But the Summer Tree of Mörnirwood was more than all of these. Naked upon it in the blaze of day, Paul felt the ancient bark all along the planes of his body, and in that contact he apprehended power that made what strength he had its own. The Tree would not break him; instead he felt it reaching out, pulling him into itself, taking everything. Claiming him. He knew as well, somehow, that this was only the beginning, not even the second night. It was scarcely awake.

The God was coming, though. Paul could feel that slow approach along his flesh, in the running of his blood, and now there was thunder, too. Low yet, and muted, but there were two whole nights to come and all about him the Godwood vibrated soundlessly as it had not for years upon years, waiting, waiting for the God to come and claim his own, in darkness and forever, as was his due.

———◆———

The genial proprietor of the Black Boar was in a mood that bade fair to shatter his public image entirely. Under the circumstances, however, it was not entirely surprising that his countenance should display a distinctly forbidding mien as he surveyed his demesne in the morning light.

It was a festival. People drank during festivals. There were visitors in town, visitors with dry throats from the drought and a little money saved for this time. Money that might—money that *should*—be his, by all

the gods, if he hadn't been forced to close the Boar
for the day to redress the damage of the night before.

He worked them hard all day, even the ones with
broken bones and bashed pates from the brawl, and he
certainly wasted no sympathy on employees bemoan-
ing hangovers or lack of sleep. There was money being lost every moment he stayed closed, every
moment! And to add to the choler of his mood there
was a vile, vile rumor running through the capital that
bloody Gorlaes, the Chancellor, intended to slap a rationing law down on all liquids as soon as the fortnight's festival ended. Bloody drought. He attacked a
pile of debris in a corner as if it were the offending
Chancellor himself. Rationing, indeed! He'd like to
see Gorlaes try to ration Tegid's wine and ale, he'd
like to see him try! Why, the fat one had likely poured
a week's worth of beer over his posterior the night
before.

At the recollection, the owner of the Black Boar
succumbed to his first smile of the day, almost with
relief. It was hard work being furious. Eyeing the
room, hands on hips, he decided that they'd be able to
open within an hour or so of sundown; the day
wouldn't be a total loss.

So it was that as full dark cloaked the twisting lanes
of the old town, and torches and candles gleamed
through curtained windows, a bulky shadow moved
ponderously towards the recently reopened door of his
favorite tavern.

It was dark, though, in the alleys, and he was im-
peded a trifle by the effects of his wars the night before, and so Tegid almost fell as he stumbled into a
slight figure in the lane.

"By the horns of Cernan!" the great one spluttered.
"Mind your path. Few obstruct Tegid without peril!"

"Your pardon," the wretched obstacle murmured,
so low he was scarcely audible. "I fear I am in some
difficulty, and I. . . ."

The figure wavered, and Tegid put out an instinctive

hand of support. Then his bloodshot eyes finally adjusted to the shadows, and with a transcendent shock of awe, he saw the other speaker.

"Oh, Mörnir," Tegid whispered in disbelief, and then, for once, was speechless.

The slim figure before him nodded, with an effort. "Yes," he managed. "I am of the lios alfar. I—," he gasped with pain, then resumed, "—I have tidings that must . . . must reach the palace, and I am sorely hurt."

At which point, Tegid became aware that the hand he had laid upon the other's shoulder was sticky with fresh blood.

"Easy now," he said with clumsy tenderness. "Can you walk?"

"I have, so far, all day. But . . ." Brendel slipped to one knee, even as he spoke. "But as you see, I am. . . ."

There were tears in Tegid's eyes. "Come, then," he murmured, like a lover. And lifting the mangled body effortlessly, Tegid of Rhoden, named Breakwind, called the Boaster, cradled the lios alfar in his massive arms and bore him towards the brilliant glitter of the castle.

◆

"I dreamt again," Kim said. "A swan." It was dark outside the cottage. She had been silent all day, had walked alone by the lake. Throwing pebbles.

"What color?" Ysanne asked, from the rocking chair by the hearth.

"Black."

"I dreamt her as well. It is a bad thing."

"What is it? Eilathen never showed me this."

There were two candles in the room. They flickered and dwindled as Ysanne told her about Avaia and Lauriel the White. At intervals they heard thunder, far off.

◆

It was still a festival, and though the King looked haggard and desiccated in his seat at the high table,

the Great Hall gleamed richly by torchlight, festooned
as it was with hangings of red and gold silk. Despite
their morose King and his unwontedly bemused Chancellor, the court of Ailell was determined to enjoy itself. The players in the musicians' gallery overhead
were in merry form, and even though dinner had not
yet begun, the pages were being kept busy running
back and forth with wine.

Kevin Laine, eschewing both his seat at the high
table as a guest of honor and the not-very-subtle invitation of the Lady Rheva, had decided to ignore pro-
tocol by opting for a masculine enclave partway down
one of the two tables that ran along the hall. Seated
between Matt Sören and Diarmuid's big, broken-nosed
lieutenant, Coll, he attempted to preserve a cheerful
appearance, but the fact that no one had seen Paul
Schafer since last night was building into a real source
of anxiety. Jennifer, too: where the hell was she?

On the other hand, there were still many people fil-
ing into the room, and Jen, he had cause to remember,
was seldom on time for anything, let alone early. Kevin
drained his wine goblet for the third time and decided
that he was becoming altogether too much of a wor-
rier.

At which point Matt Sören asked, "Have you seen
Jennifer?" and Kevin abruptly changed his mind.

"No," he said. "I was at the Boar last night, and
then seeing the barracks and the armory with Carde
and Erron today. Why? Do you—?"

"She went riding with one of the ladies-in-waiting
yesterday. Drance was with them."

"He's a good man," Coll said reassuringly, from
the other side.

"Well, has anyone seen them? Was she in her room
last night?" Kevin asked.

Coll grinned. "That wouldn't prove much, would
it? A lot of us weren't in our beds last night." He
laughed and clapped Kevin on the shoulder. "Cheer
up!'

Kevin shook his head. Dave. Paul. Now Jen.

"Riding, you said?" He turned to Matt. "Has anyone checked the stables? Are the horses back?"

Sören looked at him. "No," he said softly. "We haven't—but I think I want to now. Come on!" He was already pushing his chair back.

They rose together and so were on their feet when the sudden babble of sound came from the east doorway, and the courtiers and ladies gathered there moved aside for the torches to reveal the enormous figure with a bloodstained body in his arms.

Everything stopped. In the silence Tegid moved slowly forward between the long tables to stand before Ailell.

"Look!" he cried, grief raw in his voice. "My lord King, here is one of the lios alfar, and see what they have done to him!"

The King was ashen. Trembling, he rose. "Na-Brendel?" he croaked. "Oh, Mörnir. Is he . . . ?"

"No," a faint, clear voice replied. "I am not dead, though I might yet wish to be. Let me stand to give my tidings."

Gently, Tegid lowered the lios to stand on the mosaic-inlaid floor, and then, kneeling awkwardly, he offered his shoulder for support.

Brendel closed his eyes and drew a breath. And when he spoke again his voice, by some act of pure will, rang out strong and clear beneath the windows of Delevan.

"Treachery, High King. Treachery and death I bring you, and tidings of the Dark. We spoke, you and I, four nights past, of svart alfar outside Pendaran Wood. High King, there have been svarts outside your walls this day, and wolves with them. We were attacked before dawn and all my people are slain!"

He stopped. A sound like the moaning of wind before a storm ran through the hall.

Ailell has sunk back into his chair, his eyes bleak and hollow. Brendel lifted his head and looked at him. "There is an empty seat at your table, High King. I must tell you that it stands empty for a traitor. Look to your own hearth, Ailell! Metran, your First Mage, is allied with the Dark. He has deceived you all!" There were cries at that, of anger and dismay.

"Hold!" It was Diarmuid, on his feet and facing the lios. His eyes flashed, but his voice was under tight control. "You said the Dark. Who?"

Once more the silence stretched. Then Brendel spoke. "I would not have ever wanted to bear this tale to the world. I spoke of svart alfar and wolves attacking us. We would not have died had it been only them. There was something else. A giant wolf, with silver on his head like a brand against the black. Then I saw him after with Metran and I knew him, for he had taken back his true form. I must tell you that the Wolflord of the andain has come among us again: Galadan has returned."

"Accursed be his name!" someone cried, and Kevin saw that it was Matt. "How can this be? He died at Andarien a thousand years ago."

"So thought we all," said Brendel, turning to the Dwarf. "But I saw him today, and this wound is his." He touched his torn shoulder. Then, "There is more. Something else came today and spoke with both of them."

Once more Brendel hesitated. And this time his eyes, dark-hued, went to Kevin's face.

"It was the black swan," he said, and a stillness fell upon stillness. "Avaia. She carried away Jennifer, your friend, the golden one. They had come for her, why I know not, but we were too few, too few against the Wolflord, and so my brethren are all dead, and she is gone. And the Dark is abroad in the world again."

Kevin, white with dread, looked at the maimed figure of the lios. "Where?" he gasped, in a voice that shocked him.

Brendel shook his head wearily. "I could not hear their words. Black Avaia took her north. Could I have stayed her flight, I would have died to do so. Oh, believe me,'' the lios alfar's voice faltered. ''Your grief is mine, and mine may tear the fabric of my soul apart. Twenty of my people have died, and it is in my heart that they are not the last. We are the Children of Light, and the Dark is rising. I must return to Daniloth. But,'' and now his voice grew strong again, ''an oath I will swear before you now. She was in my care. I shall find her, or avenge her, or die in the attempt.'' And Brendel cried then, so that the Great Hall echoed to the sound: ''We shall fight them as we did before! As we always have!''

The words rang among them like a stern bell of defiance, and in Kevin Laine they lit a fire he did not know lay within him.

''Not alone!'' he cried, his own voice pitched to carry. ''If you share my grief, I will share yours. And others here will, too, I think.''

''Aye!'' boomed Matt Sören beside him.

''All of us!'' cried Diarmuid, Prince of Brennin. ''When the lios are slain in Brennin, the High Kingdom goes to war!''

A mighty roar exploded at those words. Building and building in a wave of fury it climbed to the highest windows of Delevan and resounded through the hall.

It drowned, quite completely, the despairing words of the High King.

''Oh, Mörnir,'' whispered Ailell, clutching his hands together in his lap. ''What have I done? Where is Loren? What have I done?''

◆

There had been light, now there was not. One measured time in such ways. There were stars in the space above the trees; no moon yet, and only a thin one later, for tomorrow would be the night of the new moon.

His last night, if he lived through this one.

The Tree was a part of him now, another name, a summoning. He almost heard a meaning in the breath-

ing of the forest all around him, but his mind was
stretched and flattened, he could not reach to it, he
could only endure, and hold the wall of memory as
best he might.

One more night. After which there would be no music to be laid open by, no highways to forget, no rain,
no sirens, none, no Rachel. One more night at most,
for he wasn't sure he could survive another day like
the last.

Though truly he would try: for the old King, and
the slain farmer, and the faces he'd seen on the roads.
Better to die for a reason, and with what one could
retain of pride. Better, surely, though he could not say
why.

Now I give you to Mörnir, Ailell had said. Which
meant he was a gift, an offering, and it was all waste
if he died too soon. So he had to hold to life, hold the
wall, hold for the God, for he was the God's to claim,
and there was thunder now. It seemed at times to come
from within the Tree, which meant, in the way of
things, from within himself. If only there could be rain
before he died, he might find some kind of peace at
the end. It had rained, though, when *she* died, it had
rained all night.

His eyes were hurting now. He closed them, but that
was no good, either, because she was waiting there,
with music. Once, earlier, he had wanted to call her
name in the wood, as he had not beside the open grave,
to feel it on his lips again as he had not since; to burn
his dry soul with her. Burn, since he could not cry.

Silence, of course. One did not do any such thing.
One opened one's eyes instead on the Summer Tree,
in the deep of Mörnirwood, and one saw a man come
forward from among the trees.

It was very dark, he could not see who it was, but
the faint starlight reflected from silver hair and so he
thought. . . .

"Loren?" he tried, but scarcely any sound escaped
his cracked lips. He tried to wet them, but he had no

moisture, he was dry. Then the figure came nearer, to stand in the starlight below where he was bound, and Paul saw that he had been wrong. The eyes that met his own were not those of the mage, and, looking into them, he did know fear then, for it should not end so, truly it should not. But the man below stood as if cloaked in power, even in that place, even in the glade of the Summer Tree, and in the dark eyes Paul saw his death.

Then the figure spoke. "I cannot allow it," he said, with finality. "You have courage, and something else, I think. Almost you are one of us, and it might have been that we could have shared something, you and I. Not now, though. This I cannot allow. You are calling a force too strong for the knowing, and it must not be wakened. Not when I am so near. Will you believe," the voice said, low and assured, "that I am sorry to have to kill you?"

Paul moved his lips. "Who?" he asked, the sound a scrape in his throat.

The other smiled at that. "Names matter to you? They should. It is Galadan who has come, and I fear it is the end."

Bound and utterly helpless, Paul saw the elegant fig-ure draw a knife from his belt. "It will be clean, I promise you," he said. "Did you not come here for release? I will give it to you." Their eyes locked once more. It was a dream, it was so like a dream, so dark, blurred, shadowed. He closed his eyes; one closed one's eyes to dream. She was there, of course, but it was ending, so all right then, fine, let it end on her.

A moment passed. No blade, no severing. Then Galadan spoke again, but not to him, and in a different voice.

"You?" he said. "Here? Now I understand."

For reply there came only a deep, rumbling growl. His heart leaping, Paul opened his eyes. In the clear-ing facing Galadan was the grey dog he had seen on the palace wall.

Gazing at the dog, Galadan spoke again. "It was written in wind and fire long ago that we should meet," he said. "And here is as fit a place as any in all the worlds. Would you guard the sacrifice? Then your blood is the gateway to my desire. Come, and I shall drink it now!"

He placed a hand over his heart and made a twisting gesture, and after a brief blurring of space, there stood a moment later, where he had been, a wolf so large it dwarfed the grey figure of the dog. And the wolf had a splash of silver between its ears.

One endless moment the animals faced each other, and Paul realized that the Godwood had gone deathly still. Then Galadan howled so as to chill the heart, and leaped to attack.

There took place then a battle foretold in the first depths of time by the twin goddesses of war, who are named in all the worlds as Macha and Nemain. A portent it was to be, a presaging of the greatest war of all, this coming together in darkness of the wolf, who was a man whose spirit was annihilation, and the grey dog, who had been called by many names but was always the Companion.

The battle the two goddesses foreknew—for war was their demesne—but not the resolution. A portent then, a presaging, a beginning.

And so it came to pass that wolf and dog met at last in Fionavar, first of all the worlds, and below the Summer Tree they ripped and tore at one another with such fury that soon dark blood soaked the glade under the stars.

Again and again they hurled themselves upon each other, black on grey, and Paul, straining to see, felt his heart go out to the dog with all the force of his being. He remembered the loss he had seen in its eyes, and he saw now, even in the shadows, as the animals rolled over and over, biting and grappling, engaging and recoiling in desperate frenzy, that the wolf was too large.

They were both black now, for the light grey fur of the dog was matted and dark with its own blood. Still it fought, eluding and atacking, summoning a courage, embodying a gallantry of defiance that hurt to see, it was so noble and so doomed.

The wolf was bleeding, too, and its flesh was ripped and torn, but it was so much larger; and more, more than that, Galadan carried within himself a power that went far deeper than tooth and gashing claw.

Paul became aware that his bound hands were torn and bleeding. Unconsciously he had been struggling to free himself, to go to the aid of the dog who was dying in his defence. The bonds held, though, and so, too, did the prophecy, for this was to be wolf and dog alone, and so it was.

Through the night it continued. Weary and scored with wounds, the grey dog fought on; but its attacks were parried more easily now, its defences were more agonizing, more narrowly averting the final closing of jaw on jugular. It could only be a question of time, Paul realized, grieving and forced to bear witness. It hurt so much, so much. . . .

"Fight!" he screamed suddenly, his throat raw with effort. "Go on! I'll hold if you can—I'll make it through tomorrow night. In the name of the God, I swear it. Give me till tomorrow and I'll bring you rain."

For a moment the animals were checked by the force of his cry. Then, limp and drained, Paul saw with agony that it was the wolf who lifted a head to look at him, a terrible smile distorting its face. Then it turned back, back for the last attack, a force of fury, of annihilation. Galadan who had returned. It was a charge of uncoiled power, not to be denied or withstood.

And yet it was.

The dog, too, had heard Paul's cry; without the strength to raise its head in reply, it found yet in the words, in the desperate, scarcely articulate vow, a pure white power of its own; and reaching back, far back into its own long history of battle and loss, the grey dog met the wolf for the last time with a spirit of utmost denial, and the earth shook beneath them as they crashed together.

Over and over on the sodden ground they rolled, indistinguishable, one contorted shape that embodied all the endless conflict of Light and Dark in all the turning worlds.

Then the world turned enough, finally, for the moon to rise above the trees.

Only a crescent she was, the last thin, pale sliver before the dark of tomorrow. But she was still there, still glorious, a light. And Paul, looking up, understood then, from a deep place in his soul, that just as the Tree belonged to Mörnir, so did the moon to the Mother; and when the crescent moon shone above the Summer Tree, then was the banner of Brennin made real in that wood.

In silence, in awe, in deepest humility, he watched at length as one dark, blood-spattered animal disengaged from the other. It limped, tail down, to the edge of the glade, and when it turned to look back, Paul saw a splash of silver between its ears. With a snarl of rage, Galadan fled the wood.

The dog could barely stand. It breathed with a sucking heave of flank and sides that Paul ached to see. It was so terribly hurt, it was scarcely alive; the blood so thick upon it he could not see an untorn patch of fur.

But it *was* alive, and it came haltingly over to gaze up at him, lifting its torn head under the light and succor of the moon it had waited for. In that moment, Paul Schafer felt his own cracked, dry soul open up again to love as he looked down upon the dog.

For the second time their eyes met, and this time Paul did not back away. He took in the loss he saw, all of it, the pain endured for him and endured long before him, and with the first power of the Tree, he made it his own.

"Oh, brave," he said, finding that he could speak. "There can never have been a thing so brave. Go now, for it is my turn, and I will keep faith. I'll hold now, until tomorrow night, for you as much as anything."

The dog looked at him, the eyes clouded with pain, but still deep with intelligence, and Paul knew he was understood.

"Goodbye," he whispered, a kind of caress in the word.

And in response the grey dog threw back its proud head and howled: a cry of triumph and farewell, so loud and clear it filled all the Godwood and then echoed far beyond it, beyond the bounds of the worlds, even, hurtling into time and space, that the goddesses might hear it, and know.

———◆———

In the taverns of Paras Derval, the rumor of war spread like a fire in dry grass. Svarts had been seen, and giant wolves, and lios alfar had walked in the city and been slain in the land. Diarmuid, the Prince, had sworn vengeance. All over the capital, swords and spears were rescued from places where they had rusted long years. Anvil Lane would resound in the morning to the clanging sound of fevered preparation.

For Karsh, the tanner, though, there was other news that eclipsed even the rumors, and on the crest of it he was engaged in drinking himself happily to incapacity, and buying, with profoundly uncharacteristic largess, drinks for every man in earshot.

He had cause, they all agreed. It wasn't every day that saw a man's daughter initiated as an acolyte in the Temple of the Mother. The more so, when Jaelle, the High Priestess herself, had summoned her.

It was an honor, they all chorused, toasting Karsh amid the bustle of war talk. It was more, the tanner said, toasting back: for a man with four daughters, it was a blessing from the gods. From the Goddess, he corrected himself owlishly, and brought everyone another round with money marked until that day for her dowry.

In the sanctuary the newest acolyte drifted towards the sleep of the utterly exhausted. In her fourteen years she had never known a day like the one just past. Tears and pride, unexpected fear, and then laughter had all been part of it.

The ceremony she had barely understood, for they had given her a drink that made the domed room spin softly, though not unpleasantly. The axe she remembered, the chanting of the grey-clad priestesses of whose number she would soon be one, and then the voice, cold and powerful, of the High Priestess in her white robe.

She didn't remember when she had been cut, but the wound on her wrist throbbed under the cloth bandage. It was necessary, they had explained: blood to bind.

Leila hadn't bothered telling them that she had always known that.

Long past midnight Jaelle woke in the stillness of the Temple. High Priestess of Brennin, and one of the Mormae of Gwen Ystrat, she could not fail to hear, though no one else in Paras Derval would, the supernatural howling of a dog, as the moon shone down upon the Summer Tree.

She could hear it, but she did not understand, and lying in her bed she chafed and raged at her inability. There was something happening. Forces were abroad. She could feel power gathering like a storm.

She needed a Seer, by all the names of the Mother, she needed one. But there was only the hag, and she had sold herself. In the darkness of her room, the High Priestess clenched her long fingers in deep, unending bitterness. She had *need,* and was being denied. She was blind.

Lost and forever, she cursed again, and lay awake all the rest of the night, feeling it gathering, gathering.

---◆---

Kimberly thought she was dreaming. The same dream as two nights before, when the howling had shattered her vision of Paul and Ailell. She heard the dog, but this time she did not wake. Had she done so, she would have seen the Baelrath glowering ominously on her hand.

In the barn, among the close, familiar smells of the animals, Tyrth the servant did awaken. One moment he lay motionless, disbelieving, as the inner echoes of that great cry faded, then an expression crossed his face that was composed of many elements, but had more of longing than anything else. He swung out of bed, dressed quickly, and left the barn.

He limped across the yard and through the gate, closing it behind him. Only when he was in the strand of trees, and so hidden from the cottage, did the limp disappear. At which point he began to run, very swiftly, in the direction of the thunder.

Alone of those who heard the dog, Ysanne the Seer, awake in her bed as well, knew what that cry of pain and pride truly meant.

She heard Tyrth cross the yard, limping west, and she knew what that meant, too. There were so many unexpected griefs, she thought, so many different things to pity.

Not least, what she had now, at last, to do. For the storm was upon them, that cry in the wood was the harbinger, and so it was full time, and this night would see her do what she had seen long ago.

Not for herself did she grieve; there had been true fear at her first foreknowledge, and an echo of it when she had seen the girl in the Great Hall, but it had passed. The thing was very dark, but no longer terrifying; long ago she had known what would come.

It would be hard, though, for the girl. It would be hard in every way, but against what had begun tonight with the dog and the wolf. . . . It was going to be hard for all of them. She could not help that; one thing only, she could do.

There was a stranger dying on the Tree. She shook her head; that, that was the deepest thing of all, and he was the one she had not been able to read, not that it mattered now. As to that, only the sporadic thunder mattered, thunder in a clear, starry sky. Mörnir would walk tomorrow, if the stranger held, and no one, not one of them could tell what that might mean. The God was outside of them.

But the girl. The girl was something else, and her Ysanne could see, had seen many times. She rose quietly and walked to stand over Kim. She saw the vellin stone on the slim wrist, and the Baelrath glowing on one finger, and she thought of Macha and Red Nemain and their prophecy.

She thought of Raederth then, for the first time that night. An old, old sorrow. Fifty years, but still. Lost once, fifty years ago on the far side of Night, and now. . . . But the dog had howled in the wood, it was full, fullest time, and she had known for very long what was to come. There was no terror any more, only loss, and there had always been loss.

Kimberly stirred on her pillow. So young, the Seer thought. It was all so sad, but she knew, truly, of no other way, for she had lied the day before: it was not merely a matter of time before the girl could know the woven patterns of Fionavar as she needed to. It could not be. Oh, how could it ever be?

The girl was needed. She was a Seer, and more. The crossing bore witness, the pain of the land, the testimony in Eilathen's eyes. She was needed, but not ready, not complete, and the old woman knew one way, and only one, to do the last thing necessary.

The cat was awake, watching her with knowing eyes from the window sill. It was very dark; tomorrow there would be no moon. It was time, past time.

She laid a hand then, and it was very steady, upon Kimberly's forehead, where the single vertical line showed when she was distressed. Ysanne's fingers, still beautiful, traced a sign lightly and irrevocably on the unfurrowed brow. Kimberly slept. A gentle smile lit the Seer's face as she withdrew.

"Sleep child," she murmured. "You have need, for the way is dark and there will be fire ere the end, and a breaking of the heart. Grieve not in the morning for my soul; my dream is done, my dreaming. May the Weaver name you his, and shield you from the Dark all your days."

Then there was silence in the room. The cat watched from the window. *"It is done,"* Ysanne said, to the room, the night, the summer stars, to all her ghosts, and to the one loved man, now to be lost forever among the dead.

With care she opened the secret entrance to the chamber below, and went slowly down the stone stairs to where Colan's dagger lay, bright still in its sheath of a thousand years.

———◆———

There was a very great deal of pain now. The moon has passed from overhead. His last moon, he realized, though thought was difficult. Consciousness was going to become a transient condition, a very hard thing, and already, with a long way yet to go, he was beginning to hallucinate. Colors, sounds. The trunk of the Tree seemed to have grown fingers, rough like bark, that wrapped themselves around him. He was touching the Tree everywhere now. Once, for a long spell, he thought he was inside it, looking out, not bound upon it. He thought he *was* the Summer Tree.

He was truly not afraid of dying, only of dying too soon. He had sworn an oath. But it was so hard to hold onto his mind, to hold his will to living another night. So much easier to let go, to leave the pain behind. Already the dog and wolf seemed to have been half dreamt, though he knew the battle had ended only hours before. There was dried blood on his wrists from when he had tried to free himself.

When the second man appeared before him, he was sure it was a vision. He was so far gone. *Popular attraction,* a faint, fading capacity of his mind mocked. *Come see the hanging man!*

This man had a beard, and deep-set dark eyes, and didn't seem about to change into an animal. He just stood there, looking up. A very boring vision. The trees were loud in the wind; there was thunder, he could feel it.

Paul made an effort, moving his head back and forth to clear it. His eyes hurt, for some reason, but he could see. And what he saw on the face of the figure below was an expression of such appalling, balked desire that the hair rose up on his neck. He should know who this was, he should. If his mind were working, he would know, but it was too hard, it was hopelessly beyond him.

"You have stolen my death," the figure said.

Paul closed his eyes. He was too far away from this. Too far down the road. He was incapable of explaining, unable to do more than try to endure.

An oath. He had sworn an oath. What did an oath mean? A whole day more, it meant. And a third night.

Some time later his eyes seemed to be open again and he saw, with uttermost relief, that he was alone. There was grey in the eastern sky; one more, one last.

And this was the second night of Pwyll the Stranger on the Summer Tree.

Chapter 9

In the morning came something unheard of: a hot, dry wind, bitter and unsettling, swept down into Paras Derval from the north.

No one could remember a hot north wind before. It carried with it the dust of bone-bare farms, so the air darkened that day, even at noon, and the high sun shone balefully orange through the obscuring haze.

The thunder continued, almost a mockery. There were no clouds.

"With all respect, and such-like sentiments," Diarmuid said from by the window, his tone insolent and angry, "We are wasting time." He looked dishevelled and dangerous; he was also, Kevin realized with dismay, a little drunk.

From his seat at the head of the council table, Ailell ignored his heir. Kevin, still not sure why he'd been invited here, saw two bright spots of red on the cheeks of the old King. Ailell looked terrible; he seemed to have shrivelled overnight.

Two more men entered the room: a tall, clever-looking man, and beside him, a portly, affable fellow. The other mage, Kevin guessed: Teyrnon, with Barak, his source. Gorlaes, the Chancellor, made the introductions and it turned out he was right, except the innocuous-seeming fat man was the mage, and not the other way around.

Loren was still away, but Matt was in the room, and so, too, were a number of other dignitaries. Kevin recognized Mabon, the Duke of Rhoden, Ailell's cousin, and beyond him was Niavin of Seresh. The ruddy man with the salt-and-pepper beard was Ceredur, who had been made North Warden after Diarmuid's brother was exiled. He'd seen them at last night's banquet. Their expressions were very different now.

It was Jaelle, they were waiting for, and as the moments passed, Kevin, too, began to grow impatient with apprehension.

"My lord," he said abruptly to the King, "while we wait—who is Galadan? I feel completely ignorant."

It was Gorlaes who answered. Ailell was sunken in silence, and Diarmuid was still sulking by the window. "He is a force of Darkness from long ago. A very great power, though he did not always serve the Dark," the Chancellor said. "He is one of the andain—child of a mortal woman and a god. In older days there were not a few such unions. The andain are a difficult race, moving easily in no world at all. Galadan became their Lord, by far the most powerful of them all, and said to be the most subtle mind in Fionavar. Then something changed him."

"An understatement, that," murmured Teyrnon.

"I suppose," said Gorlaes. "What happened is that he fell in love with Lisen of the Wood. And when she rejected him and bound herself instead to a mortal, Amairgen Whitebranch, first of the mages, Galadan vowed the most complete vengeance ever sworn." The Chancellor's voice took on a note of awe. "Galadan swore that the world that witnessed his humiliation would cease to exist."

There was a silence. Kevin could think of nothing to say. Nothing at all.

Teyrnon took up the tale. "In the time of the Bael Rangat he was first lieutenant to Rakoth and most terrible of his servants. He had the power to take on the shape of a wolf, and so he commanded them all.

His purposes, though, were at odds with his master's, for though the Unraveller sought rule for lust of power and domination, Galadan would have conquered to utterly destroy.''

"They fought?'' Kevin hazarded.

Teyrnon shook his head. "One did not pitch oneself against Rakoth. Galadan has very great powers, and if he has joined the svart alfar to his wolves in war upon us, then we are in danger indeed; but Rakoth, whom the stones bind, is outside the Tapestry. There is no thread with his name upon it. He cannot die, and none could ever set his will against him.''

"Amairgen did,'' said Diarmuid from the window.

"And died,'' Teyrnon replied, not ungently.

"There are worse things,'' the Prince snapped.

At that, Ailell stirred. Before he could speak, though, the door opened and Jaelle swept into the room. She nodded briefly to the King, acknowledged no one else, and slipped into the chair left for her at one end of the long table.

"Thank you for hurrying,'' Diarmuid murmured, coming to take his chair at Ailell's right hand. Jaelle merely smiled. It was not a pleasant smile.

"Well, now,'' said the King, clearing his throat, "it seems to me that the best way to proceed is to spend this morning in a careful review—''

"In the name of the Weaver and the Loom, Father!'' Diarmuid's fist crashed on the table. "We all know what has happened! What is there to review? I swore an oath last night we would aid the lios, and—''

"A premature oath, Prince Diarmuid,'' Gorlaes interrupted. "And not one within your power to swear.''

"No?'' said the Prince softly. "Then let me remind you—let us indeed carefully review,'' he amended delicately, "what has happened. One of my men is dead. One of the ladies of this court is dead. A svart alfar was within the palace grounds six nights ago.'' He was ticking them off on his fingers. "Lios alfar have died in Brennin. Galadan has returned. Avaia has returned.

Our First Mage is a proven traitor. A guest-friend of
this House has been torn away from us—a guest-friend,
I pause to point out, of our radiant High Priestess as
well. Which should mean something, unless she takes
such things to be meaningless.''

"I do not," Jaelle snapped through clenched teeth.

"No?" the Prince said, his eyebrows raised. "What
a surprise. I thought you might regard it as of the same
importance as arriving to a War Council on time."

"It isn't yet a Council of War," Duke Ceredur said
bluntly. "Though to be truthful, I am with the Prince—
I think we should have the country on war footing
immediately."

There was a grunt of agreement from Matt Sören.
Teyrnon, though, shook his round honest head. "There
is too much fear in the city," he demurred, "and it is
going to spread within days throughout the country."
Niavin, Duke of Seresh, was nodding agreement.
"Unless we know exactly what we are doing and what
we face, I think we must take care not to panic them,"
the chubby mage concluded.

"We *do* know what we face!" Diarmuid shot back.
"Galadan was seen. He was *seen!* I say we summon
the Dalrei, make league with the lios, and seek the
Wolflord wherever he goes and crush him now!"

"Amazing," Jaelle murmured drily in the pause that
ensued, "how impetuous younger sons tend to be, especially when they have been drinking."

"Go gently, sweetling," the Prince said softly. "I
will not brook that from anyone. You, least of all, my
midnight moonchild."

Kevin exploded. "Will you two listen to yourselves?
Don't you understand: Jennifer is gone! We've got to
do something besides bicker, for God's sake!"

"I quite agree," Teyrnon said sternly. "May I suggest that we invite our friend from Daniloth to join us
if he is able. We should seek the views of the lios on
this."

"You may seek their views," said Ailell dan Art,

suddenly rising to tower above them all, "and I would
have his thoughts reported to me later, Teyrnon. But I
have decided to adjourn this Council until this same
time tomorrow. You all have leave to go."

"Father—" Diarmuid began, stammering with con-
sternation.

"No words!" Ailell said harshly, and his eyes
gleamed in his bony face. "I am still High King in
Brennin, let all of you remember it!"

"We do, my dearest lord," said a familiar voice
from the door. "We all do," Loren Silvercloak went
on, "but Galadan is far too great a power for us to
delay without cause."

Dusty and travel-stained, his eyes hollow with exhaustion, the mage ignored the fierce reaction to his
arrival and gazed only at the King. There was, Kevin
realized, a sudden surge of relief in the room; he felt
it within himself. Loren was back. It made a very great
difference.

Matt Sören had risen to stand beside the mage, eyeing his friend with a grimly worried expression. Lor-
en's weariness was palpable, but he seemed to gather
his resources, and turned among all that company to
look at Kevin.

"I am sorry," he said simply. "I am deeply sorry."

Kevin nodded jerkily. "I know," he whispered. That
was all; they both turned to the King.

"Since when need the High King explain himself?" Ailell said, but his brief assertion of control
seemed to have drained him; his tone was querulous,
not commanding.

"He need not, my lord. But if he does, his subjects
and advisers may sometimes be of greater aid." The
mage had come several steps into the room.

"Sometimes," the King replied. "But at other times
there are things they do not and should not know."
Kevin saw Gorlaes shift in his seat. He took a chance.

"But the Chancellor knows, my lord. Should not

your other counsellors? Forgive my presumption, but a woman I love is gone, High King.''

Ailell regarded him for a long time without speaking. Then he gave a small nod. "Well spoken," he said. "Indeed, the only person here who truly has a right to be told is you, but I will do as you ask.''

"My lord!" Gorlaes began urgently.

Ailell raised a hand, quelling him.

In the ensuing silence there came a distant roll of thunder.

"Can you not hear it?" the High King whispered on a rising note. "Listen! The God is coming. If the offering holds, he comes tonight. This will be the third night. How can we act before we know?"

They were all on their feet.

"Someone is on the Tree," Loren said flatly.

The King nodded.

"My brother?" asked Diarmuid, his face ashen.

"No," said Ailell, and turned to Kevin.

It took a moment, then everything fell into place. "Oh, God," Kevin cried. "It's Paul!" and he lowered his face into his hands.

———◆———

Kimberly woke knowing.

Who kills without love shall surely die, Seithr the Dwarf-King had said to Colan the Beloved long ago. And then, lowering his voice, he had added for only the son of Conary to hear, "Who dies with love may make of his soul a gift to the one marked with the pattern on the dagger's haft.''

"A rich gift," had murmured Colan.

"Richer than you know. Once given, the soul is gone. It is lost to time. There can be no passage beyond the walls of Night to find light at the Weaver's side.''

Conary's son had bowed very low. "I thank you," he said. "Double-edged the knife, and double-edged the gift. Mörnir grant us the sight to use it truly.''

* * *

Even before she looked, Kim knew that her hair was white. Lying in bed that first morning she cried, though silently and not for long. There was much to be done. Even with the vellin on her wrist, she felt the day like a fever. She would be unworthy of the gift if she were undone by mourning.

So she rose up, Seer of Brennin, newest dreamer of the dream, to begin what Ysanne had died to allow her to do.

More than died.

There are kinds of action, for good or ill, that lie so far outside the boundaries of normal behavior that they force us, in acknowledging that they have occurred, to restructure our own understanding of reality. We have to make room for them.

This, Kim thought, is what Ysanne had done. With an act of love so great—and not just for her—it could scarcely be assimilated, she had stripped her soul of any place it held in time. She was gone, utterly. Not just from life, but more, much more, as Kim now knew—from death as well; from what lay after in the patterns of the Weaver for his children.

Instead, the Seer had given all she could to Kim, had given all. No longer could Kim say she was not of Fionavar, for within her now pulsed an intuitive understanding of this world more deep even than the knowledge of her own. Looking now at a bannion, she would know what it was; she understood the vellin on her wrist, something of the wild Baelrath on her finger; and one day she would know who was to bear the Circlet of Lisen and tread the darkest path of all. Raederth's words; Raederth whom Ysanne had lost again, that Kim might have this.

Which was so unfair. What right, what possible right had the Seer had to make such a sacrifice? To impose with this impossible gift, such a burden? How had she presumed to decide for Kim?

The answer, though, was easy enough after a while: she hadn't. Kim could go, leave, deny. She could cross home as planed and dye her hair, or leave it as it was and go New Wave if she preferred. Nothing had changed.

Except, of course, that everything had. *How can you tell the dancer from the dance?* she had read somewhere. Or the dreamer from the dream, she amended, feeling a little lost. Because the answer to that was easiest of all.

You can't.

Some time later she laid her hand, in the way she now knew, upon the slab below the table, and saw the door appear.

Down the worn stone stairs she went, in her turn. Lisen's Light showed her the way. The dagger would be there, she knew, with red blood on the silver-blue thieren of the blade. There would be no body, though, for Ysanne the Seer, having died with love and by that blade, had taken herself beyond the walls of time, where she could not be followed. Lost and forever. It was final, absolute. It was ended.

And she was left here in the first world of them all, bearing the burden of that.

She cleaned Lökdal and sheathed it to a sound like a harpstring. She put it back in the cabinet. Then she went up the stairs again towards the world that needed her, all the worlds that needed what it seemed she was.

———◆———

"Oh, God," Kevin said. "It's Paul!"

A stunned silence descended, overwhelming in its import. This was something for which none of them could have prepared. I should have known, Kevin was thinking, though. I should have figured it out when he first told me about the Tree. A bitterness scaling towards rage pulled his head up. . . .

"That must have been some chess game," he said savagely to the King.

"It was," Ailell said simply. Then, "He came to

me and offered. I would never have asked, or even thought to ask. Will you believe this?''

And of course he did. It fit too well. The attack was unfair, because Paul would have done what he wanted to, exactly what he wanted to, and this was a better way to die than falling from a rope down a cliff. As such things were measured, and he supposed they could be measured. It hurt, though, it really hurt, and—

"No!" said Loren decisively. "It must be stopped. This we cannot do. He is not even one of us, my lord. We cannot lay our griefs upon him in this way. He must be taken down. This is a guest of your House, Ailell. Of our world. What were you thinking of?''

"Of our world. Of my House. Of my people. He came to me, Silvercloak.''

"And should have been refused!''

"Loren, it was a true offering.'' The speaker was Gorlaes, his voice unwontedly diffident.

"You were there?'' the mage bristled.

"I bound him. He walked past us to the Tree. It was as if he were alone. I know not how, and I am afraid here speaking of it, as I was in the Godwood, but I swear it is a proper offering.''

"No," Loren said again, his face sharp with emotion. "He cannot possibly understand what he is doing. My lord, he must be taken down before he dies.''

"It is his own death, Loren. His chosen gift. Would you presume to strip it from him?'' Ailell's eyes were so old, so weary.

"I would," the mage replied. "He was not brought here to die for us.''

It was time to speak.

"Maybe not,'' Kevin said, forcing the words out, stumbling and in pain. "But I think that is why he came.'' He was losing them both. Jennifer. Now Paul, too. His heart was sore. "If he went, he went knowing, and because he wanted to. Let him die for you, if he can't live for himself. Leave him, Loren. Let him go.''

He didn't bother trying to hide the tears, not even from Jaelle, whose eyes on his face were so cold.

"Kevin," said the mage gently, "it is a very bad death. No one lasts the three—it will be waste and to no point. Let me take him down.''

"It is not for you to choose, Silvercloak," Jaelle spoke then. "Nor for this one, either.''

Loren turned, his eyes hard as flint. "If I decide to bring him down,'' he said driving the words into her, "then it will be necessary for you to kill me to prevent it.''

"Careful, mage,'' Gorlaes cautioned, though mildly. "That is close to treason. The High King has acted here. Would you undo what he has done?''

None of them seemed to be getting the point. "No one has acted but Paul,'' Kevin said. He felt drained now, but completely unsurprised. He really should have known this was coming. "Loren, if anyone understood this, it was him. If he lasts three nights, will there be rain?''

"There might be.'' It was the King. "This is wild magic, we cannot know.''

"Blood magic,'' Loren amended bitterly.

Teyrnon shook his head. "The God is wild, though there may be blood.''

"He can't last, though,'' Diarmuid said, his voice sober. He looked at Kevin. "You said yourself, he's been ill.''

A cracked, high laugh escaped Kevin at that.

"Never stopped him,'' he said fiercely, feeling it so hard. The stubborn, brave, son of a bitch!''

The love in the harsh words reached through to all of them, it could not help but do so; and it had to be acknowledged. Even by Jaelle and, in a very different way, by Loren Silvercloak.

"Very well,'' said the mage at last. He sank into a

chair. "Oh, Kevin. They will sing of him here as long as Brennin lasts, regardless of the end."

"Songs," said Kevin. "Songs only mess you up." It was too much effort not to ache; he let it sweep over him. Sometimes, his father had said, you can't do anything. *Oh, Abba,* he thought, far away and alone inside the hurt.

"Tomorrow," Ailell the High King said, rising again, gaunt and tall. "I will meet you here at sunrise tomorrow. We will see what the night brings."

It was a dismissal. They withdrew, leaving the King sitting at the last alone in his council chamber with his years, his self-contempt, and the image of the stranger on the Tree in his name, in the name of the God, in his name.

They went outside into the central courtyard, Diarmuid, Loren, Matt, and Kevin Laine. In silence they walked together, the same face in their minds, and Kevin was grateful for the presence of friends.

The heat was brutal, and the sour wind abraded them under the sickly, filtered sun. A prickly tension seemed woven into the texture of the day. And then, suddenly, there was more.

"Hold!" cried Matt the Dwarf, whose people were of the caverns of the earth, the roots of mountains, the ancient rocks. "Hold! Something comes!

And in the same instant, north and west of them, Kim Ford rose, a blinding pulse in her head, an apprehension of enormity, and moved, as if compelled, out back of the cottage where Tyrth was laboring. "Oh, God," she whispered. "Oh my God!" Seeing with distorted vision the vellin bracelet writhing on her wrist, knowing it could not ward what was coming, what had been coming for so long, so terribly, what none of them had seen, none, what was *here, now, right now!* She screamed, in overwhelming agony.

And the roof of the world blew up.

Far, far in the north among the ice, Rangat Cloud-Shouldered rose up ten miles into the heavens, towering above the whole of Fionavar, master of the world, prison of a god for a thousand years.

But no more. A vast geyser of blood-red fire catapulted skyward with a detonation heard even in Cathal. Rangat exploded with a column of fire so high the curving world could not hide it. And at the apex of its ascent the flame was seen to form itself into the five fingers of a hand, taloned, oh, taloned, and curving southward on the wind to bring them all within its grasp, to tear them all to shreds.

A gauntlet hurled, it was, a wild proclamation of release to all the cowering ones who would be his slaves forever after now. For if they had feared the svart alfar, trembled before a renegade mage and the power of Galadan, what would they do now to see the fingers of this fire raking heaven?

To know Rakoth Maugrim was unchained and free, and could bend the very Mountain to his vengeance?

And on the north wind there came then the triumphant laughter of the first and fallen god, who was coming down on them like a hammer bringing fire, bringing war.

The explosion hit the King like a fist in the heart. He tottered from the window of the council chamber and fell into a chair, his face grey, his hands opening and closing spasmodically as he gasped for breath.

"My lord?" Tarn the page rushed into the room and knelt, terror in his eyes. *"My lord?"*

But Ailell was beyond speech. He heard only the laughter on the wind, saw only the fingers curving to clutch them, enormous and blood-colored, a death cloud in the sky, bringing not rain but ruin.

He seemed to be alone. Tarn must have run for aid. With a great effort Ailell rose, breathing in high short gasps, and made his way down the short hallway to his rooms. There he stumbled to the inner door and opened it.

Down the familiar corridor he went. At the end of the passageway, the King stopped before the viewing slot. His vision was troubled: there seemed to be a girl beside him. She had white hair, which was unnatural. Her eyes were kind, though, as Marrien's had been at the end. He had managed to win love there after all. It was patience that power taught. He had told that to the stranger, he remembered. After ta'bael. Where was the stranger? He had something else to say to him, something important.

Then he remembered. Opening the slot, Ailell the King looked into the Room of the Stone and saw that it was dark. The fire was dead, the sacred naal fire; the pillar carved with images of Conary bore nothing upon its crown, and on the floor, shattered forever into fragments like his heart, lay the stone of Ginserat.

He felt himself falling. It seemed to take a very long time. The girl was there; her eyes were so sorrowful. He almost wanted to comfort her. Aileron, he thought. Diarmuid. Oh, Aileron. Very far off, he heard thunder. A god was coming. Yes, of course, but what fools they all were—it was the wrong god. It was so funny, so funny, it was.

And on that thought he died.

So passed, on the eve of war, Ailell dan Art, High King of Brennin, and the rule passed to his son in a time of darkness, when fear moved across the face of all the lands. A good King and wise, Ysanne the Seer had called him once.

What he had fallen from.

———◆———

Jennifer was flying straight at the Mountain when it went up.

A harsh cry of triumph burst from the throat of the black swan as the blast of fire rose far above to separate high in the air and form the taloned hand, bending south like smoke on the wind, but not dissolving, hanging there, reaching.

There was laughter in the sky all around her. *Is the*

person under the mountain dead? Paul Schafer had asked before they crossed. He wasn't dead, nor was he under the Mountain anymore. And though she didn't understand, Jennifer knew that he wasn't a person, either. You had to be something more to shape a hand of fire and send mad laughter down the wind.

The swan increased her speed. For a day and a night Avaia had borne her north, the giant wings beating with exquisite grace, the odor of corruption surrounding her, even in the high, thin reaches of the sky. All through this second day they flew, but late that night they set down on the shores of a lake north of the wide grasslands that had unrolled beneath their flight.

There were svart alfar waiting for them, a large band this time, and with them were other creatures, huge and savage, with fangs and carrying swords. She was pulled roughly from the swan and thrown on the ground. They didn't bother tying her—she couldn't move in any case, her limbs were brutally stiff with cramp after so long bound and motionless.

After a time they brought her food: the half-cooked carcass of some prairie rodent. When she shook her head in mute refusal, they laughed.

Later they did tie her, tearing her blouse in the process. A few of them began pinching and playing with her body, but some leader made them stop. She hardly registered it. A far corner of her mind, it seemed to be as remote as her life, said that she was in shock, and that it was probably a blessing.

When morning came, they would bind her to the swan again and Avaia would fly all that third day, angling northwest now so the still-smoldering mountain gradually slid around towards the east. Then, toward sunset, in a region of great cold, Jennifer would see Starkadh, like a giant ziggurat of hell among the ice, and she would begin to understand.

———◆———

For the second time, Kimberly came to in her bed in the cottage. This time, though, there was no Ysanne to watch over her. Instead, the eyes gazing at her were the dark ones, deepset, of the servant, Tyrth.

As awareness returned she became conscious of a pain on her wrist. Looking, she saw a scoring of black where the vellin bracelet had twisted into her skin. That she remembered. She shook her head.

"I think I would have died without this." She made a small movement of her hand to show him.

He didn't reply but a great tension seemed to dissolve from his compact, muscled frame as he heard her speak. She looked around; by the shadows it was late afternoon.

"That's twice now you've had to carry me here," she said.

"You must not let that bother you, my lady," he said in his rough, shy voice.

"Well, I'm not in the habit of fainting."

"I would never think that." He cast his eyes down.

"What happened with the Mountain?" she asked, almost unwilling to know.

"It is over," he replied. "Just before you woke." She nodded. That made sense.

"Have you been watching me all day?"

He looked apologetic. "Not always, my lady. I am sorry, but the animals were frightened and. . . ."

At that she smiled inwardly. He was pushing it a bit.

"There is boiling water," Tyrth said after a short silence. "Could I make you a drink?"

"Please."

She watched as he limped to the fire. With neat, economical motions he prepared a pot of some herbal infusion and carried it back to the table by the bed.

It was, she decided, time.

"You don't have to fake the limp anymore," she said.

He was very cool, you had to give him credit. Only the briefest flicker of uncertainty had touched the dark eyes, and his hands pouring her drink were absolutely steady. Only when he finished did he sit down for the first time and regard her for a long time in silence.

"Did she tell you?" he asked finally, and she heard his true voice for the first time.

"No. She lied, actually. Said it wasn't her secret to tell." She hesitated. "I learned from Eilathen by the lake."

"I watched that. I wondered."

Kim could feel her forehead creasing with its incongruous vertical line.

"Ysanne is gone, you know." She said it as calmly as she could.

He nodded. "That much I know, but I don't understand what has happened. Your hair. . . ."

"She had Lökdal down below," Kim said bluntly. Almost, she wanted to hurt him with it. "She used it on herself."

He did react, and she was sorry for the thought behind her words. A hand came up to cover his mouth, a curious gesture in such a man. "No," he breathed. "Oh, Ysanne, no!" She could hear the loss.

"You understand what she has done?" she asked. There was a catch in her voice; she controlled it. There was so much pain.

"I know what the dagger does, yes. I didn't know she had it here. She must have come to love you very much."

"Not just me. All of us." She hesitated. "She dreamt me twenty-five years ago. Before I was born." Did that make it easier? Did anything?

His eyes widened. "That I never knew."

"How could you?" He seemed to regard gaps in his awareness as deeply felt affronts. But there was something else that had to be said. "There is more," Kim said. *His name is not to be spoken,* she thought, then: "Your father died this afternoon, Aileron."

There was a silence.

"Old news," the elder Prince of Brennin said. "Listen."

And after a moment she heard them: all the bells in Paras Derval tolling. The death bells for the passing of a King.

"I'm sorry," she said.

His mouth twitched, then he looked out the window. *You cold bastard,* she thought. *Old news.* He deserved more than that, surely; surely he did. She was about to say as much when Aileron turned back to her, and she saw the river of tears pouring and pouring down his face.

Dear God, she thought shakily, enduring a paroxysm of self-condemnation. He may be hard to read, but how can you be *that* far off? It would have been funny, a Kim Ford classic, except that people were going to be relying on her now for so much. It was no good, no good at all. She was an impulsive, undisciplined, halfway-decent intern from Toronto. What the *hell* was she going to do?

Nothing, at any rate, for the moment. She held herself very still on the bed, and after a minute Aileron lifted his tanned, bearded face and spoke.

"After my mother died, he was never the same. He . . . dwindled. Will you believe that he was once a very great man?"

This she could help him with. "I saw by the lake. I know he was, Aileron."

"I watched him until I could hardly bear it," he said, under control now. "Then factions formed in the palace that wanted him to step aside for me. I killed two men who spoke of it in my presence, but my father grew suspicious and frightened. I could not talk to him anymore."

"And Diarmuid?"

The question seemed to genuinely surprise him. "My brother? He was drunk most of the time, and taking ladies to South Keep the rest. Playing March Warden down there."

"There seems to be more to him than that," Kim said mildly.

"To a woman, perhaps."

She blinked. "That," she said, "is insulting."

He considered it. "I suppose it is," he said. "I'm sorry." Then he surprised her again. "I am not good," Aileron said, his eyes averted, "at making myself liked. Men will usually end up respecting me, if against their will, because at some things they value I have . . . a little skill. But I have no skill with women." The eyes, almost black, swung back to hers. "I am also hard to shake from desires I have, and I am not patient with interference."

He was not finished. "I tell you these things, not because I expect to change, but so you will know I am aware of them. There will be people I must trust, and if you are a Seer, then you must be one of them, and I'm afraid you will have to deal with me as I am."

A silence followed this, not surprisingly. For the first time she noticed Malka and called her softly. The black cat leaped to the bed and curled up on her lap.

"I'll think about it," she said finally. "No promises; I'm fairly stubborn myself. May I point out, on the original issue, that Loren seems to value your brother quite a bit, and unless I've missed something, Silvercloak isn't a woman." *Too much asperity,* she thought. *You must go carefully here.*

Aileron's eyes were unreadable. "He was our teacher as boys," he said. "He has hopes still of salvaging something in Diarmuid. And in fairness, my brother does elicit love from his followers, which must mean something."

"Something," she echoed gravely. "You don't see anything to salvage?" It was ironic, actually: she hadn't liked Diarmuid at all, and here she was. . . .

Aileron, for reply, merely shrugged expressively.

"Leave it, then," she said. "Will you finish your story?"

"There is little left to tell. When the rains receded last year, and stopped absolutely this spring, I suspected it was not chance. I wanted to die for him, so

I would not have to watch him fading. Or see the expression in his eyes. I couldn't live with him mistrusting me. So I asked to be allowed to go to the Summer Tree, and he refused. Again I asked, again he refused. Then word came to Paras Derval of children dying on the farms, and I asked again before all the court and once more he refused to grant me leave. And so. . . ."

"And so you told him exactly what you thought." She could picture the scene.

"I did. And he exiled me."

"Not very effectively," she said wryly.

"Would you have me leave my land, Seer?" he snapped, the voice suddenly commanding. It pleased her; he had some caring, then. More than some, if she were being fair. So she said, "Aileron, he did right. You must know that. How could the High King let another die for him?"

And knew immediately that there was something wrong.

"You don't know, then." It was not a question. The sudden gentleness in his voice unsettled her more than anything.

"What? Please. You had better tell me."

"My father did let another go," Aileron said. "Listen to the thunder. Your friend is on the Tree. Pwyll. He has lasted two nights. This is the last, if he is still alive."

Pwyll. Paul.

It fit. It fit too perfectly. She was brushing tears away, but others kept falling. "I saw him," she whispered. "I saw him with your father in my dream, but I couldn't hear what they said, because there was this music, and—"

Then that, too, fell into place.

"Oh, Paul," she breathed. "It was the Brahms, wasn't it? Rachel's Brahms piece. How could I not have remembered?"

"Would you have changed anything?" Aileron asked. "Would you have been right to?"

Too hard, that one, just then. She concentrated on the cat. "Do you hate him?" she asked in a small voice, surprising herself with the question.

It drove him to his feet with a startled, exposed gesture. He strode to the window and looked out over the lake. There were bells. And then thunder. A day so charged with power. And it wasn't over. Night to come, the third night. . . .

"I will try not to," he said at last, so softly Kim could scarcely hear it.

"Please," she said, feeling that somehow it mattered. If only to her, to ease her own gathering harvest of griefs. She rose from the bed, holding the cat in both arms.

He turned to face her. The light was strange behind him.

Then, "It is to be my war," said Aileron dan Ailell. She nodded.

"You have seen this?" he pushed.

Again she nodded. The wind had died outside; it was very quiet. "You would have thrown it away on the Tree."

"Not thrown away. But yes, it was a foolishness. In me, not in your friend," he added after a moment. "I went to see him there last night. I could not help myself. In him it is something else."

"Grief. Pride. A dark kind."

"It is a dark place."

"Can he last?"

Slowly, Aileron shook his head. "I don't think so. He was almost gone last night."

Paul. When, she thought, had she last heard him laugh?

"He's been sick," she said. It sounded almost irrelevant. Her own voice was funny, too.

Aileron touched her shoulder awkwardly. "I will not hate him, Kim." He used her name for the first time. "I cannot. It is so bravely done."

"He has that," she said. She was *not* going to cry

again. "He has that," she repeated, lifting her head. "And we have a war to fight."

"We?" Aileron asked, and in his eyes she could see the entreaty he would not speak.

"You're going to need a Seer," she said matter-of-factly. "I seem to be the best you've got. And I have the Baelrath, too."

He came a step towards her. "I am . . ." He took a breath. "I am . . . pleased," he managed.

A laugh escaped her, she couldn't help it. "God," she said on a rising note. "God, Aileron, I've never met anyone who had so much trouble saying thank-you. What do you do when someone passes you the salt?"

His mouth opened and closed. He looked very young.

"Anyhow," she said briskly, "you're welcome. And now we'd better get going. You should be in Paras Derval tonight, don't you think?"

It seemed that he had already saddled the horse in the barn, and had only been waiting for her. While Aileron went out back to bring the stallion around, she set about closing up the cottage. The dagger and the Circlet would be safest in the chamber down below. She knew that sort of thing now, it was instinctive.

She thought of Raederth then, and wondered if it was folly to sorrow for a man so long dead. But it wasn't, she knew, she now knew; for the dead are still in time, they are travelling, they are not lost. Ysanne was lost. She still needed a long time alone, Kim realized, but she didn't have it, so there was no point even thinking. The Mountain had taken that kind of luxury away from all of them.

From all of them. She did pause, at that. She was numbering herself among them, she realized, even in her thoughts. *Are you aware,* she asked herself, with a kind of awe, *that you are now the Seer of the High Kingdom of Brennin in Fionavar?*

She was. *Holy cow,* she thought, *talk about over-achievers!* But then her mind swung back to Aileron, and the flared levity faded. Aileron, whom she was going to help become King if she could, even though his brother was the heir. She would do it because her blood sang to her that this was right, and that, she knew by now, was part of what being a Seer meant.

She was quiet and ready when he came round the side on the horse. He had a sword now, and a bow slung in the saddle, and he rode the black charger with an easy grace. She was, she had to admit, impressed.

There was a slight issue at the outset over her refusal to leave Malka behind, but when she threatened to walk, Aileron, a stony expression on his face, reached a hand down and swung her up behind him. With the cat. He was very strong, she realized.

He also had a scratched shoulder a minute later. Malka, it seemed, didn't like riding horseback. Aileron, it also seemed, could be remarkably articulate when swearing. She told him as much, sweetly, and was rewarded with a quite communicative silence.

With the dying of the wind, the haze of the day seemed to be lifting. It was still light, and the sun, setting almost directly behind them, cast its long rays along the path.

Which was one reason the ambush failed.

They were attacked at the bend where she and Matt had first seen the lake. Before the first of the svarts had leaped to the road, Aileron, some sixth sense triggered, had already kicked the stallion into a gallop.

There were no darts this time. They had been ordered to take the white-haired woman alive, and she had only one servant as a guard. It should have been easy. There were fifteen of them.

Twelve, after the first rush of the horse, as Aileron's blade scythed on both sides. She was hampering him, though. With a concise movement he leaped from the saddle, killing another svart as he landed.

"Go on!" he shouted.

Of its own accord, the horse sped into a trot and then a gallop down the path. *No way,* Kim thought, and, holding the terrified cat as best she could, grappled for the reins and pulled the stallion to a halt.

Turning, she watched the battle, her heart leaping into her throat, though not with fear.

By the light of the setting sun, Kimberly bore witness to the first battle of Aileron dan Ailell in his war, and a stunning, a nearly debilitating grace was displayed for her then upon that lonely path. To see him with a sword in his hand was almost heartbreaking. It was a dance. It was more. Some men, it seemed, were born to do a thing; it was true.

Because awesomely, stupefyingly, she saw that it had been a mismatch from the first. Fifteen of them, with weapons and sharp teeth for close fighting, against the one man with the long blade flashing in his hand, and she understood that he was going to win. Effortlessly, he was going to win.

It didn't last very long. Not one of the fifteen svart alfar survived. Breathing only a little quickly, he cleaned his sword and sheathed it, before walking toward her up the path, the sun low behind him. It was very quiet now. His dark eyes, she saw, were sombre.

"I told you to go," he said.

"I know. I don't always do what I'm told. I thought I warned you."

He was silent, looking up at her.

"A 'little' skill," she mimicked quite precisely.

His face, she saw with delight, had suddenly gone shy.

"Why," Kim Ford asked, "did that take you so long?"

For the first time she heard him laugh.

They reached Paras Derval at twilight, with Aileron hooded for concealment. Once inside the town they made their way quickly and quietly to Loren's quarters. The mage was there, with Matt and Kevin Laine.

Kim and Aileron told their stories as succinctly as they could; there was little time. They spoke of Paul, in whispers, hearing the thunder gathering in the west.

And then, when it became clear that there was something important neither she nor the Prince knew, they were told about Jennifer.

At which point it was made evident that notwithstanding a frightened cat, or a kingdom that needed her, the new Seer of Brennin could still fall apart with the best of them.

◆

Twice during the day he thought it was the end. There was very great pain. He was badly sunburned now, and so dry. Dry as the land, which, he had thought earlier—how much earlier?—was probably the point. The nexus. It all seemed so simple at times, it came down to such basic correspondences. But then his mind would start to spin, to slide, and with the slide, all the clarity went, too.

He may have been the only person in Fionavar who didn't see the Mountain send up its fire. The sun was fire enough for him. He heard the laughter, but was so far gone he placed it elsewhere, in his own hell. It hurt there, too; he was not spared.

That time it was the bells that brought him back. He was lucid then for an interval, and knew where they were ringing, though not why. His eyes hurt; they were puffy with sunburn, and he was desperately dehydrated. The sun seemed to be a different color today. Seemed. What did he know? He was so skewed, nothing could be taken for what it was.

Though the bells were ringing in Paras Derval, he was sure of that. Except . . . except that after a while, listening, he seemed to hear a harp sounding, too, and that was very bad, as bad as it could be, because it was a thing from his own place, from behind the bolted door. It wasn't out there. The bells were, yes, but they were fading. He was going again, there was nothing to grab hold of, no branch, no hand. He was bound and dry, and sliding, going under. He saw the bolts shatter, and the door opening, and the room. *Oh, lady, lady, lady,* he thought. Then no bolts anymore, nothing to bar the door. Under. Undersea down. . . .

They were in bed. The night before his trip. Of course. It would be that memory. Because of the harp, it would be.

His room. Spring night; almost summer weather. Window open, curtains blowing, her hair around them both, the covers back so he could see her by candlelight. Her candle, a gift. The very light was hers.

"Do you know," Rachel said, "that you are a musician, after all."

"I wish," he heard himself say. "You know I can't even sing."

"But no," she said pursuing a conceit, playing with the hairs on his chest. "You are. You're a harper, Paul. You have harper's hands."

"Where's my harp, then?" Straight man.

And Rachel said, "Me, of course. My heart's your harpstring."

What could he do but smile? The very light.

"You know," she said, "when I play next month, the Brahms, it'll be for you."

"No. For yourself. Keep that for yourself."

She smiled. He couldn't see it, but he knew by now when Rachel smiled.

"Stubborn man." She touched him lightly with her mouth. "Share it, then. Can I play the second movement for you? Will you take that? Let me play that part because I love you. To tell."

"Oh, lady," he had said.

Hand of the harper. Heart of the harpstring.

Lady, lady, lady.

What had brought him back this time, he didn't know. The sun was gone, though. Dark coming down.

Fireflies. Third night then. Last. *For three nights, and forever,* the King had said.

The King was dead.

How did he know that? And after a moment it seemed that very far down, below the burnt, strung-out place of pain he had become, a part of him remained that could fear.

How did he know Ailell was dead? The Tree had told him. It knew the passing of High Kings, it always did. It had been rooted here to summon them far back in the soil of time. From Iorweth to Ailell they were the Children of Mörnir, and the Tree knew when they died. And now he knew as well. He understood. *Now I give you to Mörnir;* the other part of the consecration. He was given. He was becoming root, branch. He was naked there, skin to bark; naked in all the ways there were, it seemed, because the dark was coming down inside again, the door unbolting. He was so open the wind could pass through him, light shine, shadow fall.

Like a child again. Light and shade. Simplicity.

When had all the twisting started?

He could remember (a different door, this) playing baseball on the street as darkness fell. Playing even after the streetlights kicked on, so that the ball would come flashing like a comet out of brightness and into dark, elusive but attainable. The smell of cut grass and porch flowers, the leather of a new fielder's glove. Summer twilight, summer dark. All the continuities. When had it turned? Why did it have to turn? The process changing to disjunctions, abortings, endings, all of them raining down like arrows, unlit and inescapable.

And then love, love, the deepest discontinuity.

Because it seemed that this door had turned into the other one after all, the one he couldn't face. Not even childhood was safe anymore, not tonight. Nowhere would be safe tonight. Not here at the end, naked on the Tree.

And he understood then, finally: understood that it

had to be naked, truly so, that one went to the God. It was the Tree that was stripping him, layer by layer, down to what he was hiding from. To what—hadn't there once been a thing called irony?—he had come here hiding from. Music. Her name. Tears. Rain. The highway.

He was skewed again, going down; the fireflies among the trees had become headlights of approaching cars, which was so absurd. But then it wasn't, after all, because now he was in the car, driving her eastward on Lakeshore Boulevard in the rain.

It had rained the night she died.

I don't, I don't want to go here, he thought, clinging to nothing, his mind's last despairing effort to pull away. *Please, just let me die, let me be rain for them.*

But no. He was the Arrow now. The Arrow on the Tree, of Mörnir, and he was to be given naked or not at all.

Or not at all. There was that, he realized. He could die. That was still his choice, he could let go. It was there for him.

And so on the third night Paul Schafer came to the last test, the one that was always failed, the opening. Where the Kings of Brennin, or those coming in their name, discovered that the courage to be here, the strength to endure, even love of their land were none of them enough. On the Tree one could no longer hide from the living or the dead, from one's own soul. Naked or not at all, one went to Mörnir. And oh, that was too much for them, too hard, too unfair after all that had been endured, to be forced to go into the darkest places then, so weak, so impossibly vulnerable.

And so they would let go, brave Kings of the sword, wise ones, gallant Princes, all would turn away from so much nakedness and die too soon.

But not that night. Because of pride, of pure stubbornness, and because, most surely, of the dog, Paul Schafer found the courage not to turn. Down he went.

Arrow of the God. So open, the wind could pass, light shine through him.

Last door.

"The Dvořák," he heard. His own voice, laughing. "The Dvořák with the Symphony. Kincaid, are you a star!"

She laughed nervously. "It's only at Ontario Place. Outdoors, with a baseball game in the background at the stadium. No one will hear a thing."

"Wally will hear. Wally loves you already."

"Since when have you and Walter Langside been so close?"

"Since the recital, lady. Since his review. He's my main man now, Wally." She had won everything, won them all. She had dazzled. All three papers had been there, because of advance rumor of what she was. It was unheard-of for a graduate recital. The second movement, Langside of the *Globe* had written, could not be played more beautifully.

She had won everything. Had eclipsed every cellist ever to come out of Edward Johnson Hall. And today the Toronto Symphony had called. The Dvořák Cello Concerto. August 5, at Ontario Place. Unheard-of. So they had gone to Winston's for dinner, to blow a hundred dollars of his bursary money from the history department.

"It'll probably rain," she said. The wipers slapped their steady tattoo on the windshield. It was really coming down.

"The bandstand's covered," he replied airily, "and the first ten rows. Besides, if it rains, you don't have to fight the Blue Jays. Can't lose, kid."

"Well, you're pretty high tonight."

"I am, indeed," he heard the person he had been say, "pretty high tonight. I am very high."

He passed a laboring Chevy.

"Oh, shit," Rachel said.

Please, a lost, small voice within the Godwood

pleaded. His. *Oh, please.* But he was inside it now, had taken himself there, all the way. There was no pity on the Summer Tree. How could there be? So open, he was, the rain could fall through him.

"Oh, shit," she said.

"What?" he heard himself say, startled. Saw it start right then, right there. The moment. Wipers at the top of their sweep. Lakeshore East. Just past a blue Chevrolet.

She was silent. Glancing, he could see her hands clasped tightly together. Her head was down. *What was this?*

"I've got something to tell you."

"Evidently." Oh, God, his defences.

She looked over at that. Dark eyes. Like no one else. "I promised," she said. "I promised I'd talk to you tonight."

Promised? He tried, watched himself try. "Rachel, what is it?"

Eyes front again. Her hands.

"You were away for a month, Paul."

"I was away for a month, yes. You know why." He'd gone four weeks before her recital. Had convinced them both it made sense—the time was too huge for her, it meant too much. She was playing eight hours a day; he wanted to let her focus. He flew to Calgary with Kev and drove his brother's car through the Rockies and then south down the California coast. Had phoned her twice a week.

"You know why," he heard himself say again. It had begun.

"Well, I did some thinking."

"One should always do some thinking."

"Paul, don't be like—"

"What do you want from me?" he snapped. "What *is* this, Rach?"

So, so, so. "Mark asked me to marry him."

Mark? Mark Rogers was her accompanist. Last-year

piano student, good-looking, mild, a little effeminate. It didn't fit. He couldn't make it fit.

"All right," he said. "That happens. It happens when you've got a common goal for a while. Theatre romance. He fell in love. Rachel, you're easy to fall in love with. But why are you telling me this way?"

"Because I'm going to say yes."

No warning at all. Point-blank. Nothing had ever prepared him for this kick. Summer night, but God, he was so cold. So cold, suddenly.

"Just like that?" Reflex.

"No! Not just like that. Don't be so cold, Paul."

He heard himself make a sound. A gasp, a laugh: halfway. He was actually shivering. *Don't be so cold, Paul.*

"That's just the sort of thing," she said, twisting her hands together. "You're always so controlled, thinking, figuring out. Like figuring out I needed to be alone a month, or why Mark fell in love with me. So much logic: Mark's not so strong. He *needs* me. I can see the ways he needs me. He cries, Paul."

Cries? Nothing held together anymore. What did crying have to do with it?

"I didn't know you liked a Niobe number." It was important to stop shivering.

"I *don't*. Please don't be nasty, I can't handle it. . . . Paul, it's that you never truly let go, you never made me feel I was indispensable. I guess I'm not. But Mark . . . puts his head on my chest sometimes, after."

"Oh, Jesus, Rachel, don't!"

"It's true!" It was raining harder. Trouble breathing now.

"So he plays harp, too? Versatile, I must say." God, such a kick; he was so cold.

She was crying. "I didn't want it to be. . . ."

She didn't want it to be like this. How had she wanted it to be? Oh, lady, lady, lady.

"It's okay," he found himself saying, incredibly.

Where had that come from? Trouble breathing still. Rain on the roof, on the windshield. "It'll be all right."

"No," Rachel said, weeping still, rain drumming. "Sometimes it can't be all right."

Smart, smart girl. Once he would have reached to touch her. Once? Ten minutes ago. Only that, before the cold.

Love, love, the deepest discontinuity.

Or not quite the deepest.

Because this, precisely, was when the Mazda in front blew a tire. The road was wet. It skidded sideways and hit the Ford in the next lane, then rebounded and three-sixtied as the Ford caromed off the guard rail.

There was no room to brake. He was going to plough them both. Except there was a foot, twelve inches' clearance if he went by on the left. He knew there'd been a foot, had seen the movie in slow motion in his head so many times. Twelve inches. Not impossible; very bad in rain, but.

He went for it, sliced the whirling Mazda, banged the rail, spun, and rolled across the road and into the sliding Ford.

He was belted; she wasn't.

That was all there was to it, except for the truth.

The truth was that there had indeed been twelve inches, perhaps ten, as likely, fourteen. Enough. Enough if he had gone for it as soon as he saw the hole. But he hadn't, had he? By the time he'd moved, there were three inches clear, four, not enough at night, in rain, at forty miles an hour. Not nearly.

Question: how did one measure time there, at the end? Answer: by how much room there was. Over and over he'd watched the film in his mind; over and over he'd seen them roll. Off the rail, into the Ford. Over.

Because he hadn't moved fast enough.

And why—*Do pay attention, Mr. Schafer*—why hadn't he moved fast enough?

Well, class, modern techniques now allow us to ex-
amine the thought patterns of that driver in the scintilla—lovely word, that—of time between the seeing
and the moving. Between the desire and the spasm, as
Mr. Eliot so happily put it once.

And where, on close examination, was the desire?

Not that we can be sure, class, this is *most* hazardous terrain (it was raining, after all), but careful scru-
tiny of the data does seem to elicit a curious lacuna in
the driver's responses.

He moved, oh, yes indeed, he did. And in fairness—
do let's be fair—faster than most drivers would have
done. But was it—and there's the rub—was it as fast
as he could move?

Is it possible, just a hypothesis now, but is it possible that he delayed that scintilla of time—only that,
no more; but still—because he wasn't entirely sure he
wanted to move? The desire and the spasm. *Mr.
Schafer, your thoughts?* Was there perhaps a slight,
shall we say, lag in the desire?

Dead on. St. Michael's Emergency Ward.

The deepest discontinuity.

"It should have been me," he'd said to Kevin. You
had to pay the price, one way or another. You certainly
weren't allowed to weep. Too much hypocrisy, that
would be. Part of the price, then: no tears, no release.
What had crying to do with it? he had asked her. Or
no, he had thought that. Niobe, he had said. A Niobe
number. Witty, witty, defenses up so fast. Seatbelt
buckled. So cold, though, he'd been, so very cold.
Crying, it seemed, had a lot to do with it, after all.

But there was more. One played the tape. Over and
over, like the inner film, like the rolling car: over and
over, the tape of her recital. And one listened, always, in
the second movement, for the lie. His, she had said. That
part because she loved him. So it had to be a lie. One
should be able to hear that, despite Walter Langside and
everyone else. Surely one could hear the lie?

Not so. Her love for him in that sound, that perfect

sound. Incandescent. And this was beyond him; how it could be done. And so each time there came a point where he couldn't listen anymore and not cry. And he wasn't permitted to cry, so.

So she had left him and he had killed her, and you weren't allowed to weep when you have done that. You pay the price, so.

So he had come to Fionavar.

To the Summer Tree.

Class dismissed. Time to die.

This time it was the silence. Complete and utter stillness in the wood. The thunder had stopped. He was cinder, husk: what is left, at the end.

At the end one came back because, it seemed, this much was granted: that one would go in one's own self, from this place, knowing. It was an unexpected dispensation. Drained, a shell, he could still feel gratitude for dignity allowed.

It was unnaturally silent in the darkness. Even the pulsing of the Tree itself had stopped. There was no wind, no sound. The fireflies had gone. Nothing moved. It was as if the earth itself had stopped moving.

Then it came. He saw that, inexplicably, a mist was rising from the floor of the forest. But no, not inexplicably: a mist was rising because it was meant to rise. What could be explained in this place?

With difficulty he turned his head, first one way, then the other. There were two birds on the branches, ravens, both of them. I know these, he thought, no longer capable of surprise. They are named Thought and Memory. I learned this long ago.

It was true. They were named so in all the worlds, and this was their nesting place. They were the God's.

Even the birds were still, though, each bright yellow eye steady, motionless. Waiting, as the trees were waiting. Only the mist was moving; it was higher now. There was no sound. The whole of the Godwood

seemed to have gathered itself, as if time were somehow opening, making a place—and only then, finally,
did Paul realize that it was not the God they were
waiting for, it was something else, not truly part of
the ritual, something outside . . . and he remembered
an image then (thought, memory) of something far
back, another life it seemed, another person almost
who had had a dream . . . no, a vision, a searching,
yes, that was it . . . of mist, yes, and a wood, and
waiting, yes, waiting for the moon to rise, when something, something. . . .

But the moon could not rise. It was the dark of
moon, new moon night. The last crescent had saved
the dog the night before. Had saved him for this. They
were waiting, the Godwood, the whole night was waiting, coiled like a spring, but there could be no moonrise that night.

And then there was.

Above the eastern trees of the glade of the Summer
Tree, there came the rising of the Light. And on the
night of the new moon there shone down on Fionavar
the light of a full moon. As the trees of the forest
began to murmur and sway in the sudden wind, Paul
saw that the moon was red, like fire or blood, and
power shaped that moment to its name: Dana, the
Mother, come to intercede.

Goddess of all the living in all the worlds; mother,
sister, daughter, bride of the God. And Paul saw then,
in a blaze of insight, that it didn't matter which, all
were true: that at this level of power, this absoluteness
of degree, hierarchies ceased to signify. Only the
might did, the awe, the presence made manifest. Red
moon in the sky on new moon night, so that the glade
of the Godwood could shine and the Summer Tree be
wrapped below in mist, above in light.

Paul looked up, beyond surprise, beyond disbelief;
the sacrifice, the shell. Rain to be. And in that moment it seemed to him as if he heard a voice, in the
sky, in the wood, in the running of his own moon-

colored blood, and the voice spoke so that all the trees vibrated like living wands to the sound:

It was not so, will not have been so.

And when the reverberations ceased, Paul was on the highway again, Rachel with him in the rain. And once more he saw the Mazda blow and skid into the Ford. He saw the spinning, impossible obstruction.

He saw twelve inches' clearance on the left.

But Dana was with him now, the Goddess, taking him there to truth. And in a crescendo, a heart-searing blaze of final dispensation, he saw that he had missed the gap, and only just, oh, only just, not because of any hesitation shaped by lack of desire, by death or murder wish, but because, in the end, he was human. Oh, lady, he was. Only, only human, and he missed because of hurt, grief, shock, and rain. Because of these, which could be forgiven.

And were, he understood. Truly, truly were.

Deny not your own mortality. The voice was within him like a wind, one of her voices, only one, he knew, and in the sound was love, he was loved. *You failed because humans fail. It is a gift as much as anything else.*

And then, deep within him like the low sound of a harp, which no longer hurt, this last: *Go easy, and in peace. It is well.*

His throat ached. His heart was a bound, constrained thing too large for him, for what was left of his body. Dimly, through the risen mist, he saw a figure at the edge of the glade: in the form of a man, but bearing the proud antlers of a stag, and through the mist he saw the figure bow to him and then disappear.

Time was.

The pain was gone. His being was shaped of light, he knew his eyes were shining. He had not killed her, then: it was all right. It was loss, but loss was allowed, it was demanded. So much light, there seemed to be, even in that moment when the mist rose to his feet.

And at last it came, at last, sweet, sweet release of

mourning. He thought of Kevin's song then, remembered it with love: *There will come a tomorrow when you weep for me.*

Tomorrow. And so. So. It seemed that this was tomorrow, and here at the end, at the last, he was weeping for Rachel Kincaid who had died.

So Paul cried on the Summer Tree.

And there came then a roll of thunder like the tread of doom, of worlds cracking asunder, and the God was there in the glade, he had come. And he spoke again, in his place, in the one unchanging voice that was his, and forged by the power of that thundering, the mist began to flow together then, faster and faster, to the one place, to the Summer Tree.

Upwards it boiled, the mist of the Godwood, up through the sacrifice, the great trunk of the Tree, hurled into the night sky by the God like a spear.

And in the heavens above Brennin, as the thunder crashed and rolled, suddenly there were clouds piling higher and higher upon each other, spreading from the Mörnirwood to cover all the land.

Paul felt it going. Through him. His. His and the God's. Whose he was. He felt the tears on his face. He felt himself claimed, going, mist boiling through him, ravens rising to fly, the God in the Tree, in him, the moon above the clouds riding in and out, never lost, Rachel, the Summer Tree, the wood, the world, and oh, the God, the God. And then one last thing more before the dark.

Rain, rain, rain, rain, rain.

------◆------

In Paras Derval that night the people went down into the streets. In villages all over Brennin they did so, and farmers bore their children out of doors, only half awake, that they might see the miraculous moon that was answer of the Mother to the fire of Maugrim, and that they might feel upon their faces and remember, though it might seem to them a dream, the return of rain, which was the blessing of the God upon the Children of Mörnir.

In the street, with Loren and Matt, with Kim and the exiled Prince, Kevin Laine wept in his turn, for he knew what this must mean, and Paul was the closest thing to a brother he'd ever had.

"He did it," whispered Loren Silvercloak, in a voice choked and roughened with awe. Kevin saw, with some surprise, that the mage, too, was crying. "Oh, bright," Loren said. "Oh, most brave."

Oh, Paul.

But there was more. "Look," Matt Sören said. And turning to where the Dwarf was pointing, Kevin saw that when the red moon that should never have been shone through the scudding clouds, the stone in the ring Kim wore leaped into responding light. It burned on Kim's finger like a carried fire, the color of the moon.

"What is this?" Aileron asked.

Kim, instinctively raising her hand high so that light could speak to light, realized that she both knew and didn't know. The Baelrath was wild, untamed; so was that moon.

"The stone is being charged," she said quietly. "That is the war moon overhead. This is the Warstone." The others were silent, hearing her. And suddenly her own voice intoning, her role, seemed so heavy; Kim reached back, almost desperately, for some trace of the lightness that had once defined her.

"I think," she tried, hoping that Kevin, at least, would catch it, would play along, help her, please, to remember what she was, "I think we'd better have a new flag made."

Kevin, wrestling with things of his own, missed it completely. All he heard was Kim saying "we" to this new Prince of Brennin.

Looking at her, he thought he was seeing a stranger.

* * *

In the courtyard behind the sanctuary, Jaelle, the High Priestess, lifted her face to the sky and gave praise. And with the teachings of Gwen Ystrat in her heart, she looked at the moon, understanding far better than anyone else west of Lake Leinan what it meant. She gave careful thought for a time, then called six of her women to her, and led them secretly out of Paras Derval, westward in the rain.

In Cathal, too, they had seen the Mountain's fire in the morning, and trembled to hear the laughter on the wind. Now the red moon shone above Larai Rigal as well. Power on power. A gauntlet hurled into the sky, and answered in the sky. This, Shalhassan could understand. He summoned a Council in the dead of night and ordered an embassy to leave for Cynan and then Brennin immediately. No, not in the morning, he snapped in response to a rash question. Immediately. One did not sleep when war began, or one slept forever when it ended.

A good phrase, he thought, dismissing them. He made a mental note to dictate it to Raziel when time allowed. Then he went to bed.

Over Eridu the red moon rose, and the Plain, and down upon Daniloth it cast its light. And the lios alfar, alone of all the guardian peoples, had lore stretching back sufficiently far to say with certainty that no such moon had ever shone before.

It was a reply to Rakoth, their elders agreed, gathered before Ra-Tenniel on the mound at Atronel, to the one the younger gods had named Sathain, the Hooded One, long, long ago. It was an intercession as well, the wisest of them added, though for what, or as to what, they could not say.

Nor could they say what the third power of the moon was, though all the lios knew there was a third.

The Goddess worked by threes.

* * *

There was another glade in another wood. A glade where one man alone had dared to walk in ten centuries since Amairgen had died.

The glade was small, the trees of the grove about were very old, extremely tall. The moon was almost overhead before she could shine down upon Pendaran's sacred grove.

When she did, it began. A play of light first, a shimmering, and then a sound following, unearthly like a flute among the leaves. The air itself seemed to quiver to that tune, to dance, to form and reform, coalesce, to shape finally a creature of light and sound, of Pendaran and the moon.

When it was ended, there was silence, and something stood in the glade where nothing had stood before. With the wide eyes of the newly born, dewed so that her coat glistened in the birthing light, she rose on unsteady legs, and stood a moment, as one more sound like a single string plucked ran through Pendaran Wood.

Slowly then, delicately as all her kind, she moved from the glade, from the sacred grove. Eastward she went, for though but newly birthed, she knew already that to the west lay the sea.

Lightly, lightly did she tread the grass, and the powers of Pendaran, all the creatures gathered there, grow still as she passed, more beautiful, more terrible than any one of them.

The Goddess worked by threes; this was the third.

To the highest battlement he had climbed, so that all of black Starkadh lay below him. Starkadh rebuilt, his fortress and his fastness, for the blasting of Rangat had not signified his freedom—though let the fools think so yet awhile—he had been free a long time now. The Mountain had been exploded because he was ready at last for war, with the place of his power rising anew to tower over the northland, over Daniloth, a blur to the south, where his heart's hate would forever lie.

But he did not look down upon it.

Instead his eyes were riveted on the impossible response the night sky held up to him, and in that moment he tasted doubt. With his one good hand, he reached upwards as if his talons might rake the moon from heaven, and it was a long time before his rage passed.

But he had changed in a thousand years under Rangat. Hate had driven him to move too fast the last time. This time it would not.

Let the moon shine tonight. He would have it down before the end. He would smash Brennin like a toy and uproot the Summer Tree. The Riders would be scattered, Larai Rigal burned to waste, Calor Diman defiled in Eridu.

And Gwen Ystrat he would level. Let the moon shine, then. Let Dana try to show forth empty signs in heavens choked with his smoke. Her, too, he would have kneeling before him. He had had a thousand years to consider all of this.

He smiled then, for the last was best. When all else was done, when Fionavar lay crushed beneath his fist, only then would he turn to Daniloth. One by one he would have them brought to him, the lios alfar, the Children of Light. One by one by one to Starkadh.

He would know what to do with them.

The thunder was almost spent, the rain a thin drizzle. The wind was wind, no more. A taste of salt on it from the sea, far away. The clouds were breaking up. The red moon stood directly over the Tree.

"Lady," said the God, muting the thunder of his voice, "Lady, this you have never done before."

"It was needful," she replied, a chiming on wind. "He is very strong this time."

"He is very strong," the thunder echoed. "Why did you speak to my sacrifice?" A slight reproach.

The Lady's voice grew deeper, woven of hearth smoke and caves. "Do you mind?" she murmured.

There came a sound that might have been a god amused. "Not if you beg forgiveness, no. It has been long, Lady." A deeper sound, and meaningful.

"Do you know what I have done in Pendaran?" she asked, eluding, voice gossamer like dawn.

"I do. Though for good or ill I do not know. It may burn the hand that lays hold of it."

"All my gifts are double-edged," the Goddess said, and he was aware of ancient blood in that tone. There was a silence, then she was finest lace again, cajoling: "I have interceded, Lord, will you not do so?"

"For them?"

"And to please me," said the moon.

"Might we please each other?"

"We might so."

A roll of thunder then. Laughter.

"I have interceded," Mörnir said.

"Not the rain," she protested, sea-sound. "The rain was bought."

"Not the rain," the God replied. "I have done what I have done."

"Let us go, then," said Dana.

The moon passed away behind the trees to the west.

Shortly thereafter the thunder ceased, and the clouds began to break up overhead.

And so at the last, at the end of night, in the sky above the Summer Tree, there were only the stars to look down upon the sacrifice, upon the stranger hanging naked on the Tree, only the stars, only them.

Before dawn it rained again, though the glade was empty by then, and silent, save for the sound of water falling and dripping from the leaves.

And this was the last night of Pwyll the Stranger on the Summer Tree.

PART III

The Children
of Ivor

Chapter 10

He landed badly, but the reflexes of an athlete took him rolling through the fall, and at the end of it he was on his feet, unhurt. Very angry, though.

He had opted out, damn it! What the hell right did Kim Ford have to grab his arm and haul him to another world? What the. . . .

He stopped; the fury draining as realization came down hard. She had, she really *had* taken him to another world.

A moment ago he had been in a room in the Park Plaza Hotel, now he found himself outdoors in darkness with a cool wind blowing, and a forest nearby; looking the other way, he saw wide rolling grasslands stretching away as far as he could see in the moonlight.

He looked around for the others, and then as the fact of isolation slowly came home, Dave Martyniuk's anger gave way to fear. They weren't friends of his, that was for sure, but this was no time or place to have ended up alone.

They couldn't be far, he thought, managing to keep control. Kim Ford had had his arm; surely that meant she couldn't be far away, her and the others, and that Lorenzo Marcus guy who'd got him into this in the first place. And was going to get him out, or deal with severe bodily pain, Martyniuk vowed. Notwithstanding the provisions of the Criminal Code.

Which reminded him: looking down, he saw that he was still clutching Kevin Laine's Evidence notes.

The absurdity, the utter incongruousness in this night place of wind and grass acted, somehow, to loosen him. He took a deep breath, like before the opening jump in a game. It was time to get his bearings. Boy Scout time.

Paras Derval where Ailell reigns, the old man had said. Any cities on the horizon? As the moon slipped from behind a drift of cloud, Dave turned north into the wind and saw Rangat clear.

He was not, as it happened, anywhere near the others. All Kim had been able to do with her desperate grab for his arm was keep him in the same plane as them, the same world. He was in Fionavar, but a long way north, and the Mountain loomed forty-five thousand feet up into the moonlight, white and dazzling.

"Holy Mother!" Dave exclaimed involuntarily.

It saved his life.

Of the nine tribes of the Dalrei, all but one had moved east and south that season, though the best grazing for the eltor was still in the northwest, as it always was in summer. The messages the auberei brought back from Celidon were clear, though: svart alfar and wolves in the edgings of Pendaran were enough for most Chieftains to take their people away. There had been rumors of urgach among the svarts as well. It was enough. South of Adein and Rienna they went, to the leaner, smaller herds, and the safety of the country around Cynmere and the Latham.

Ivor dan Banor, Chieftain of the third tribe, was, as often, the exception. Not that he did not care for the safety of his tribe, his children. No man who knew him could think that. It was just that there were other things to consider, Ivor thought, awake late at night in the Chieftain's house.

For one, the Plain and the eltor herds belonged to the Dalrei, and not just symbolically. Colan had given them to Revor after the Bael Rangat, to hold, he and his people, for so long as the High Kingdom stood.

It had been earned, by the mad ride in terror through
Pendaran and the Shadowland and a loop in the thread
of time to explode singing into battle on a sunset field
that else had been lost. Ivor stirred, just thinking on
it: for the Horsemen, the Children of Peace, to have
done this thing. . . . There had been giants in the old
days.

Giants who had earned the Plain. To have and to
hold, Ivor thought. Not to scurry to sheltered pockets
of land at the merest rumor of danger. It stuck in Ivor's
craw to run from svart alfar.

So the third tribe stayed. Not on the edge of Pendaran—that would have been foolhardy and unnecessary. There was a good camp five leagues from the
forest, and they had the dense herds of the eltor to
themselves. It was, the hunters agreed, a luxury. He
noticed that they still made the sign against evil,
though, when the chase took them within sight of the
Great Wood. There were some, Ivor knew, who would
rather have been elsewhere.

He had other reasons, though, for staying. It was
bad in the south, the auberei reported from Celidon;
Brennin was locked in a drought, and cryptic word had
come from his friend Tulger of the eighth tribe that
there was trouble in the High Kingdom. What, Ivor
thought, did they need to go into that for? After a
harsh winter, what the tribe needed was a mild, sweet
summer in the north. They needed the cool breeze and
the fat herds for feasting and warm coats against the
coming of fall.

There was another reason, too. More than the usual
number of boys would be coming up to their fasts this
year. Spring and summer were the time for the totem
fasts among the Dalrei, and the third tribe had always
been luckiest in a certain copse of trees here in the
northwest. It was a tradition. Here Ivor had seen his
own hawk gazing with bright eyes back at him from
the top of an elm on his second night. It was a good
place, Faelinn Grove, and the young ones deserved to

lie there if they could. Tabor, too. His younger son was fourteen. Past time. It might be this summer. Ivor had been twelve when he found his hawk; Levon, his older son—his heir, Chieftain after him—had seen his totem at thirteen.

It was whispered, among the girls who were always competing for him, that Levon had seen a King Horse on his fast. This, Ivor knew, was not true, but there *was* something of the stallion about Levon, in the brown eyes, the unbridled carriage, the open, guileless nature, even his long, thick yellow hair, which he wore unbound.

Tabor, though, Tabor was different. Although that was unfair, Ivor told himself—his intense younger son was only a boy yet, he hadn't had his fasting. This summer, perhaps, and he wanted Tabor to have the lucky wood.

And above and beyond all of these, Ivor had another reason still. A vague presence at the back of his mind, as yet undefined. He left it there. Such things, he knew from experience, would be made clear to him in their time. He was a patient man.

So they stayed.

Even now there were two boys in Faelinn Grove. Gereint had spoken their names two days ago, and the shaman's word began the passage from boy to man among the Dalrei.

There were two in the wood then, fasting; but though Faelinn was lucky, it was also close to Pendaran, and Ivor, father to all his tribe, had taken quiet steps to guard them. They would be shamed, and their fathers, if they knew, so it had been only with a look in his eye that he had alerted Torc to ride out with them unseen.

Torc was often away from the camps at night. It was his way. The younger ones joked that his animal had been a wolf. They laughed too hard at that, a little afraid. Torc: he did look like a wolf, with his lean body, his long, straight, black hair, and the dark, unrevealing eyes. He never wore a shirt, or moccasins; only his eltor skin leggings, dyed black to be unseen at night.

The Outcast. No fault of his own, Ivor knew, and resolved for the hundredth time to do something about that name. It hadn't been any fault of Torc's father, Sorcha, either. Just sheerest bad luck. But Sorcha had slain an eltor doe that was carrying young. An accident, the hunters agreed at the gathering: the buck he'd slashed had fallen freakishly into the path of the doe beside it. The doe had stumbled over him and broken her neck. When the hunters came up, they had seen that she was bearing.

An accident, which let Ivor make it exile and not death. He could not do more. No Chieftain could rise above the Laws and hold his people. Exile, then, for Sorcha; a lonely, dark fate, to be driven from the Plain. The next morning they had found Meisse, his wife, dead by her own hand. Torc, at eleven, only child, had been left doubly scarred by tragedy.

He had been named by Gereint that summer, the same summer as Levon. Barely twelve, he had found his animal and had remained ever after a loner on the fringes of the tribe. As good a hunter as any of Ivor's people, as good even, honesty made Ivor concede, as Levon. Or perhaps not quite, not *quite* as good.

The Chieftan smiled to himself in the dark. That, he thought, was self-indulgent. Torc was his son as well, the whole tribe were his children. He liked the dark man, too, though Torc could be difficult; he also trusted him. Torc was discreet and competent with tasks like the one tonight.

Awake beside Leith, his people all about him in the camp, the horses shut in for the night, Ivor felt better knowing Torc was out there in the dark with the boys. He turned on his side to try to sleep.

After a moment, the Chieftain recognized a muffled sound, and realized that someone else was awake in the house. He could hear Tabor's stifled sobbing from

the room he shared with Levon. It was hard for the
boy, he knew; fourteen was late not to be named, especially for the Chieftain's son, for Levon's brother.

He would have comforted his younger son, but knew
it was wiser to leave the boy alone. It was not a bad
thing to learn what hurt meant, and mastering it alone
helped engender self-respect. Tabor would be all right.

In a little while the crying stopped. Eventually Ivor,
too, fell asleep, though first he did something he'd not
done for a long time.

He left the warmth of his bed, of Leith sound asleep
beside him, and went to look in on his children. First
the boys; fair, uncomplicated Levon, nut-brown, wiry
Tabor; and then he walked into Liane's room.

Cordeliane, his daughter. With a bemused pride he
gazed at her dark brown hair, at the long lashes of her
closed eyes, the upturned nose, laughing mouth . . .
even in sleep she smiled.

How had he, stocky, square, plain Ivor, come to
have such handsome sons, a daughter so fair?

All of the third tribe were his children, but these,
these.

Torc had been having a bad night. First the two id-
iots who had come to fast had managed to end up,
totally oblivious, within twenty feet of each other on
precisely opposite sides of a clump of bushes in the
wood. It was ridiculous. What sort of babies were they
sending out these days?

He had managed, with a series of snuffling grunts
that really were rather unnerving, to scare one of them
into moving a quarter of a mile away. It was an interference with the ritual, he supposed, but the fast had
barely begun, and in any case, the babies needed all
the help they could get: the man smell in those bushes
had been so strong they'd have likely ended up finding
only each other for totem animals.

That, he thought, was funny. Torc didn't find many
things funny, but the image of two fasting thirteen-

year-olds becoming each other's sacred beasts made
him smile in the dark.

He stopped smiling when his sweep of the grove
turned up a spoor he didn't recognize. After a moment, though, he realized that it had to be an urgach,
which was worse than bad. Svart alfar would not have
disturbed him unless there were a great many. He had
seen small numbers of them on his solitary forays
westward towards Pendaran. He'd also found the trail
of a very large band, with wolves among them. It had
been a week before, and they were moving south fairly
quickly. It had not been a pleasant thing to find, and
he'd reported it to Ivor, and to Levon as leader of the
hunt, but it was, for the time being, no direct concern
of theirs.

This was. He'd never seen one of the urgach, no one
in the tribe had, but there were legends enough and
night stories to make him very cautious indeed. He
remembered the tales very well, from before the bad
time, when he'd been only a child in the third tribe, a
child like all the others, shivering with pleasurable fear
by the fire, dreading his mother's summons to bed,
while the old ones told their stories.

Kneeling over the spoor, Torc's lean face was grim.
This was not Pendaran Wood, where creatures of
Darkness were known to walk. An urgach, or more
than one in Faelinn Grove, the lucky wood of the third
tribe, was serious. It was more than serious: there were
two babies fasting tonight.

Moving silently, Torc followed the heavy, almost
overpowering spoor and, dismayed, he saw that it led
eastward out of the grove. Urgach on the Plain! Dark
things were abroad. For the first time, he wondered
about the Chieftain's decision to stay in the northwest
this summer. They were alone. Far from Celidon, far
from any other tribe that might have joined numbers
with them against what evils might be moving here.
The Children of Peace, the Dalrei were named, but
sometimes peace had been hard won.

Torc had no problems with being alone, he had been so all his adult life. Outcast, the young ones called him, in mockery. The Wolf. Stupid babies: wolves ran in packs. When had he ever? The solitude had made for some bitterness, for he was young yet, and the memory of other times was fresh enough to be a wound. It had also given him a certain dour reflectiveness born of long nights in the dark, and an outsider's view of what humans did. Another kind of animal. If he lacked tolerance, it was not a surprising flaw.

He had very quick reflexes.

The knife was in his hand, and he was low to the gully and crawling from the trees as soon as he glimpsed the bulky shadow in a brief unsheathing of moonlight. There were clouds, or else he would have seen it earlier. It was very big.

He was downwind, which was good. Moving with honed speed and silence, Torc traversed the open ground towards the figure he'd seen. His bow and sword were on his horse; a stupidity. Can you kill an urgach with a knife, a part of him wondered.

The rest of him was concentrating. He had moved to within ten feet. The creature hadn't noticed him, but it was obviously angry and it was very large—almost a foot taller than he was, bulking hugely in the shadows of the night.

He decided to wait for moonlight and throw for the head. One didn't stop to talk with creatures from one's nightmares. The size of it made his heart race—tearing fangs on a creature that big?

The moon slanted out; he was ready. He drew back his arm to throw: the dark head was clearly outlined against the silvered plain, looking the other way, north.

"Holy Mother!" the urgach said.

Torc's arm had already begun its descent. With a brutal effort he retained control of the dagger, cutting himself in the process.

Creatures of evil did not invoke the Goddess, not in that voice. Looking again in the bright moonlight, Torc saw that the creature before him was a man; strangely garbed, and very big, but he seemed to be unarmed.

Drawing breath, Torc called out in a voice as courteous as the circumstances seemed to permit, "Move slowly and declare yourself."

At the snarled command, Dave's heart hit his throat and jack-knifed back into his rib-cage. *Who the hell?* Rather than pursue this inquiry, however, he elected to move slowly and declare himself.

Turning toward the voice with his hands outspread and bearing only Evidence notes, he said, as levelly as he could, "My name is Martyniuk. Dave Martyniuk. I don't know where I am, and I'm looking for someone named Loren. He brought me here."

A moment passed. He felt the wind from the north ruffling his hair. He was, he realized, very frightened.

Then a shadow rose from a hollow he hadn't even seen, and moved towards him.

"Silvercloak?" the shadow asked, materializing in the moonlight as a young man, shirtless despite the wind, barefoot, and clad in leggings of black. He carried a long, quite lethal-looking blade in his hand.

Oh, God, Dave thought. *What have they done to me?* Carefully, his eyes on the knife, he replied, "Yes, Loren Silvercloak. That's his name." He took a breath, trying to calm down. "Please don't misunderstand anything. I'm here in peace. I don't even want to be here. I got separated . . . we're supposed to be in a place called Paras Derval. Do you know it?"

The other man seemed to relax a little. "I know it. How is it that you don't?"

"Because I'm not from here," Dave exclaimed, frustration hitting his voice. "We crossed from my world. Earth?" he said hopefully, then realized how stupid that was.

"Where is Silvercloak, then?"

"Aren't you listening?" Martyniuk exploded. "I told you, I got separated. I need him to go home. All

I want to do is get home as fast as I can. Can't you understand that?''

There was another silence.

"Why," the other man asked, "shouldn't I just kill you?''

Dave's breath escaped in a hiss. He hadn't handled this too well, it seemed. God, he wasn't a diplomat. Why hadn't Kevin Laine been separated from the others? Dave considered jumping the other man, but something told him this lean person knew how to use that blade extremely well.

He had a sudden inspiration. "Because," he gambled, "Loren wouldn't like it. I'm his friend; he'll be looking for me." *You are too quick to renounce friendship,* the mage had said, the night before. Not always, Dave thought, not tonight, boy.

It seemed to work, too. Martyniuk lowered his hands slowly. "I'm unarmed," he said. "I'm lost. Will you help me, please?''

The other man sheathed his blade at last. "I'll take you to Ivor," he said, "and Gereint. They both know Silvercloak. We'll go to the camp in the morning."

"Why not now?''

"Because," the other said, "I have a job to do, and I suppose you'll have to do it with me now."

"How? What?''

"There are two babies in that wood fasting for their animals. We've got to watch over them, make sure they don't cut themselves or something." He held up a bleeding hand. "Like I did, not killing you. You are among the Dalrei. Ivor's tribe, the third. And lucky for you he is a stubborn man, or the only thing you would find here would be eltor and svart alfar, and the one would flee you and the other kill. My name," he said, "is Torc. Now come."

The babies, as Torc insisted on calling the two thirteen-year-olds, seemed to be all right. If they were lucky, Torc explained, they would each see an animal before dawn. If not, the fast would continue, and he would have to watch another night. They were sitting with their backs against a tree in a small clearing midway between the two boys. Torc's horse, a small dark gray stallion, grazed nearby.

"What are we watching for?" Dave asked, a little nervously. Night forests were not his usual habitat.

"I told you: there are svart alfar around here. Word of them has driven all the other tribes south."

"There was a svart alfar in our world," Dave volunteered. "It followed Loren. Matt Sören killed it. Loren said they weren't dangerous, and there weren't many of them."

Torc raised his eyebrows. "There are more than there used to be," he said, "and though they may not be dangerous to a mage, they were bred to kill and they do it very well."

Dave had an uncomfortable, prickly feeling suddenly. Torc spoke of killing with disquieting frequency.

"The svarts would be enough to worry about," Torc went on, "but just before I saw you, I found the spoor of an urgach—I took you for it, back there. I was going to kill first and investigate after. Such creatures have not been seen for hundreds of years. It is very bad that they are back; I don't know what it means."

"What are they?"

Torc made a strange gesture and shook his head. "Not at night," he said. "We shouldn't be talking of them out here." He repeated the gesture.

Dave settled back against the tree. It was late, he supposed he should try to sleep, but he was far too keyed up. Torc no longer seemed to be in a talking mood; that was okay by him.

On the whole, it looked all right. Could have been a lot worse. He appeared to have landed among people who knew the mage. The others couldn't be too far away; it would probably work out, if he didn't get eaten by something in these woods. On the other hand, Torc obviously knew what he was doing. Roll with it, he thought.

After about three-quarters of an hour, Torc rose to check on his babies. He looped east, and came back ten minutes later, nodding his head.

"Barth is all right, and well hidden now, too. Not as stupid as most of them." He continued west to look in on the other one. A few minutes later, he reappeared again.

"Well—" Torc began, approaching the tree.

Only an athlete could have done it. With purest reflex, Dave launched himself at the apparition that had emerged from the trees beside Torc. He hit the hairy, ape-like creature with the hardest cross-body block he could throw, and the sword swinging to decapitate Torc was deflected away.

Sprawled flat with the breath knocked out of him, Dave saw the huge creature's other hand coming down. He managed to parry with his left forearm, and felt a numbing sensation from the contact. God, he thought, staring into the enraged red eyes of what had to be the urgach, this sucker is strong! He didn't even have time to be afraid: rolling clumsily away from the urgach's short-range sword thrust, he saw a body hurtle past him.

Torc, knife in hand, had hurled himself straight at the creature's head. The urgach dropped its awkward sword, and with a terrifying snarl, easily blocked Torc's arm. Shifting its grip, it threw the Rider bodily away, to smash into a tree, senseless for a moment.

One on one, Dave thought. Torc's dive had given him time to get to his feet, but everything was moving so fast. Whirling, he fled to where Torc's tethered horse was neighing in terror, and he grabbed the sword resting by the saddle-cloth. *A sword?* he thought. *What the hell do I do with a sword?*

Parry, like crazy. The urgach, weapon reclaimed, was right on top of him, and it levelled a great two-handed sweep of its own giant blade. Dave was a strong man, but the jarring impact of blocking that blow made his right arm go almost as numb as his left; he staggered backwards.

"Torc!" he cried desperately. "I can't—"

He stopped, because there was suddenly no need to say anything more. The urgach was swaying like a toppling rock, and a moment later it fell forward with a crash, Torc's dagger embedded to the hilt in the back of its skull.

The two men gazed at each other across the dead body of the monstrous creature.

"Well," said Torc finally, still breathing hard, "now I know why I didn't kill you."

What Dave felt then was so rare and unexpected, it took him a moment to recognize it.

◆

Ivor, up with the sun and watching by the southwest gate, saw Barth and Navon come walking back together. He could tell—it was not hard—from the way they moved that they had both found something in the wood. Found, or been found by, as Gereint said. They had gone out as boys and were coming back to him, his children still, but Riders now, Riders of the Dalrei. So he lifted his voice in greeting, that they should be welcomed by their Chieftain back from the dream-world to the tribe.

"Hola!" cried Ivor, that all should hear. "See who comes! Let there be rejoicing, for see the Weaver sends two new Riders to us!"

They all rushed out then, having waited with suppressed excitement, so that the Chieftain should be first to announce the return. It was a tradition of the third tribe since the days of Lahor, his grandfather.

Barth and Navon were welcomed home with honor and jubilation. Their eyes were wide yet with wonder, not yet fully returned from the other world, from the visions that fasting and night and Gereint's secret drink had given them. They seemed untouched, fresh, which was as it should be.

Ivor led them, one on either side, letting them walk beside him now, as was fit for men, to the quarters set apart for Gereint. He went inside with them and watched as they knelt before the shaman, that he might confirm and consecrate their animals. Never had one of Ivor's children tried to dissemble about his fast, to claim a totem when there had been none, or pretend in his mind that an eltor had been an eagle or a boar. It was still the task of the shaman to find in them the truth of their vigil, so that in the tribe Gereint knew the totems of every Rider. It was thus in all the tribes. So it was written at Celidon. So was the Law.

At length Gereint lifted his head from where he sat cross-legged on his mat. He turned unerringly to where Ivor stood, the light from outside silhouetting him.

"Their hour knows their name," the shaman said.

It was done. The words that defined a Rider had been spoken: the hour that none could avoid, and the sanctity of their secret name. Ivor was assailed suddenly by a sense of the sweep, the vastness of time. For twelve hundred years the Dalrei had ridden on the Plain. For twelve hundred years each new Rider had been so proclaimed.

"Should we feast?" he asked Gereint formally.

"Indeed we should," came the placid reply. "We should have the Feast of the New Hunters."

"It shall be so," Ivor said. So many times he and Gereint had done this, summer after summer. Was he getting old?

He took the two newest Riders and led them into the sunlight, to where all the tribe was gathered before the door of the shaman's house.

"Their hour knows," he said, and smiled to hear the roar that went up.

He gave Navon and Barth back to their families at last. "Sleep," he urged them both, knowing what the morrow would be like, knowing he would not be heeded. Who slept on this day?

Levon had, he remembered; but he had been three

nights in the grove and had come out, at the last, hollowed and other-worldly. A difficult, far-voyaging fast it had been, as was fitting for one who would one day lead the tribe.

Thinking so, he watched his people stream away, then ducked back into the darkness of Gereint's house. There was never any light in that house, no matter which camp they occupied.

The shaman had not moved.

"It is well," Ivor said, hunkering down beside the old one.

Gereint nodded. "It is well, I think. They should both do, and Barth may be something more." It was the closest he ever came to giving the Chieftain a hint of what he had seen in the new ones. Always Ivor marvelled at the shaman's gift, at his power.

He still remembered the night they had blinded Gereint. A child, Ivor had been, four summers from his hawk, but as Banor's only son, he had been taken out with the men to see it done. Power for him all his life would be symbolized by deep-voiced chanting and torches weaving on the night plain under the stars of midsummer.

For some moments the two men sat quietly, each wrapped in his own thoughts, then Ivor rose. "I should speak to Levon about tomorrow's hunt," he said "Sixteen, I think."

"At least," the shaman said in an aggrieved tone. "I could eat a whole one myself. We haven't feasted in a long time, Ivor."

Ivor snorted. "A very long time, you greedy old man. Twelve whole days since Walen was named. Why aren't you fat?"

"Because," the wisest one explained patiently, "you never have enough food at the feasts."

"Seventeen, then!" Ivor laughed. "I'll see you in the morning before they go. It's up to Levon, but I'm going to suggest east."

"East," Gereint agreed gravely. "But you'll see me later today."

This, too, Ivor had grown accustomed to.

The Sight comes when the light goes, the Dalrei said. It was not Law, but had the same force, it seemed to Ivor at times. They found their totems in the dark, and all their shamans came to their power in blindness with that ceremony on midsummer night, the bright torches and the stars suddenly going black.

He found Levon with the horses, of course, tending to a mare with a bad fetlock. Levon rose at his father's footstep and came over, pushing the yellow hair back from his eyes. It was long, and he never tied it back. Seeing Levon lifted Ivor's heart; it always did.

He remembered, probably because he'd been thinking of it earlier, the morning Levon had returned from his three-day fast. All day he had slept, bone-weary, the fair skin almost translucent with exhaustion. Late at night he had arisen and sought his father.

Ivor and his thirteen-year-old son had walked out alone into the sleeping camp.

"I saw a cerne, father," Levon had said suddenly. A gift to him, the deepest, rarest gift. His animal, his secret name. A cerne was very good, Ivor thought with pride. Strong and brave, proudly horned like the god for which it was named, legendary for how it would defend its young. A cerne was as good as could be.

He nodded. There had been a difficulty in his throat. Leith was always teasing him about how quick he was to cry. He wanted to put an arm about the boy, but Levon was a Rider now, a man, and had given him a man's gift.

"Mine was a hawk," Ivor had said, and had stood beside his son, their shoulders touching as they looked together at the summer sky above their sleeping people.

"Eastward, right?" Levon said now, coming up. There was laughter in his brown eyes.

"I think," Ivor replied. "Let's not be foolhardy. It's up to you, though," he added quickly.

"I know. East is fine. I'll have the two new ones, anyhow. It's easier country to hunt. How many?"

"I thought sixteen, but Gereint wants an eltor to himself."

Levon threw back his head and laughed. "And he complained about not enough feasting, didn't he?"

"Always," his father chuckled. "How many hunters, then, for seventeen?"

"Twenty," Levon said immediately.

It was five fewer than he would have taken. It put great pressure on the hunters, especially with the two new ones in the band, but Ivor held his peace. The hunting was Levon's now, and his son knew the horses and hunters, and the eltor like no one else did. He believed in putting pressure on them, too, Ivor knew. It kept them sharp. Revor was said to have done the same thing.

So "Good" was all he said. "Choose well. I'll see you at home later." Levon raised a hand; he was already turning back to the mare.

Ivor hadn't eaten yet, or talked to Leith, and the sun was already high. He went home. They were waiting for him in the front room. Because of Gereint's parting words, he wasn't totally surprised.

"This," said Torc, without ceremony, "is Davor. He crossed from another world with Loren Silvercloak last night, but was separated from him. We killed an urgach together in Faelinn last night."

Yes, Ivor thought, *I knew there was something more.* He looked at the two young men. The stranger, a very big man, bristled with a certain aggressiveness, but was not truly so, Ivor judged. Torc's terse words had both frightened and pleased the Chieftain. An urgach was unheard-of news, but the Outcast's saying "we" made Ivor smile inwardly. The two of them had shared something in that killing, he thought.

"Welcome," he said to the stranger. And then, formally, "Your coming is a bright thread in what is woven for us. You will have to tell me as much as you care to of your story. Killing an urgach—that was bravely done. We shall eat first, though," he added hastily, knowing Leith's rules with guests. "Liane?" he called.

His daughter materialized instantaneously. She had, of course, been listening behind the door. Ivor suppressed a smile. "We have guests for the morning meal," he said. "Will you find Tabor and have him request Gereint to come? Levon, too."

"Gereint won't want to," she said impertinently. "It's too far, he'll say." Ivor observed that she was keeping her back to Torc. It was shameful that a child of his should treat a tribesman so. He would have to speak to her of it. This business of the Outcast must be ended.

For the moment he said merely, "Have Tabor say that he was right this morning."

"About what?" Liane demanded.

"Go, child," Ivor said. There were limits.

With a predictable toss of her hair, Liane spun and left the room. The stranger, Ivor saw, had an amused look on his face, and no longer clutched the sheaf of papers he carried quite so defensively. It was well, for the moment.

Loren Silvercloak, though, and an urgach in Faelinn Grove? Not for five hundred years had such a creature been reported to Celidon. *I knew,* Ivor thought, *there was another reason why we stayed.*

This, it seemed, was it.

Chapter 11

They had found a horse for him, not an easy task. The Dalrei tended to be smallish people, quick and wiry, and their mounts were much the same. In winter, though, they traded with the men of Brennin in the land where the High Kingdom ran into the Plain near the Latham, and there were always one or two larger mounts in every tribe, used usually for carrying goods from camp to camp. Riding the placid-tempered grey they had given him, and with Ivor's younger son, Tabor, as a guide, Dave had come out at dawn with Levon and the hunters to watch an eltor chase.

His arms were in pretty rough shape, but Torc had to be just as bad, or worse, and he was hunting; so Dave figured he could manage to ride a horse and watch.

Tabor, skinny and tanned dark brown, rode a chestnut pony beside him. He wore his hair tied back like Torc and most of the Riders, but it wasn't really long enough for that, and the tied part stuck up on the back of his head like a tree stump. Dave remembered himself at fourteen and found an uncharacteristic empathy for the kid beside him. Tabor talked a lot—in fact, he hadn't shut up since they'd ridden out—but Dave was interested and didn't mind, for once.

"We used to carry our houses with us when we moved," Tabor was saying as they jogged along. Up front, Levon was setting an easy pace eastward into the rising sun. Torc was beside him and there seemed to be about twenty other riders. It was a glorious, mild summer morning.

"They weren't houses like we have now, of course," Tabor went on. "We made them of eltor skin and poles, so they were easy to carry."

"We have things like that in my world, too," Dave said. "Why did you change?"

"Revor did it," Tabor explained.

"Who's he?"

The boy looked pained, as if appalled to discover that the fame of this Revor hadn't reached Toronto yet. Fourteen was a funny age, Dave thought, suppressing a grin. He was surprised at how cheerful he felt.

"Revor is our brightest hero," Tabor explained reverently. "He saved the High King in battle during the Bael Rangat, by riding through Daniloth, and was rewarded with the land of the Plain for the Dalrei forever. After that," Tabor went on, earnestly, "Revor called a great gathering of all the Dalrei at Celidon, the mid-Plain, and said that if this was now our land, we should have some mark of ourselves upon it. So the camps were built in those days, that our tribes might have true homes to come to as they followed the eltor about the Plain."

"How far back?" Dave asked.

"Oh, forever and ever," Tabor replied, waving a hand.

"Forever and Revor?" said Dave, surprising himself. Tabor looked blank for a second, then giggled. He was a good kid, Dave decided. The ponytail was hilarious, though.

"The camps have been rebuilt many times since then," Tabor resumed his lecture. He was taking his guide duties seriously. "We always cut wood when we are near a forest—except Pendaran, of course—and we carry it to the next camp when we move. Sometimes the camps have been completely destroyed. There are fires when the Plain is dry."

Dave nodded; it made sense. "And I guess you have

to clear out the damage the weather and animals do in between times, anyway.''

"Weather, yes,'' Tabor said. "But never the animals. The shamans were given a spell as a gift from Gwen Ystrat. Nothing wild ever enters the camps.''

That, Dave still had problems with. He remembered the old, blind shaman, Gereint, being led into the Chieftain's house the morning before. Gereint had trained his sightless eye sockets right on him. Dave had met the look as best he could—a staring duel with a blind man—but when Gereint had turned away, expressionless, he'd felt like crying out, *"What did you see, damn you?"*

The whole thing unnerved him. It had been the only bad moment, though. Ivor, the Chieftain, a small, leathery guy with crinkly eyes and a considered way of speaking, had been all right.

"If Silvercloak was going to Paras Derval,'' he'd said, "then that is where he'll be. I will send word of you with the auberei to Celidon, and a party of us will guide you south to Brennin. It will be a good thing for some of our younger men to make that journey, and I have tidings for Ailell, the High King.''

"The urgach?'' a voice had said then from by the door, and Dave had turned to see Liane again, Ivor's brown-haired daughter.

Levon had laughed. "Father,'' he'd said, "we may as well make her part of the tribal council. She's going to listen anyhow.''

Ivor had looked displeased and proud, both. It was at that point that Dave had decided he liked the Chieftain.

"Liane,'' Ivor had said, "doesn't your mother need you?''

"She said I was in her way.''

"How can you be in her way? We have guests, there must be things for you to do,'' Ivor had said bemusedly.

"I break dishes," Liane had explained. "Is it the urgach?"

Dave had laughed aloud, then flushed at the look she'd given him.

"Yes," Ivor had said. But then he added, looking levelly at Liane, "My daughter, you are being indulged because I dislike chastising my children before guests, but you go too far. It ill becomes you to listen at doors. It is the action of a spoiled child, not a woman."

Liane's flippant manner had disappeared completely. She paled, and her lip trembled. "I'm sorry," she had gasped, and spinning on her heel, had fled the home.

"She hates missing things," Levon had said, stating the obvious.

"There they are."

Tabor was pointing southeast, and Dave, squinting into the sun, saw the eltor moving northward across their path. He had been expecting buffalo, he now realized, for what he saw made him catch his breath, in sudden understanding of why the Dalrei spoke not of a herd, but of a swift of eltor.

They were like antelope: graceful, many-horned, sleek, and very, very fast. Most were colored in shadings of brown, but one or two were purest white. The speed of their sweep across the plain was dazzling. There had to be five hundred of them, moving like wind over the grass, their heads carried high, arrogant and beautiful, the hair of their manes lifting back in the wind of their running.

"A small swift," Tabor said. The kid was trying to be cool, but Dave could hear the excitement in his voice, even as he felt his own heartbeat accelerate. God, they were beautiful. The Riders around him, in response to Levon's concise command, picked up speed and changed approach slightly to intersect the swift at an angle.

"Come!" Tabor said, as their slower mounts fell behind. "I know where he will have them do it." He cut away sharply northward, and Dave followed. In a moment they crested a small knoll in the otherwise level sweep of the prairie; turning back, Dave saw the eltor swift and the hunters converge, and he watched the Dalrei hunt, as Tabor told him of the Law.

An eltor could be killed by knife blade only. Nothing else. Any other killing meant death or exile to the man who did so. Such, for twelve hundred years, had been the Law inscribed on the parchments at Celidon.

More: one eltor to one man, and one chance only for the hunter. A doe could be killed, but at risk, for a bearing doe's death meant execution or exile again.

This, Dave learned, was what had happened to Torc's father. Ivor had exiled him, having no other mercy to grant, for in the preservation of the great eltor swifts lay the preservation of the Dalrei themselves. Dave nodded to hear it; somehow, out here on the Plain under that high sky, harsh, clear laws seemed to fit. It was not a world shaped for nuance or subtlety.

Then Tabor drew silent, for one by one, in response to Levon's gesture, the hunters of the third tribe set out after their prey. Dave saw the first of them, low and melded to his flying horse, intersect the edge of the racing swift. The man picked his target, slid into place beside it; then Dave, his jaw dropping, saw the hunter leap from horse to eltor, dagger flashing, and, with a succinct slash, sever the beast's jugular. The eltor fell, the weight of the Dalrei pulling it away from the body of the swift. The hunter disengaged from the falling beast, hit the ground himself at frightening speed, rolled, and was up, his dagger raised in red triumph.

Levon raised his own blade in response, but most of the other men were already flying alongside the swift. Dave saw the next man kill with a short, deadly throw. His eltor fell, almost in its tracks. Another hunter, riding with unbelievable skill, held to his mount with his legs only, leaning far out over the back of a madly racing eltor, to stab from horseback and bring down his beast.

"Uh-oh," Tabor said sharply. "Navon's trying to be fancy." Shifting his glance, Dave saw that one of the boys he'd guarded the night before was showing off on his first hunt. Riding his horse while standing up, Navon smoothly cut in close to one of the eltor. Taking careful aim, he threw from his standing position—and missed. The flung blade whipped just over the neck of the prey and fell harmlessly.

"Idiot!" Tabor exclaimed, as Navon slumped down on his mount. Even at a distance Dave could see the young Rider's dejection.

"It was a good try," he offered.

"No," Tabor snapped, his eyes never leaving the hunters. "He shouldn't be doing that on his first hunt, especially when Levon has trusted him by taking only twenty for seventeen. Now if anyone else is unlucky. . . ."

Turning back to the hunt, Dave picked out the other new Rider. Barth, on a brown stallion, went in with cool efficiency, picked out his eltor and, wasting no time, pulled alongside, leaped from his horse, and stabbing, as the first hunter had done, brought his beast down.

"Good," Tabor muttered, a little grudgingly. "He did well. See, he even pulled it down to the outside, away from the others. The leap is the surest way, though you can get hurt doing it."

And sure enough, though Barth rose holding a dagger aloft, it was in his left hand, and his right hung down at his side. Levon saluted him back. Dave turned to Tabor to ask a question, but was stopped cold by the stricken expression on his companion's face.

"Please," Tabor whispered, almost a prayer. "Let it be soon. Oh, Davor, if Gereint doesn't name me this summer, I will die of shame!"

Dave couldn't think of a single thing to say. So, after

a moment, he just asked his question. "Does Levon go in, too, or will he just watch?"

Tabor collected himself. "He only kills if the others have failed, then he must make up the numbers himself. It is a shameful thing, though, if the leader must kill, which is why most tribes take many more hunters than they need." There was pride in Tabor's voice again. "It is a thing of great honor to take only a few extra Riders, or none, though no one does that. The third tribe is known now over all the Plain for how bold we are on the hunt. I wish, though, that Levon had been more careful with two new ones today. My father would have—*oh, no!*"

Dave saw it, too. The eltor picked out by the fifteenth Rider stumbled, just as the hunter threw, and the blade hit an antler only and glanced away. The eltor recovered and raced off, head high, its mane blown gracefully back.

Tabor was suddenly very still, and after a quick calculation Dave realized why: no one else could miss. Levon had cut it very fine.

The sixteenth hunter, an older man, had already peeled off from the small group remaining. Dave saw that the Riders who had already killed were racing along on the far side of the swift. They had turned the eltor so the beasts were now running back south along the other side of the knoll. All the kills, he realized, would be close together. It was an efficient process, well judged. If no one else missed.

The sixteenth hunter played no games. In fast, his blade high, he picked a slower animal, leaped, and stabbed, pulling it clear. He rose, dagger lifted.

"A fat one," Tabor said, trying to mask his tension. "Gereint'll want that one tonight."

The seventeenth man killed, too, throwing from almost directly over top of his eltor. He made it look easy.

"Torc won't miss," Dave heard Tabor say, and saw the now familiar shirtless figure whip past their knoll.

Torc singled out an eltor, raced south with it for several strides, then threw with arrogant assurance. The eltor dropped, almost at their feet. Torc saluted briefly, then sped off to join the other Riders on the far side of the swift. Seeing that throw, Dave remembered the urgach falling two nights before. He felt like cheering for Torc, but there was one more to go, and he could feel Tabor's anxiety.

"Cechtar's very good," the boy breathed. Dave saw a big man on a chestnut horse leave Levon's side—the leader was alone now, just below them. Cechtar galloped confidently towards the racing swift that the others were steering past the knoll. His knife was drawn already, and the man's carriage on his horse was solid and reassuring.

Then the horse hit a tummock of grass and stumbled. Cechtar kept his seat, but the damage was done—the knife, prematurely upraised, had flown from his hand to fall harmlessly short of the nearest animal.

Hardly breathing, Dave turned to see what Levon would do. Beside him, Tabor was moaning in an agony of distress. "Oh no, oh no," he repeated. "We are shamed. It's a disgrace for all three Riders, and Levon especially for misjudging. There's nothing he can do. I feel sick!"

"He has to kill now?"

"Yes, and he will. But it doesn't make any difference, there's nothing he can—oh!"

Tabor stopped, for Levon, moving his horse forward very deliberately, had shouted a command to Torc and the others. Watching, Dave saw the hunters race to turn the eltor yet again, so that after a wide arc had been described, the swift, a quarter of a mile away now, were flying back north, five hundred strong on the east side of the knoll.

"What's he doing?" Dave asked softly.

"I don't know, I don't understand. Unless . . ."
Levon began to ride slowly eastward, but after a few

strides he turned his horse to stand motionless, square in the path of the swift.

"What the hell?" Dave breathed.

"Oh, Levon, no!" Tabor screamed suddenly. The boy clutched Dave's arm, his face white with terrified understanding. "He's trying Revor's Kill. He's going to kill himself!"

Dave felt his own rush of fear hit, as he grasped what Levon was trying to do. It was impossible, though; it was insanity. Was the hunt leader committing suicide out of shame?

In frozen silence they watched from the knoll as the massed swift, slightly wedge-shaped behind a huge lead animal, raced over the grass towards the still figure of Tabor's yellow-haired brother. The other hunters, too, Dave was dimly aware, had stopped riding. The only sound was the rapidly growing thunder of the onrushing eltor.

Unable to take his eyes away from the hunt leader, Dave saw Levon, moving without haste, dismount to stand in front of his horse. The eltor were very close now, flying; the sound of the drumming hooves filled the air.

The horse was utterly still. That, too, Dave registered, then he saw Levon unhurriedly draw his blade.

The lead eltor was fifty yards away.

Then twenty.

Levon raised his arm and, without pausing, the whole thing one seamless motion, threw.

The blade hit the giant animal directly between the eyes; it broke stride, staggered, then fell at Levon's feet. Right at Levon's feet.

His fists clenched tightly with raw emotion, Dave saw the other animals instantly scythe out away from the fallen leader and form two smaller swifts, one angling east, one west, dividing in a cloud of dust precisely at the point where the fallen eltor lay.

Where Levon, his yellow hair blowing free, stood quietly stroking his horse's muzzle, having stolen in that moment, with an act of incandescent gallantry, great honor for his people from the teeth of shame. As a leader should.

Dave became aware that he was shouting wildly, that Tabor, tears in his eyes, was hugging him fiercely and pounding his sore shoulders, and that he had an arm around the boy and was hugging him back. It was not, it never had been the sort of thing he did, but it was all right now, it was more than all right.

Ivor was astonished at the fury he felt. A rage such as this he could not remember. Levon had almost died, he told himself, that was why. A foolhardy piece of bravado, it had been. Ivor should have insisted on twenty-five Riders. He, Ivor, was still Chieftain of the third tribe.

And that vehement thought gave him pause. Was it only fear for Levon that sparked his anger? After all, it was over now; Levon was fine, he was better than fine. The whole tribe was afire with what he had done. Revor's Kill. Levon's reputation was made; his deed would dominate the midwinter gathering of the nine tribes at Celidon. His name would soon be ringing the length of the Plain.

I feel old, Ivor realized. *I'm jealous. I've got a son who can do Revor's Kill.* What did that make him? Was he just Levon's father now, the last part of his name?

Which led to another thought: did all fathers feel this way when their sons became men? Men of achievement, of names that eclipsed the father's? Was there always the sting of envy to temper the burst of pride? Had Banor felt that way when twenty-year-old Ivor had made his first speech at Celidon and earned the praise of all the elders for the wisdom of his words?

Probably, he thought, remembering his father with love. Probably he had, and, Ivor realized, it didn't matter. It really didn't. It was part of the way of things, part of the procession all men made towards the knowing hour.

If he had a virtue, Ivor reflected, something of his nature he wanted his sons to have, it was tolerance. He smiled wryly. It would be ironic if that tolerance could not be extended to himself.

Which reminded him. His sons; and his daughter. He had to have a talk with Liane. Feelingly decidedly better, Ivor went looking for his middle child.

Revor's Kill. Oh, by Ceinwen's bow, he was proud!

The Feast of the New Hunters started formally at sundown, the tribe gathering in the huge central area of the camp, from where the smell of slowly roasting game had been wafting all afternoon. Truly, this would be a celebration: two new Riders and Levon's deed that morning. A feat that had obliterated the failures before. No one, not even Gereint, could remember the last time it had been done. "Not since Revor himself!" one of the hunters had shouted, a little drunkenly.

All the hunters from the morning were a little drunk; they had started early, Dave among them, on the clear, harsh liquor the Dalrei brewed. The mood of mingled relief and euphoria on the ride home had been completely infectious and Dave had let himself go with it. There didn't seem to be any reason to hold back.

Through it all, drinking round for round with them, Levon seemed almost unaffected by what he had done. Looking for it, Dave could find no arrogance, no hidden sense of superiority in Ivor's older son. It had to be there, he thought, suspicious, as he always was. But looking one more time at Levon as he walked between him and Ivor to the feast—he was guest of honor, it seemed—Dave found himself reluctantly changing his mind. Is a horse arrogant or superior? He didn't think so. Proud, yes; there was great pride in the bay stallion that had stood so still with Levon that morning, but it wasn't a pride that diminished anything or anyone else. It was simply part of what the stallion was.

Levon was like that, Dave decided.

It was one of his last really coherent thoughts, for with the sunset the feast began. The eltor meat was superlative; broiled slowly over open fires, seasoned with spices he didn't recognize, it was better than anything he'd ever tasted in his life. When the sizzling slices of meat started to go around, the drinking among the tribesmen got quite serious as well.

Dave was seldom drunk; he didn't like surrendering the edge of control, but he was in a strange space that evening, a whole other country. A whole other world, even. He didn't hold back.

Sitting by Ivor's side, he suddenly realized that he hadn't seen Torc since the hunt. Looking around the firelit pandemonium, he finally spotted the dark man standing by himself, off on the edge of the circle of light cast by the fires.

Dave rose, not too steadily. Ivor raised an inquiring eyebrow. "It's Torc," Dave mumbled. "Why's he on his own? Shouldn't be. He should be here. Hell, we . . . we killed an urgach together, me and him." Ivor nodded, as if the stumbling discourse had been lucid explanation.

"Truly," the Chieftain said quietly. Turning to his daughter, who was serving him just then, he added, "Liane, will you go and bring Torc to sit by me?"

"Can't," Liane said. "Sorry. Have to go get ready for the dancing." And she was gone, quick, mercurial, into the confused shadows. Ivor, Dave saw, did not look happy.

He strode off to fetch Torc himself. Stupid girl, he thought, with some anger, she's avoiding him because his father was exiled and she's chief's daughter.

He came up to Torc in the half-dark, just beyond the cast glow of the many fires. The other man, chewing on an eltor haunch, merely grunted a hello. That was okay. Didn't need to talk; talkers bugged Dave anyhow.

They stood awhile in silence. It was cooler beyond the fires; the wind felt easy, refreshing. It sobered him a little.

"How do you feel?" he asked finally.

"Better," Torc said. And after a moment, "Your shoulder?"

"Better," Dave replied. When you didn't say a lot, he thought, you said the important things. In the shadows with Torc, he felt no real desire to go back to the center of the clearing. It was better here, feeling the wind. You could see the stars, too. You couldn't in the firelight; or in Toronto, either, he thought.

On impulse he turned around. There it was. Torc turned to look with him. Together they gazed at the white magnificence of Rangat.

"There's someone under there?" Dave asked softly.

"Yes," said Torc briefly. "Bound."

"Loren told us."

"He cannot die."

Which was not comforting. "Who is he?" Dave asked with some diffidence.

For a moment Torc was silent, then: "We do not name him by his name. In Brennin they do, I am told, and in Cathal, but it is the Dalrei who dwell under the shadow of Rangat. When we speak of him, it is as Maugrim, the Unraveller."

Dave shivered, though it wasn't cold. The Mountain was shining in the moonlight, its peak so high he had to tilt his head back to take it in. He wrestled then with a difficult thought.

"It's so great," he said. "So tremendous. Why'd they put him under something so beautiful? Now every time you look at it, you have to think about. . . ." He trailed off. Words were too tough, sometimes. Most of the time.

Torc was looking at him with sharp understanding,

though. "That," he said softly, "is why they did it."
And he turned back to the lights.

Turning with him, Dave saw that some of the fires
were being put out, leaving a ring of flame, around
which the Dalrei were gathering. He looked at Torc.

"Dancing," his companion said. "The women and
boys."

And a moment later Dave saw a number of young
girls enter the ring of fire and begin an intricate, weaving dance to a tune laid down by two old men with
curiously shaped stringed instruments. It was pretty,
he supposed, but dancing wasn't really his thing. His
eyes wandered away, and he spotted the old shaman,
Gereint. Gereint was holding a piece of meat in each
hand, one light, one dark. He was taking turns biting
from each. Dave snorted and nudged Torc to look.

Torc laughed, too, softly. "He should be fat," he
said. "I don't know why he isn't." Dave grinned. Just
then Navon, still looking sheepish about his failure
that morning, came by with a flask. Dave and Torc
each drank, then watched the new Rider walk off. Still
a boy, Dave thought, but he's a hunter now.

"He'll be all right," Torc murmured. "I think he
learned his lesson this morning."

"He wouldn't be around to have learned it if you
didn't use a knife as well as you do. That," Dave said
for the first time, "was some throw the other night."

"I wouldn't have been around to throw it if you
hadn't saved my life," Torc said. Then after a moment
he grinned, his teeth white in the darkness. "We did
all right back there."

"Damn right," said Dave, grinning back.

The young girls had gone, to cheerful applause. A
larger operation began now, with the older boys joining a number of the women. Dave saw Tabor move to
the center of the circle, and after a moment he realized
that they were dancing the morning's hunt. The music
was louder now, more compelling. Another man had
joined the two musicians.

They danced it all, with stylized, ritual gestures. The women, their hair loose and flowing, were the eltor, and the boys mimed the Riders they would one day be. It was beautifully done, even to the individual quirks and traits of the hunters. Dave recognized the characteristic head tilt of the second Rider in the boy who imitated him. There was enthusiastic applause for that, then there was laughter as another boy danced Navon's flashy failure. It was indulgent laughter, though, and even the other two misses were greeted with only brief regret, because everyone knew what was coming.

Tabor had untied his hair for this. He looked older, more assured—or was it just the role, Dave wondered, as he saw Ivor's younger son dance, with palpable pride and surprisingly graceful restraint, his older brother's kill.

Seeing it again in the dance, Dave cheered as loudly as everyone else when the young woman dancing the lead eltor fell at Tabor's feet, and all the other women streamed around him, turning at the edge of the circle defined by the fires to form a whirling kaleidoscope of movement about the still figure of Tabor dan Ivor. It was well done, Dave thought, really well done. A head taller than everyone there, he could see it all. When Tabor glanced at him across the massed people in between, Dave gave him a high, clenched-fist gesture of approval. He saw Tabor, despite his role, flush with pleasure. Good kid. Solid.

When it ended, the crowd grew restive again; the dancing seemed to be over. Dave looked at Torc and mimed a drinking motion. Torc shook his head and pointed.

Looking back, Dave saw that Liane had entered the circle of fire.

She was dressed in red and had done something to her face; her color was high and striking. She wore golden jewelry on each arm and about her throat; it glinted and flashed in the firelight as she moved, and it seemed to Dave as if she had suddenly become a creature of flame herself.

The crowd grew quiet as she waited. Then Liane, instead of dancing, spoke. "We have cause to celebrate," she sang out. "The kill of Levon dan Ivor will be told at Celidon this winter, and for many winters after." There was a roar of approval; Liane let it die down. "That kill," she said, "may not be the brightest deed we have reason to honor tonight." The crowd hushed in perplexity. "There was another act of courage done," Liane continued, "a darker one, in the night wood, and it should be known and celebrated by all of the third tribe."

What? Dave thought. *Uh-oh.*

It was all he had time for. "Bring forth Torc dan Sorcha," cried Liane, "and with him Davor, our guest, that we may honor them!"

"Here they are!" a high voice cried from behind Dave, and suddenly goddamn Tabor was pushing him forward, and Levon, smiling broadly, had Torc by the arm, and the two sons of Ivor led them through the parting crowd to stand beside the Chieftain.

With excruciating self-consciousness, Dave stood exposed in the light of the fires, and heard Liane continue in the rapt silence.

"You do not know," she cried to the tribe, "of what I speak, so I will dance it for you." *Oh, God,* Dave thought. He was, he knew, beet-red. "Let us do them honor," Liane said, more softly, "and let Torc dan Sorcha no more be named Outcast in this tribe, for know you that these two killed an urgach in Faelinn Grove two nights ago."

They hadn't known, Dave realized, wishing he could find a place to disappear, knowing Torc felt the same. From the electric response of the tribe, it was clear that they hadn't had a clue.

Then the music began, and gradually his color receded, for no one was looking at him anymore: Liane was dancing between the fires.

She was doing it all, he marveled, spellbound, doing it all herself. The two sleeping boys in the wood, Torc, himself, the very texture, the mood of Faelinn Grove at night—and then somehow, unbelievably, whether it was alcohol or firelight or some alchemy of art, he saw the urgach again, huge, terrifying, swinging its giant sword.

But there was only a girl in the ring of fire, only a girl and her shadow, dancing, miming, becoming the scene she shaped, offering it to all of them. He saw his own instinctive leap, then Torc's, the urgach's brutal blow that had sent Torc smashing into a tree. . . .

She had it dead-on, he realized, astonished. Then he smiled, even through his wonder and stirring pride: of course, she'd listened in while they told Ivor. He felt like laughing suddenly, like crying, like some kind, *any* kind of articulation of emotion as he watched Liane dance his own desperate parry of the urgach's sword, and then, finally, Torc's hurled dagger—she was Torc, she was the blade, and then the toppling, like a mighty tree, of the beast. She was all of it, entire, and she wasn't a stupid girl after all.

Ivor saw the urgach sway and fall, and then the dancer was herself again, Liane, and she was whirling between the fires, her bare foot flying, jewelry flashing on her arms, moving so fast her hair, short as it was, lifted behind her as she exploded in a wild celebration of dance, of the deed in the night wood, of this night, and the next, and the days, all of them, of everything there was before the hour came that knew your name.

With a lump in his throat he saw her slow, the motion winding down until she stopped, her hands across her breasts, her head lowered, motionless, the still point between the fires; between the stars, it seemed to him.

A moment the third tribe was still with her, then there came an explosion of cheering that must have rocketed beyond the camp, Ivor thought, beyond the lights of men, far out into the wide dark of the night plain.

He looked for Leith in that moment, and saw her standing among the women on the other side of the fires. No tears for her; she was not that sort of woman. But he knew her well enough after so many years to read the expression on her face. Let the tribe think the Chieftain's wife cool, efficient, unruffled; he knew better. He grinned at her, and laughed when she flushed and looked away, as if unmasked.

The tribe was still buzzing with the catharsis of the dance and the killing that had led to it. Even in this, Liane had been wilful, for he was not at all sure this was how he would have chosen to tell them of the urgach, and it was his place to decide. It couldn't be kept hidden, for the auberei would have to take word on their ride to Celidon tomorrow, but once more, it seemed, his middle child had gone her own way.

How could he be angry, though, after this? It was always so hard, Ivor found, to stay angry with Liane. Leith was better at it. Mothers and daughters; there was less indulgence there.

She had judged it rightly, though, he thought, watching her walk over to Torc and the stranger and kiss them both. Seeing Torc redden, Ivor decided that not the least cause for joy this night might be the reclaiming of the outcast by this tribe.

And then Gereint rose.

It was remarkable how tuned the tribe was to him. As soon as the blind shaman moved forward into the space between the fires, some collective thread of instinct alerted even the most intoxicated hunter. Gereint never had to gesture or wait for silence.

He'd looked silly before, Ivor reflected, watching the shaman move unassisted between the flames. Not anymore. However he might look with eltor juice dripping from his chin, when Gereint rose in the night to address the tribe, his voice was the voice of power.

He spoke for Ceinwen and Cernan, for the night wind and the dawn wind, all the unseen world. The hollowed sockets of his eyes gave testimony. He had paid the price.

"Cernan came to me with the greyness of dawn," Gereint said quietly. *Cernan,* thought Ivor, god of the wild things, of wood and plain, Lord of the eltor, brother and twin to Ceinwen of the Bow.

"I saw him clear," Gereint went on. "The horns upon his head, seven-tined for a King, the dark flash of his eyes, the majesty of him." A sound like wind in tall grass swept through the tribe.

"He spoke a name to me," Gereint said. "A thing that has never happened in all my days. Cernan named to me this morning Tabor dan Ivor, and called him to his fast."

Tabor. And not just named by the shaman after a dream. Summoned by the god himself. A thrill of awe touched Ivor like a ghostly finger in the dark. For a moment he felt as if he were alone on the Plain. There was a shadow with him, only a shadow, but it was the god. Cernan knew his name; Tabor dan Ivor, he had called.

The Chieftain was brought unceremoniously back to the reality of the camp by the high scream of a woman. Liane, of course. He knew without looking. Flying across the ring, almost knocking over the shaman in her haste, she sped to Tabor's side, no longer a red spirit of dance and flame, only a quicksilver, coltish girl fiercely hugging her brother. Levon was there, too, Ivor saw; more quietly, but as fast, his open face flashing a broad smile of delight. The three of them together. Fair and brown and brown. His.

So Tabor was in Faelinn tomorrow. At that thought, he looked over and saw Torc gazing at him. He received a smile and a reassuring nod from the dark man, and then, with surprise and pleasure, another from giant Davor, who had been so lucky for them. Tabor would be guarded in the wood.

He looked for Leith again across the ring of fire. And with a twist in his heart, Ivor saw how beautiful she was, how very beautiful still, and then he saw the tears in her eyes. Youngest child, he thought, a mother and her youngest. He had a sudden overwhelming sense of the wonder, the strangeness, the deep, deep richness of things. It filled him, it expanded within his breast. He couldn't hold it in, it was so much, so very much.

Moving within the ring to a music of his own, Ivor, the Chieftain, not so old after all, not so very, danced his joy for his children, all of them.

Chapter 12

Tabor, at least, was no baby. Ivor's son, Levon's brother, he knew where to lie in the wood at night. He was sheltered and hidden and could move easily at need. Torc approved.

He and Davor were in Faelinn Grove again. Their guest had, surprisingly, elected to delay his journey south in order to watch over the boy with him. Tabor, Torc thought, had made a strong impression. It wasn't unusual: he liked the boy himself. Characteristically, Torc gave no thought to the possibility that he himself might be another reason for Dave's reluctance to leave.

Torc had other things to think about. In fact, he had been of two minds about being accompanied that night. He had been looking forward to solitude and dark since the festival. Too much had happened there, and too quickly. Too many people had come over to embrace him after Liane's dance. And in the night, long after the fires had burned down, Kerrin dal Ragin had slipped into the room Levon had insisted he take in the camp. Levon had been smiling when they talked, and when Kerrin appeared in the doorway, Torc had belatedly understood why. Kerrin was very pretty, and much talked about among the hunters; her giggling, scented arrival was not the sort of thing an outcast grew accustomed to.

It had been very nice, more than that, in fact. But what had followed her arrival in his bed did not admit of leisure or tranquillity to let him reflect on all that had occurred.

He'd needed to be alone, but Davor's company was the next best thing. The big man was inclined to silence himself, and Torc could sense that the stranger had things of his own to think about. In any case, they were there to guard Tabor, and he'd not have wanted to meet another urgach alone. The Chieftain had given Davor an axe—the best weapon for one of his size, without training in the sword.

So, weapons to hand this time, the two of them had settled down against a pair of trees close to where Tabor lay. It was a mild easy night. Torc, outcast no longer, it seemed, let his mind go back, past Kerrin's fair, silken hair, past the naming of Tabor by the god, the tumult of the tribe's response to what he and Davor had done, to the still point, the heart of everything, the moment for which he needed the dark and solitude.

Liane had kissed him when her dance was done.

Fingering the haft of his axe, enjoying the balanced, solid feel of it, Dave realized that he even liked the name they had given him.

Davor. It sounded far more formidable than Dave. Davor of the Axe. Axewielder. Davor dan Ivor—

Which stopped him. From that thought he could feel himself backing away; it was too exposed to even let it surface inside.

Beside him, Torc sat quietly, his dark eyes hidden; he seemed lost in reverie. Well, Dave thought, I guess he won't be an outcast anymore, not after last night.

Which took him back. His, too, had been a tiring night. Three girls, no less, had made their way through Ivor's doorway to the room where Dave slept. Or didn't, after all, sleep.

God, he remembered thinking at one point, I'll bet there's a lot of kids born nine months after one of these feasts. A good life, he decided, being a Rider of the Dalrei, of the third tribe, of the children of Ivor—

He sat up abruptly. Torc glanced at him, but made

no comment. *You have a father,* Dave told himself sternly. *And a mother and brother. You're a law student in Toronto, and a basketball player, for God's sake.*

"In that order?" he remembered Kim Ford teasing, the first time they'd met; or had Kevin Laine put it the other way around? He couldn't remember. Already the time before the crossing seemed astonishingly remote. The Dalrei were real, Martyniuk thought. This axe, the wood, Torc—his kind of person. And there was more.

His mind looped back again to the night before, and this time it zeroed in on the thing that mattered much more than it should, more, he knew, than he could allow it to. Still, it did. He leaned back against the tree again, going with the memory.

Liane had kissed him when her dance was done.

They heard it at the same time: something crashing loudly through the trees. Torc, child of night and woods, knew immediately—only someone who wanted to be heard would make so much noise. He didn't bother moving.

Dave, however, felt his heart lurch with apprehension. "What the hell is that?" he whispered fiercely, grabbing for his axe.

"Her brother, I think," Torc said, inadvisedly, and felt himself go crimson in the dark.

Even Dave, far from a perceptive man, could hardly miss that one. When Levon finally emerged through the trees, he found the two of them sitting in an awkward silence.

"I couldn't sleep," he offered apologetically. "I thought I might watch with you. Not that you need me, but . . ."

There was truly no guile, no hauteur in Levon. The man who had just done Revor's Kill, who would one day lead the tribe, was sheepishly requesting their indulgence.

"Sure," Dave said. "He's your brother. Come sit down."

Torc managed a short nod. His heartbeat was slowing, though, and after a time he decided he didn't really mind if Davor knew. *I've never had a friend,* he thought suddenly. *This is the sort of thing you talk to friends about.*

It was all right that Levon had come; Levon was unlike anyone else. And he had done something the morning before that Torc was not sure he would have dared to try. The realization was a hard one for a proud man, and a different person might have hated Levon for it. Torc, however, measured out his respect in terms of such things. *Two friends,* he thought, *I have two friends here.*

Though he could only speak of her to one of them.

That one was having problems. Torc's slip had registered, and Dave felt a need to walk the implications out. He rose. "I'm going to check on him," he said. "Right back."

He didn't do much thinking, though. This wasn't the sort of situation Dave Martyniuk could handle, so he ducked it. He carried the axe, careful not to make a noise with it; he tried to move as quietly as Torc did in the wood. *It's not even a situation,* he told himself abruptly. *I'm leaving tomorrow.*

He had spoken aloud. A night bird whirred suddenly from a branch overhead, startling him.

He came to the place where Tabor was hidden—and well hidden, too. It had taken Torc almost an hour to find him. Even looking straight at the spot, Dave could barely make out the shape of the boy in the hollow he'd chosen. Tabor would be asleep, Torc had explained earlier. The shaman had made a drink that would ensure this, and open the mind to receive what might come to wake him.

Good kid, Dave thought. He'd never had a younger brother, wondered how he would have behaved toward one. A lot better than Vince did, the bitter thought came. A hell of a lot better than Vincent.

A moment longer he watched Tabor's hollow, then, assured there was no danger to be seen, he turned away. Not quite ready to rejoin the other two, Dave took an angled route back through the grove.

He hadn't seen the glade before. He almost stumbled into it, checked himself barely in time. Then he crouched down, as silently as he could.

There was a small pool, glittering silver in the moonlight. The grass, too, was tinted silver, it seemed dewy and fragrant, new somehow. And there was a stag, a full-grown buck, drinking from the pool.

Dave found he was holding his breath, keeping his body utterly still. The moonlit scene was so beautiful, so serene, it seemed to be a gift, a bestowing. He was leaving tomorrow, riding south to Paras Derval, the first stage of the road home. He would never be here again, see anything like this.

Should I not weep? he thought, aware that even such a question was a world away from the normal workings of his mind. But he was, he was a world away.

And then, as the hairs rose up on the back of his neck, Dave became aware that there was someone else beside the glade.

He knew before he even looked, which is what caused the awe: her presence had been made manifest in ways he scarcely comprehended. The very air, the moonlight, now reflected it.

Turning, in silence and dread, Dave saw a woman with a bow standing partway around the glade from where he crouched in darkness. She was clad in green, all in green, and her hair was the same silver as the moonlight. Very tall she was, queenly, and he could not have said if she was young or old, or the color of her eyes, because there was a light in her face that made him avert his face, abashed and afraid.

It happened very quickly. A second bird flew suddenly, flapping its wings loudly, from a tree. The stag raised its head in momentary alarm, a magnificent creature, a king of the wood. Out of the corner of his eye—for he dared not look directly—Dave saw the woman string an arrow to her bow. A moment, a bare pulsation of time, slipped past as the frieze held: the stag with its head high, poised to flee, the moonlight on the glade, on the water, the huntress with her bow.

Then the arrow was loosed and it found the long, exposed throat of the stag.

Dave hurt for the beast, for blood on that silvered grass, for the crumpled fall of a thing so noble.

What happened next tore a gasp of wonder from the core of his being. Where the dead stag lay, a shimmer appeared in the glade, a sheen of moonlight it seemed at first; then it darkened, took shape and then substance, and finally Dave saw another stag, identical, stand unafraid, unwounded, majestic, beside the body of the slain one. A moment it stood thus, then the great horns were lowered in homage to the huntress, and it was gone from the glade.

It was a thing of too much moonlit power, too much transcendency; there was an ache within him, an appalled awareness of his own—

"Stand! For I would see you before you die."

Of his own mortality.

With trembling limbs, Dave Martyniuk rose to stand before the goddess with her bow. He saw, without surprise, the arrow leveled on his heart, knew with certainty that he would not rise to bow to her once that shaft was in his breast.

"Come forward."

A curious, other-worldly calm descended upon Dave as he moved into the moonlight. He dropped the axe before his feet; it glittered on the grass.

"Look at me."

Drawing a deep breath, Dave raised his eyes and looked, as best he could, upon the shining of her face. She was beautiful, he saw, more beautiful than hope.

"No man of Fionavar," the goddess said, "may see Ceinwen hunt."

It gave him an out, but it was cheap, shallow, demeaning. He didn't want it.

"Goddess," he heard himself say, wondering at his own calm, "it was not intentional, but if there is a price to be paid, I will pay it."

A wind stirred the grass. "There is another answer you could have made, Dave Martyniuk," Ceinwen said.

Dave was silent.

An owl suddenly burst from the tree behind him, cutting like a shadow across the crescent of the moon and away. The third one, a corner of his mind said.

Then he heard the bowstring sing. *I am dead,* he had time, amazingly, to think, before the arrow thudded into the tree inches above his head.

His heart was sore. There was so much. He could feel the quivering of the long shaft; the feathers touched his hair.

"Not all need die," Green Ceinwen said. "Courage will be needed. You have sworn to pay a price to me, though, and one day I will claim it. Remember."

Dave sank to his knees; his legs would not bear him up before her any longer. There was such a glory in her face, in the shining of her hair.

"One thing more," he heard her say. He dared not look up. *"She is not for you."*

So his very heart lay open, and how should it be otherwise? But this, this he had decided for himself; he wanted her to know. He reached for the power of speech, a long way.

"No," he said. "I know. She's Torc's."

And the goddess laughed. "Has she no other choice?" Ceinwen said mockingly, and disappeared.

Dave, on his knees, lowered his head into his hands. His whole body began to shake violently. He was still like that when Torc and Levon came looking for him.

* * *

When Tabor woke, he was ready. There was no disorientation. He was in Faelinn, and fasting, and he was awake because it was time. He looked about, opening himself, prepared to receive what had come, his secret name, the ambit of his soul.

At which point, disorientation did set in. He was still in Faelinn, still in his hollow, even, but the wood had changed. Surely there had been no cleared space before him; he would never have chosen such a place. there *was* no such place near this hollow.

Then he saw that the night sky had a strange color to it, and with a tremor of fear he understood that he was still asleep, he was dreaming, and would find his animal in the strange country of this dream. It was not usual, he knew; usually you woke to see your totem. Mastering fear as best he could, Tabor waited.

It came from the sky.

Not a bird. No hawk or eagle—he had hoped, they all did—nor even an owl. No, his heart working strangely, Tabor realized then that the clearing was needed for the creature to land.

She did, so lightly the grass seemed scarcely to be supporting her. Lying very still, Tabor confronted his animal. With an effort, then, a very great effort, he stretched himself out, mind and soul, to the impossible creature that had come for him. It did not exist, this exquisite thing that stood gazing calmly back at him in the strangely hued night. It did not exist, but it would, he knew, as he felt her enter him, become a part of him as he of her, and he learned her name even as he learned what it was the god had summoned him to find and be found by.

For a last moment, the very last, the youngest child of Ivor heard, as if someone else were speaking, a part of himself whisper, "An eagle would have been enough."

It was true. It would have been more than enough, but it was not so. Standing very still before him, the creature appeared to understand his thought. He felt her then, gently, in his mind. *Do not reject me,* he heard as from within, while her great, astonishing eyes never left his own. *We will have only each other at the last.*

He understood. It was in his mind, and then in his heart also. It was very deep; he hadn't known he went so deep. In response he stretched forth a hand. The creature lowered her head, and Tabor touched the offered horn.

"Imraith-Nimphais," he said, remembered saying, before the universe went dark.

"Hola!" cried Ivor joyously. "See who comes! Let there be rejoicing, for see, the Weaver sends a new Rider to us."

But as Tabor drew nearer, Ivor could see that it had been a difficult fast. He had found his animal—such was written in every movement he made—but he had clearly gone a long way. It was not unusual, it was good, even. A sign of a deeper merger with the totem.

It was only when Tabor walked up close to him that Ivor felt the first touch of apprehension.

No boy came back from a true fast looking quite the same; they were boys no longer, it had to show in their faces. But what he saw in his son's eyes chilled Ivor to the core, even in the morning sunshine of the camp.

No one else seemed to notice; the tumult of welcome resounded as it always did, louder even, for the son of the Chieftain who had been called by the god.

Called to what, Ivor was thinking, as he walked beside his youngest child towards Gereint's house. Called to what?

He smiled, though, to mask his concern, and saw that Tabor did so as well; with his mouth only, not the eyes, and Ivor could feel a muscle jumping spasmodically where he gripped his son's arm.

Arriving at Gereint's door he knocked, and the two of them entered. It was dark inside, as always, and the noise from without faded to a distant murmur of anticipation.

Steadily, but with some care, Tabor walked forward and knelt before the shaman. Gereint touched him affectionately on the shoulder. Then Tabor lifted his head.

Even in the darkness Ivor saw Gereint's harshly checked motion of shock. He and Tabor faced each other, for what seemed a very long time.

At length Gereint spoke, but not the words of ritual. "This does not exist," the shaman said. Ivor clenched his fists.

Tabor said, "Not yet."

"It is a true finding," Gereint went on, as if he hadn't heard. "But there is no such animal. You have encompassed it?"

"I think so," Tabor said, and in his voice now was utter weariness. "I tried. I think I did."

"I think so, too," Gereint said, and there was wonder in his voice. "It is a very great thing Tabor dan Ivor."

Tabor made a gesture of deprecation; it seemed to drain what reserves of endurance he had left. "It just came," he said, and toppled sideways to his father's feet.

As he knelt to cradle his unconscious son, Ivor heard the shaman say in his voice of ritual, "His hour knows his name." And then, differently, "May all the powers of the Plain defend him."

"From what?" Ivor asked, knowing he should not.

Gereint swung to face him. "This one I would tell you if I could, old friend, but truly I do not know. He went so far the sky was changed."

Ivor swallowed. "Is it good?" he asked the shaman, who was supposed to know such things. "Is it good, Gereint?"

After too long a silence Gereint only repeated, "It is a very great thing," which was not what he needed to hear. Ivor looked down at Tabor, almost weightless in his arms. He saw the tanned skin, straight nose, unlined brow of youth, the unruly shock of brown hair, not long enough to tie properly, too long to wear loose—it always seemed to be that way with Tabor, he thought.

"Oh, my son," Ivor murmured, and then again, rocking him back and forth as he always used to, not so many years ago.

Chapter 13

Towards sundown they pulled the horses to a halt in a small gully, only a depression, really, defined by a series of low tummocks on the plain.

Dave was a little unnerved by all the openness. Only the dark stretch of Pendaran brooding to the west broke the long monotony of the prairie, and Pendaran wasn't a reassuring sight.

The Dalrei were undisturbed, though; for them, clearly, this exposed spot on the darkening earth was home. The Plain was their home, all of it. For twelve hundred years, Dave remembered.

Levon would allow no fires; supper was cold eltor meat and hard cheese, with river water in flasks to wash it down. It was good, though, partly because Dave was ravenous after the day's ride. He was brutally tired as well, he realized, unfolding his sleeping roll beside Torc's.

Overtired, he soon amended, for once inside the blanket he found that sleep eluded him. Instead he lay awake under the wide sky, his mind circling restlessly back over the day.

Tabor had still been unconscious when they left in the morning. "He went far," was all the Chieftain would say, but his eyes could not mask concern, even in the dark of Gereint's house.

But then the question of Tabor was put aside for a moment, as Dave told his own story of the night glade

and the Huntress, except for the very last, which was
his alone. There was a silence when he was done.

Cross-legged on his mat, Gereint asked, " 'Courage will be needed'—she said exactly that?''

Dave nodded, then remembered it was the shaman,
and grunted a yes. Gereint rocked back and forth after
that, humming tunelessly to himself for a long time.
So long that it startled Dave when he finally spoke.

"You must go south quickly, then, and quietly, I
think. Something grows, and if Silvercloak brought
you, then you should be with him.''

"It was only for the King's festival,'' Dave said.
Nervousness made it sound sharper than he meant.

"Perhaps,'' Gereint said, "but there are other
threads appearing now.''

Which wasn't all that wonderful.

Turning on his side, Dave could see the raised silhou-
ette of Levon against the night sky. It was deeply comforting to have that calm figure standing guard. Levon
hadn't wanted to come at first, he remembered. Concern
for his brother had left him visibly torn.

It was the Chieftain, asserting himself with absolute
firmness, who had settled the issue. Levon would be
useless at home. Tabor was being cared for. It was
not, in any case, unusual for a faster to sleep a long
time on his return. Levon, Ivor reminded his older
son, had done the same. Cechtar could lead the hunt
for ten days or two weeks—it would be good for him
in any case, after the loss of face caused by his failure
two days ago.

No, Ivor had said decisively, given Gereint's injunc-
tion as to speed and secrecy, it was important to get
Dave—Davor, he said, as they all did—south to Paras
Derval safely. Levon would lead, with Torc beside him
in a band of twenty. It was decided.

Logical and controlling, Dave had thought, and
coolly efficient. But then he remembered his own last
conversation with Ivor.

The horses had been readied. He had bidden formal, slightly stiff farewells to Leith and then Liane—he was very bad at goodbyes. He'd been embarrassed, too, by the knot of girls standing nearby. Ivor's daughter had been elusive and remote.

After, he'd looked in on Tabor. The boy was feverish, and restless with it. Dave wasn't good with this, either. He'd made a confused gesture to Leith, who'd come in with him. He hoped she'd understand, not that he could have said exactly what he'd wanted to convey.

It was after this that Ivor had taken him for that last stroll around the perimeter of the camp.

"The axe is yours," the Chieftain had begun. "From what you have described, I doubt you will have great use for it in your own world, but perhaps it will serve to remind you of the Dalrei." Ivor had frowned then. "A warlike remembrance, alas, of the Children of Peace. Is there anything else you would . . . ?"

"No," Dave had said, flustered. "No, it's fine. It's great. I'll ah, treasure it." Words. They had walked a few paces in silence, before Dave thought of a thing he did want to say.

"Say goodbye to Tabor for me, eh? I think . . . he's a good kid. He'll be all right, won't he?"

"I don't know," Ivor had replied with disturbing frankness. They had turned at the edge of the camp to walk north, facing the Mountain. By daylight Rangat was just as dazzling, the white slopes reflecting the sunlight so brightly it hurt the eye to see.

"I'm sure he'll be fine," Dave had said lamely, aware of how asinine that sounded. To cover it, he pushed on. "You've been, you know, really good to me here. I've . . . learned a lot." As he said it, he realized it was true.

For the first time Ivor smiled. "That pleases me," he said. "I like to believe we have things to teach."

"Oh, yeah, for sure," Dave said earnestly. "Of course you do. If I could stay longer. . . ."

"If you could stay," Ivor had said, stopping and

looking directly at Dave, "I think you would make a Rider."

Dave swallowed hard, and flushed with intense, self-conscious pleasure. He was speechless; Ivor had noticed. "If," the Chieftain had added, with a grin, "we could ever find a proper horse for you!"

Sharing the laugh, they resumed their walk. *God,* Dave was thinking, *I really, really like this man.* It would have been nice to be able to say it.

But then Ivor had thrown him the curve. "I don't know what your encounter last night means," he had said softly, "but it means a good deal, I think. I am sending Levon south with you, Davor. It is the right thing, though I hate to see him go. He is young yet, and I love him very much. Will you take care of him for me?"

Mean, unbalancing curve ball. "What?" Dave had exclaimed, bridling reflexively at the implications. "What are you talking about? *He's* the one who knows where he's going! You want me to guard him? Shouldn't it be the other way around?"

Ivor's expression was sad. "Ah, my son," he had said gently, "you have far to go in some ways. You, too, are young. Of course I told him to guard you as well, and with everything he has. I tell you both. Don't you see, Davor?"

He did see. Too late, of course. And clearly, he'd been an idiot, again. Again. And with no time to make it up, for they had looped full circle by then, and Levon, Torc, and seventeen other Riders were already mounted, with what seemed to be the whole third tribe turning out to see them off.

So there had been no last private word. He'd hugged Ivor hard, though, hoping the Chieftain would somehow know that it meant a lot for him to do that. Hoping, but not knowing if.

Then he had left, south for Brennin and the way home, the axe at his saddle side, sleeping roll behind, a few other things behind as well, too far behind for anything to be done.

On the starlit dark of the Plain, Dave opened his eyes again. Levon was still there, watching over them, over him. Kevin Laine would have known how to handle that last talk, he thought, surprisingly, and slept.

On the second day they started just before sunrise. Levon set a brisk but not a killing pace; the horses would have to last, and the Dalrei knew how to judge these things. They rode in a tight cluster, with three men, rotating every second hour, sent ahead a half-mile. Quickly and quietly, Gereint had advised, and they all knew Torc had seen svart alfar heading south two weeks before. Levon might take calculated risks on the hunt, but he was not a rash man; Ivor's son could hardly be so. He kept them moving in a state of watchful speed, and the trees at the outreaches of Pendaran rolled steadily by on their right as the sun climbed in the sky.

Gazing at the woods, less than a mile away, Dave was bothered by something. Kicking his horse forward, he caught up with Levon at the head of the main party.

"Why," he asked, without preamble, "are we riding so close to the forest?"

Levon smiled. "You are the seventh man to ask me that," he said cheerfully. "It isn't very complex. I'm taking the fastest route. If we swing farther east we'll have to ford two rivers and deal with hilly land between them. This line takes us to Adein west of the fork where Rienna joins it. Only one river, and as you see, the riding is easy."

"But the forest? It's supposed to be. . . ."

"Pendaran is deadly to those who enter it. No one does. But the Wood is angry, not evil, and unless we trespass, the powers within it will not be stirred by our riding here. There are superstitions otherwise, but I have been taught by Gereint that this is so."

"What about an ambush, like from those svart alfar?"

Levon was no longer smiling. "A svart would sooner
die than enter Pendaran," he said. "The Wood for-
gives none of us."

"For what?" Dave asked.

"Lisen," Levon said. "Shall I tell the story?"

"I'm not going anywhere," said Dave.

"I have to explain magic to you first, I think. You
were brought here by Silvercloak. You would have seen
Matt Sören?"

"The Dwarf? Sure."

"Do you know how they are bound to each other?"

"Haven't a clue. Are they?"

"Assuredly," said Levon, and as they rode south
over the prairie, Dave learned, as Paul Schafer had
four nights before, about the binding of mage and
source, and how magic was made of that union.

Then as Levon began his tale, Torc came up quietly
on his other side. The three of them rode together,
bound by the rhythm and cadence of Lisen's tragedy.

"It is a long story," Levon began, "and much of
import comes into it, and has grown out of it. I do not
know nearly the whole, but it begins in the days before
the Bael Rangat.

"In those days, the days before magic was as I have
told you it now is, Amairgen, a counselor to Conary,
the High King in Paras Derval, rode forth alone from
Brennin.

"Magic in that time was governed by the earthroot,
the avarlith, and so it was within the domain of the
Priestesses of the Mother in Gwen Ystrat, and jeal-
ously they guarded their control. Amairgen was a
proud and brilliant man, and he chafed at this. So he
went forth one morning in the spring of the year, to
see if it need always be so.

"In time he came, after many adventures that are
all part of the full tale—though most of them I do not
know—to the sacred grove in Pendaran. The Wood

was not angry then, but it was a place of power, and never one that welcomed the presence of men, especially in the grove. Amairgen was brave, though, and he had been journeying long without answer to his quest, so he dared greatly, and passed a night alone in that place.

"There are songs about that night: about the three visitations he had, and his mind battle with the earth demon that came up through the grass; it was a long and terrible night, and it is sung that no man else would have lived or been whole of mind to see the dawn.

"Be that as it may, just before morning there came a fourth visitation to Amairgen, and this one was from the God, from Mörnir, and it was beneficent, for it taught to Amairgen the runes of the skylore that freed the mages ever after from the Mother.

"There was war among the gods after that, it is told, for the Goddess was wrathful at what Mörnir had done, and it was long before she would let herself be placated. Some say, though I would not know if it is true, that it was the discord and the chaos of this conflict that gave Maugrim, the Unraveller, the chance to slip from the watch of the younger gods. He came from the places where they have their home and took root in the north lands of Fionavar. So some songs and stories have it. Others say he was always here, or that he slipped into Fionavar when the Weaver's eye was dimmed with love at the first emergence of the lios alfar—the Children of the Light. Still others tell that it was as the Weaver wept, when first man slew his brother. I know not; there are many stories. He is here and he cannot be killed. The gods grant he be always bound.

"Be all of that as it may, in the morning when Amairgen rose up, the runes in his heart and great power waiting there, he was in mortal danger yet; for the Wood, having its own guardians, was greatly angered at his having dared the grove at night, and Lisen was sent forth to break his heart and kill him.

"Of that meeting there is one song only. It was made not long after, by Ra-Termaine, greatest of all singers, Lord then of the lios alfar, and he crafted it in homage and remembrance of Amairgen. It is the most beautiful lay ever fashioned, and no poet since has ever touched the theme.

"There were very mighty peoples on the earth in those days, and among them all, Lisen of the Wood was as a Queen. A wood spirit she was, a deiena, of which there are many, but Lisen was more. It is said that on the night she was born in Pendaran, the evening star shone as brightly as the moon, and all the goddesses from Ceinwen to Nemain gave grant of their beauty to that child in the grove, and the flowers bloomed at night in the shining that arose when they all came together in that place. No one has ever been or will be more fair than was Lisen, and though the deiena live very long, Dana and Mörnir that night, as their joint gift, made her immortal that this beauty might never be lost.

"These gifts she was given at her birth, but not even the gods may shape exactly what they will, and some say that this truth is at the heart of the whole long tale. Be that so, or not, in the morning after his battles she came to Amairgen to break him with her beauty and slay him for his presumption of the night. But, as Ra-Termaine's song tells, Amairgen was as one exalted that morning, clothed in power and lore, and the presence of Mörnir was in his eyes. So did the design of the God act to undo the design of the God, for coming to him then, wrapped in her own beauty like a star, Lisen fell in love and he with her, and so their doom was woven that morning in the grove.

"She became his source. Before the sun had set that day, he had taught her the runes. They were made mage and source by the ritual, and the first sky magic was wrought in the grove that day. That night they lay

down together, and as the one song tells, Amairgen
slept at length a second night in the sacred grove, but
this time within the mantle of her hair. They went
forth together in the morning from that place, bound
as no living creatures to that day had been. Yet because Amairgen's place was at the right hand of Conary, and there were other men to whom he had to teach
the skylore, he returned to Paras Derval and founded
the Council of the Mages, and Lisen went with him
and so left the shelter of the Wood.''

Levon was silent. They rode thus for a long time.
Then, ''The tale is truly very complex now, and it
picks up many other tales from the Great Years. It was
in those days that the one we call the Unraveler raised
his fortress of Starkadh in the Ice and came down on
all the lands with war. There are so many deeds to tell
of from that time. The one the Dalrei sing is of Revor's
Ride, and it is very far from the least of the great
things that were done. But Amairgen Whitebranch, as
he came to be called, for the staff Lisen found for him
in Pendaran, was ever at the center of the war, and
Lisen was at his side, source of his power and his soul.

''There are so many tales, Davor, but at length it
came to pass that Amairgen learned by his art that
Maugrim had taken for his own a place of great power,
hidden far out at sea, and was drawing upon it might-
ily for his strength.

''He determined then that this island must be found
and wrested away from the Dark. So Amairgen gathered to him a company of one hundred lios alfar and
men, with three mages among them, and they set sail
west from Taerlindel to find Cader Sedat, and Lisen
was left behind.''

''What? Why?'' Dave rasped, stunned.

It was Torc who answered. ''She was a deiena,'' he
said, his own voice sounding difficult. ''A deiena dies
at sea. Her immortality was subject to the nature of
her kind.''

''It is so,'' Levon resumed quietly. ''They built in

that time for her the Anor Lisen at the westernmost part of Pendaran. Even in the midst of war, men and lios alfar and the powers of the Wood came together to do this for her out of love. Then she placed upon her brow the Circlet of Lisen, Amairgen's parting gift. The Light against the Dark, it was called, for it shone of its own self, and with that light upon her brow—so great a beauty never else having been in any world—Lisen turned her back on the war and the Wood and, climbing to the summit of the tower, she set her face westward to the sea, that the Light she bore might show Amairgen the way home.

''No man knows what happened to him or those who sailed in that ship. Only that one night Lisen saw, and those who stood guard beside the Anor saw as well, a dark ship sailing slowly along the coast in the moonlight. And it is told that the moon setting west in that hour shone through its tattered sails with a ghostly light, and it could be seen that the ship was Amairgen's, and it was empty. Then, when the moon sank into the sea, that ship disappeared forever.

''Lisen took the Circlet from her brow and laid it down; then she unbound her hair that it might be as it was when first they had come together in the grove. Having done these things, she leaped into the darkness of the sea and so died.''

The sun was high in the sky, Dave noticed. It seemed wrong, somehow, that this should be so, that the day should be so bright. ''I think,'' Levon whispered, ''that I will go ride up front for a time.'' He kicked his horse to a gallop. Dave and Torc looked at each other. Neither spoke a word. The Plain was east, the Wood west, the Sun was high in the sky.

Levon took a double shift up front. Late in the day Dave went forward himself to relieve him. Towards sunset they saw a black swan flying north almost directly overhead, very high. The sight filled them all

with a vague, inexplicable sense of disquiet. Without
a word being spoken, they picked up speed.

As they continued south, Pendaran gradually began
to fall away westward. Dave knew it was there, but by
the time darkness fell, the Wood could no longer be
seen. When they stopped for the night, there was only
grassland stretching away in every direction under the
profligate dazzle of the summer stars, scarcely dimmed
by the last thin crescent of the moon.

Later that night a dog and a wolf would battle in
Mörnirwood, and Colan's dagger, later still, would be
unsheathed with a sound like a harpstring in a stone
chamber underground beside Eilathen's lake.

At dawn the sun rose red, and a dry, prickly heat
came with it. From first mounting, the company was
going faster than before. Levon increased the point
men to four and pulled them back a little closer, so
both parties could see each other all the time.

Late in the morning the Mountain exploded behind
them.

With the deepest terror of his life, Dave turned with
the Dalrei to see the tongue of flame rising to master
the sky. They saw it divide to shape the taloned hand,
and then they heard the laughter of Maugrim.

"The gods grant he be always bound," Levon had
said, only yesterday.

No dice, it seemed.

There was nothing within Dave that could surmount
the brutal sound of that laughter on the wind. They
were small, exposed, they were open to him and he
was free. In a kind of trance, Dave saw the point men
galloping frantically back to join them.

"Levon! Levon! We must go home!" one of them
was shouting as he came nearer. Dave turned to Ivor's
son and, looking at him, his heart slowed towards nor-
mality, and he marveled again. There was no expression on Levon's face, his profile seemed chiseled from
stone as he gazed at the towering fire above Rangat.

But in that very calm, that impassive acceptance, Dave found a steadfastness of his own. Without moving a muscle, Levon seemed to be growing, to be willing himself to grow large enough to match, to overmatch the terror in the sky and on the wind. And somehow in that moment Dave had a flashing image of Ivor doing the selfsame thing, two days' ride back north, under the very shadow of that grasping hand. He looked for Torc and found the dark man gazing back at him, and in Torc's eyes Dave saw not the stern resistance of Levon, but a fierce, bright, passionate defiance, a bitter hatred of what that hand meant, but not fear.

Your hour knows your name, Dave Martyniuk thought, and then, in that moment of apocalypse, had another thought: *I love these people.* The realization hit him, for Dave was what he was, almost as hard as the Mountain had. Struggling to regain his inner balance, he realized that Levon was speaking, quelling the babble of voices around him.

"We do not go back. My father will be caring for the tribe. They will go to Celidon, all the tribes will. And so will we, after Davor is with Silvercloak. Two days ago Gereint said that something was coming. This is it. We go south as fast as we can to Brennin, and there," said Levon, "I will take counsel with the High King."

Even as he spoke, Ailell dan Art was dying in Paras Derval. When Levon finished, not another word was said. The Dalrei regrouped and began riding, very fast now and all together. They rode henceforth with a hard, unyielding intensity, turning their backs on their tribe without a demurrer to follow Levon, though every one of them knew, even as they galloped, that if there was war with Maugrim, it would be fought on the Plain.

It was that alert tension that gave them warning, though in the end it would not be enough to save them.

Torc it was who, late in the afternoon, sped a distance ahead; bending sideways in his saddle, he rode

low to the ground for a time before wheeling back to
Levon's side. The Wood was close again, on their
right. "We are coming to trouble," Torc said shortly.
"There is a party of svart alfar not far ahead of us."

"How many?" Levon asked calmly, signaling a
halt.

"Forty. Sixty."

Levon nodded. "We can beat them, but there will
be losses. They know we are here, of course."

"If they have eyes," Torc agreed. "We are very
exposed."

"Very well. We are close to Adein, but I do not
want a fight now. It will waste us some time, but we
are going to flank around them and cross both rivers
farther east."

"I don't think we can, Levon," Torc murmured.

"Why?" Levon had gone very still.

"Look."

Dave turned east with Levon to where Torc was
pointing, and after a moment he, too, saw the dark
mass moving over the grass, low, about a mile away,
and coming nearer.

"What are they?" he asked, his voice tight.

"Wolves," Levon snapped. "Very many." He drew
his sword. "We can't go around—they will slow us by
the rivers for the svarts. We must fight through south
before they reach us." He raised his voice. "We fight
on the gallop, my friends. Kill and ride, no lingering.
When you reach Adein, you cross. We can outrun them
on the other side." He paused, then: "I said before
there would be war. It seems that we are to fight the
first battle of our people. Let the servants of Maugrim
now learn to fear the Dalrei again, as they did when
Revor rode!"

With an answering shout, the Riders, Dave among
them, loosed their weapons and sprang into gallop.
His heart thudding, Dave followed Levon over a low
tummock. On the other side he could see the river
glistening less than a mile away. But in their path stood

the svart alfar, and as soon as the Dalrei crested the
rise a shower of arrows was launched towards them.
A moment later, Dave saw a Rider fall beside him,
blood flowering from his breast.

A rage came over Dave then. Kicking his horse to
greater speed, he crashed, with Torc and Levon on
either side, into the line of svarts. Leaning in the saddle, he whistled the great axe down to cleave one of
the ugly, dark green creatures where it stood. Light-
headed with fury, he pulled the axe clear and turned
to swing it again.

"No!" Torc screamed. "Kill and ride! Come on!"
The wolves, Dave saw in a flying glance, were less
than half a mile away. Wheeling hard, he thundered
with the others towards the Adein. They were through,
it seemed. One man dead, two others nursing wounds,
but the river was close now and once across they would
be safe.

They would have been. They should have been. It
was only sheerest, bitterest bad luck that the band of
svarts that had ambushed Brendel and the lios alfar
were there waiting.

They were, though, and there were almost a hundred of them left to rise from the shallows of Adein
and block the path of the Dalrei. So with the wolves
on their flank, and svarts before and behind, Levon
was forced into a standing fight.

Under that red sun the Children of Peace fought
their first battle in a thousand years. With courage
fueled by rage they fought on their land, launching
arrows of their own, angling their horses in jagged
lethal movements, scything with swords soon red with
blood.

"Revor!" Dave heard Levon scream, and the very
name seemed to cow the massed forces of the Dark.
Only for a moment, though, and there were so many.
In the chaos of the melee, Dave saw face after face of
the nightmare svarts appear before him with lifted
swords and razor teeth bared, and in a frenzy of battle

fury he raised and lowered the axe again and again. All he could do was fight, and so he did. He scarcely knew how many svarts had died under his iron, but then, pulling the axe free from a mashed skull, Dave saw that the wolves had come, and he suddenly understood that death was here, by the Adein River on the Plain. Death, at the hands of these loathsome creatures, death for Levon, for Torc. . . .

"No!" Dave Martyniuk cried then, his voice a mighty bellow over the battle sounds, as inspiration blasted him. "To the Wood! Come on!"

And punching Levon's shoulder, he reined his own horse so that it reared high above the encircling enemy. On the way down he swung the axe once on either side of the descending hooves, and on each side he killed. For a moment the svarts hesitated, and using the moment, Dave kicked his horse again and pounded into them, the axe sweeping red, once, and again, and again; then suddenly he was clear, as their ranks broke before him, and he cut sharply away west. West, where Pendaran lay, brooding and unforgiving, where none of them, man or svart alfar or even the giant, twisted wolves of Galadan, dared go.

Three of them did dare, though. Looking back, Dave saw Levon and Torc knife through the gap his rush had carved and follow him in a flat-out race west, with the wolves at their heels and arrows falling about them in the growing dark.

Three only, no more, though not for lack of courage. The rest were dead. Nor had there been a scanting of gallant bravery in any one of the Dalrei who died that day, seventeen of them, by Adein where it runs into Llewenmere by Pendaran Wood.

They were devoured by the svart alfar as the sun went down. The dead always were. It was not the same as if it were the lios they had killed, of course, but blood was blood, and the red joy of killing was thick within them all that night. After, the two groups of them, so happily come together, made a pile of all the bones, clean-picked and otherwise, and started in, letting the wolves join them now, on their own dead.

Blood was blood.

There was a lake on their left, dark waters glimpsed through a lattice of trees as they whipped by. Dave had a fleeting image of hurtful beauty, but the wolves were close behind and they could not linger. At full tilt they hurtled into the outreaches of the forest, leaping a fallen branch, dodging sudden trees, not slacking pace at all, until at last Dave became aware that the wolves were no longer chasing them.

The twisting half-trail they followed became rougher, forcing them to slow, and then it was merely an illusion, not really a path. The three of them stopped, breathing with harsh effort amid the lengthening shadows of trees.

No one spoke. Levon's face, Dave saw, was like stone again, but not as before. This he recognized: not the steadfastness of resolution, but a rigid control locking the muscles, the heart, against the pain inside. You held it in, Dave thought, had always thought. It didn't belong to anyone else. He couldn't look at Levon's face very long, though; it twisted him somehow, on top of everything else.

Turning to Tore, he saw something different. "You're bleeding," he said, looking at the blood welling from the dark man's thigh. "Get down, let's have a look."

He, of course, hadn't a clue what to do. It was Levon, glad of the need for action, who tore his sleeping roll into strips and made a tourniquet for the wound, which was messy but, after cleaning, could be seen to be shallow.

By the time Levon finished, it was dark, and they had all been deeply conscious for some moments of something pulsing in the woods around them. Nor was there anything remotely vague about it: what they sensed was anger, and it could be heard in the sound of the leaves, felt in the vibrations of the earth beneath their feet. They were in Pendaran, and men, and the Wood did not forgive.

"We can't stay here!" Torc said abruptly. It sounded loud in the dark; for the first time, Dave heard strain in his voice.

"Can you walk?" Levon asked.

"I will," said Torc grimly. "I would rather be on my feet and moving when we meet whatever is sent for us." The leaves were louder now, and there seemed—or was that imagination?—to be a rhythm to their sound.

"We will leave the horses, then," Levon said. "They will be all right. I agree with you—I don't think we can lie down tonight. We will walk south, until we meet what—"

"Until we're out!" Dave said strongly. "Come on, both of you. Levon, you said before, this place isn't evil."

"It doesn't have to be, to kill us," said Torc. "Listen." It was not imagination; there *was* a pattern to the sound of the leaves.

"Would you prefer," Dave snapped, "to go back and try to make nice to the wolves?"

"He's right, Torc," Levon said. In the dark, only his long yellow hair could be seen. Torc, in black, was almost invisible. "And Davor," Levon went on, in a different voice, "you wove something very bright back there. I don't think any man in the tribe could have forced that opening. Whatever happens after, you saved our lives then."

"I just swung the thing," Dave muttered.

At which Torc, astonishingly, laughed aloud. For a moment the listening trees were stilled. No mortal had laughed in Pendaran for a millennium. "You are," said Torc dan Sorcha, "as bad as me, as bad as him. Not one of us can deal with praise. Is your face red right now, my friend?"

Of course it was, for God's sake. "What do you

think?'' he mumbled. Then, feeling the ridiculousness of it, hearing Levon's snort of amusement, Dave felt something let go inside, tension, fear, grief, all of them, and he laughed with his friends in the Wood where no man went.

It lasted for some time; they were all young, had fought their first battle, seen comrades slaughtered beside them. There was a cutting edge of hysteria to the moment.

Levon took them past it. ''Torc is right,'' he said finally. ''We are alike. In this, and in other ways. Before we leave this place, there is a thing I want to do. Friends of mine have died today. It would be good to have two new brothers. Will you mingle blood with me?''

''I have no brothers,'' Torc said softly. ''It would be good.''

Dave's heart was racing. ''For sure,'' he said.

And so the ritual was enacted in the Wood. Torc made the incisions with his blade and they touched their wrists, each to each, in the dark. No one spoke. After, Levon made bandages, then they freed the horses, took their gear and weapons, and set forth together south through the forest, Torc leading, Levon last, Dave between his brothers.

As it happened, they had done more than they knew. They had been watched, and Pendaran understood these things, bindings wrought of blood. It did not assuage the anger or the hate, for she was forever lost who should never have died; but though these three had still to be slain, they could be spared madness before the end. So it was decided as they walked, oblivious to the meaning of the whispering around them, wrapped in it, though, as in a net of sound.

For Torc, nothing had ever been so difficult or shaken him so deeply as that progression. Over and above the horrors of the slaughter by Adein, the deep terror of being in Pendaran, there was another thing for him: he was a night mover, a woods person, this was his milieu, and all he had to do was lead his companions south.

Yet he could not.

Roots appeared, inexplicably, for him to stumble over, fallen branches blocked paths, other trails simply ended without apparent cause. Once, he almost fell.

South, that's all! he snarled to himself, oblivious in his concentration to the aching of his leg. It was no good, though—every trail that seemed to hold promise soon turned, against all sense or reason, to the west. Are the trees moving? he asked himself once, and pulled sharply away from the implications of that. Or am I just being incredibly stupid?

For whichever cause, supernatural or psychological, after a little while it was clear to him that hard as he might try—cutting right through a thicket once—to keep them on the eastern edges of the Great Wood, they were being drawn, slowly, very patiently, but quite inescapably, westward into the heart of the forest.

It was not, of course, his fault at all. None of what happened was. Pendaran had had a thousand years to shape the paths and patterns of its response to intrusions such as theirs.

It is well, the trees whispered to the spirits of the Wood.

Very well, the deiena replied.

Leaves, leaves, Torc heard. Leaves and wind.

For Dave that night walk was very different. He was not of Fionavar, knew no legends of the Wood to appal, beyond the story Levon had told the day before, and that was more sorrowful than frightening. With Torc before and Levon behind, he felt quite certain that they were going as they should. He was blissfully unaware of Torc's desperate maneuverings ahead of him, and after a time he grew accustomed to, even sedated by, the murmurings all around them.

So sedated, that he had been walking alone, due west, for about ten minutes before he realized it.

"Torc!" he cried, as sudden fear swept over him. *"Levon!"* There was, of course, no reply. He was utterly alone in Pendaran Wood at night.

Chapter 14

Had it been any other night, they would have died.

Not badly, for the forest would do this much honor to their exchange of blood, but their deaths had been quite certain from the moment they had ridden past haunted Llewenmere into the trees. One man alone had walked in Pendaran and come out alive since Maugrim, whom the powers called Sathain, had been bound. All others had died, badly, screaming before the end. Pity was not a thing the Wood could feel.

Any other night. But away south of them in another wood, this was Paul Schafer's third night on the Summer Tree.

Even as the three intruders were being delicately separated from each other, the focus of Pendaran was torn utterly away from them by something impossible and humbling, even for the ancient, nameless powers of the Wood.

A red moon rose in the sky.

In the forest it was as if a fire had started. Every power and spirit of the wild magic, of tree and flower or beast, even the dark, oldest ones that seldom woke and that all the others feared, the powers of night and the dancing ones of dawn, those of music and those who moved in deadly silence, all of them began a mad rush away, away, to the sacred grove, for they had to be there before that moon was high enough to shed her light upon the glade.

* * *

Dave heard the whispering of the leaves stop. It frightened him, everything did now. But then there came a swift sense of release, as if he were no longer being watched. In the next instant he felt a great sweep, as of wind but not wind, as something rushed over him, through him, hurtling away to the north.

Understanding nothing, only that the Wood seemed to be simply a wood now, the trees merely trees, Dave turned to the east, and he saw the full moon resting, red and stupefying, atop the highest trees.

Such was the nature of the Mother's power that even Dave Martyniuk, alone and lost, unspeakably far from home and a world he somewhat comprehended, could look upon that moon and take heart from it. Even Dave could see it for an answer to the challenge of the Mountain.

Not release, only an answer, for that red moon meant war as much as anything ever could. It meant blood and war, but not a hopeless conflict now, not with Dana's intercession overhead, higher than even Rangat's fires could be made to climb.

All this was inchoate, confused, struggling for some inner articulation in Dave that never quite came together; the sense was there, though, the intuitive awareness that the Lord of the Dark might be free, but he would not be unopposed. It was thus with most of those across Fionavar who saw that symbol in the heavens: the Mother works, has always worked, along the tracings of the blood so that we know things of her we do not realize we know. In very great awe, hope stirring in his heart, Dave looked into the eastern sky, and the thought that came to him with absolute incongruity was that his father would have liked to see this thing.

For three days Tabor had not opened his eyes. When the Mountain unleashed its terror, he only stirred on his bed and murmured words that his mother, watching, could not understand. She adjusted the cloth on his forehead and the blankets over him, unable to do more.

She had to leave him for a while after that, for Ivor had given orders, swift and controlled, to quell the panic caused by the laughter riding on the wind. They were starting east for Celidon at first light tomorrow. They were too alone here, too exposed, under the very palm, it seemed, of the hand that hung above Rangat.

Even through the loud tumult of preparation, with the camp a barely contained whirlwind of chaos, Tabor slept.

Nor did the rising of a red full moon on new moon night cause him to wake, though all the tribe stopped what they were doing, wonder shining in their eyes, to see it swing up above the Plain.

"This gives us time," Gereint said, when Ivor snatched a minute to talk with him. The work continued at night, by the strange moonlight. "He will not move quickly now, I think."

"Nor will we," Ivor said. "It is going to take us time to get there. I want us out by dawn."

"I'll be ready," the old shaman said. "Just put me on a horse and point it the right way."

Ivor felt a surge of affection for Gereint. The shaman had been white-haired and wrinkled for so long he seemed to be timeless. He wasn't, though, and the rapid journey of the coming days would be a hardship for him.

As so often, Gereint seemed to read his mind. "I never thought," he said, very low, "I would live so long. Those who died before this day may be the fortunate ones."

"Maybe so," Ivor said soberly. "There will be war."

"And have we any Revors or Colans, any Ra-Termaines or Seithrs among us? Have we Amairgen or Lisen?" Gereint asked painfully.

"We shall have to find them," Ivor said simply. He

laid a hand on the shaman's shoulder. "I must go. Tomorrow."

"Tomorrow. But see to Tabor."

Ivor had planned to supervise the last stages of the wagon loading, but instead he detailed Cechtar to that and went to sit quietly by his son.

Two hours later Tabor woke, though not truly. He rose up from his bed, but Ivor checked his cry of joy, for he saw that his son was wrapped in a waking trance, and it was known to be dangerous to disturb such a thing.

Tabor dressed, quickly and in silence, and left the house. Outside the camp was finally still, asleep in troubled anticipation of grey dawn. The moon was very high, almost overhead.

It was, in fact, now high enough. West of them a dance of light was beginning in the clearing of the sacred grove, while the gathered powers of Pendaran watched.

Walking very quickly, Tabor went around to the stockade, found his horse, and mounted. Lifting the gate, he rode out and began to gallop west.

Ivor, running to his own horse, leaped astride, bareback, and followed. Alone on the Plain, father and son rode towards the Great Wood, and Ivor, watching the straight back and easy riding of his youngest child, felt his heart grow sore.

Tabor had gone far indeed. It seemed he had farther yet to go. *The Weaver shelter him,* Ivor prayed, looking north to the now quiescent glory of Rangat.

More than an hour they rode, ghosts on the night plain, before the massive presence of Pendaran loomed ahead of them, and then Ivor prayed again: *Let him not go into it. Let it not be there, for I love him.*

Does that count for anything, he wondered; striving to master the deep fear the Wood always aroused in him.

It seemed that it might, for Tabor stopped his horse fifty yards from the trees and sat quietly, watching the

dark forest. Ivor halted some distance behind. He felt
a longing to call his son's name, to call him back from
wherever he had gone, was going.

He did not. Instead, when Tabor, murmuring something his father could not hear, slipped from his mount
and walked into the forest, Ivor did the bravest deed
of all his days, and followed. No call of any god could
make Ivor dan Banor let his son walk tranced into Pendaran Wood alone.

And thus did it come to pass that father and both
sons entered into the Great Wood that night.

Tabor did not go far. The trees were thin yet at the
edge of the forest, and the red moon lit their path with
a strangely befitting light. None of this, Ivor thought,
belonged to the daylight world. It was very quiet. Too
quiet, he realized, for there was a breeze, he could
feel it on his skin, and yet it made no sound among
the leaves. The hair rose up on the back of Ivor's neck.
Fighting for calm in the enchanted silence, he saw
Tabor suddenly stop ten paces ahead, holding himself
very still. And a moment later Ivor saw a glory step
from the trees to stand before his son.

Westward was the sea, she had known that, though
but newly born. So east she had walked from the birthing place she shared with Lisen—though that she did
not know—and as she passed among the gathered
powers, seen and unseen, a murmur like the forest's
answer to the sea had risen up and fallen like a wave
in the Wood.

Very lightly she went, knowing no other way to tread
the earth, and on either side the creatures of the forest
did her homage, for she was Dana's, and a gift in time
of war, and so was much more than beautiful.

And as she traveled, there came a face into the eye
of her mind—how, she knew not, nor would ever—but
from the time that was before she was, a face appeared
to her, nut-brown, very young, with dark unruly hair,
and eyes she needed to look into. Besides, and more
than anything, this one knew her name. So here and

there her path turned as she sought, all unknowing, delicate and cloaked in majesty, a certain place within the trees.

Then she was there and he was there before her, waiting, a welcome in those eyes, and a final acceptance of what she was, all of her, both edges of the gift.

She felt his mind in hers like a caress, and nudged him back as if with her horn. *Only each other, at the last,* she thought, her first such thought. Whence had it come?

I know, his mind answered her. *There will be war.*

For this was I birthed, she replied, aware of a sudden of what lay sheathed within the light, light grace of her form. It frightened her.

He saw this and came nearer. She was the color of the risen moon, but the horn that brushed the grass when she lowered her head for his touch was silver.

My name? she asked.

Imraith-Nimphais, he told her, and she felt power burst within her like a star.

Joyously she asked, *Would you fly?*

She felt him hesitate.

I would not let you fall, she told him, a little hurt.

She felt his laughter then. *Oh, I know, bright one,* he said, *but if we fly you may be seen and our time is not yet come.*

She tossed her head impatiently, her mane rippling. The trees were thinner here, she could see the stars, the moon. She wanted them. *There is no one to see but one man,* she told him. The sky was calling her.

My father, he said. *I love him.*

Then so will I, she answered, *but now I would fly. Come!*

And within her then he said, *I will,* and moved to mount astride her back. He was no weight at all; she was very strong and would be stronger yet. She bore him past the other, older man, and because Tabor loved him, she lowered her horn to him as they went by.

Then they were clear of the trees, and there was
open grass and oh, the sky, all the sky above. For the
first time she released her wings and they rose in a
rush of joy to greet the stars and the moon whose child
she was. She could feel his mind within hers, the ex-
ulting of his heart, for they were bound forever, and
she knew that they were glorious, wheeling across the
wide night sky, Imraith-Nimphais and the Rider who
knew her name.

When the chestnut unicorn his son rode lowered her
head to him as they passed, Ivor could not keep the
tears from his eyes. He always cried too easily, Leith
used to scold, but this, surely this transcendency . . . ?
And then, turning to follow them, he saw it become
even more, for the unicorn took flight. Ivor lost all
track of time then, seeing Tabor and the creature of
his fast go soaring across the night. He could almost
share the joy they felt in the discovery of flight, and
he felt blessed in his heart. He had walked into Pendaran and come out alive to see this creature of the
Goddess bear his son like a comet above the Plain.

He was too much a Chieftain and too wise to forget
that there was a darkness coming. Even this creature,
this gift, could not be an easy thing, not colored as
she was like the moon, like blood. Nor would Tabor
ever be the same, he knew. But these sorrows were for
the daylight—tonight he could let his heart fly with the
two of them, the two young ones at play in the wind
between him and the stars. Ivor laughed, as he had not
in years, like a child.

After an unknown time they came down gently, not
far from where he stood. He saw his son lay his head
against that of the unicorn, beside the silver shining
of its horn. Then Tabor stepped back, and the creature
turned, moving with terrible grace, and went back into
the darkness of the Wood.

When Tabor turned to him, his eyes were his own

again. Wordlessly, for there were no words, Ivor held out his arms and his youngest child ran into them.

"You saw?" Tabor asked finally, his head against his father's chest.

"I did. You were glorious."

Tabor straightened, his eyes reclaiming their dance, their youth. "She bowed to you! I didn't ask. I just said you were my father and I loved you, so she said she would love you, too, and she bowed."

Ivor's heart was full of light. "Come," he said gruffly, "it is time to go home. Your mother will be weeping with anxiety."

"Mother?" Tabor asked in a tone so comical Ivor had to laugh. They mounted and rode back, slowly now, and together, over their Plain. On this eve of war a curious peace seemed to descend upon Ivor. Here was his land, the land of his people for so long that the years lost meaning. From Andarien to Brennin, from the mountains to Pendaran, all the grass was theirs. The Plain *was* the Dalrei, and they, it. He let that knowledge flow through him like a chord of music, sustaining and enduring.

It would have to endure in the days to come, he knew, the full power of the Dark coming down. And he also knew that it might not. Tomorrow, Ivor thought, I will worry tomorrow; and riding in peace over the prairie beside his son, he came back to the camp and saw Leith waiting for them by the western gate.

Seeing her, Tabor slipped from his horse and ran into her arms. Ivor willed his eyes to stay dry as he watched. Sentimental fool, he castigated himself; she was right. When Leith, still holding the boy, looked a question up at him he nodded as briskly as he could.

"To bed, young man," she said firmly. "We're riding in a few hours. You need sleep."

"Oh, Mother," Tabor complained, "I've done nothing *but* sleep for the—"

"Bed!" Leith said, in a voice all her children knew.

"Yes, Mother," Tabor replied, with such pure happiness that even Leith smiled watching him go into the camp. Fourteen, Ivor thought, regardless of everything. Absolutely regardless.

He looked down at his wife. She met the look in silence. It was, he realized, their first moment alone since the Mountain.

"It was all right?" she asked.

"It was. It is something very bright."

"I don't think I want to know, just yet."

He nodded, seeing once more, discovering it anew, how beautiful she was.

"Why did you marry me?" he asked impulsively.

She shrugged. "You asked."

Laughing, he dismounted, and with each of them leading a horse, his and Tabor's, they went back into the camp. They put the animals in the stockade and turned home.

At the doorway Ivor looked up for the last time at that moon, low now in the west, over where Pendaran was.

"I lied," Leith said quietly. "I married you because no other man I know or can imagine could have made my heart leap so when he asked."

He turned from the moon to her. "The sun rises in your eyes," he said. The formal proposal. "It always, always has, my love."

He kissed her. She was sweet and fragrant in his arms, and she could kindle his desire so. . . .

"The sun rises in three hours," she said, disengaging. "Come to bed."

"Indeed," said Ivor.

"To sleep," she said, warningly.

"I am not," Ivor said, "fourteen years old. Nor am I tired."

She looked at him sternly a moment, then the smile lit her face as from within.

"Good," said Leith, his wife. "Neither am I." She took his hand and drew him inside.

———————◆———————

Dave had no idea where he was, nor, beyond a vague notion of heading south, where to go. There weren't likely to be signposts in Pendaran Wood indicating the mileage to Paras Derval.

On the other hand, he was absolutely certain that if Torc and Levon were alive, they'd be looking for him, so the best course seemed to be to stay put and call out at intervals. This raised the possibility of other things answering, but there wasn't a lot he could do about that.

Remembering Torc's comments on the "babies" in Faelinn Grove, he sat down against a tree on the upwind side of a clearing, where he could see anything coming across, with a chance of hearing or smelling something approaching from behind. He then proceeded to negate this bit of concealment by shouting Levon's name several times at the top of his voice.

He looked around afterwards, but there was nothing stirring. Indeed, as the echoes of his cry faded, Dave became deeply aware of the silence of the forest. That wild rush, as of wind, seemed to have carried everything with it. He appeared to be very much alone.

But not quite. "You make it," a deep voice sounded, from almost directly beneath him, "very hard for honest folk to sleep."

Leaping violently to his feet, Dave raised his axe and watched apprehensively as a large fallen tree trunk was rolled aside to reveal a series of steps leading down, and a figure emerging to look up at him.

A long way up. The creature he'd awakened resembled a portly gnome more than anything else. A very long white beard offset a bald crown and rested comfortably on a formidable paunch. The figure wore some sort of loose, hooded robe, and the whole ensemble stood not much more than four feet high.

"Could you trouble yourself," the bass voice continued, "to summon this Levon person from some other locality?"

Checking a bizarre impulse to apologize, and another to swing first and query later, Dave raised the axe to shoulder height and growled, "Who are you?"

Disconcertingly, the little man laughed. "Names already? Six days with the Dalrei should have taught you to go slower with a question like that. Call me Flidais, if you like, and put that down."

The axe, a live thing suddenly, leaped from Dave's hands and fell on the grass. Flidais hadn't even moved. His mouth open, Dave stared at the little man. "I am testy when awakened," Flidais said mildly. "And you should know better than to bring an axe in here. I'd leave it there if I were you."

Dave found his voice. "Not unless you take it from me," he rasped. "It was a gift from Ivor dan Banor of the Dalrei and I want it."

"Ah," said Flidais. "Ivor." As if that explained a good deal. Dave had a sense, one that always irritated him, that he was being mocked. On the other hand, he didn't seem in a position to do much about it.

Controlling his temper, he said, "If you know Ivor, you know Levon. He's in here somewhere, too. We were ambushed by svart alfar and escaped into the forest. Can you help me?"

"I am pied for protection, dappled for deception," Flidais replied with sublime inconsequentiality. "How do you know I'm not in league with those svarts?"

Once more Dave forced himself to be calm. "I don't," he said, "but I need help, and you're the only thing around, whoever you are."

"Now that, at least, is true," Flidais nodded sagely. "All the others have gone north to the grove, or," he amended judiciously, "south to the grove if they were north of it to start with."

Cuckoo, Dave thought. I have found a certifiable loon. Wonderful, just wonderful.

"I have been the blade of a sword," Flidais confided, confirming the hypothesis. "I have been a star at night, an eagle, a stag in another wood than this. I have been in your world and died, twice; I have been a harp and a harper both.''

In spite of himself Dave was drawn into it. In the red-tinted shadows of the forest, there was an eerie power to the chant.

"I know," Flidais intoned, "how many worlds there are, and I know the skylore that Amairgen learned. I have seen the moon from undersea, and I heard the great dog howl last night. I know the answer to all the riddles there are, save one, and a dead man guards that gateway in your world, Davor of the Axe, Dave Martyniuk.''

Against his will, Dave asked, "What riddle is that?" He hated this sort of thing. God, did he hate it.

"Ah," said Flidais, tilting his head. "Would you come to salmon knowledge so easily? Be careful or you will burn your tongue. I have told you a thing already, forget it not, though the white-haired one will know. Beware the boar, beware the swan, the salt sea bore her body on.''

Adrift in a sea of his own, Dave grabbed for a floating spar. "Lisen's body?" he asked.

Flidais stopped and regarded him. There was a slight sound in the trees. "Good," Flidais said at last. "Very good. For that you may keep the axe. Come down and I will give you food and drink.''

At the mention of food, Dave became overwhelmingly aware that he was ravenous. With a sense of having accomplished something, though by luck as much as anything else, he followed Flidais down the crumbling earthen stairs.

At the bottom there opened out a catacomb of chambers, shaped of earth and threaded through twisting tree roots. Twice he banged his head before following his small host into a comfortable room with a rough table and stools around it. There was a cheery light, though from no discernible source.

"I have been a tree," Flidais said, almost as if answering a question. "I know the earthroot's deepest name."

"Avarlith?" Dave hazarded, greatly daring.

"Not that," Flidais replied, "but good, good." He seemed to be in a genial mood now as he puttered about domestically.

Feeling curiously heartened, Dave pushed a little. "I came here with Loren Silvercloak and four others. I got separated from them. Levon and Torc were taking me to Paras Derval, then there was that explosion and we got ambushed."

Flidais looked aggrieved. "I *know* all that," he said, a little petulantly. "There shall be a shaking of the Mountain."

"Well, there was," Dave said, taking a pull at the drink Flidais offered. Having done which, he pitched forward on the table, quite unconscious.

Flidais regarded him a long time, a speculative look in his eye. He no longer seemed quite so genial, and certainly not mad. After a while, the air registered the presence he'd been awaiting.

"Gently," he said. "This is one of my homes, and tonight you owe me."

"Very well." She muted a little the shining from within her. "Is it born?"

"Even now," he replied. "They will return soon."

"It is well," she said, satisfied. "I am here now and was here at Lisen's birth. Where were you?" Her smile was capricious, unsettling.

"Elsewhere," he admitted, as if she had scored a point. "I was Taliesen. I have been a salmon."

"I know," she said. Her presence filled the room as if a star were underground. Despite his request, it was still hard to look upon her face. "The one riddle," she said. "Would you know the answer?"

He was very old and extremely wise, and he was half a god himself, but this was the deepest longing of his soul. "Goddess," he said, a helpless streaming of hope within him, "I would."

"So would I," she said cruelly. "If you find the summoning name, do not fail to tell me. And," said Ceinwen, letting a blinding light well up from within her so that he closed his eyes in pain and dread, "speak not ever to me again of what I owe. I owe nothing, ever, but what has been promised, and if I promise, it is not a debt, but a gift. Never forget."

He was on his knees. The brightness was overpowering. "I have known," Flidais said, a trembling in his deep voice, "the shining of the Huntress in the Wood."

It was an apology; she took it for such. "It is well," she said for the second time, muting her presence once more, so that he might look upon her countenance. "I go now," she said. "This one I will take. You did well to summon me, for I have laid claim to him."

"Why, goddess?" Flidais asked softly, looking at the sprawled form of Dave Martyniuk.

Her smile was secret and immortal. "It pleases me," she said. But just before she vanished with the man, Ceinwen spoke again, so low it was almost not a sound. "Hear me, forest one: if I learn what name calls the Warrior, I will tell it thee. A promise."

Stricken silent, he knelt again on his earthen floor. It was, had always been, his heart's desire. When he looked up he was alone.

———————◆———————

They woke, all three of them, on soft grass in the morning light. The horses grazed nearby. They were on the very fringes of the forest; southward a road ran from east to west, and beyond it lay low hills. One farmhouse could be seen past the road, and overhead birds sang as if it were the newest morning of the world. Which it was.

In more ways than the obvious, after the cataclysms that the night had known. Such powers had moved across the face of Fionavar as had not been gathered since the worlds were spun and the Weaver named the gods. Iorweth Founder had not endured that blast of

Rangat, seen that hand in the sky, nor had Conary
known such thunder in Mörnirwood, or the white
power of the mist that exploded up from the Summer
Tree, through the body of the sacrifice. Neither Revor
nor Amairgen had ever seen a moon like the one that
had sailed that night, nor had the Baelrath blazed so
in answer on any other hand in the long telling of its
tale. And no man but Ivor dan Banor had ever seen
Imraith-Nimphais bear her Rider across the glitter of
the stars.

Given such a gathering, a concatenation of powers
such that the worlds might never be the same, how
small a miracle might it be said to be that Dave awoke
with his friends in the freshness of that morning on
the southern edge of Pendaran, with the high road from
North Keep to Rhoden running past, and a horn lying
by his side.

A small miracle, in the light of all that had shaken
the day and night before, but that which grants life
where death was seen as certain can never be incon-
sequential, or even less than wondrous, to those who
are the objects of its intercession.

So the three of them rose up, in awe and great joy,
and told their stories to each other while morning's
bird-song spun and warbled overhead.

For Torc, there had been a blinding flash, with a
shape behind it, apprehended but not seen, then darkness until this place. Levon had heard music all around
him, strong and summoning, a wild cry of invocation
as of a hunt passing overhead, then it had changed, so
gradually he could not tell how or when, but there
came a moment when it was so very sad and restful
he had to sleep—to wake with his new brothers on the
grass, Brennin spread before them in a mild sunlight.

"Hey, you two!" cried Dave exuberantly. "Will you
look at this?" He held up the carved horn, ivory-
colored, with workmanship in gold and silver, and
runes engraved along the curve of it. In a spirit of

euphoria and delight, he set the horn to his lips and blew.

It was a rash, precipitate act, but one that could cause no harm, for Ceinwen had intended him to have this and to learn the thing they all learned as that shining note burst into the morning.

She had presumed, for this treasure was not truly hers to bestow. They were to blow the horn and learn the first property of it, then ride forth from the place where it had lain so long. That was how she had intended it to be, but it is a part of the design of the Tapestry that not even a goddess may shape exactly what she wills, and Ceinwen had reckoned without Levon dan Ivor.

The sound was Light. They knew it, all three of them, as soon as Dave blew the horn. It was bright and clean and carrying, and Dave understood, even as he took it from his lips to gaze in wonder at what he held, that no agent of the Dark could ever hear that sound. In his heart this came to him, and it was a true knowing, for such was the first property of that horn.

"Come on," said Torc, as the golden echoes died away. "We're still in the Wood. Let's move." Obediently Dave turned to mount his horse, still dazzled by the sound he had made.

"Hold!" said Levon.

There were perhaps five men in Fionavar who might have known the second power of that gift, and none in any other world. But one of the five was Gereint, the shaman of the third tribe of the Dalrei, who had knowledge of many lost things, and who had been the teacher of Levon dan Ivor.

She had not known or intended this, but not even a goddess can know all things. She had intended a small gift. What happened was otherwise, and not small. For a moment the Weaver's hands were still at his Loom, then Levon said:

"There should be a forked tree here."

And a thread came back with his words into the Tapestry of all the worlds, one that had been lost a very long time.

It was Torc who found it. An enormous ash had been split by lightning—they could have no glimmering how long ago—and its trunk lay forked now, at about the height of a man.

In silence, Levon walked over, Dave beside him, to where Torc was standing. Dave could see a muscle jumping in his face. Then Levon spoke again:

"And now the rock."

Standing together the three of them looked through the wishbone fork of the ash. Dave had the angle. "There," he said, pointing.

Levon looked, and a great wonder was in his eyes. There was indeed a rock set flush into a low mound at the edge of the Wood. "Do you know," he said in a hushed whisper, "that we have found the Cave of the Sleepers."

"I don't understand," said Torc.

"The Wild Hunt," Levon replied. Dave felt a prickling at the back of his neck. "The wildest magic that ever was lies in that place asleep." The strain in Levon's usually unruffled voice was so great it cracked. "Owein's Horn is what you just blew, Davor. If we could ever find the flame, they would ride again. Oh, by all the gods!"

"Tell me," Dave pleaded; he, too, was whispering.

For a moment Levon was silent; then, as they stared at the rock through the gap in the ash, he began to chant:

> *The flame will wake from sleep*
> *The Kings the horn will call,*
> *But though they answer from the deep*
> *You may never hold in thrall*
> *Those who ride from Owein's Keep*
> *With a child before them all.*

"The Wild Hunt," Levon repeated as the sound of his chanting died away. "I have not words to tell how far beyond the three of us this is." And he would say no more.

They rode then from that place, from the great stone and the torn tree with the horn slung at Dave's side. They crossed the road, and by tacit agreement rode in such a way as to be seen by no men until they should come to Silvercloak and the High King.

All morning they rode, through hilly farmland, and at intervals a fine rain fell. It was badly needed, they could see, for the land was dry.

It was shortly after midday that they crested a series of ascending ridges running to the southeast, and saw, gleaming below them, a lake set like a jewel within the encircling hills. It was very beautiful, and they stopped a moment to take it in. There was a small farmhouse by the water, more a cottage really, with a yard and a barn behind it.

Riding slowly down, they would have passed by, as they had all the other farms, except that as they descended, an old, white-haired woman came out in back of the cottage to gaze at them.

Looking at her as they approached, Dave saw that she was not, in fact, so old after all. She made a gesture of her hand to her mouth that he seemed, inexplicably, to know.

Then she was running towards them over the grass, and with an explosion of joy in his heart, Dave leaped, shouting, from his horse, and ran and ran and ran until Kimberly was in his arms.

PART IV

The Unraveller

Chapter 15

Diarmuid, the Prince, as Warden of South Keep, had a house allocated to him in the capital, a small barracks, really, for those of his men who might, for any reason, be quartered there. It was here that he preferred to spend his own nights when in Paras Derval, and it was here that Kevin Laine sought him out in the morning after the cataclysms, having wrestled with his conscience a good part of the night.

And it was still giving him trouble as he walked from the palace in the rain. He couldn't think very clearly, either, for grief was a wound in him that dawn. The only thing keeping him going, forcing resolution, was the terrible image of Jennifer bound to the black swan and flying north into the grasp of that hand the Mountain had sent up.

The problem, though, was *where* to go, where loyalty took him. Both Loren and Kim, unnervingly transformed, were clearly supporting this grim, prepossessing older Prince who had suddenly returned.

"It is my war," Aileron had told Loren, and the mage had nodded quietly. Which, on one level, left Kevin with no issue at all to wrestle with.

On the other hand, Diarmuid was the heir to the throne and Kevin was, if he was anything at all here, one of Diarmuid's band. After Saeren and Cathal, after, especially, the look he and the Prince had exchanged when he'd finished his song in the Black Boar.

He needed Paul to talk it over with, God, he needed

him. But Paul was dead, and his closest friends here
were Erron and Carde and Coll. And their Prince.

So he entered the barracks and asked, as briskly as
he could, "Where's Diarmuid?" Then he stopped dead
in his tracks.

They were all there: Tegid, the company from the
journey south, and others he didn't know. They were
sitting soberly around the tables in the large front
room, but they rose when he entered. Every one of
them was dressed in black, with a red band on his left
arm.

Diarmuid, too. "Come in," he said. "I see you
have news. Let it wait, Kevin." There was quiet emotion in the usually acerbic voice. "The grief, I know,
is yours most of all, but the men of the South Marches
have always worn a red armband when one of their
own dies, and we have lost two now. Drance and
Pwyll. He was one of us—we all feel it here. Will you
let us mourn for Paul with you?"

There was no briskness left in Kevin, only a com-
pounding of sorrows. He nodded, almost afraid to
speak. He collected himself, though, and said, swallowing hard, "Of course, and thank you. But there is
business first. I have information, and you should know
it now."

"Tell me, then," the Prince said, "though I may
know it already."

"I don't think so. Your brother came back last
night."

Sardonic amusement registered in Diarmuid's face.
But it had indeed been news, and the mocking reaction
had been preceded by another expression.

"Ah," said the Prince, in his most acid tones. "I
should have guessed from the grayness of the sky. And
of course," he went on, ignoring the rising murmur
from his men, "there is now a throne up for the taking. He would return. Aileron likes thrones."

"It is *not* up for the taking!" The speaker, red-faced

and vehement, was Coll. "Diar, you are the heir! I
will cut him apart before I see him take it from you."

"No one," said Diarmuid, playing delicately with
a knife on the table, "is going to take anything from
me at all. Certainly not Aileron. Is there more,
Kevin?"

There was, of course. He told them about Ysanne's
death, and Kim's transformation, and then, reluctantly, about Loren's tacit endorsement of the older
Prince. Diarmuid's eyes never left his own, nor did the
hint of laughter sheathed in their depths ever quite disappear. He continued to toy with the dagger.

When Kevin had finished, there was a silence in the
room, broken only by Coll's furious pacing back and
forth.

"I owe you again," said Diarmuid at length. "I
knew none of this."

Kevin nodded. Even as he did, there came a knocking at the door. Carde opened it.

In the entranceway, rain dripping from his hat and
cloak, stood the broad, square figure of Gorlaes, the
Chancellor. Before Kevin could assimilate his presence there, Gorlaes had stepped into the room.

"Prince Diarmuid," he said, without preamble,
"my sources tell me your brother has returned from
exile. For the Crown, I think. You, my lord, are the
heir to the throne I swore to serve. I have come to
offer you my services."

And at that Diarmuid's laughter exploded, un-
checked and abrasive in a room full of mourners. "Of
course you have!" he cried. "Come in! Do come in,
Gorlaes. I have great need of you—we're short a cook
at South Keep!"

Even as the Prince's sarcastic hilarity filled the room,
Kevin's mind cut back to the pulse beat of time that
had followed his first announcement of Aileron's return. There had been sharp irony in Diarmuid then,
too, but only after the first instant. In the first instant,
Kevin thought he had seen something very different

flash across the Prince's face, and he was almost certain he knew what it was.

◆

Loren and Matt had gone with Teyrnon and Barak to bring the body home from the Tree. The Godwood was not a place where soldiers would willingly go, and in any case, on the eve of war the last two mages in Paras Derval saw it as fit that they walk together with their sources, apart from other men, and share their thoughts on what would lie in the days ahead.

They were agreed on the kingship, though in some ways it was a pity. For all Aileron's harsh abrasiveness, there was in his driven nature the stuff of a war king of old. Diarmuid's mercurial glitter made him simply too unreliable. They had been wrong about things before, but not often in concert. Barak concurred. Matt kept his own counsel, but the other three were used to that.

Besides, they were in the wood by then and, being men acquainted with power, and deeply tuned to what had happened in the night, they walked in silence to the Summer Tree.

And then, in a different kind of silence, walked back away, under leaves dripping with the morning rain. It was taught, and they all knew the teachings, that Mörnir, if he came for the sacrifice, laid claim only to the soul. The body was husk, dross, not for the God, and it was left behind.

Except it hadn't been.

A mystery, but it was solved when Loren and Matt returned to Paras Derval and saw the girl, in the dun robes of an acolyte of the sanctuary, waiting outside their quarters in the town.

"My lord," she said, as they walked up, "the High Priestess bade me tell you to come to her in the Temple so soon as you might."

"Tell him?" Matt growled.

The child was remarkably composed. "She did say that. The matter is important."

"Ah," said Loren. "She brought back the body."

The girl nodded.

"Because of the moon," he went on, thinking aloud. "It fits."

Surprisingly, the acolyte nodded again. "Of course it does," she said coolly. "Will you come now?"

Exchanging a raised-eyebrows look, the two of them followed Jaelle's messenger through the streets to the eastern gate.

Once beyond the town, she stopped. "There is something I would warn you about," she said.

Loren Silvercloak looked down from his great height upon the child. "Did the Priestess tell you to do so?"

"Of course not." Her tone was impatient.

"Then you should not speak other than what you were charged to say. How long have you been an acolyte?"

"I am Leila," she replied, gazing up at him with tranquil eyes. Too tranquil; he wondered at the answer. Was her mind touched? Sometimes the Temple took such children.

"That isn't what I asked," he said kindly.

"I know what you asked," she said with some asperity. "I am Leila. I called Finn dan Shahar to the Longest Road four times this summer in the ta'kiena."

His eyes narrowed; he had heard about this. "And Jaelle has made you an acolyte?"

"Two days ago. She is very wise."

An arrogant child. It was time to assert control. "Not," he said sternly, "if her acolytes presume to judge her, and her messengers offer messages of their own."

It didn't faze her. With a shrug of acceptance, Leila turned and continued up the slope to the sanctuary.

He wrestled with it for several strides, then admitted a rare defeat. "Hold," Loren said, and heard Matt's snort of laughter beside him. "What is your news?"

The Dwarf, he was aware, was finding this whole exchange richly amusing. It was, he supposed.

"He is alive," Leila said, and suddenly there was nothing amusing about anything at all.

◆

There had been darkness. A sense of movement, of being moved. The stars very close, then impossibly far away, and receding. Everything receding.

The next time there was an impression, blurred as through rain on glass, of candles wavering, with gray shapes moving ambiguously beyond their arc. He was still now, but soon he felt himself slipping back again, as a tide withdraws to the dark sea wherein there lie no discontinuities.

Except the fact of his presence.

Of his being alive.

Paul opened his eyes, having come a long way. And it seemed, after all the journeying, that he was lying on a bed in a room where there were, indeed, candles burning. He was very weak. There was astonishingly little physical pain, though, and the other kind of pain was so newly allowed it was almost a luxury. He took one slow breath that meant life, and then another to welcome back sorrow.

"Oh, Rachel," he breathed, scarcely a sound. Forbidden once, the most forbidden name. But then intercession had come, before he died, and absolution allowing grief.

Except that he hadn't died. A thought like a blade pierced him at that: was he alive because he'd failed? Was that it? With an effort he turned his head. The movement revealed a tall figure standing by the bed gazing down at him from between the candles.

"You are in the Temple of the Mother," Jaelle said. "It is raining outside."

Rain. There was a bitter challenge in her eyes, but it couldn't touch him in that moment. He was beyond her. He turned his head away. It was raining; he was alive. Sent back. Arrow of the God.

He felt the presence of Mörnir then, within himself, latent, tacit. There was a burden in that, and soon it would have to be addressed, but not yet, not yet. Now was for lying still, tasting the sense of being himself again for the first time in so very long. Ten months. And three nights that had been forever. Oh, he could go with joy a little ways, it was allowed. Eyes closed, he sank deep into the pillow. He was desperately weak, but weakness was all right now. There was rain.

"Dana spoke to you."

He could hear the vivid rage in her voice. Too much of it; he ignored her. *Kevin,* he thought. *I want to see Kev. Soon,* he told himself, *after I sleep.*

She slapped him hard across the face. He felt a raking nail draw blood.

"You are in the sanctuary. Answer!"

Paul Schafer opened his eyes. With cold scorn of his own, he confronted her fury. This time, Jaelle looked away.

After a moment she spoke, gazing at one of the long candles. "All my life I have dreamt of hearing the Goddess speak, of seeing her face." Bitterness had drained her voice. "Not me, though. Not anything at all. Yet you, a man, and one who turned from her entirely for the God in his wood, have been allowed grant of her grace. Do you wonder why I hate you?"

The utter flatness of her tone made the words more chilling than any explosion of anger would have been. Paul was silent a moment, then he said, "I am her child, too. Do not begrudge the gift she offered me."

"Your life, you mean?" She was looking at him again, tall and slender between the candles.

He shook his head; it was still an effort. "Not that. In the beginning, perhaps, but not now. It was the God who gave me this."

"Not so. You are a greater fool than I thought if you know not Dana when she comes."

"Actually," he said, but gently, for it was a matter too high for wrangling, "I do know. In this case, better than you, Priestess. The Goddess was there, yes, and she did intercede, though not for my life. For something else before the end. But it was Mörnir who saved me. It was his to choose. The Summer Tree is the God's, Jaelle.''

For the first time he read a flicker of doubt in the wide-set eyes. ''She was there, though? She did speak? Tell me what she said.''

''No,'' said Paul, with finality.

''You must.'' But it was not a command now. He had a vague sense that there was something he should, something he wanted to say to her, but he was so weary, so utterly drained. Which triggered a completely different realization.

''You know,'' he said, with feeling, ''that I haven't had food or drink for three days. Is there . . . ?''

She stood still a moment, but when she moved, it was to a tray on a low table by the far wall. She brought a bowl of cool soup to the bed. Unfortunately it seemed that his hands didn't work very well yet. He thought she would send for one of the gray-clad priestesses, but in the end she sat stiffly on the bed beside him and fed him herself.

He ate in silence, leaning back against the pillows when he was done. She made as if to get up, but then, with an expression of distaste, used the sleeve of her white gown to wipe the blood from his cheek.

She did rise then, to stand tall and queenly by his bed, her hair the color of the candlelight. Looking up at her, he felt at a disadvantage suddenly.

''Why,'' he asked, ''am I here?''

''I read the signs.''

''You didn't expect to find me alive?''

She shook her head. ''No, but it was the third night, and then the moon rose. . . .''

He nodded. ''But why?'' he asked. ''Why bother?''

Her eyes flashed. ''Don't be such a child. There is a war now. You will be needed.''

He felt his heart skip. "What do you mean? What war?"

"You don't know?"

"I've been somewhat out of touch," he said sharply. "What has happened?"

It may have taken an effort, but her voice was controlled. "Rangat exploded yesterday. A hand of fire in the sky. The wardstone is shattered. Rakoth is free."

He was very still.

"The King is dead," she said.

"That I know," he said. "I heard the bells."

But for the first time now, her expression was strained; something difficult moved in her eyes. "There is more," said Jaelle. "A party of lios alfar were ambushed here by svarts and wolves. Your friend was with them. Jennifer. I am sorry, but she was captured and taken north. A black swan bore her away."

So. He closed his eyes again, feeling the burdens coming down. It seemed they could not be deferred after all. Arrow of the God. Spear of the God. Three nights and forever, the King had said. The King was dead. And Jen.

He looked up again. "Now I know why he sent me back."

As if against her will, Jaelle nodded. "Twiceborn," she murmured.

Wordlessly, he asked with his eyes.

"There is a saying," she whispered, "a very old one: *No man shall be Lord of the Summer Tree who has not twice been born.*"

And so by candlelight in the sanctuary, he heard the words for the first time.

"I didn't ask for this," Paul Schafer said.

She was very beautiful, very stern, a flame, as the candles were. "Are you asking me for pity?"

His mouth crooked wryly at that. "Hardly, at this point." He smiled a little. "Why is it so much easier for you to strike a defenseless man than to wipe the blood from his face?"

Her reply was formal, reflexive, but he had seen her eyes flinch away. "There is mercy in the Goddess sometimes," she said, "but not gentleness."

"Is that how you know her?" he asked. "What if I tell you that I had from her last night a compassion so tender there are no words to compass it?"

She was silent.

"Aren't we two human beings first?" he went on. "With very great burdens, and support to share. You are Jaelle, surely, as well as her Priestess."

"There you are wrong," she said. "I am only her Priestess. There is no one else."

"That seems to me very sad."

"You are only a man," Jaelle replied, and Paul was abashed by what blazed in her eyes before she turned and left the room.

◆

Kim had lain awake for most of the night, alone in her room in the palace, achingly aware of the other, empty bed. Even inside, the Baelrath was responding to the moon, glowing brightly enough to cast shadows on the wall: a branch outside the window swaying in the rain wind, the outline of her own white hair, the shape of a candle by the bed, but no Jen, no shadow of her. Kim tried. Utterly unaware of what her power was, of how to use the stone, she closed her eyes and reached out in the wild night, north as far as she might, as clearly as she might, and found only the darkness of her own apprehensions.

When the stone grew dim again, only a red ring on her finger, she knew the moon had set. It was very late then, little left of the night. Kim lay back in weariness and dreamt of a desire she hadn't known she had.

It is in your dreams that you must walk, Ysanne had said, was saying still, as she dropped far down into the dream again.

And this time she knew the place. She knew where lay those jumbled mighty arches of broken stone, and who was buried there for her to wake.

Not him, not the one she sought. Too easy, were it so. That path was darker even than it was now, and it led through the dead in the dreaming place. This she now knew. It was very sad, though she understood that the gods would not think it so. The sins of the sons, she thought in her dream, knowing the place, feeling the wind rising, and, her hair, oh, her white hair, blown back.

The way to the Warrior led through the grave and the risen bones of the father who had never seen him alive. What was she that she should know this?

But then she was somewhere else, with no space to wonder. She was in the room under the cottage where the Circlet of Lisen still shone, Colan's dagger beside it, where Ysanne had died, and more than died. The Seer was with her, though, was within her, for she knew the book, the parchment page within the book where the invocation could be found to raise the father whole from his grave, and make him name the name of his son to the one who knew the place of summoning. There was no peace, no serenity anywhere. She carried none, had none to grant, she wore the Warstone on her hand. She would drag the dead from their rest, and the undead to their doom.

What was she that this should be so?

At the morning's first light she made them take her back in the rain. An armed guard of thirty men went with her; troops from North Keep who had been Aileron's before he was exiled. With cool efficiency they compassed her about on the ride to the lake. At the last curve the bodies of Aileron's victims still lay on the path.

"Did he do that alone?" the leader of the guard asked when they were past. His voice was reverent.

"Yes," she said.

"He will be our king?"

"Yes," she said.

They waited by the lake while she went inside, and

then down the now familiar stairs into the glow cast
by Lisen's Light. She left it where it lay, though; and,
walking to the table, she opened one of the books.
Oh, it was a glory and a terror that she knew where
to look, but she did, and sitting there alone, she slowly
read the words that she would have to speak.

But only when she knew the place that no one knew.
The tumbled stones were only the starting point. There
was a long way yet to walk along this path; a long
way, but she was on it now. Preoccupied, tangled
among interstices of time and place, the Seer of Brennin went back up the stairs. Aileron's men awaited
her, in disciplined alertness by the lake.

It was time to go. There was a very great deal to be
done. She lingered, though, in the cottage, seeing the
fire, the hearth, the worn table, the herbs in jars along
the wall. She read the labels, unstoppered one con-
tainer to smell its contents. There was so much to be
done, the Seer of Brennin knew, but still she lingered,
tasting the aloneness.

It was bittersweet, and when she moved at last,
Kimberly went out the back door, still alone, into the
yard, away from where the soldiers were, and she saw
three men picking their way on horseback down the
slope north of her, and one of them she knew, oh, she
knew. And it seemed that amid all the burdens and
sorrows, joy could still flower like a bannion in the
wood.

———◆———

They buried Ailell dan Art in a time of rain. It fell
upon the windows of Delevan high above the Great
Hall where the King lay in state, robed in white and
gold, his sword upon his breast, his great, gnarled
hands closed upon the hilt; it fell softly upon the gor-
geous woven covering of the bier when the nobility of
Brennin, who had gathered for celebration and stayed
for mourning and war, bore him out of the palace and
to the doors of the Temple where the women took him;
it fell, too, upon the dome of that sanctuary while

Jaelle, the High Priestess, performed the rites of the Mother, to send back home to her one of the Kings.

No man was in that place. Loren had taken Paul away. She'd had hopes of seeing Silvercloak shaken, but had been disappointed, for the mage had shown no surprise at all, and she had been forced to cloak her own discomfiture at that, and at his bowing to the Twiceborn.

No man was in that place, save for the dead King, when they lifted the great axe from its rest, and no man saw what they did then. Dana was not mocked nor denied when she took her child home, whom she had sent forth so long ago on the circling path that led ever back to her.

It was the place of the High Priestess to bury the High King, and so Jaelle led them forth when the rites were done. Into the rain she went, clad in white among all the black, and they bore Ailell shoulder-high behind her to the crypt wherein the Kings of Brennin were laid to rest.

East of the palace it lay, north of the Temple. Before the body went Jaelle with the key to the gates in her hands. Behind the bier, fair and solitary, walked Diarmuid, the King's Heir, and after him came all the lesser nobility of Brennin. Among them there walked, though with aid, a Prince of the lios alfar, and there were come as well two men of the Dalrei, from the Plain; and with these walked two men from another world, one very tall and dark, another fair, and between them was a woman with white hair. The common folk lined the path, six deep in the rain, and they bowed their heads to see Ailell go by.

Then they came to the great gates of the burying place, and Jaelle saw that they were open already and that a man clad in black stood waiting there for them, and she saw who it was.

"Come," said Aileron, "let us lay my father by my mother, whom he loved."

And while she was trying to mask her shock, another voice spoke. "Welcome home, exile," Diarmuid said, his tone mild, unsurprised, and he moved lightly past her to kiss Aileron on the cheek. "Shall we lead him back to her?"

It was greatly wrong, for she had right of precedence here, but in spite of herself the High Priestess felt a strange emotion to see the two of them, the dark son and the bright, pass through the gates of the dead, side by side, while all the people of Brennin murmured behind them in the falling rain.

On a spur of hill high above that place, three men watched. One would be First Mage of Brennin before the sun had set, one had been made King of the Dwarves by a sunrise long ago, and the third had caused the rain and been sent back by the God.

◆

"We are gathered," Gorlaes began, standing beside the throne but two careful steps below it, "in a time of sorrow and need."

They were in the Great Hall, Tomaz Lal's masterpiece, and there were gathered that afternoon all the mighty of Brennin, save one. The two Dalrei, and Dave as well, so fortuitously arrived, had been greeted with honor and shown to their chambers, and even Brendel of Daniloth was absent from this assemblage, for what Brennin had now to do was matter for Brennin alone.

"In any normal time our loss would demand space for mourning. But this is no such time. It is needful for us now," the Chancellor continued, seeing that Jaelle had not contested his right to speak first, "to take swift counsel amongst one another and go forth from this hall united, with a new King to lead us into—"

"Hold, Gorlaes. We will wait for Silvercloak." It was Teyrnon, the mage, and he had risen to stand, with Barak, his source, and Matt Sören. Trouble already, and they had not even begun.

"Surely," Jaelle murmured, "it is rather his duty

to be here when others are. We have waited long enough.''

''We will wait longer,'' the Dwarf growled. ''As we waited for you, yesterday.'' There was something in his tone that made Gorlaes glad it was Jaelle who'd raised objection, and not himself.

''Where is he?'' Niavin of Seresh asked.

''He is coming. He had to go slowly.''

''Why?'' It was Diarmuid. He had stopped his feline pacing at the edges of the hall and come forward.

''Wait,'' was all the Dwarf replied.

Gorlaes was about to remonstrate, but someone else came in first.

''No,'' said Aileron. ''For all the love I bear him, I will not wait on this. There is, in truth, little to discuss.''

Kim Ford, in that room as the newest, the only, Seer of Brennin, watched him stride to stand by Gorlaes.

And a step above him, directly before the throne. *He will always be like this,* she thought. *There is only the force of him.*

And with force, cold, unyielding force, Aileron looked over them all and spoke again. ''In time of council Loren's wisdom will be sorely needed, but this is not a time of council, whatever you may have thought.''

Diarmuid was no longer pacing. He had moved, at Aileron's first words, to stand directly in front of his brother, an unruffled contrast to Aileron's coiled intensity.

''I came here,'' said Aileron dan Ailell flatly, ''for the Crown, and to lead us into war. The Throne is mine''—he was looking directly at his brother—''and I will kill for it, or die for it before we leave this hall.''

The rigid silence that followed this was broken a moment later by the jarring sound of one man clapping.

''Elegantly put, my dear,'' said Diarmuid as he continued to applaud. ''So utterly succinct.'' Then he lowered his hands. The sons of Ailell faced each other as if alone in the vast hall.

"Mockery," said Aileron softly, "is easy. It was ever your retreat. Understand me, though, brother. This, for once, is no idle sport. I want your fealty this hour, in this place, or there are six archers in the musicians' gallery who will kill you if I raise my hand."

"No!" Kim exclaimed, shocked out of silence.

"This is preposterous!" Teyrnon shouted at the same time, striding forward. "I forbid—"

"You cannot forbid me!" Aileron rode over him. "Rakoth is free. What lies ahead is too large for me to trifle with."

Diarmuid had cocked his head quizzically to one side, as if considering an abstract proposition. Then he spoke, his voice so soft they had to strain to hear. "You would truly do this thing?"

"I would," Aileron replied. With no hesitation at all.

"Truly?" Diarmuid asked a second time.

"All I have to do is raise my arm," Aileron said. "And I will if I must. Believe it."

Diarmuid shook his head slowly back and forth; he sighed heavily. Then:

"Coll," he said, and pitched it to carry.

"My lord Prince." The big man's voice boomed instantly from overhead. From the musicians' gallery.

Diarmuid lifted his head, his expression tranquil, almost indifferent. "Report."

"He did do it, my lord." Coll's voice was thick with anger. He moved forward to the railing. "He really did. There were seven men up here. Say the word and I will slay him now."

Diarmuid smiled. "That," he said, "is reassuring." Then he turned back to Aileron and his eyes were no longer so aloof. The older brother had changed, too; he seemed to have uncoiled himself into readiness. And he broke the silence.

"I sent six," Aileron said. "Who is the seventh?"

They were all scrambling to grasp the import of this when the seventh leaped from the gallery overhead.

It was a long jump, but the dark figure was lithe and, landing, rolled instantly and was up. Five feet from Diarmuid with a dagger back to throw.

Only Aileron moved in time. With the unleashed reflexes of a pure fighter, he grabbed for the first thing that came to hand. As the assassin's dagger went back, Aileron flung the heavy object hard across the space between. It hit the intruder square in the back; the flung blade was sent awry, just awry. Enough so as not to pierce the heart it was intended for.

Diarmuid had not even moved. He stood, swaying a little, with a peculiar half-smile on his face and a jeweled dagger deep in his left shoulder. He had time, Kim saw, to murmur something very low, indistinguishable, as if to himself, before all the swords were out and the assassin was ringed by steel. Ceredur of North Keep drew back his blade to kill.

"Hold swords!" Diarmuid ordered sharply. "Hold!" Ceredur slowly lowered his weapon. The only sound in the whole great room was made by the object Aileron had flung, rolling in diminishing circles on the mosaic-inlaid floor.

It happened to be the Oak Crown of Brennin.

Diarmuid, with a frightening glint of hilarity in his face, bent to pick it up. He bore it, his footsteps echoing, to the long table in the center of the room. Setting it down, he unstoppered a decanter, using one hand only. They all watched as he poured himself a drink, quite deliberately. Then he carried his glass slowly back towards them all.

"It is my pleasure," said Diarmuid dan Ailell, Prince of Brennin, "to propose a toast." The wide mouth smiled. There was blood dripping from his arm. "Will you all drink with me," he said, raising high the glass, "to the Dark Rose of Cathal?"

And walking forward, he lifted his other arm, with

obvious pain, and removed the cap and pins she wore, so that Sharra's dark hair tumbled free.

◆

Having Devorsh killed had been a mistake, for two reasons. First, it gave her father far too much leverage in his campaign to foist one of the lords on her. The lordlings. Leverage he had already begun to use.

Secondly, he was the wrong man.

By the time Rangat sent up its fiery hand—visible even in Cathal, though the Mountain itself was not— her own explosion of rage had metamorphosed into something else. Something quite as deadly, or even more so, since it was sheathed within exquisitely simulated repentance.

She had agreed that she would walk the next morning with Evien of Lagos in the gardens, and then receive two other men in the afternoon; she had been agreeing to everything.

But when the red moon rose that night, she bound up her hair, knowing her father very, very well, and in the strangely hued darkness and the haste of departure, she joined the embassy to Paras Derval.

It was easy. Too easy, a part of her thought as they rode to Cynan; discipline was shockingly lax among the troops of the Garden Country. Still, it served her purpose now, as had the Mountain and the moon.

For whatever the larger cataclysms might mean, whatever chaos lay before them all, Sharra had her own matter to deal with first, and the falcon is a hunting bird.

At Cynan there was pandemonium. When they finally tracked down the harbor-master, he flashed a code of lights across the delta to Seresh and was quickly answered. He took them across himself, horses and all, on a wide river barge. From the familiarity of the greetings exchanged on the other side of Saeren, it was clear that rumors of quite improper intercourse between the river fortresses were true. It was increasingly evident how certain letters had gotten into Cathal.

There had been rumblings of thunder in the north as they rode to Cynan, but as they came ashore in Seresh in the dark hours before dawn, all was still and the red moon hung low over the sea, sailing in and out of scudding clouds. All about her flowed the apprehensive murmurings of war, mingled with a desperate relief among the men of Brennin at the rain that was softly falling. There had been a drought, she gathered.

Shalhassan's emissaries accepted, with some relief, an invitation from the garrison commander at Seresh to stay for what remained of the night. The Duke, they learned, was in Paras Derval already, and something else they learned: Ailell was dead. This morning. Word had come at sundown. There would be a funeral and then a coronation on the morrow.

Who? Why, Prince Diarmuid, of course. The heir, you know. A little wild, the commander conceded, but a gallant Prince. There were none in Cathal to match him, he'd wager. Only a daughter for Shalhassan. What a shame, that.

She slipped from the party as it rode towards Seresh castle and, circling the town to the northeast, set out alone on the road to Paras Derval.

She reached it late in the morning. It was easy there, too, amid the hysteria of an interrupted, overcrowded festival, a dead King, and the terror of Rakoth unchained. She should, a part of her mind said, be feeling that terror, too, for as Shalhassan's heir she had an idea of what was to come, and she had seen her father's face as he looked upon the shattered wardstone. Shalhassan's frightened face, which never, ever showed his thought. Oh, there was terror enough to be found, but not yet.

She was on a hunt.

The doors of the palace were wide open. The funeral had so many people coming and going back and forth that Sharra was able to slip inside without trouble. She thought, briefly, of going to the tombs, but there would be too many people there, too great a press.

Fighting the first numbings of fatigue, she forced herself to clarity. They were having a coronation after the burial. They would have to; in time of war there was no space to linger. Where? Even in Cathal the Great Hall of Tomaz Lal was a byword. It would have to be there.

She had spent all her life in palaces. No other assassin could have navigated with such instinctive ease the maze of corridors and stairwells. Indeed, it was the very certainty of her bearing that precluded any challenge.

All so very easy. She found the musicians' gallery, and it was even unlocked. She could have picked the lock in any case; her brother had taught her how, years and years ago. Entering, she sat down in a dark corner and composed herself to wait. From the high shadows she could see servants below making ready glasses and decanters, trays of food, deep chairs for nobility.

It was a fine hall, she conceded, and the windows were indeed something rare and special. Larai Rigal was better, though. Nothing matched the gardens she knew so well.

The gardens she might never see again. For the first time, now that she was, unbelievably, here, and had only to wait, a tendril of fear snaked insidiously through her mind. She banished it. Leaning forward, she gauged the leap. It was long, longer than from high branches of familiar trees, but it could be done. It would be done. And he would see her face before he died, and die knowing. Else there was no point.

A noise startled her. Pressing quickly back into her corner, she caught her breath as six archers slipped through the unlocked door and ranged themselves along the gallery. It was wide and deep; she was not seen, though one of them was very close to her. In silence she crouched in the corner, and so learned,

from their low talk, that there was more than a simple
coronation to take place that day, and that there were
others in that hall with designs on the life she had
claimed as her own.

She had a moment to think on the nature of this returned Prince, Aileron, who could send men hither with
orders to kill his only brother on command. Briefly
she remembered Marlen, her own brother, whom she
had loved and who was dead. Only briefly, though, because such thoughts were too soft for what she had
still to do, despite this new difficulty. It had been easy
to this point, she had no right to have expected no hin-
drance at all.

In the next moments, though, difficulty became
something more, for ten men burst through the two
doors of the high gallery; in pairs they came, with
knives and swords drawn, and in cold, efficient silence
they disarmed the archers and found her.

She had the presence of mind to keep her head down
as they threw her together with the six archers. The
gallery had been designed to be shadowed and torchlit, with only the flames visible from below, so that
music emanating therefrom would seem disembodied,
born of fire. It was this that saved her from being exposed in the moments before the nobles of Brennin
began to file in over the mosaic-inlaid floor below
them.

Every man in that gallery, and the one woman,
watched, absorbed, as the foreshortened figures moved
to the end of the hall where stood a carved wooden
throne. It was oak, she knew, and so was the crown
resting on the table beside it.

Then he came forward into view from the perimeter
of the room and it was clear that he had to die, because
she was still, in spite of all, having trouble breathing
at the sight of him. The golden hair was bright above
the black of his mourning. He wore a red armband;
so, she abruptly realized, did the ten men encircling
her and the archers. An understanding came then and,

though she fought it very hard, a sharp pleasure at his mastery. Oh, it was clear, it was clear he had to die.

The broad-shouldered man with the Chancellor's seal about his neck was speaking now. Then he was interrupted once, and, more intensely, a second time. It was hard to hear, but when a dark-bearded man strode to stand in front of the throne she knew it was Aileron, the exile returned. He didn't look like Diarmuid.

"Kevin, by all the gods, I want his blood for this!" the leader of her captors hissed fiercely.

"Easy," a fair-haired man replied. "Listen."

They all did. Diarmuid, she saw, was no longer pacing; he had come to stand, his posture indolent, before his brother.

"The Throne is mine," the dark Prince announced. "I will kill for it or die for it before we leave this hall." Even in the high gallery, the intensity of it reached them. There was a silence.

Raucously broken by Diarmuid's lazy applause. "God," the one called Kevin murmured. *I could have told you,* she thought, and then checked it brutally.

He was speaking now, something too soft to be caught, which was maddening, but Aileron's reply they all heard, and stiffened: "There are six archers in the musicians' gallery," he said, "who will kill you if I raise my hand."

Time seemed to slow impossibly. It was upon her, she knew. Words were spoken very softly down below, then more words, then: *"Coll,"* Diarmuid said clearly, and the big man moved forward to be seen and speak, and say, as she had known he would:

"There were seven men up here."

It all seemed to be quite peculiarly slow; she had a great deal of time to think, to know what was about to happen, long, long it seemed, before Aileron said, "I sent six. Who is the seventh?"—and she jumped, catching them utterly by surprise, drawing her dagger even as she fell, so slowly, with so much clarity, to land and roll and rise to face her lover.

She had intended to give him an instant to recognize her; she prayed she had that much time before they killed her.

He didn't need it. His eyes were wide on hers, knowing right away, knowing probably even as she fell, and, oh, curse him forever, quite unafraid. So she threw. She had to throw, before he smiled.

It would have killed him, for she knew how to use a dagger, if something had not struck her from behind as she released.

She staggered, but kept her feet. So did he, her dagger in his left arm to the hilt, just above the red armband. And then, in a longed-for, terrifying access to what lay underneath the command and the glitter, she heard him murmur, so low no one else could possibly hear, "Both of you?"

And in that moment he was undisguised.

Only for the moment, so brief, she almost doubted it had taken place, because immediately he was smiling again, elusive, controlling. With vivid laughter in his eyes, he took the crown his brother had thrown to save his life, and set it down. Then he poured his wine and came back to salute her extravagantly, and set free her hair so that she was revealed, and though her dagger was in his arm, it seemed that it was he who held her as a small thing in the palm of his hand, and not the other way around at all.

"Both of them!" Coll exclaimed. "They both wanted him dead, and now he has them both. Oh, by the gods, he will do it now!"

"I don't think so," said Kevin soberly. "I don't think he will."

"What?" demanded Coll, taken aback.

"Watch."

"We will treat this lady," Diarmuid was saying, "with all dignity due to her. If I am not mistaken, she comes as the vanguard of an embassy from Shalhassan of Cathal. We are honored that he sends his daughter and heir to consult with us.''

It was so smoothly done that he took them all with him for a moment, standing the reality on its head.

"But," spluttered Ceredur, red-faced with indignation, "she tried to kill you!"

"She had cause," Diarmuid replied calmly.

"Will you explain, Prince Diarmuid?" It was Mabon of Rhoden. Speaking with deference, Kevin noted.

"Now," said Coll, grinning again.

Now, thought Sharra. *Whatever happens, I will not live with this shame.*

Diarmuid said, "I stole a flower from Larai Rigal four nights ago in such a way that the Princess would know. It was an irresponsible thing, for those gardens, as we all know, are sacred to them. It seems that Sharra of Cathal valued the honor of her country above her own life—for which we in turn must honor her."

Sharra's world spun for a dizzy instant, then righted itself. She felt herself flushing; tried to control it. He was giving her an out, setting her free. But, she asked herself, even then, with a racing heart, of what worth was freedom if it came only as his gift?

She had no time to pursue it, for Aileron's voice cut abrasively through his brother's spell, just as Diarmuid's applause had destroyed his own, moments before: "You are lying," the older Prince said tersely. "Even you would not go through Seresh and Cynan as King's Heir, risking so much exposure for a flower. Do not toy with us!"

Diarmuid, eyebrows raised, turned to his brother. "Should I," he said in a voice like velvet, "kill you instead?"

Score one, Kevin thought, seeing, even high as he was, how Aileron paled at that. *And a neat diversion, too.*

"As it happens," Diarmuid went on, "I didn't go near the river fortresses."

"You flew, I suppose?" Jaelle interjected acidly.

Diarmuid bestowed his most benign smile upon her. "No. We crossed Saeren below the Dael Slope, and climbed up the handholds carved in the rock on the other side."

"This is disgraceful!" Aileron snapped, recovering. "How can you lie at such a time?" There was a murmur among the gathering.

"As it happens," Kevin Laine called down, moving forward to be seen, "he's telling the truth." They all looked up. "The absolute truth," Kevin went on, pushing it. "There were nine of us."

"Do you remember," Diarmuid asked his brother, "the book of Nygath that we read as boys?"

Reluctantly, Aileron nodded.

"I broke the code," Diarmuid said cheerfully. "The one we could never solve. It told of steps carved into the cliff in Cathal five hundred years ago by Alorre, before he was King. We crossed the river and climbed them. It isn't quite as foolish as it sounds—it was a useful training expedition. And something more."

She kept her head high, her eyes fixed on the windows. But every timbre of his voice registered within her. *Something more.* Is a falcon not a falcon if it does not fly alone?

"How did you cross the river?" Duke Niavin of Seresh asked, with no little interest. He had them all now, Kevin saw; the first great lie now covered with successive layers of truth.

"With Loren's arrows, actually, and a taut rope across. But don't tell him," Diarmuid grinned easily, despite a dagger in his arm, "or I'll never, ever hear the end of it."

"Too late!" someone said from behind them, halfway down the hall.

They all turned. Loren was there, clad for the first time since the crossing in his cloak of power, shot through with many colors that shaded into silver. And beside him was the one who had spoken.

"Behold," said Loren Silvercloak, "I bring you the Twiceborn of the prophecy. Here is Pwyll the Stranger who has come back to us, Lord of the Summer Tree."

He had time to finish, barely, before there came an utterly undecorous scream from the Seer of Brennin, and a second figure hurtled over the balcony of the overhead gallery, shouting with relief and joy as he fell.

Kim got there first, to envelop Paul in a fierce, strangling embrace that was returned, as hard, by him. There were tears of happiness in her eyes as she stepped aside to let Kevin and Paul stand face to face. She was grinning, she knew, like a fool.

"Amigo," said Paul, and smiled.

"Welcome back," said Kevin simply, and then all the nobility of Brennin watched in respectful silence as the two of them embraced.

Kevin stepped back, his eyes bright. "You did it," he said flatly. "You're clear now, aren't you?" And Paul smiled again.

"I am," he said.

Sharra, watching, not understanding anything beyond the intensity, saw Diarmuid walk forward then to the two of them, and she marked the pleasure in his eyes, which was unfeigned and absolute.

"Paul," he said, "this is a bright thread unlooked-for. We were mourning you."

Schafer nodded. "I'm sorry about your father."

"It was time, I think," said Diarmuid. They, too, embraced, and as they did so, the stillness of the hall was shattered by a great noise over their heads as Diarmuid's men roared and clattered their swords. Paul raised a hand to salute them back.

Then the mood changed, the interlude was over, for Aileron had come forward, too, to stand in front of Paul as Diarmuid stepped aside.

For what seemed like forever, the two men gazed at each other, their expressions equally unreadable. No one there could know what had passed between them in the Godwood two nights before, but what lay in the room was palpable, and a thing very deep.

"Mörnir be praised," Aileron said, and dropped to his knees before Paul.

A moment later, everyone in the room but Kevin Laine and the three women had done the same. His heart tight with emotion, Kevin suddenly understood a truth about Aileron. This, this was how he led, by pure force of example and conviction. Even Diarmuid, he saw, had followed his brother's lead.

His eyes met Kim's across the heads of the kneeling brothers. Not clearly knowing what it was he was acquiescing to, he nodded, and was moved to see the relief that showed in her face. She wasn't, it seemed, such a stranger after all, white hair notwithstanding.

Aileron rose again, and so did all the others. Paul had not moved or spoken. He seemed to be conserving his strength. Quietly the Prince said, "We are grateful beyond measure for what you have woven."

Schafer's mouth moved in what was only half a smile. "I didn't take your death after all," he said.

Aileron stiffened; without responding, he spun and walked back to the throne. Ascending the steps, he turned again to face them all, his eyes compelling. "Rakoth is free," he said. "The stones are broken and we are at war with the Dark. I say to all of you, to you, my brother"—a sudden rawness in the voice— "I tell you that this conflict is what I was born for. I have sensed it all my life without knowing. Now I know. It is my destiny. It is," cried Aileron, passion blazing in his face, "my war!"

The power of it was overwhelming, a cry of conviction torn whole from the heart. Even Jaelle's bitter eyes held a kind of acceptance, and there was no mockery at all in Diarmuid's face.

"You arrogant bastard," Paul Schafer said.

It was like a kick in the teeth. Even Kevin felt it. He saw Aileron's head snap back, his eyes go wide with shock.

"How presumptuous can you get?" Paul went on, stepping forward to stand before Aileron. "Your death. Your crown. Your destiny. Your war. *Your* war?" His voice skirled upward. He put a hand on the table for support.

"Pwyll," said Loren. "Paul, wait."

"No!" Schafer snapped. "I hate this, and I hate giving in to it." He turned back to Aileron. "What about the lios alfar?" he demanded. "Loren tells me twenty of them have died already. What about Cathal? Isn't it their war, too?" He pointed to Sharra. "And Eridu? And the Dwarves? Isn't this Matt Sören's war? And what about the Dalrei? There are two of them here now, and seventeen of them have died. Seventeen of the Dalrei are dead. Dead! Isn't it their war, Prince Aileron? And look at us. Look at Kim—*look* at her, at what she's taken on for you. And"—his voice roughened—"think about Jen, if you will, just for a second, before you lay sole claim to this."

There was a difficult silence. Aileron's eyes had never left Paul's while he spoke, nor did they now. When he began to speak, his tone was very different, a plea almost. "I understand," he said stiffly. "I understand all of what you are saying, but I cannot change what else I know. Pwyll, I was born into the world to fight this war."

With a strange light-headedness, Kim Ford spoke then for the first time in public as Seer of Brennin. "Paul," she said, "everyone, I have to tell you that I've seen this. So did Ysanne. That's why she sheltered him. Paul, what he's saying is true."

Schafer looked at her, and the crusading anger she remembered from what he had been before Rachel died faded in the face of her own certitude. *Oh, Ysanne,* she thought, seeing it happen, *how did you stand up under so much weight?*

"If you tell me, I will believe it," Paul said, obviously drained. "But you know it remains his war even

if he is not High King of Brennin. He's still going to
fight it. It seems a wrong way to choose a King."

"Do you have a suggestion?" Loren asked, surprising them all.

"Yes, I do," Paul said. He let them wait, then, "I
suggest you let the Goddess decide. She who sent the
moon. Let her Priestess speak her will," said the Arrow of the God, looking at Jaelle.

They all turned with him. It seemed, in the end, to
have a kind of inevitability to it: the Goddess taking
back one King and sending forth another in his stead.

She had been waiting, amid the tense dialogue back
and forth, for the moment to stop them all and say this
thing. Now he had done it for her.

She gazed at him a moment before she rose, tall and
beautiful, to let them know the will of Dana and Gwen
Ystrat, as had been done long ago in the naming of
the Kings. In a room dense with power, hers was not
the least, and it was the oldest, by far.

"It is a matter for sorrow," she began, blistering
them with a glance, "that it should take a stranger to
Fionavar to remind you of the true order of things. But
howsoever that may be, know ye the will of the Goddess—"

"No," said Diarmuid. And it appeared that there
was nothing inevitable after all. "Sorry, sweetling.
With all the reference to the dazzle of your smile, I don't
want to know ye the will of the Goddess."

"Fool!" she exclaimed. "Do you want to be
cursed?"

"I have been cursed," Diarmuid said with some
feeling. "Rather a good deal lately. I have had quite a
lot happen to me today and I need a pint of ale very
badly. It has only just occurred to me that as High
King I couldn't very easily drop in to the Boar at night,
which is what I propose to do as soon as we've
crowned my brother and I get this dagger out of my
arm."

Even Paul Schafer was humbled by the relief that

flashed in that moment across the bearded face of Aileron dan Ailell, whose mother was Marrien of the Garantae, and who would be crowned later that day by Jaelle, the Priestess, as High King of Brennin to lead that realm and its allies into war against Rakoth Maugrim and all the legions of the Dark.

◆

There was no banquet or celebration; it was a time of mourning and of war. And so at sundown Loren gathered the four of them, with the two young Dalrei Dave refused to be parted from, in the mages' quarters in the town. One of the Dalrei had a leg wound. That, at least, his magic had been able to deal with. A small consolation, given how much seemed to be beyond him of late.

Looking at his guests, Loren counted it off inwardly. Eight days; only eight days since he had brought them here, yet so much had overtaken them. he could read changes in Dave Martyniuk's face, and in the tacit bonds that united him to the two Riders. Then, when the big man told his story, Loren began to understand, and he marveled. Ceinwen. Flidais in Pendaran. And Owein's Horn hanging at Dave's side.

Whatever power had been flowing through him when he chose to bring these five had been a true one, and deep.

There had been five, though, not four; there were only four in the room, however, and absence resonated among them like a chord.

And then was given voice. "Time to start thinking about how to get her back," Kevin Laine said soberly. It was interesting, Loren noted, that it was still Kevin who could speak, instinctively, for all of them.

It was a hard thing, but it had to be said. "We will do everything we can," Loren stated flatly. "But you must be told that if the black swan bore her north, she has been taken by Rakoth himself."

There was a pain in the mage's heart. Despite his premonitions, he had deceived her into coming, given her over to the svart alfar, bound her beauty as if with his own hands to the putrescence of Avaia, and consigned her to Maugrim. If there was a judgement waiting for him in the Weaver's Halls, Jennifer would be someone he had to answer for.

"Did you say a swan?" the fair-haired Rider asked. Levon. Ivor's son, whom he remembered from fully ten years ago as a boy on the eve of his fast. A man now, though young, and bearing the always difficult weight of the first men killed under his command. They were all so young, he realized suddenly, even Aileron. *We are going to war against a god,* he thought, and tasted a terrible doubt.

He masked it. "Yes," he said, "a swan. Avaia the Black she was named, long ago. Why do you ask?"

"We saw her," Levon said. "The evening before the Mountain's fire." For no good reason, that seemed to make it hurt even more.

Kimberly stirred a little, and they turned to her. The white hair above the young eyes was still disturbing. "I dreamt her," she said. "So did Ysanne."

And with that, there was another lost woman in the room for Loren, another ghost. *You and I will not meet again on this side of the Night,* Ysanne had told Ailell.

On this side, or on the other now, it seemed. She had gone so far it could not be compassed. He thought about Lökdal. Colan's dagger, Seithr's gift. Oh, the Dwarves did dark things with power under their mountains.

Kevin, straining a little, punctured the grimness of the silence. "Ye gods and little fishes!" he exclaimed. "This is some reunion. We've got to do better than this!"

A good try, Dave Martyniuk thought, surprising himself with how well he understood what Kevin was trying to do. It wasn't going to get more than a smile, though. It wasn't—

Access to inspiration came then with blinding suddenness.

"Uh-uh," he said slowly, choosing his words. "Can't do it, Kevin. We've got another problem here." He paused, enjoying a new sensation, as their concerned eyes swung to him.

Then, reaching into the pocket of his saddle-bag on the floor beside him, he withdrew something he'd carried a long way. "I think you've misinterpreted the judgement in the *McKay* case," he told Kevin, and tossed the travel-stained Evidence notes down on the table.

Hell, Dave thought, watching them all, even Levon, even Torc, give way to hilarity and relief. There's nothing to this! A wide grin, he knew, was splashed across his face.

"Funny, funny man," Kevin Laine said, with unstinted approval. He was still laughing. "I need a drink," Kevin exclaimed. "We all do. And you," he pointed to Dave, "haven't met Diarmuid yet. I think you'll like him even more than you like me."

Which was a funny kind of dig, Dave thought as they rose to go, and one he'd have to think about. He had a feeling, though, that this, at least, would turn out to be all right.

The five young men departed for the Black Boar. Kim, however, following an instinct that had been building since the coronation, begged off and returned to the palace. Once there, she knocked at a door down the corridor from her own. She made a suggestion, which was accepted. A short while later, in her own room, it emerged that her intuitions on this sort of thing had not been affected at all by anything in Fionavar.

Matt Sören closed the door behind them. He and Loren looked at each other, alone for the first time that day.

"Owein's Horn now," the mage said finally, as if concluding a lengthy exchange.

The Dwarf shook his head. "That is deep," he said. "Will you try to wake them?"

Loren rose and crossed to the window. It was raining again. He put out his hand to feel it like a gift on his palm.

"I won't," he said at last. "But they might."

The Dwarf said softly, "You have been holding yourself back, haven't you?"

Loren turned. His eyes, deep-set under the thick gray eyebrows, were tranquil, but there was power in them still. "I have," he said. "There is a force flowing through all of them, I think, the strangers and our own. We have to give them room."

"They are very young," Matt Sören said.

"I know they are."

"You are sure of this? You are going to let them carry it?"

"I am sure of nothing," the mage said. "But yes, I am going to let them carry it."

"We will be there?"

Silvercloak smiled then. "Oh, my friend," he said, "we will have our battle, never fear. We must let the young ones carry it, but before the end, you and I may have to fight the greatest battle of them all."

"You and I," the Dwarf growled in his deep tones. By which the mage understood a number of things, not least of which was love.

In the end, the Prince had had a great many pints of ale. There were an infinity of reasons, all good.

He had been named Aileron's heir in the ceremony that afternoon. "This," he'd said, "is getting to be a habit." The obvious line. They were quoting it all over the Black Boar, though. He drained another pint. Oh, an infinity of reasons, he had.

Eventually it seemed that he was alone, and in his own chambers in the palace, the chambers of Prince Diarmuid dan Ailell, the King's Heir in Brennin. Indeed.

It was far too late to bother going to sleep. Using the outer walls, though with difficulty because of his arm, he made his way to Sharra's balcony.

Her room was empty.

On a hunch, he looped two rooms along to where Kim Ford was sleeping. It was hard work, with the wound. When he finally climbed up over the balustrade, having to use the tree for awkward leverage, he was greeted by two pitchers of icy water in the face. No one deflected them either, or the laughter of Shalhassan's daughter and the Seer of Brennin, who were a long way down the road to an unexpected friendship.

Mourning his fate somewhat, the heir to the throne finally slipped back into the palace and made his way, dripping, to the room of the Lady Rheva.

One took comfort where one could, at times like this.

He did, in fact, eventually fall asleep. Looking complacently down on him, Rheva heard him murmur as in a dream, "Both of them." She didn't really understand, but he had praised her breasts earlier, and she was not displeased.

Kevin Laine, who might have been able to explain it to her, was awake as well, hearing a very long, very private story from Paul. Who could talk again, it seemed, and who wanted to. When Schafer was done, Kevin spoke himself, also for a long time.

At the end of it, they looked at each other. Dawn was breaking. Eventually, they had to smile, despite Rachel, despite Jen, despite everything.

Chapter 16

He came for her in the morning.

She thought she had sounded the depths of despair the night before, when the swan had set down before the iron gates of Starkadh. From the air she had seen it a long way off, a brutally superimposed black upon the white plateaus of the glaciers. Then as they flew nearer, she had felt herself almost physically battered by the nature of it: the huge, piled slabs of windowless stone, lightless, unyielding. Fortress of a god.

In the darkness and the cold his servants had unbound her from the swan. With grasping hands she had been dragged—for her legs were numb—into the bowels of Starkadh, where the odor was of decay and corrupting flesh, even among the cold, and the only lights gleamed a baneful green. They had thrown her into a room alone, and filthy, exhausted, she had fallen onto the one stained pallet on the icy floor. It smelt of svart alfar.

She lay awake, though, shivering with the bitter cold for a long time. When she did sleep, it was fitfully, and the swan flew through her dreams crying in cold triumph.

When she woke, it was to the certitude that the terrors she had endured were but a shelf on the long way down, and the bottom was invisible yet in the darkness, but waiting. She was going there.

It wasn't dark in the room now, though. There was a bright fire blazing on the opposite wall, and in the middle of the room she saw a wide bed standing, and with a constriction of the heart she recognized her parents' bed. A foreboding came upon her, complete and very clear; she was here to be broken, and there was no mercy in this place. There was a god.

And in that moment he was there, he had come, and she felt her mind shockingly peeled open like a fruit. For an instant she fought it, and then was enveloped, stricken by the ease with which she was exposed. She was in his fortress. She was his, it was made known to her. She would be smashed on the anvil of his hate.

It ended, as suddenly as it had begun. Her sight returned, slowly, blurred; her whole body trembled violently, she had no control over it. She turned her head and saw Rakoth.

She had vowed not to cry out, but all vows in this place were as nothing before what he was.

From out of time he had come, from beyond the Weaver's Halls, and into the pattern of the Tapestry. A presence in all the worlds he was, but incarnate here in Fionavar, which was the First, the one that mattered.

Here he had set his feet upon the Ice, and so made the northland the place of his power, and here he had raised up jagged Starkadh. And when it was full-wrought, a claw, a cancer in the north, he had risen to the topmost tower and screamed his name that the wind might bear it to the tamed gods whom he feared not, being stronger by far than any one of them.

Rakoth Maugrim, the Unraveller.

It was Cernan, the stag-horned forest god, who set the trees whispering in mockery of that claim, and in mockery they named him otherwise: Sathain, the Hooded One, and Mörnir of the Thunder sent lightning down to drive him from the tower.

And all the while the lios alfar, newly wakened, sang in Daniloth of Light, and Light was in their eyes, their name, and he hated them with an undying hate.

Too soon had he attacked, though the years may have seemed long to mortal men. And indeed there were men in Fionavar then, for Iorweth had come from oversea, in answer to a dream sent by Mörnir with sanction of the Mother, to found Paras Derval in Brennin by the Summer Tree, and his son had ruled, and his son's son, and then Conary had ascended to the throne.

And in that time had Rakoth come down in fury from the Ice.

And after bitter war been beaten back. Not by the gods—for in the waiting time, the Weaver had spoken, the first and only time he had done so. He said that the worlds had not been woven to be a battleground for powers outside of time, and that if Maugrim were to be mastered, it would be by the Children, with only mildest intercession of the gods. And it had been so. They had bound him under the Mountain, though he could not die, and they had shaped the wardstones to burn red if he but assayed the smallest trial of his powers.

This time it would be otherwise. Now his patience would bear ripe fruit for the crushing, for this time he had been patient. Even when the circle of the guardians had been broken, he had lain still under Rangat, enduring the torment of the chain, savoring it then to sweeten the taste of vengeance to come. Not until Starkadh had been raised high again from the rubble of its fall had he come out from under the Mountain, and with red exploding triumph, let them know he was free.

Oh, this time he would go slowly. He would break them all, one by one. He would crush them with his hand. His one hand, for the other lay, black and festering, under Rangat, with Ginserat's unbroken chain around it still, and for that as much as anything would they pay full, fullest measure before they were allowed to die.

Starting with this one, who knew nothing, he saw, and so was trash, a toy, first flesh for his hunger, and fair like the lios, a presaging of his oldest desire. He reached into her, it was so easy in Starkadh, he knew her whole, and began.

She had been right. The bottom was so far down, the truest depths of night lay beyond where she could ever have apprehended them to be. Facing hate in that moment, a blank, obliterating power, Jennifer saw that he was huge, towering over her, with one hand taloned, gray like disease, and the other gone, leaving only a stump that forever dripped black blood. His robe was black, darker even, somehow, a swallowing of light, and within the hood he wore there was—most terrible—no face. Only eyes that burned her like dry ice, so cold they were, though red like hellfire. Oh, what sin, what sin would they say had been hers that she be given over to this?

Pride? For she was proud, she knew, had been raised to be so. But if that was it, then be it so still, here at the end, at the fall of Dark upon her. A sweet child she had been, strong, a kindness in her nature, if hidden behind caution, not opening easily to other souls, because she trusted only her own. A pride in that, which Kevin Laine, first of all men, had seen for what it was, and laid open for her to understand before he stepped back to let her grow in that understanding. A gift, and not without pain for himself. A long way off, he was, and what, oh, what did any of it matter in this place? What did it matter why? It didn't, clearly, except that at the end we only have ourselves anyway, wherever it comes down. So Jennifer rose from the mattress on the floor, her hair tangled, filthy, the odor of Avaia on her torn clothes, her face stained, body bruised and cut, and she mastered the tremor in her voice and said to him, "You will have nothing of me that you do not take."

And in that foul place, a beauty blazed like Light unleashed, white with courage and fierce clarity.

But this was the stronghold of the Dark, the deepest place of his power, and he said, "But I will take everything,'' and changed his shape before her eyes to become her father.

And after that it was very bad.

You send your mind away, she remembered reading once; when you're tortured, when you're raped, you send your mind after a while into another place, far from where pain is. You send it as far as you can. To love, the memory of it, a spar for clinging to.

But she couldn't, because everywhere she went he was there. There was no escape to love, not even in childhood, because it was her father naked on the bed with her—her mother's bed—and there was nothing clean in any place. "You wanted to be Princess One," James Lowell whispered tenderly. "Oh, you are now, you are. Let me do this to you, and this, you have no choice, you always wanted this."

Everything. He was taking everything. And through it all he had one hand only, and the other, the rotting stump, dripped his black blood on her body and it burned wherever it fell.

Then he started the changes, again and again, tracking her through all the corridors of her soul. Nowhere, nowhere to even try to hide. For Father Laughlin was above her then, tearing her, excoriating her, penetrating, whose gentleness had been an island all her life. And after him, she should have been prepared, but oh, Mary Mother, what was her sin, what had she done that evil could have power over her like this? For now it was Kevin, brutal, ravaging, burning her with the blood of his missing hand. Nowhere for her to go, where else was there in all the worlds? She was so far, so far, and he was so vast, he was all places, everywhere, and the only thing he could not do was reclaim his hand, and what good would that do her, oh, what good?

It went on so long that time unhinged among the pain, the voices, the probing of her deepest places as with a trowel, effortlessly. Once he was a man she did not know, very tall, dark, a square-jawed face, distorted now with hatred, brown eyes distended—but she did not know him, she knew she did not know. And then he was, most shockingly, himself at the end, giant upon her, the hood terribly thrown back and nothing there, only the eyes, endlessly, only them, raking her into shreds, first sweet fruit of his long revenge.

It had been over for a long time before she became aware. She kept her eyes closed. She breathed, she was still alive. And *no,* she told herself, her soul on a spar in a darkest place, the only light her own and so dim. But *no,* she said again within her being; and, opening her eyes, she looked full upon him and spoke for the second time. "You can take them," Jennifer said, her voice a scrape of pain, "but I will not give them to you, and every one of them has two hands."

And he laughed, for resistance here was a joy, an intensifying of pleasure unimagined. "You shall," he said, "give all of yourself for that. I shall make of your will my gift."

She didn't understand, but a time later there was someone else in the room, and for a hallucinatory instant she thought it was Matt Sören.

"When I leave this room," said Rakoth, "you are Blöd's, for he brought me a thing I coveted." The Dwarf, who was not Matt after all, smiled. There was a hunger in his expression. She was naked, she knew. Open.

"You will give him everything he asks," the Unraveller said. "He need take nothing, you will give and give again until you die." He turned to the Dwarf. "She pleases you?"

Blöd could only nod; his eyes were terrifying.

Rakoth laughed again, it was the laughter on the wind. "She will do anything you ask. At morning's end you are to kill her, though. Any way you like, but she must die. There is a reason." And moving forward as he spoke, Sathain, the Hooded One, touched her once, with his one hand, between the eyes.

And oh, it was not over after all. For the spar was gone, the clinging place for what she was, for Jennifer.

He left the room. He left her with the Dwarf. What was left of her.

Blöd wet his lips. "Get up," he said, and she rose. She could not do otherwise. There was no spar, there was no light.

"Beg me," he said, and oh, what sin had it been? Even as the pleading spilled helplessly from her, as his filthy abuse rained down, and then real pain, which excited him—even through it all she found something. Not a spar of light, for there was no light anymore, it was drowned; but here, at the last, the very last thing was pride. She would not scream, she would not go mad, unless he said for her to do so, and if he did that, it was still being taken, after all, she was not giving it.

But at length he tired and, mindful of his instructions, turned his mind to killing her. He was inventive, and it appeared after a time that pain did impose impossibilities. Pride can only carry one so far, and golden girls can die, so when the Dwarf began to truly hurt her, she started to scream after all. No spar, no light, no name, nothing left but the Dark.

◆

When the embassy from Cathal entered the Great Hall of Paras Derval in the morning, it was with a degree of stupefaction quite spectacular that they discovered their Princess waiting to greet them.

Kim Ford was fighting a shameful case of the giggles. Sharra's description of the probable reactions on the part of the embassy dovetailed so wonderfully with the reality that she knew with certainty that if she but glanced at the Princess, she would disgrace herself. She kept her eyes carefully lowered.

Until Diarmuid strolled up. The business with the water pitchers the night before had generated the sort of hilarity between the two women that cements a developing friendship. They had laughed for a long time.

It was only afterwards that Kim had remembered that he was a wounded man, and perhaps in more ways than one. He had also acted in the afternoon to save both Sharra's life and her pride, and he had told them to crown his brother. She should have remembered all of that, she supposed, but then she couldn't, she simply *could not* be serious and sensitive all the time.

In any case, the Prince showed no traces of affliction at the moment. Using the drone of Gorlaes's voice as cover—Aileron had, a little surprisingly, re-appointed the Chancellor—he approached the two of them. His eyes were clear, very blue, and his manner gave no hint of extreme intoxication a few hours before, unless it lay in the slightly edged quality of his gaze.

"I hope," he murmured to Sharra, "that yesterday discharged all your impulses to throw things at me."

"I wouldn't count on it," Sharra said defiantly.

He was very good at this, Kim realized. He paused to flick her with a brief, sardonic glance, as to an erring child, before turning back to the Princess. "That," he said simply, "would be a pity. Adults do have better things to do." And he moved off, elegant and assured, to stand beside his brother, as the heir to the throne should.

Kim felt obscurely chastened; the water had been awfully childish. On the other hand, she abruptly recalled, he had been climbing into their rooms! He deserved whatever he got, and more.

Which, though manifestly true, didn't seem to count for much. She still felt like a kid at the moment. *God, he's cool,* she thought, and felt a stirring of sympathy for her newest friend. Sympathy and, because she was honest with herself, the slightest flicker of envy.

In the meantime, she was beginning to understand why Gorlaes was still Chancellor. No one else would have put such a flourish into the necessary rituals that accompanied procedures of this sort. Or even remembered them, for that matter. He was still going, and Aileron was waiting with surprising patience, when a second man, in his own way as handsome as the first, came up to her.

"What," asked Levon, without preamble or greeting, direct as wind, "is the ring you have?"

This was different. It was the Seer of Brennin who looked up at him appraisingly. "The Baelrath," she answered quietly. "The Warstone, it is called. It is of the wild magic."

He reacted to that. "Forgive me, but why are you wearing it?"

"Because the last Seer gave it to me. She dreamt it on my hand."

He nodded, his eyes widening. "Gereint told me of such things. Do you know what it is?"

"Not entirely. Do you?"

Levon shook his head. "No. How should I? It is far from my world, Lady. I know the eltor and the Plain. But I have one thought. May we talk after?"

He really was extraordinarily attractive, a restless stallion in the confines of the hall. "Sure," she said.

As it happened, they never got the chance.

Kevin, standing with Paul beside one of the pillars opposite the women, was quietly pleased at how clear-headed he felt. They'd done a lot of ale the night before. Paying close attention, he saw Gorlaes and then Galienth, the Cathalian emissary, conclude their formal speeches.

Aileron rose. "I thank you," he said levelly, "for coming here, and for your gracious words about my father. We are grateful to Shalhassan that he saw fit to send his daughter and heir to take counsel with us. It is a trust we honor, and it is an emblem of the trust we all must share in the days to come."

The emissary, who, Kevin knew, was utterly clueless as to how Sharra had got there, nodded sage agreement. The King, still standing, spoke again.

"In this counsel-taking, all shall be granted speech, for it cannot be otherwise. It comes to me, though, that first right of address here belongs not to myself, but rather to the eldest of us and the one whose people best know the fury of Rakoth. Na-Brendel of Daniloth, will you speak for the lios alfar?'' For a moment after he had ended, Aileron's glance met that of Paul Schafer in an enigmatic exchange.

Then all eyes were on the lios. Still limping from his wounds, Brendel advanced, and with him for support came the one who had seldom left his side in three days. Tegid took Brendel carefully forward, and then withdrew, unwontedly diffident, and the lios alfar stood alone in the midst of them all, his eyes the color of the sea under rain.

"I thank you, High King," he said. "You do me and my people honor in this hall." He paused. "The lios have never been known for brevity of discourse, since time runs more slowly for us than for you, but there is urgency upon us now, and I will not be overlong. Two thoughts I have." He looked around.

"There were five guardian peoples named, one thousand years ago before the Mountain. Four are here today: Brennin and Cathal, the Dalrei and the lios alfar. None of our wardstones turned red, yet Rakoth is free. We had no warning at all. The circle was broken, my friends, and so—," he hesitated, then spoke aloud the thought they all shared, "—and so we must beware of Eridu."

Eridu, Kim thought, remembering it from Eilathen's whirling vision. Wild, beautiful land where lived a race of dark, fierce, violent men.

And the Dwarves. She turned, to see Matt Sören gazing at Brendel with an impassive face.

"That is my first counsel," the lios continued. "The other is more to the point. If Rakoth is but newly free, then even with his power, black Starkadh cannot be raised again for some time. He has announced himself too soon. We must attack before that fortress anchors his might in the Ice again. I say to all of you that we should go forth from this Council and carry war to the

Unraveller ourselves. We bound him once, and we will do so again!''

He was a flame; he fired them all with the burning in him. Even Jaelle, Kevin saw, had a blaze of color in her face.

"No one," said Aileron, rising again, "could have spoken more clearly my own thought. What say the Dalrei?"

In the now charged ambience, Levon walked forward, uncomfortable but not abashed, and Dave felt a surge of pride to hear his new brother say, "Never in our long history have the Riders failed the High Kingdom in time of need. I can say to you all that the sons of Revor will follow the sons of Conary and Colan into the Rük Barrens and beyond against Maugrim. Aileron, High King, I pledge my life to you, and my sword; do with them what you will. The Dalrei shall not fail you."

Quietly Torc stepped forward. "And I," he said. "My life, my sword."

Stern and erect, Aileron nodded to them, accepting it. He looked a king, Kevin thought. In that moment he came into it.

"And Cathal?" Aileron asked, turning to Galienth. But it was another voice that answered him.

"A thousand years ago," said Sharra, daughter of Shalhassan, heir of Shalhassan, "the men of the Garden Country fought and died in the Bael Rangat. They fought at Celidon and among the tall trees of Gwynir. They were at Sennett Strand when the last battle began and at Starkadh when it ended. They will do as much again." Her bearing was proud before them all, her beauty dazzling. "They will fight and die. But before I accede to this counsel of attack, there is another voice I would hear. Throughout Cathal the wisdom of the lios alfar is a byword, but so, too, and often it has been said with a woven curse, is the knowledge of the followers of Amairgen. What say the mages of Brennin? I would hear the words of Loren Silvercloak."

And with a jolt of dismay, Kevin realized that she was right. The mage hadn't said a thing. He had barely made his presence known. And only Sharra had noticed.

Aileron, he saw, seemed to have followed the same line of thought. He wore a sudden expression of concern.

And even now, Loren was hesitating. Paul gripped Kevin's arm. "He doesn't want to speak," Schafer whispered. "I think I'm going to—"

But whatever intervention he had planned was forestalled, for there came then a loud hammering on the great doors at the end of the hall, and as they turned, startled, the doors were opened, and a figure walked with two of the palace guard between the high pillars towards them all. He walked with the flat, halting steps of absolute exhaustion, and as he drew nearer, Kevin saw that it was a Dwarf.

In the loud silence, it was Matt Sören who stepped forward. "Brock?" he whispered.

The other Dwarf did not speak. He just kept walking and walking, as if by will-power alone, until he had come the length of the Great Hall to where Matt stood. And there he dropped to his knees at last, and in a voice of rawest grief, cried aloud, "Oh, my king!"

In that moment the one eye of Matt Sören truly became a window to his soul. And in it they all saw a hunger unassuageable, the deepest, bitterest, most forsaken longing of the heart.

"Why, Matt?" Kim remembered asking after her tranced vision of Calor Diman on that first walk to Ysanne's lake. "Why did you leave?"

And now, it seemed they were to learn. A chair had been set for Brock before the throne, and he had collapsed into it. It was Matt who spoke, though, as they gathered around the two Dwarves.

"Brock has a tale to tell," Matt Sören said in his deep tones, "but I fear it will mean little to you unless

I first tell you mine. It seems the time for privacy is past. Listen, then.

"In the time of the passing of March, King of the Dwarves, in his one-hundred-and-forty-seventh year, only one man could be found who would assay the test of full moon night by Calor Diman, the Crystal Lake, which is how we choose our King, or have the powers choose him for us.

"Know you that he who would rule under the twin mountains must first lie at full moon night beside the lake. If he lives to see the dawn and is not mad, he is crowned under Banir Lök. It is a dark ordeal, though, and many of our greatest warriors and artisans have been broken shards when the sun rose on their vigil."

Kim began to feel the first pulsings of a migraine behind her eyes. Blocking it as best she could, she focused hard on what Matt was saying.

"When March, to whom I was sister-son, died, I gathered what courage I had—a youthful courage it was, I confess—and according to the ritual, I shaped a crystal of my own devising and dropped it as a token of intention in Crystal Lake on new moon night.

"Two weeks later the door from Banir Tal, which is the one entrance to the meadow by Calor Diman, was opened for me and then bolted behind my back."

Matt's voice had dropped almost to a whisper. "I saw the full moon rise above that lake," he said. "I saw many things besides. I . . . did not go mad. In the end I offered and was bound to the waters. They crowned me King two days after."

It was building up to a grandfather of a headache, Kim realized. She sat down on the steps before the throne and put her head in her hands, listening, straining to concentrate.

"I did not fail by the lake," Matt said, and they could all hear the bitterness, "but in every other way I did fail, for the Dwarves were not what once we had been."

"Not your fault," Brock murmured, looking up. "Oh, my lord, truly not your fault."

Matt was silent a moment, then shook his head in rejection. "I was King," he said shortly. Just like that, Kevin thought. He looked at Aileron.

But Matt was continuing. "Two things the Dwarves have always had," he said. "A knowledge of secret things in the earth, and a lust to know more.

"In the last days of King March, a faction formed within our halls around two brothers, foremost of our artisans. Their desire, which became a passion and then, in the first weeks of my reign, a crusade, was to find and unlock the secrets of a dark thing: the Cauldron of Khath Meigol."

A murmur rose in the hall at that. Kim had her eyes closed; there was a lot of pain, and the light was hurting now, lancing against her eyeballs. She bent all her will to Matt. What he was saying was too important to lose because of a headache.

"I ordered them to stop," the Dwarf said. "They did, or so I thought. But then I found Kaen, the older, combing the oldest books again, and his brother had gone away without my leave. I grew wrathful then, and in my folly and pride I called a gathering of all Dwarves in the Moot Hall and demanded they choose between Kaen's desires and my own, which were to let the black thing lie where it was lost, while we moved from spells and powers of the old ways and sought the Light I had been shown by the lake.

"Kaen spoke after me. He said many things. I do not care to repeat them before—"

"He lied!" Brock exclaimed fiercely. "He lied and he lied again!"

Matt shrugged. "He did it well, though. In the end the Dwarfmoot chose that he be allowed to go on with his search, and they voted as well that all our energies should be bent to his aid. I threw down my scepter," Matt Sören said. "I left the Moot Hall, and the twin mountains, and I vowed I would not come back. They might search for the key to this dark thing, but not while I was King under Banir Lök."

God, it was hurting. Her skin felt too tight. Her mouth was dry. She pressed her hands to her eyes and held her head as motionless as she could.

"Wandering in the mountains and the wooded slopes that summer," Matt continued, "I met Loren, who was not yet Silvercloak, nor yet a mage, though his training was done. What passed between us is still matter for we two alone, but in the end I told the one lie of my life to him, because it involved a pain I had resolved to bear alone.

"I told Loren that I was free to become his source, that I wanted nothing more. And indeed, there was already something woven into our coming together. A night by Calor Diman had taught me to see that. But it had given me something else—something I lied about. Loren could not have known it. Indeed, until I met Kimberly, I thought no one who was not a Dwarf could know this thing."

Kim lifted her head, feeling the movement like a knife. They would be looking at her, though, so she opened her eyes for a moment, trying to mask the nausea flooding over her. When she thought no one was watching, she closed her eyes again. It was very bad, and getting worse.

"When the King is bound to Crystal Lake," Matt was explaining softly, "he is forever bound. There is no breaking it. He may leave but he is not free. The lake is in him like another heartbeat and it never stops calling. I lie down at night fighting this and rise up in the morning fighting it, and it is with me through the day and the evening and will be until I die. This is my burden, and it is mine alone, and I would have you know, else I would not have spoken before you, that it was freely chosen and is not regretted."

The Great Hall was silent as Matt Sören fixed each

of them in challenge with his one dark eye. All but
Kim, who couldn't even look up now. She was seriously wondering if she was going to pass out.

"Brock," said Matt at length, "you have tidings for
us. Are you able to tell them now?"

The other Dwarf looked at him, and, noting the
regained composure in his eyes, Kevin realized that
there had been a second reason why Matt had spoken
first and at length. Within himself, he still felt the
deep hurting of Sören's tale, and it was as an echo of
his own thought that he heard Brock murmur, "My
King, will you not come back to us? It has been forty
years."

But Matt was ready for it this time; once only would
he expose his soul. "I am," he said, "source to Loren
Silvercloak, First Mage to the High King of Brennin.
Kaen is King of the Dwarves. Tell us your news,
Brock."

Brock looked at him. Then said, "I would not add
to your burdens, but I must tell you that what you say
is untrue. Kaen reigns in Banir Lök, but he is not
King."

Matt raised a hand. "Do you tell me he has not slept
by Calor Diman?"

"I do. We have a ruler, but not a King, unless it be
you, my lord."

"Oh, by Seithr's memory!" Matt Sören cried.
"How far have we fallen from what we were?"

"Very far," Brock said in a harsh whisper. "They
found the Cauldron at the last. They found it and restored it."

There was something in his voice; something terrible.

"Yes?" Matt said.

"There was a price," Brock whispered. "Kaen
needed help in the end."

"Yes?" Matt said again.

"A man came. Metran was his name, a mage from

Brennin, and together he and Kaen unlocked the power of the Cauldron. Kaen's soul, I think, had been twisted utterly by then. There was a price and he paid it."

"What price?" asked Matt Sören.

Kim knew. Pain was splintering her mind.

"He broke the wardstone of Eridu," said Brock, "and delivered the Cauldron to Rakoth Maugrim. We did it, my King. The Dwarves have freed the Unraveller!" And casting his cloak over his face, Brock wept as if his heart would break.

In the uproar that followed, the terror and the fury, Matt Sören turned slowly, very slowly, as if the world were a calm, still place, and looked at Loren Silvercloak, who was looking back at him.

We will have our battle, Loren had said the night before. *Never fear.* And now, most terribly, it was clear what that battle would be.

Her head was being torn apart. There were white detonations within her brain. She was going to scream.

"What is it?" a voice whispered urgently at her side.

A woman, but not Sharra. It was Jaelle who knelt beside her. She was too agonized to feel surprise. Leaning on the other woman, she whispered on a thin-stretched note, "Don't know. My head. As if— something's cracking in I don't "

"Open your eyes," Jaelle commanded. "Look at the Baelrath!"

She did. The pain was almost blinding. But she could see the stone on her hand throbbing with red fire, pulsing to the rhythm of the explosions behind her eyes, and looking into it, her hand held close to her face, Kim saw something else then, a face, a name written in fire, a room, a crescendo of dark, of Dark, and—

"Jennifer!" she screamed. *"Oh, Jen, no!"*

She was on her feet. The ring was a wild, burning, uncontrollable thing. She staggered, but Jaelle supported her. Hardly knowing what she was doing, she screamed again, "Loren! I need you!"

Kevin was there. "Kim? What?"

She shook her head, tore away from his touch. She was blind with agony; she could scarcely speak. "Dave," she scraped. "Paul. Come on . . . the circle. *Now!*" There was so much urgency. They seemed to move so slowly, and Jen, Jen, oh, Jen. *"Come on!"* she screamed again.

Then they were around her, the three of them, and Loren and Matt, unquestioning, were beside them. And she held up the ring again, instinctively, and opening herself, her mind, cutting through the claws of pain she found Loren and linked to him and then— oh, a gift—Jaelle was there as well, tapping into the avarlith for her, and with the two of them as ballast, as bedrock, she cast her mind, her soul, to its farthest, most impossible compassing. Oh, far, and there was so much Dark between, so much hate, and oh, so very great a power in Starkadh to stay her.

But there was also a spar of light. A dying spar, so nearly gone, but it was there, and Kim reached with everything she had, with all she was, to the lost island of that light and she found Jennifer.

"Oh, love," she said, inside and aloud. "Oh, love, I'm here. Come!"

The Baelrath was unleashed, it was so bright they had to close their eyes against the blazing of that wildest magic as Kimberly pulled them out, and out, all the way out, with Jennifer held to the circle only by her mind, the spar, pride, last dying light, and love.

Then as the shimmering grew in the Great Hall, and the humming before the crossing time, as they started to go, and the cold of the space between worlds entered the five of them, Kim drew one breath again and cried the last desperate warning, not knowing, oh not, if she was heard:

"Aileron, don't attack! He's waiting in Starkadh!"

And then it was cold, cold, and completely dark, as she took them through alone.

Here ends THE SUMMER TREE,
the first book of
THE FIONAVAR TAPESTRY

About the Author

Guy Gavriel Kay is the author of the acclaimed *Fionavar Tapestry*, comprising *The Summer Tree*, *The Wandering Fire*, and *The Darkest Road*. Translated into eight languages, the trilogy has won awards and accolades all over the world. He can be found on the Web at www.brightweavings.com.